UNCAGED

THE SINGULAR MENACE · BOOK 1

UNCAGED

JOHN SANDFORD & MICHELE COOK

EMBER

Text copyright © 2014 by John Sandford and Michele Cook
Cover photograph copyright © 2014 by Zmeel/Getty Images

All rights reserved. Published in the United States by Ember, an imprint of Random House Children's Books, a division of Penguin Random House LLC, New York. Originally published in hardcover in the United States by Alfred A. Knopf, an imprint of Random House Children's Books, New York, in 2014.

Ember and the E colophon are registered trademarks of Penguin Random House LLC.

Visit us on the Web! randomhouseteens.com

Educators and librarians, for a variety of teaching tools, visit us at RHTeachersLibrarians.com

The Library of Congress has cataloged the hardcover edition of this work as follows:
Sandford, John.
Uncaged / John Sandford & Michele Cook. — First edition.
p. cm. — (The singular menace ; book 1)
Summary: When an animal rights action at a research lab goes wrong, a terrible secret is exposed, and Shay must find her brother Odin before the researchers at Singular Corp. can silence both of them.
ISBN 978-0-385-75306-7 (trade) — ISBN 978-0-385-75307-4 (lib. bdg.) — ISBN 978-0-385-75308-1 (ebook)
[1. Adventure and adventurers—Fiction. 2. Animals—Treatment—Fiction. 3. Protest movements—Fiction. 4. Brothers and sisters—Fiction. 5. Science fiction.] I. Cook, Michele. II. Title.
PZ7.S21628Unc 2014
[Fic]—dc23
2013044491

ISBN 978-0-385-75305-0 (pbk.)

Printed in the United States of America

First Ember Edition 2015

Random House Children's Books supports the First Amendment and celebrates the right to read.

UNCAGED

IN THE END . . .

The naked girl stared at herself in the motel mirror, a little sick with what she was about to do. She was slender, with muscles in her arms and shoulders, and red hair that fell to her waist. A scratch trailed from her hairline down to one eyebrow; her lower lip was swollen, raw on the inside where her teeth had cut into it. She had the salty taste of blood in her mouth.

She'd just gotten out of the shower, where she'd scrubbed someone else's blood off her clothes and body.

Now for the hair. *Has to be done,* she thought.

She shook out the Walgreens bag. A pair of shears, a comb, and a box of Clairol Nice 'n Easy clattered down onto the Formica counter beside the sink. Behind her, the gray, wolflike dog was on its feet, watching her, picking up on the stress; the dog made a rumbling sound in its throat.

She turned and said, "You're gonna get it too."

The motel was a dump, built a half century earlier, twenty rooms stretched along a broken-blacktop parking lot. The room smelled of cigarette smoke, sweat, urine, whiskey, and disinfectant. The windows were glazed with dirt, and the venetian blinds were yellow with age. The bed was short and lumpy, covered with a shiny maroon bedspread that she didn't want to touch.

Instead of throwing her clothes on the bed, she'd hung them on a hook by the shower. The wooden handle of a wicked knife stuck out of a sheath tucked inside the back pocket of the jeans.

An ancient television sat on a corner table. It didn't work. The room had one solid appliance: the big chain on the door, which, she thought, it probably needed.

The motel office was down at the far end of the building. When she'd walked in a half hour earlier, the clerk, a too-thin, windburnt man in his forties with a hard, bobbing Adam's apple, had said, "We don't usually take dogs."

She ignored the comment. "How much for the room?"

He looked her over. She wore a hoodie pulled down over her forehead, and sunglasses. The bottom part of her face was pretty, except for a bruised lip. Her only luggage was a man's leather briefcase.

"Could be free, depending," he said, trying to be cool about it.

He failed. The office looked like it hadn't been cleaned since the place was built, with paper trash everywhere. A dusty box of Snickers candy bars was propped next to the cash register, the same cash register that had a trucker's bumper sticker stuck to it that read ASS, GRASS OR CASH, NOBODY RIDES FREE. Somebody had crossed out the RIDES with a Magic Marker and written above it SLEEPS.

"I don't want free," the girl said. She dug a twenty-dollar bill out of her jeans, held it up with two fingers. "For me and the dog. I only want the room for a couple of hours, for a shower and a nap. I don't need a receipt."

He looked her over again, then reached under the counter and produced a key on a tag. "You're in room eighteen. Be out by one o'clock. You bring in any guys, I get a cut."

"Won't be any guys," she said. She snapped the bill down onto the counter, took the key, and was out of there.

Standing naked in front of the mirror, she picked up the shears and ran her fingers through her hair. No more sentimental moments; she started cutting. When she was done, long curls of red hair lay in the sink, like streaks of blood.

In the mirror, she'd changed: she looked lighter, thinner, almost elfin; the short hair emphasized her high cheekbones. She'd cut it just short of punk.

Now for the color. She took two bottles, a tube of conditioner, and some gloves out of the Clairol box, read the instructions, poured the color into the activator, and began working the black dye through her hair. Because her hair was so short, she'd need less than half of it. Behind her, the dog whimpered.

"Smells like cat pee, huh?"

When she was finished, she picked up the comb, got the bottle, and said, "C'mere boy."

The dog whimpered again.

An hour later, they were done. She pulled on her damp shirt, put the comb and shears in the briefcase, and used the last of the motel towels to dry her hair and the dog's. He was contributing a whole new stink to the smelly room.

"Let's get your collar back on," she said. "You look undressed."

The dog had been a silver gray. She'd used the comb to drag the color through the hair on his forehead, back, and sides, but hadn't tried to get all of it. He looked pretty good in black and gray: like an off-brand German shepherd.

She looked off-brand herself. Different. So different that after she buckled the collar on the dog, she turned and examined herself in the mirror for a long minute, getting used to it.

Shay Remby was gone. Who was this new girl?

She moved the sheath and knife to the small of her back, pulled on her hoodie, and picked up the briefcase. The dog was already at the door. She clipped on his leash, tossed the room key on the table next to the TV, and then they were out of the motel and walking down the street, moving fast.

There had to be good parts of Stockton, California, she thought, but this wasn't one of them. The streets were rough, the buildings decrepit. Broken windows were everywhere; the ones that weren't broken were covered with bars or heavy mesh screens. A gang was busy tagging the bare concrete walls and every other flat place they could find.

She turned the corner and saw Spartan Assembly straight ahead. She had no idea what was done there. A factory of some kind, she thought, with fifty cars parked outside. The best place to hide a car, she'd learned in the last few days, is a crowded parking lot.

"You're gonna smell up the Jeep," she said to the dog. "I love you anyway."

The dog rumbled at her.

The black Jeep Rubicon, almost new, sat in the middle row of the parking lot. She popped the door, let the dog jump into the driver's seat, then pushed him over to the passenger side. A moment later, they were moving, the girl and the dog turning their heads to look out the windshield, the side and back windows.

On guard against the world.

Running.

1

IN THE BEGINNING . . .

The leader of the group had the Taser, a snub-nosed stun gun that looked like a miniature Super Soaker. There were six baseball bats and two commercial bolt cutters scattered among them, hung on loops beneath casual jackets. A seventeen-year-old boy, muscled up from white-water kayaking, had the ten-pound sledgehammer. They all carried ski masks and heavy work gloves.

Twelve young people altogether, male and female in equal numbers, most still in their teens. If they were stopped by the police, there would be no defense for the gear, so they were on edge, jumpy, looking around as they walked.

Ready to run.

But the distance from the cars was short, and the exposure was brief. A risk that had to be taken.

They had one big fence to get through.

The fence was twelve feet high, with razor wire on the top: they couldn't climb it. The bottom of the fence was set in a band of concrete: they couldn't dig under it. They couldn't cut through it, or even touch it, because of a spiderweb of motion alarms.

There was one possible entry, at a back gate. The gate, which was almost never used, was secured with an electronic lock that opened only with the right magnetic card.

They didn't have one of those. They did have a deck of obsolete cards, kept by the son of a former researcher. The boy was a computer hacker who'd studied the cards for years and claimed to have found the algorithm by which the codes were updated.

Eventually, one of the women in the group had paid attention to what he was saying. She'd led him through cyber attacks on several animal lab facilities, and the damage had been impressive. The woman took the high school senior as a lover to tie him more tightly to the group.

Two weeks earlier, he'd stuck a recorder card into the electronic lock to get a reading on the current lock code. A few hours later, he'd produced a new card that he swore would open the gate and silence the alarms around it.

Some of the members of the group had their doubts, but the boy didn't. He was ultimately convincing.

All twelve of the raiders were committed, some more committed than others. At least two would give great sighs of relief if the card failed and they couldn't get in.

The target was a research laboratory near the university in Eugene, Oregon, a heavy user of live animals: the usual mice and rats, but also rabbits, cats, and rhesus monkeys. The lab's website was glossy and vague—a lot of PR double-talk about searching for a cure for Parkinson's disease. But they had an insider who told them that something else was going on, something a lot stranger and meaner. The animals, he said, were being used and abused in ways that had no relevance to Parkinson's or any other disease.

"They're trying to make robots out of living beings" is the way he put it. "I don't know why, but I think they're planning to make robots out of people. They've killed hundreds of those monkeys, and they're killing more all the time."

The raiders were ready to believe. They'd all been involved in tree sitting, and tree spiking, and then more extreme environmental sabotage actions. They all knew each other and their various levels of commitment. Five of the twelve had been to jail at least once. The others had been luckier.

Or faster.

They crossed the parking lot in three groups, through the dense, fishy odor of the Willamette River, and converged on an alley between two anonymous warehouse buildings. The alley was the riskiest part, the part where it'd be almost impossible to run, where they could be trapped.

They saw no one.

Emerging from the alley, they moved sideways down the back of one of the buildings to three large Dumpsters that smelled of rotting vegetables and spoiled milk. The Dumpsters were fifty feet from the gate and provided temporary concealment.

The leader checked the power level on the Taser, then said, "Masks, everyone."

The black knit ski masks came out of their jacket pockets. Sixteen-year-old Aubrey Calder giggled nervously as she fitted the breathing hole around her lip-glossed mouth and whispered, "I'm seriously wetting my pants."

Time enough to do a lot of damage.

The leader put the cell phone to his face again, stepped over the threshold, and said, "Go!"

The raiders streamed across the tarmac, through the gate, across the grass, into the building. They knew exactly where they were going. They went down the hall, running, up the back stairs, through a fire door, and down another hall.

The steel door between the hall and the first animal containment unit was kept locked, but there were so many people coming and going that the lab workers left the key on a chain hanging on a coat peg inside the lunchroom. A security violation, but who'd ever know about it?

Their insider did. He'd also told them that the office doors, and the lunchroom door, were locked, but made of wood.

"This is it," the leader said to Christopher, the sledge guy, as they stood outside the lunchroom door. "Hit it right, because when you do, they'll be coming."

"I'll hit it," Christopher said. He'd done it before, and was already buzzed from the adrenaline. He looked back at the others. "Everybody ready?" And without waiting for a response, he raised the sledge and said, "Here we go."

He swung, and the door smashed open, the small inset windows shattering into the hallway like diamonds on the concrete floor. An alarm fired, shrieking down the halls, adding an air of panic and energy.

Ignoring the alarm, the leader stepped past the broken door, looked to his right. A half-dozen coat pegs were set into the wall, with white lab coats hanging off them. He started pulling the coats off, found the key under the fourth one, dashed back to the containment area door, fitted the key in the lock, turned it, and pushed the door open.

Another raider, eighteen-year-old Danny, who had a stopwatch on a loop of parachute cord around his neck, bellowed over the siren: "Time's running: three minutes fifty seconds."

The idea was not to liberate the animals, but to wreck the experiments. To do that, the animals didn't have to be freed, but simply set loose to contaminate each other and themselves. Lab animals were carefully separated to prevent infection by stray viruses or bacteria, which would uncontrollably alter any experimental results.

Nor did the raiders have any illusions about permanently stopping the experimentation—the forces pushing it were simply too powerful. But they could demonstrate, with YouTube videos, what was done to the animals in the name of science. Or just in the name of better cosmetics. Danny, the stopwatch monitor, was also operating a high-res Sony video camera, catching the chaos as it spread through the lab.

And people shouted over the noise of the destruction:

"Gimme a crowbar, I need a crowbar. . . ."

"Cutters, cutters, where the hell are the cutters?"

"Sledge, where's the sledge?"

One girl smashed a plastic-front cage, and a piece of the plastic, sharp as glass, cut her hand, not badly, but the sight of the blood running down her arm pushed the others even harder.

• • •

The raiders went through the first containment unit like a hurricane. The experimental animals—all rodents in this first room—were held in plastic cages stacked one atop another in three lines of steel racks. Some raiders smashed the plastic doors with their baseball bats while others scooped the panicked animals out of their cages. In thirty seconds, hundreds and then thousands of rats and mice were scurrying between the raiders' feet and sometimes up their legs.

Christopher, the sledge carrier, had been smashing every piece of expensive-looking lab gear that he could find, then began battering open the screened windows, knocking out the wire grids between the glass and the outside. Some of the raiders began scooping up binfuls of mice and shoveling them out the windows.

The alarm sirens screamed on.

Then they entered the primate unit, and the pandemonium momentarily stopped as they reacted in stunned horror to what they found: A hundred or more pink-faced, humanlike rhesus monkeys were isolated in separate Plexiglas cages. The tops of their skulls had been cut away and replaced with glass or plastic caps, and computer modules were strapped to the animals' backs. A dozen of the monkeys lay in quivering heaps, as though near death, or simply paralyzed with fear or pain; the others screamed and scampered to the backs of their cages. A baby monkey with a missing skullcap clung to its mother, who'd been similarly altered.

The raiders used bolt cutters to slice the locks off the cage doors, and then, protected by thick leather work gloves, they began pulling the mutilated animals from their cages. One girl—Laura—started screaming, and never did stop, as she reached inside again and again, the monkeys' eyes blank or wild, some shaking uncontrollably and without pause, defecating and urinating in fear and pain and what might have been anger.

Christopher was smashing out the exterior windows, and one of the experimental monkeys, which had been scampering down the hallway between the legs of the raiders, jumped onto the window ledge and then dropped out of sight. Another one saw it go, and followed.

The noise was terrific—the sirens, the screaming girls, the screaming animals, and the smashing of the cages, which sounded like an army of men beating on garbage cans with steel pipes. People continued to call for help: "Gimme a bat, we need a bat over here. Watch that monkey, he's a biter. . . ."

Danny, the timekeeper, looked at his stopwatch and yelled, "Two minutes," and the fury continued: smash, smash, smash, scream, smash, scream . . .

And the sirens wailed like banshees.

Rachel, wild brown hair curling out from under her ski mask, got Christopher to break a door marked DR. LAWRENCE JANES.

Inside, she found a secretary's desk near the door and an enclosed space at the back. She went straight to a double-wide four-drawer file cabinet. The cabinet was locked, but she pulled a short crowbar out of her belt, wedged it into the lip of the drawer, and then stood back while Christopher gave the bar a whack.

The door popped loose, revealing a line of hanging folders. She pulled three of them out, carried them to the desk, and shook them. An envelope containing a thumb drive popped out of each.

They'd been told by their insider that the thumb drives contained backup files and reports on the research being done at the facility. She went back for more folders, shaking out the thumb drives.

"Rachel!" A thin, awkward teen stepped in, banging his hip on the desk but holding fast to a maimed rat. His voice was cool, but the anger clawed through. "Look at this! Look what they're doing. They cut off her legs! How could they do that?"

The woman barely looked up. "Not *how*—*why*?" she said, and dumped four more drives onto the desk. "Put that thing down and stick these drives in your pockets."

The boy tipped the rat gently onto one hand and started picking up drives with the other. "It's pointless—they're gonna be encrypted."

She paused in her search. "You couldn't decrypt them?"

"The CIA couldn't decrypt them if the encryption is strong." He unconsciously scratched the rat between the ears and glanced around the room. "The thing is . . . you don't want to jump through your butt when you need the files, either. The decryption software is probably on one of these machines."

She looked around, waved at the enclosed space at the back of the office. "That's gotta be Janes's working space. See what you can do in two minutes."

"All right." The boy walked away with the rat and came back fifteen seconds later with a compact tower computer under his arm. "If it's on here, we got it."

He was still holding the rat in his other hand.

"You can't take the rat," Rachel said. "Ethan loves your key card, but he doesn't love any of us enough to change the rules. The rat's called *evidence*."

She went back to rifling the last drawer. They'd gotten twelve thumb drives in all. Down the hall, the timekeeper screamed, "Ninety seconds."

The boy turned away.

"Hey," she called before he plunged back into the pandemonium. "Take this with you. Hide it." She handed him the crowbar.

Whatever Rachel meant to him, Odin was sorry, but he was taking the rat.

In the weeks since she'd become his first-ever girlfriend, he'd helped her crash the systems in a couple of animal labs, but tonight was his first raid involving actual live animals. The suffering made him physically ill. The only reason he was still functioning was because he'd zeroed in on one living thing, one tortured rat, that he could save.

When he left the containment units, he was headed for the stairs and then back to the van, to hide the rat. He pushed through two doors, to the stairs. There, just before he was about to start down, he saw a flickering reddish light coming from beneath a door farther down the hall.

Curiosity got the best of him; he still had a minute. He walked down the hall and peered through the door's hand-sized window. He could see racks of laboratory glass and high-tech electronic equipment, but nothing else. He tried the doorknob, but the door was locked. He'd turned away, back toward the stairs, when he heard a strangled howl.

"What?" He said it aloud, to nobody.

He put the computer and rat on the floor, jammed the blade of the crowbar against the door's strike plate, and threw his weight against it. The door splintered, and after a couple of more hacks, he

At the sight of the raiders, he scrolled through the contacts list on his cell phone until he got to the *S*'s and the head security honcho he'd never personally met: Sync.

He called the number on the landline and heard two beeps just like the two beeps he'd heard during the company's simulated emergency drills. He blurted, "Eugene lab, Code White! We've got all kinds of people busting out the animals. I repeat, Code White!"

He hung up and dialed 911. An operator came on and asked, "Is this an emergency?"

"Yes!" he shouted. "I'm at the EDT Lab on Franklin and we've got people in the building smashing open the cages for the lab animals. They're wrecking the place. Lots of people, they've got weapons. I need backup right now."

"Could you give us your name?" The voice was calm, even remote.

Still shouting: "Darrell McClane, I'm the security guard. I need cops. I'm armed. I'm going in, but I need some cops."

"We have a car on the way."

"There are a lot of them, we need more than one car," he shouted. "I'm going in." He dropped the phone and pulled his pistol.

He was carrying his favorite piece, a Model 1911A1 Colt .45. He was so excited that he nearly forgot to jack a round into the chamber—he did that only when he was out the door and halfway to the elevator.

McClane was overweight, an out-of-shape fifty-four, a resolute smoker and former drinker, but he'd studied all the Bruce Willis movies, some of which featured a cop who was also named McClane.

A movie star would have rushed the stairs, but under it all, the real McClane knew that if he rushed the stairs, he'd probably have a heart attack. So he stood at the elevator, and waited, and then, inside the car, waited some more, impatiently pushing the CLOSE DOOR button, until the elevator began slowly heading for the second floor.

At the top, when the doors opened, he did a quick peek and then slid down the hall to the first locked door. He unlocked it with his key card, and then went to the next door and unlocked it, back always to the wall, so that he was more or less walking sideways, the gun out front.

That all took time, and the longer it took, the more scared he got, until finally, with his heart pounding like a steam engine, his gun clenched in his right hand, he turned the last corner.

At the other end of the hall, he saw a tall man in a black mask and two others behind him, also masked, and the tall man saw him and shouted, "Security, security! Let's go!" and all three of them disappeared down the next hall, and he could hear more people screaming, "Security!"

McClane went after them, face red as a beet, and at the corner of the next hall, looked down and saw a half-dozen people crowding toward a stairwell door and more still coming out of the animal containment facility.

McClane screamed, "Halt!" and brought the gun up, jerked off a shot, which went through the ceiling fifteen feet in front of him.

The shot was like a thunderclap in the tile hallway, and McClane rocked back, astonished by what he'd done. He was disoriented, screamed, "Halt!" again, and fired another shot, which also went into the ceiling. At that moment, the leader stepped through an office door behind McClane, fifteen feet away, with the Taser.

McClane was already into his third shot and fired it, and saw a masked raider at the stairwell go down, and then his world blew up as the Taser element buried itself in his hip.

The sixteen-year-old nervous giggler, the honors student Aubrey Calder, took McClane's last shot. The bullet hit her in the back, blew through a shoulder blade, broke her collarbone on the way out, and then smashed through a window down the hall. She fell faceup, her eyes half closed, stunned. She was awake for ten seconds, then began to shake, her eyes rolling up, not understanding, feeling no pain or anything like regret, and then she passed out.

A boy her own age stood over her shouting, "Oh jeez, oh jeez! Aubrey!" and unconsciously smacking his head with his fists. The older raider, who'd fired the Taser into McClane's hip, hopped over the twitching body of the security guard, ran down the corridor, stooped over her.

"We've got to leave her," he said urgently to the boy. "We've got to leave! She's hurt bad, but she's not going to die if they get her to a hospital. Leaving her is the fastest way—the cops will be here in two minutes."

He pushed the boy away from the downed girl, pushed him again, and again—and then the boy pushed back and said, "Fuck you, I'm staying! I'm staying with her!"

He ripped off his jacket, ski mask, and T-shirt, then folded the T-shirt and packed it against the wound; the leader, the Taser shooter, looked back once as he fled toward the stairs and shouted, "Don't tell them who we are!"

The remaining raiders streamed out of the building. Sirens: they were close and coming fast, but they had known that would happen. They had time . . .

In the building's security lights, they could see monkeys scattered across the lawn, struggling to walk, to crawl, monkeys screaming at the darkness in pain and despair, metal wires glittering in their exposed brains. Two other monkeys stood silhouetted in the second-floor lab windows, apparently unwilling to jump.

The raiders threaded through the gate and disappeared down the alley.

By the time the cops got to the building, McClane had pushed himself into an upright seated position, leaning against a wall, his nerves still jangled by the high-voltage Taser pulse. Two deranged and bloodied monkeys were fighting a few feet away, paying no attention to him; the hall stank of fecal matter and urine and blood. A thousand white rats and mice scampered aimlessly down the tile hallway.

At the stairwell door, a half-naked boy seemed to be praying over the body of a fallen raider.

The cops came in with their pistols drawn, saw McClane, leveled their guns, and shouted, "Push the gun away."

"I'm security," McClane shouted back.

"Sir, push the gun away," a cop shouted again. "Push the gun away or we will shoot you."

McClane realized that the cops didn't like the idea of his having a gun, and he slid it down the hall toward them. One of the cops, his gun never wavering from a point on McClane's chest, eased down the hall, kicked the gun farther away. "You have any other weapons?"

"No. Listen, I'm the guy who called you." He pointed at the boy and unmoving body. "They were with them. They were wrecking the place—"

"Sir, I want you to lie flat, put your hands behind you."

"But I'm security—"

"Sir, I want you to lie flat. . . ." One cop watched McClane while the other focused on the two figures on the floor down the hall.

When they had him cuffed, McClane strained his head around to look at them and said, "They pointed a gun at me. I had to shoot . . ."

Two more cops moved past him—one crying out in fear when a rat ran up his pant leg—until they got to the boy and the body. A bloody ski mask lay on the floor next to the fallen girl. The boy looked up, fear in his eyes, and said, "She's hurt bad. Please help me, that asshole shot her . . ."

The cops said, "Back away, lie flat, put your hands behind you—now!"

He did, and one of the cops knelt by the fallen girl and said, "She's hurt; we gotta get her going, we need paramedics right now."

"On the way . . . ," the second cop said.

McClane called, "Is he dead?"

One of the cops had a daughter of his own, a girl who sometimes snuck a little dope and misbehaved. He stood up and snarled, "It's not a *he,* it's a *she.* And no, she's not dead yet. You shot a pretty little high school girl, you fuckin' moron."

By the time the cops got to Aubrey Calder, the leadership van was a mile away and moving out of the city.

"Nothing is worth that," said a girl in the back. "Aubrey was my friend."

"Nothing like that's ever happened before," said the leader. He was in the passenger seat upfront, stuffing a garbage bag with the gloves and masks they'd worn in the raid. From between his feet, he picked up a bottle of bleach and emptied it into the bag, closed the bag, and squeezed it until the contents were soaked; bleach destroys DNA. "Nothing even close to that. There was no reason for that rent-a-cop to go and shoot. We weren't threatening anybody."

The young woman with the wild brown hair, Rachel, was at the wheel and glanced back at her. "Ethan's right—it wasn't our fault and it's awful. I'm sure she'll be okay." She held up a thumb drive. "When we find out what's on these, what was really going on in there, you'll see. This is the greatest thing we've ever done. Legendary."

The girl wasn't buying it. "She was studying for her SATs," she said bitterly, and she began crying, unable to control it. She choked out, "She was trying for Stanford, she was taking all the AP classes. Now what? She's going to prison if she lives?"

"Get a grip, would you?" the woman shot back. "We can't all go losing it."

Ethan glanced up from his work. "About that—you're absolutely sure the new guy got out? 'Cause if he's still in there pocketing rats or whatever he was doing—"

Rachel broke in, defensive. "I told you, he couldn't handle the scene and took off. He's in the other van. Might have one rat with him, but the thing was basically DOA."

"Just make sure he doesn't take his microchipped lab pet to a veterinarian. That's a one-way ticket to the state pen."

Rachel rolled her eyes and Ethan told her to pull over, next to the mouth of a storm sewer. He slid the panel door open, threw the garbage bag into the sewer, then looked back at her as he pulled the door shut. "We shouldn't have taken him. From now on, he only does the computer-nerd stuff. You've got to keep him under control."

"He's not all that easy to control," Rachel said. "He's a little nuts, remember?"

"Well, use your feminine wiles, for God's sake. You're good at that," Ethan said, sarcasm riding his voice.

Rachel bared her teeth at the implication. She and Ethan had once been together. "I got him," she said.

"Good," he said, "because we went through that gate like it wasn't there. That kid is a weapon. We've needed somebody like him for a long time. Now that we've got him—"

"I got him," Rachel said.

Two miles away, Odin held the muzzled dog to his chest as the second van took a curve a little fast. He had the third-row seat all to himself, and the girl named Laura said, "We gotta figure out what to do. What if Aubrey's dead? We're gonna be in so much trouble."

"I gotta go home, this is my dad's van," the driver said, checking the rearview mirror for flashing lights. "What about you, Odin? Take you home?"

"Can't. Not with the dog," he said. "Besides, I don't really have a home. Drop me at the park, I'll hook up with Rachel later."

"I can't believe this," the driver said, and Laura started to sniffle.

Odin said, "This is what happens sometimes. We were never playing games here. These people are killers—all you have to do is see the lab. But Aubrey: jeez, I hope she's all right. Jeez, I hope she's okay."

The wolfish gray dog with the single yellow eye took it all in, but the dog hadn't known Aubrey Calder.

All the dog felt was:

Freedom.

McClane, the security guard, was read his rights and taken in handcuffs to police headquarters, the cops talking about a possible charge of aggravated assault, or even murder, if the girl died. At the police station, he was uncuffed, said he didn't need a lawyer, and gave a straightforward statement, except for one small lie. He had, he said, fired his weapon deliberately into the ceiling, and the third shot had unintentionally gone straight down the hall as a result of his being shot with a Taser.

He knew that the tasing had come after the shot, but he'd picked up enough bad feelings from the cops that he thought it best to adjust the time line.

An attorney from the prosecutor's office sat in on the interview, and made the point with detectives that it would be difficult to make a case against McClane if he fired a gun in defense of the laboratory, which was precisely what he'd been hired to do. In fact, he had been certified by the city to do just that. They released him at six o'clock in the morning, but the police kept his gun.

Two days later, when detectives reviewed the security video of the raid, they saw clearly that McClane had shot Aubrey Calder before he was tased, but by then McClane was covered by an attorney and no longer talking.

On the morning of his release, confused, frightened, and depressed, McClane went back to the laboratory. The lawn and streets around the lab were crowded with dozens of people who looked like crazed golfers, running stooped across the grass and blacktop, trying to catch ricocheting golf balls—the thousands of white mice that had been shoveled out the windows.

Inside, the entire staff was also attempting to corral loose mice and rats.

McClane was spotted by Mary Trane, the personnel director. She did a double take, then said, "Thank God. Sync has been asking for you."

"I was with the police," McClane mumbled. He'd always found Trane intimidating.

"Yes, yes, we know," she said. "Come this way."

"I didn't ... I didn't mean to shoot that girl, it was an accident. . . . Ah, God ..." McClane began to snuffle. Trane looked away.

Trane rattled down a first-floor hallway in four-inch heels—McClane had never seen her without them—not flinching when a couple of tiny black-eyed white mice dashed past her.

"This man is from San Francisco, company headquarters," she said, over her shoulder. "He flew here on the company jet. He's the one you called."

"Mr. Sync?"

"It's not 'Mr. Sync,' it's Stephen N. Creighton," she said, still half turned as she walked. "His initials are SNC and everybody calls him Sync. That's what you should call him. Sync."

"Sync," McClane repeated after her.

"One more thing, Mr. McClane," she said. She stopped to peer at him. "Do not lie to Sync. Tell him the absolute truth, whatever that is."

"I will," McClane said.

She led him down to the conference room, where a tall, silver-haired man in army-style steel-rimmed glasses and a pin-striped suit was talking to the lab director and his assistant. She stepped inside and said, "Darrell McClane, the security guard."

Sync nodded and said to the other two men, "Give me a moment alone with Mr. McClane. I'll find you up in your offices."

They left, with Trane pulling the door shut behind her.

Sync was at least six foot six, McClane thought, and looked to be in extraordinarily good shape, like a pro basketball player. He had sharp cheekbones, a squared-off chin, and the hair at the sides of his head was neatly buzzed. He had a scar on his right temple, a patch about the diameter of a quarter, that might have come from a burn. He pulled up a chair and pointed at another for McClane.

"Bad business," he said as McClane sat. "Now: I want you to tell me everything that happened, from the moment the alarms went off until you walked through the door one minute ago."

McClane told him, in detail. The recital took five minutes and then Sync cross-examined him for another five.

When they were done, Sync said, "We know this has been a shock. We want you to take a week off—but don't go anywhere. We will provide an attorney, a very good one, to handle any legal issues you may encounter, at no cost to yourself. We don't anticipate any criminal action against you, but you may be sued by this girl you shot. If you're sued, we will defend you. If you are penalized in any way, which we doubt, we will pay the penalty. In the meantime, we will increase your salary by two hundred dollars a week, ten thousand dollars a year. This disaster is not of your making. You did exactly as we expected you to do and we are pleased with your performance. So go home, and be available for that attorney."

"I really appreciate it," McClane said. Relief flooded through him: Sync was a guy who had your back. He tried to tell the story again, of how the girl had gotten shot, but Sync, showing a flash of impatience, waved him off. "Darrell, go home. Can you drive? Good. Try to get some sleep."

A man knocked at the door and stepped inside. McClane had never seen him before, but he had an air of cool efficiency. He was younger than Sync, but wore the same kind of expensive conservative suit and had the same close-cropped hair. Like Sync, he had ice-blue eyes.

Sync nodded and said, "Thorne."

Thorne was carrying a box. "I went down to one of the dorms and found some students and got them to wake up their friends. Five dollars for every mouse or rat—Janes counted, we got all the monkeys back. We've got sixty people out there now and they're all calling their friends. We'll have five hundred people here in an hour. I'm sending Lictor out there with the cash to pay them off."

He pulled the top off the box, and McClane saw that it was filled with cash. "I got fifty thousand. That should be enough."

Sync nodded. "Good. I've got Pascal and Coombs coming in to handle the PR. They should be at the airport in an hour. Get somebody to meet them." Then he turned to McClane and said, "Darrell, good work. Stay close to your house." McClane, dismissed, went out the door.

When the door closed behind him, Sync turned back to Thorne and said, "If that idiot hadn't shot the girl, this would be a hell of a lot easier to manage. We need to get that blond woman up from United Parkinson's. The good-looking one with the cleavage, the one who cries on cue. They love her on cable news. We need to get her on the air everywhere, about what a tragedy this is, the setback to research. Maybe sweeten the pot for her. Her husband runs a management consulting company. Maybe you could talk to him about a consult."

"We need to talk to those kids," Thorne said.

"Yeah, we do. But they're juveniles, and their folks have more money than Jesus Christ and all the apostles. They're all lawyered up."

"Will McClane be a risk?" Thorne asked.

"No. I don't see it," Sync said. "He knows almost nothing—one of the least curious people I've ever met. We'll cover him with an attorney, weld his mouth shut with a raise, maybe have Trane talk to him about his pension rights and what a shame it would be to lose them at his age."

The other man nodded. "If he does become a problem, I can handle it."

"I don't think that'll be necessary," Sync said. "We do need to get copies of the security videos. Harmon and I have taken a look at them, but we need more analysis. The police know about them, but Olafson told them they're all digital and he didn't know exactly how to download them. He told them we'd get the camera company in here tomorrow to retrieve them."

"Good."

"Yes," Sync said. "Now: we need to know exactly who these crazies are—we probably have their names and faces in the database, so we need to match them up. We need that dog. We really need the dog."

"We're checking with Eugene animal control, in case he's loose and someone's picked him up."

"Tell your rat catchers: a thousand bucks for the dog," said Sync. "Get that money out to Lictor and send Harmon in."

Thorne nodded and left. A moment later, a man closer to Sync's age, casually dressed in jeans, a chambray shirt, and cowboy boots, stepped through the door. He said, "Boss?"

Harmon wore dark aviators, which he didn't remove.

"We've got a problem with Janes," Sync said. "The damn fool kept copies of the research files on thumb drives, and kept the thumb drives in a regular file cabinet from Staples."

"Not locked?"

"It was locked, but it probably didn't take ten seconds to jimmy. Those drives should have been in a thousand-pound safe bolted to the floor. I need you to go up there and scare the shit out of him. Do that nervous-crazy thing you do. Shout. I need a complete reconstruction of what went out of here, and I need it fast."

"The files were encrypted, though?"

"Yeah." Sync rubbed his hands over his face, as if trying to wake himself from a bad dream. "He was using those DARPA drives. Automatic military-grade encryption. Every thumb drive has a separate password, a long password, and if he'd used a password generator, they'd probably be unbreakable. But he didn't. Janes made up the passwords as he went along. Ex-wives, girlfriends, kids, cats . . . Jesus. So they're crackable. The encryption was separate, but the encryption software was on Janes's office computer, and they took that too. If they've got the computer mojo and crack those passwords, they'll get everything."

"If they're long, how did Janes remember them? Did he write them down somewhere?"

"He says he has a password safe on his phone, and a backup on a home computer. They won't get those. If they try to crack the passwords, they'll have to do it the hard way."

Harmon nodded. "At the least, that'll give us some time."

"Yes. Now: hostile assessment," Sync said. "Let's hear it."

"These kids were pretty good," Harmon said. Not a compliment, but a professional judgment. "Gloves, masks, so no fingerprints, no faces. Had precise intel, which means they've got at least one inside source. Cracked the back gate's electronic lock, don't know how they did it. Came with the perfect equipment, they were on the clock right from the start. We found a baseball bat that somebody dropped, had a hole drilled in the handle with a leather loop tied through it so they could carry it under a jacket. They've done it before."

"Any hints?"

"We're doing a relational search on Calder and the other kid to see who they connect with. That might get us somewhere."

"We need it fast, Harmon. Find them."

Harmon stretched his arms over his head, cracked his knuckles, and said, "Man, I like this shit."

"Like it on your own time." Sync picked up a printout, a list of names of people who worked in the lab. One of them was a traitor. He crumpled the paper in one large fist and snarled at Harmon, "I want these people. I'm going to step on them like a bunch of cockroaches."

• • •

When Harmon was gone, Sync stepped over to the windows, which were covered with an electric blind. He pushed the UP button, waited as the blind rolled up, and looked outside. There were people everywhere, including a kid who was carrying a see-through plastic tub, dozens of mice scrabbling unsuccessfully to get up the sides. The kid was getting rich this morning—student rich, anyway, Sync thought.

A lot to do this day, and he needed a little silence to think about it.

The Eugene lab was critical to the interface research. They had other labs, in other countries, where they could do the kind of research that would put them in jail in the United States. But those countries didn't have the necessary intellectual or technical resources. They needed Eugene and the other secret facilities in America, but if the public learned about what they were doing there . . .

Sync and his security personnel could deal with the inevitable minor leaks. A quiet conversation with key people in the government, or the military, or the intelligence agencies, could handle the small stuff. The biggest threat to the program, to the company, and to the people running it, himself included, was the American public. If the public knew what was going on, if the wrong video should go viral . . .

The missing thumb drives, should somebody decrypt them, had enough distasteful video material to start just that kind of fire.

He became aware of the pain in his hands and looked down at his balled fists. He'd squeezed so hard that the bones stood out in pale white relief.

He relaxed them, opened them, felt the blood flow back.

So much to do, and too big a prize to let slip.

Fools. If they only knew . . .

4

Hollywood.

The young woman cut through a crowd of fashionistas, a comet of rust-red hair in a cluster of blondes. She sliced past someone she vaguely recognized as a movie star, hazel eyes tapping his before turning away in uninterest, not running but hurrying, like the White Rabbit.

She was wearing a flannel shirt, ripped blue jeans, and waterproof hiking boots. A hoodie was tied around her waist. Not exactly boy-bait clubbing gear, but not a girl who went unnoticed.

Her eyes scanned the throng around her, searching for a particular face, not finding it. The star's head craned toward her like a missile locking on a target.

"Get her number!" he barked to his bodyguard, an ex-linebacker in a suit. The star pushed past a velvet rope and took two quick hits of breath spray. "Move! I need that chick's number."

• • •

They'd seen females with knives before. Usually, they were no big problem, but this one seemed like she might know what she was doing.

She moved slowly backward, but also slipped sideways, first one way, and then the other, so she was always one-on-one, rather than between the two of them.

Knife looked nasty. Still, they had the reach on her . . .

She was moving in a crouch, and she feinted toward the one on the left, and he felt the point of the knife flick past his eyes and then come in low, toward his gut, and he managed, just barely, to jump back; he grunted, "Jesus . . ."

But the other reached out, a punch, and almost tagged her on the forehead. Not much room left. With the knife in her right hand, her left hand reached back, feeling for the wall of the Dumpster. She needed to know exactly where she was. . . .

Then a third man walked into her field of view, behind her attackers, ambling in from the mouth of the alley. He said, "What the hell? Rollo? Dick? That can't be you."

The two thugs swiveled their heads toward the voice.

In the dim light from an overhead billboard, the newcomer looked, Shay Remby thought, a little like the Cat in the Hat, one of her favorite childhood characters. Not an especially friendly cat, not this one.

He wore a shabby round-topped bowler hat, a rumpled linen jacket over a black T-shirt, and black jeans, with polished motorcycle boots. He was on the short side, even with the bowler hat and boots, and he was slender, with a three-day beard. He was leaning on a gold-headed walking stick.

His face was crossed by a scar, which started somewhere below the rim of the hat, cut over his left eyebrow and cheek, and disappeared below his jaw, as though he'd been hit with a machete. His narrow shoulders heaved with a sigh.

He said, "You can't have forgotten. I mean, how could you forget? You're banned from Hollywood. This . . ." He looked around him, as though perplexed. "This is certainly Hollywood. Isn't it?"

Rollo and Dick—Shay had their names now—stepped away from her, and Rollo said, "Watch her, watch her . . ."

Dick glanced at her and said, "Stay put or I cut your face off," and a knife flicked open in his hand. The blade was six inches long, with a serrated edge.

The four of them were now spread out in a rough diamond shape, with Rollo and Dick in the middle, their heads swiveling back and forth between Shay and the Cat in the Hat. Rollo snarled at the man: "You forget your goons? Flying solo, like Superman?"

"This saddens me," the Cat in the Hat said. He didn't seem at all afraid of the switchblade.

Shay glanced back at the Dumpster, assessing the possibility of escape with a quick jump and a pull-up. Just then, two very tall but very thin men stepped silently to the edge of it, their toes gripping the metal rim in soft Indian-style moccasins.

They perched there, over her head, like enormous owls on a low branch. One of them smiled down at her.

As the thugs had moved away from Shay, they'd focused on the Cat in the Hat and hadn't seen the newcomers.

"You gonna be a lot sadder when we cut you," Rollo said, moving off to his right, showing a razor. "Ain't gonna be enough left to feed my dogs."

Dick circled to his left, the switchblade slashing air.

"An assault on me is an insult to Dum and Dee," the Cat in the Hat said, not moving to defend himself.

"Dum and Dee?" Shay blurted. She didn't know what was going on. Hollywood had always seemed confusing, but this was ridiculous.

"Two butt-ugly goons who do his dirty work," Dick said, as if talking to himself. He never took his eyes off the Cat in the Hat. He behaved as though the small man was dangerous, though he didn't look it. "Two crazy orange-headed mothers."

Shay cocked her head. "You mean like . . . these guys?"

Dick and Rollo jerked around as the two hawk-nosed giants dropped into the alley. They were, Shay thought, at least six eight, and twins, with pockmarked complexions and, indeed, orange hair, and wearing matching outfits that might have been designed for combat in the Hollywood zone: cargo pants and black shirts, and fringed buckskin moccasins.

They each carried a club that looked like a thin, half-length baseball bat. Shay would later find out that they were Bam Bam fish bats, lead-weighted clubs normally used for killing big game fish.

Dick opened his mouth and said, "Ahhhh."

Rollo tried to run for it, but the two giants were on top of them with the bats faster than light, clubbing them down to the bricks of the alley, beating them. Bones were broken, blood spattered on the blacktop, the men screamed and rolled and crawled and tried to get up, tried to protect themselves, until Shay screamed, "Stop! You're killing them! You're killing them!"

The Cat in the Hat waved at the twins and said, "Okay. . . . Did you break Dick's leg there? I don't think you did."

One of the men—she didn't know Dum from Dee, and wondered that anyone could—stepped up with a bat and swung it like an ax down on Dick's shin and the leg broke with a crack that preceded Dick's scream by a thin nanosecond and sent an electric shiver through Shay.

She'd seen fights before, men beating on each other with their fists. She'd seen a man get cut bad in a fight outside a payday-loan store, but nothing like this. This wasn't even a fight: it was cold, calculated, almost scientific punishment, but still vicious. Dick and Rollo, large as they were and armed with blades, had no chance, and they curled up like snails and bled on the pavement.

As the beating ceased, the Cat in the Hat squatted between the two men and said, "Now: you tell Randy that if he sends you two back here, I will send Dum and Dee down to see him. They will break as many bones in his body as they can find. They might miss a few, but it won't be many."

Rollo said through bloody teeth, "When we get you—"

The Cat in the Hat didn't let him finish. His blackthorn walking stick snapped up nine or ten inches, then thumped down across the bridge of Rollo's nose, smashing it flat. Rollo screamed in renewed agony, and a gush of blood spurted from his nose and through his fingers when he tried to cover it.

Shay realized that the walking stick, with its heavy gold head, was effectively a hammer with a long handle—as nasty a weapon as Dum and Dee's clubs. She thought, *Maybe I need one of those.*

"You are not listening," the Cat in the Hat said to the two men in a quiet voice. "You're just not listening. Dee, break his wrist."

Rollo groaned, "No!" but one of the big men pinned Rollo's forearm to the ground with a giant moccasin and smashed the end of his bat into Rollo's wrist. It crunched like a walnut in a nutcracker.

"This is what happens when people like you come sniffing round my Hollywood," the Cat in the Hat said. "Now, will you give my message to Randy?"

Dick moaned something that might have been a yes.

"Good." The Cat in the Hat patted Dick on the hip. "We'll call 911 and ask them to get an ambulance down here. You fell off the roof. Hollywood roofs—they're so dangerous if you're dumb enough to climb on them."

They left the men lying there on the bloody bricks, the Cat in the Hat and Dum and Dee walking down toward the mouth of the alley, Shay trailing a safe distance behind. The man said casually, turning, "Good knife."

She said, tracking them, "Works for me." And, "Thanks for the help."

"No problem, though it wasn't entirely about you," said the Cat in the Hat. "It was more about those two. They've done some very bad things to young runaways. Very bad. We've chased them off before, but they didn't learn. They came back. As you could see."

"Pimps," she said.

"Worse than that," the Cat said. "They're more like slavers. They took a twelve-year-old girl out of here two weeks ago . . . well, never mind."

"You can't be social workers," Shay said as Dick groaned behind her.

The Cat in the Hat laughed at the thought, and Dum and Dee almost laughed, but no sound came from their oversized mouths. Shay thought that the Cat in the Hat looked like one of the happiest men she'd ever seen.

"No. We're not social workers," he said. "Where'd you learn to use the knife?"

"Around," she said.

He took in the way she was dressed and said, "Not around here."

She shrugged. "The street is the street."

"You ever stick anybody?"

"Trying to figure out how crazy I am?" Shay asked, instead of answering the question. They were getting close to the mouth of the alley, where she could break free. Behind her, she could hear one of the injured men, who'd begun to cry. He sounded like a badly injured animal—a pig, maybe.

The Cat in the Hat smiled and said, "Maybe. I basically think all women should be heavily armed." He was charming, despite the scarred face, and somewhere in his early thirties, she thought.

"Okay," she said. And, "Are you the Cat in the Hat?"

The man laughed again, and Dum and Dee did their silent laughing-like thing. The man reached into his pocket, took out a silver cigarette case, opened it, and produced a business card.

He didn't try to step closer to her, but held the card out at arm's length, where she could take it without risk of being grabbed.

The card was black, with silver script, and said:

TWIST.

Underneath that was a phone number. He said, "If you stay on the street, and stay alive, you'll hear about me. Call me when you're ready."

A tip of his hat and he was gone, the two big men behind him. Rollo groaned back in the alley and cried, "Help me."

With one backward glance, sixteen-year-old Shay Remby slipped the knife back into its sheath and was out of the alley, into the crowd.

Rollo would have to help himself.

5

Out of the alley, Shay was moving fast again, jacked up by the encounter with the pimps, or slavers, or whatever they were. She'd been on the street before, but the predators in L.A. were a whole nother thing compared to those in Eugene, who were, by comparison, gentlemen creeps.

Shay had spent her second full day in Hollywood combing storefronts and clubs looking for a face, with no luck. She needed a place to stay, she needed money, and she needed time to think about everything. One harsh thing about the street: you never had time to *think,* only to react.

Money was critical: it could buy you time, safety, even information. She had fifty-eight dollars in her pocket, and no immediate way to get more.

Shay had stashed her camping gear in an overgrown juniper behind the Del Taco on Ivar Avenue. She plucked the scuffed-up backpack from the scratchy bush and pulled it on, tightened the waist belt, and headed north on Ivar. Ahead, she could hear heavy traffic on the freeway. The famed Hollywood sign was on the mountainside beyond, but she couldn't see it. On her first night in Hollywood she'd found, to her surprise, that it wasn't lighted.

But she had a spot up ahead, safe, she thought, in some brush beneath the Hollywood Freeway overpass.

As she walked toward it, she thought about the fight. *What did the man with one name—Twist?—what did he mean,* she wondered, *when he'd said "when you're ready"?*

Ready for what?

Shay had spent her first night in a twenty-four-hour Laundromat, one eye open against a parade of men who had nothing better to do than wash their shorts at 3:00 a.m. Tonight would be better—she might actually get some sleep.

Before the sun had gone down, she'd scoped out a possible camp. She'd run away before, and had an idea of what would make her safe. She didn't go for the obvious roof-over-my-head spots—the doorways, the drainage tunnels—that would attract street people. Instead, she went for a place that looked like nothing.

Because the thing that made a female safe on the street, she'd learned, was invisibility.

After checking her backtrail and the shadows around her, she cut through a church parking lot and walked across the last street before the freeway overpass. With another quick look around, she hopped a wire-mesh fence and pushed into the brush beyond it. The stuff was tough, springy, but free of thorns.

In the center of the clump was a space long and wide enough to unroll the olive-drab bivy sack she'd taken from her foster parents' collection of camping gear. The sack was small, lightweight, and waterproof. She unrolled her summer-weight sleeping bag inside of it, climbed in, zipped up the bag, settled down, took a drink from her water bottle. She listened for a few minutes, checking for human movement. The heavy, crunchy brush was effectively a burglar alarm. Satisfied that she was alone, she pulled out a pack of saltine crackers and a jar of peanut butter.

She slipped out the knife again. Twist asked if she'd ever stuck anyone with it: she hadn't. But it worked really well for spreading peanut butter. She was neat about it, building a stack of crackers, then carefully licking off and drying the knife before eating the crackers one by one.

Twist. What was that all about? When she was ready?

Over the past two years, Shay had spent nearly a hundred nights in a tent in the mountains of Oregon and Idaho, and now was nearly as comfortable in a sleeping bag as in a regular bed. She knew the particular noises of the outdoors, and tried to settle herself by focusing on the chirping crickets, the light rustling breeze, a few nocturnal notes from a Northern mockingbird. After a while, the fight scene stopped replaying in her head and the tension leaked out of her body, but then her real worries came flooding back in . . .

Four days earlier, she'd been in Eugene, with no idea of going to Los Angeles. Three weeks before that, her brother Odin had fled their hometown and headed south, down the coast.

She'd come to find him.

• • •

Like too many nightmares, this one began with a phone call.

Shay had been in bed, asleep, at her foster parents' place when her cell phone began vibrating. It stopped before she was fully awake, then started again. She picked it off her nightstand, and the foster kid who shared the room mumbled, "Turn that thing off. Turn it off."

She looked at the screen, saw the unfamiliar number—no name—and because of that, and because of the time, knew exactly who it must be. She rolled out of bed, stepped into the hallway, closed the door behind her. "Odin . . . ," she whispered.

"Can you talk?" he asked.

"They might catch me," she said. Post-midnight calls were a violation.

"I've got to go away," Odin said. "I'm running. I don't know where, but Oates will ask about me. Tell her you didn't know I was going, or why I was going, and you don't know where I went."

Shay wasn't sure he was serious. "That's a terrible idea. What about graduation? You'll miss the ceremony—"

"Look," he broke in, "you can read about it tomorrow, but there was an accident. It was at the lab. I was there, and I did some computer stuff to get us in, and the police might find out. And the ceremony . . . I graduated, I don't need the ceremony."

"What kind of accident? This involves Rachel, doesn't it? She made you do something stupid."

"She didn't make me do anything, Shay. I'm here on my own."

"Okay, okay, okay," Shay said. "But you can't just go. You can't leave me here."

"You'll be fine," he said. "You're a lot tougher than I am. One more year and you'll be free. Maybe there'll be some of Mom's money left. You can go to college."

"Fat chance," Shay whispered, one eye on her foster parents' bedroom door. "They're draining it like vampires. . . ."

"There's still some left. More than enough, if I'm not taking any," Odin said. "I'll be eighteen in forty-three days and done with them. They won't catch me before then."

"Odin, please . . ."

There was a strange whine and Odin said, "It's okay, I'm not going to leave you. . . ."

"Is that Rachel? Let me talk to her. Odin!"

"That's not Rachel," he said. Then: "The van's here. I gotta go. Watch the news tomorrow, you'll see why I'm going. Rachel says it was worth it. I don't know. I don't know if I believe her anymore."

Shay made another protest, but Odin said, "Listen: I'll pop you a Facebook message when I can. Hey: I'm glad you're my sister."

He was gone.

Shay flew to her laptop to see if any of the local stations were posting on their websites about a lab accident. She checked twice more overnight, but there was nothing until the shocking morning newscasts: TV reporters said "radical greens" had attacked a medical laboratory in Eugene, and as they were freeing monkeys and rodents, a security guard had shot one of the raiders, who remained in serious condition.

The shooter, described by a spokeswoman for the lab's parent company, Singular Corporation, as a "highly-trained weapons handler and grandfather of four," might be charged with something, but probably not. He himself had been shot with a Taser. The wounded girl was the same age as Shay, but had attended a private high school. A yearbook photo flashed on the screen, and Shay thought Aubrey

Calder looked like the kind of person who'd be nice to her brother, and that made her a little sad.

Then the reporter added, "Police say the shooting, which occurred in the course of a crime being committed by the raiders, could mean the raiders themselves are guilty of aggravated assault."

Odin, guilty of assault?

He'd always been the sensitive one, the naive one, the one who didn't fight back when he was bullied at school; Odin, who wouldn't hurt a fly. She'd been the one to take care of business, who carried a secret knife, who went head to head with social workers and lousy foster parents. A year younger, she'd filled in for their missing parents, taking care of her sweet, mildly autistic brother.

Over the next week, Shay had gotten three messages from him, saying simply that he was okay and with friends. The messages were on fake Facebook accounts they'd set up after the county had separated them. For extra security, they'd even gone to a Starbucks, used the store's wireless to set up Gmail accounts under fake names—so not even Gmail would have an incriminating URL in their records. They'd then used the Gmail accounts to set up the Facebook pages.

When Shay wanted to leave a message, she'd turn on private browsing and leave the message on Odin's Facebook page. He'd leave his messages and replies on another page.

His three messages had been short and cheerful. He was getting closer to freedom—the magic age of eighteen—and he was traveling with people in Colorado and northern New Mexico. There were no more specifics about whom he was with, though she assumed Rachel was among them, or what they were doing.

Then the mysterious investigators had come to see her.

• • •

The men were brought in by a Child Protection worker named Cheryl Oates, who had, Shay believed, burned out on the job.

Oates was a ruddy-faced woman with tight-cut, dead-black hair and black, suspicious eyes. Her main focus in life, since she'd burned out, was to punish troublemakers—anyone who squealed, or complained, or said much of anything negative about their lives.

They were all lucky, Oates said, to have a roof over their heads. They should go to school and shut up and keep their noses clean and maybe someday they could get jobs and become useful human beings instead of the rabble and castoffs that they were.

Oates showed up while Shay and two other foster kids were cleaning up after the usual boxed macaroni dinner. She took Shay into a bedroom and said, "That idiot brother of yours is in deep trouble. Two investigators are coming to talk to you. If you know what's good for you, you'll tell them what they want to know."

Her eyes went to the laptop on Shay's bed. "They'll want to take a look at your laptop. I gave them permission."

Shay had played the humble game before. With eyes cast down, she said, "I'll help if I can. I don't know where Odin went, but whatever I can tell them . . ."

"You better," Oates snarled. "You sit here. I'm going to talk with Clarence and Mary. The investigators will be here in the next half hour."

Clarence and Mary Peters were the foster parents: two slender blond dopers looking for an easy way to get through life. They were not bad people, but not particularly good, either. Just a couple of lazy outdoor jocks whose idea of a good time was hanging off a cliff at the end of a rope.

With their house's two extra bedrooms, they could take in four foster kids, all girls, and make enough money from the arrangement to not have to work, beyond what they called their "climbing school."

The idea of foster parents who were climbers appealed to the child-welfare workers: Get the kids out in the fresh air. Teach them self-reliance. Shay learned to climb whether she wanted to or not. Somewhat to her surprise, she found that she liked it, and was good at it.

She also learned about corruption. The Peterses didn't necessarily want to drag a bunch of kids everywhere, so they all sat down and made an arrangement. They wouldn't mess with the girls any more than was necessary to maintain order, and the girls wouldn't talk about them to the Child Protection people—about their fondness for marijuana; about their occasional weeklong vacations, when they left the girls alone; about the relentless regimen of peanut butter toast and boxed noodles.

The deal was right out in the open: the kids didn't cause trouble for Clarence and Mary and gave the two foster parents good evaluations. In return, Clarence and Mary gave the girls good reports and pretty much allowed them to do as they pleased—and provided five fake sick-day excuses to the school. They were willing to stretch the curfew to midnight.

If the system worked, and it had to that point, the girls got a roof and food, and Clarence and Mary got the money. Live and let live.

As a bonus, the kids learned how to hang off a cliff on a rope, camp in a pile of thornbush, and survive on Skippy.

• • •

When Oates left to talk to Clarence and Mary, Shay grabbed her laptop and went to the Facebook page. "The police are here to ask about you. I'm worried. I'll leave another note when they're gone."

She didn't worry about leaving notes in the open. Odin might be brilliant at computers, but Shay was great at math, and she knew some simple facts: Facebook had a billion users, who sent billions of messages a day. The chances of finding any one message without knowing addresses in advance were virtually nil.

"It's not like finding a needle in a haystack," she'd told a friend. "It's like finding a needle in all the haystacks in the world."

She'd barely finished sending the message when she heard unfamiliar men's voices down the hall. She shut the MacBook down, put it back on the bed where it had been. Went to the wobbly desk she shared with her roommate, opened her calculus book, took out the problem sheet folded there, and started working on it.

A minute later, Oates knocked and then stuck her face into the room. "Shay?"

She went back into humble mode and stood up.

The investigators came in, two youngish men, tough-looking, in expensive suits. Oates introduced them as Mr. West and Mr. Cherry.

They asked about Odin, where he might be, who he might be with. She didn't know. They asked about the raid on the lab, and she told them the truth: she hadn't been involved in any of that. She supposed she didn't believe in animal testing if it was for cosmetics or something, but if it was for medicine, that was more complicated. . . .

At some point during the interview, Shay sensed that they weren't police officers. She asked Oates, "Are these investigators with the Eugene police?"

"Just cooperate," Oates said, and left the room to take a call.

"Are you with the FBI or something?" Shay persisted.

West said, "There are several agencies working on this situation. There was a shooting, and important research was destroyed."

He hadn't answered the question, Shay noticed. When they got to the computer, Cherry said, "I need to look through this."

She shrugged and said, "Okay, but all my calculus work is on it. I'm going to need it for summer school, for my college prep class. Don't mess it up. Please."

Cherry picked up the computer and walked out of the room.

West was twenty-nine years old, with broad shoulders, buzzed black hair, and soft brown eyes. Pretty cute, Shay thought, though he had muscles even in his face.

"Sit," he said, and Shay took a seat on the edge of her bed. West pulled out a desk chair and sat opposite.

"How much contact did you have with Storm?" he asked.

"Storm?" She was genuinely confused, and it showed.

"Storm, the animal rights group," he said. "Robert Overbeek, Janice Loftus, Rachel Wharton, Ethan Enquist." Shay recognized Ethan Enquist's and Rachel Wharton's names, but didn't let on; as for Storm, why hadn't her brother said something?

She said, "I . . . I . . . none. I never heard of any of those people. Who are they?"

"Crazies," West said. "We've talked to a couple of kids who took part in the raid, and they say your brother was there."

She scrambled. "He was? Are you sure? Do you know where he is now? He never even told me that he was going away."

"Then why did he call you the night he disappeared?" West asked.

They knew about the phone call.

Shay covered again. "To talk. We did that all the time." True enough. "We had a time that we called, when everybody would be asleep. If you check, you'll see we always talk at three a.m. I'd leave my phone on vibrate, so nobody else would hear it."

West peered at her, assessing her, and she realized that they knew about the other 3:00 a.m. calls too. She'd said the right thing, told the right lie. Lies, she'd learned, should always be as close as possible to the truth.

She added, "All he said that night was that he was having trouble with a bully at his foster house, and that he talked to a man from Caltech about scholarship stuff. He was trying to figure out living expenses. That's why I'm so worried. He was making plans for the future, and the next thing I know, people say he ran away."

She *was* worried, and felt tears start. She'd normally never cry in front of a stranger—or in front of anyone—but now it seemed like a good idea, so she let them come.

West said, "You ran away a couple of times—it's in your file. Why?"

She wiped the tears away. "I didn't go far. I never went farther than Portland."

"But why'd you take off?"

Shay dropped her eyes, recalling the episode. "I have trouble with people telling me what to do. Some foster parents try to control everything you do. And the second time, my foster parent then, Richard, said some things that made me uncomfortable. About us being better friends. I thought he didn't exactly want to be friends."

West gave her a quick nod and asked, "This was the guy you . . . forked?"

She had to laugh. Richard had gotten more than a little friendly one night as Shay was making scrambled eggs, and she'd stuck a fork in his hand.

"That's the guy," she said, but got serious again when she realized just how deep inside her files West had been. "You talked to him?"

"We've done numerous interviews," he said, and they both knew it was another dodge. "Did you tell Oates about what he was doing?"

Shay shrugged. "She doesn't want the details. They don't have enough foster parents. But she moved me here. Clarence, I'm happy to say, is too lazy to molest anybody."

"So that's not so bad."

"No, it's not. Clarence and Mary aren't exactly high achievers, but the thing is, I've actually learned stuff from them. About living outdoors, about climbing."

"That's cool." The man showed a thin smile, hesitated, then said, "My little sister had a college professor. He suggested that she could get an A for sleeping with him, or an F for not sleeping with him."

"That's awful," Shay said. She meant it.

"Some friends and I spoke to him. He changed his position," West said.

"He left her alone?"

"He changed his position on the planet," West said. "He moved back to England. His USA privileges have been permanently revoked."

She smiled—he'd made her like him. "Maybe you should talk to Richard," she said. "The next girl who lives with him, well . . ."

"She might not know how to use a fork?"

"That's right." Shay smiled again.

"I could do that, if you help us out." He stood up and turned away from her to look around the room, at the corkboard with its reminder notes and absence of family photos, and something about his legs . . . He moved like an athlete, a good one, but he seemed not awkward, but not quite natural.

He glanced back at her and saw her looking at his legs. "I lost my legs in Afghanistan," he said.

"Wow . . . you move like a jock," she said.

"Lost them up above the knees," he said. He hiked up one of his pant legs, above the sock, to reveal a smooth, fleshlike leg, but too smooth, and too Caucasian. "They're still working on the look of black skin. It wasn't the highest priority. The next editions may even have hair—for the men, anyway."

"Still, amazing," Shay said, and the amazement showed on her face.

"It came out of the med lab those nutsos trashed," West said, letting his pant leg slide back down. "They're now working on nerve bypasses that could help spine-damaged people. Quadriplegics and paraplegics. Give them their lives back. . . ."

Before Shay could respond, Cherry came back into the room with the laptop and handed it back to her. He said to his partner, "Nothing. If they're talking, they're doing it on Facebook or something.

She's turned off the browser history, so there's no way to tell. And she's smart. She's already finished AP Calculus BC, and she's not a senior yet."

"Well, technically I am, since the semester ended," Shay said.

West asked, "About the laptops and the cell phones. Not all foster care kids can afford them. I'm just kind of curious how you two could . . ."

"Our mom left us some money," Shay said. "We can get a few things, as long as they're educational or safety related. Phones count."

They both looked at her for a moment, then West said, "Look, Shay . . . if you see or hear from your brother, tell him to get in touch with us. We might be able to help him."

"How would he get in touch? Do you have a card?"

"My Facebook name is BlackWallpaper, from San Francisco," West said. "That's a very safe, private contact. Can you remember that?"

"Sure," she said. "He should look up BlackWallpaper, from San Francisco."

"It might save his life. The people he's moving with, they're crazy. I mean that literally. They're unbalanced. One of them has already spent time in prison. This poor little girl who got shot at the lab—they threw her away like she was a piece of toilet paper. They'll do the same to your brother when they don't need him. They could do worse, if he knows too much," West said.

"If Odin calls, I'll tell him," she said.

West followed Cherry to the door, then turned. "You are," he said with a smile, "an exceptionally good liar. Exceptionally good."

"I'm a foster kid," she said. It sounded like an admission, and he nodded.

● ● ●

Shay went out to a coffee shop an hour later and used its wireless to leave a long note on Facebook recounting the conversation, and the fact that Odin's call the night he'd run had been found, but hadn't been monitored—they didn't know what Odin had said. He shouldn't use his cell to contact her again. As soon as they could coordinate it, they needed to switch to prepaid phones with new, anonymous numbers.

She didn't hear back for thirteen days.

The text came in while she was twirling soft-serve yogurt into a cup. It was her third day on her first summer job, and the use of cell phones was strictly forbidden. She slid the phone onto the stainless-steel counter, behind a bin of waffle cones.

[ODIN] What if you and I saw the same gray whale from two different countries? It's possible. They're migrating north now and I saw four when we were in Baja.

She reached around the cones and punched in a reply:

[SHAY] WRU@

[ODIN] Secret mission. This morning, we drove by a canyon that's pretty grand.

"Miss, I'm in a hurry," a customer yelled at Shay's back. She turned and handed the man the cup of tilting yogurt, then went back to texting.

[SHAY] Grand Canyon?

[ODIN] Can't say, but I will tell you I got carded at a tavern last night and my card worked!

[SHAY] You're hanging out in bars?

The yogurt customer came back angry. "Hey, you forgot my sprinkles!"

[ODIN] For the work. Gotta go. Bye. And don't forget to tell everyone: Meat is murder.

Shay hadn't known what to think: he'd texted from his old number. She'd told him the phone was unsafe, but he'd used it anyway. She felt a jab on the shoulder.

"Are you texting?" It was the shift supervisor, a prickly girl a year ahead of her at school. "You realize you forgot his topping?"

Shay said she was sorry and that she hoped it wouldn't cost her the job, but she had a family emergency and had to run. She did, straight to a public library three blocks away. All the computers were occupied and she had to wait for five minutes, but when she finally got on, she found a message waiting for her on Facebook.

That text was a lame attempt to mislead them. We just left Arizona, but none of the people there know we're gone. That should screw up their investigation, for a while, anyway. We're working with a group in Hollywood now. I'm a little worried: there are things going on that I don't understand. Watch yourself. Ignorance is your best bet. Stay away from those two Singular guys. They are NOT cops of any kind.

Singular guys?

Did that mean West and Cherry worked for the lab's owner? That they weren't any kind of law officers? She understood a few other things, reading between the lines. Odin had never been good at social relationships, at understanding ordinary human traits like treachery, jealousy, and deceit. If he was in that kind of trouble, he wouldn't get out on his own.

● ● ●

The next day, Shay went out the door in her work uniform, lurked outside Clarence and Mary's house until she saw them leave, then went back and let herself in. She took the best stuff from a pile of camping gear kept in the basement and hit the kitchen for ramen noodles, peanut butter, and crackers, plus a few bottles of water.

She retrieved her carefully hoarded stash of cash—a lot of school lunches not eaten. Less the money for a bus, she'd have seventy-five dollars when she got to Hollywood. Her roommate had stashed another sixty. Shay knew where it was and was tempted to take that too, but the roommate had plenty of problems of her own.

When she'd packed, she got down on her knees, reached under the box spring of her bed, found the fist-sized hole, and took out the knife in its worn leather sheath. It had a clip on the back, and when she slipped it under the waistband at the back of her jeans, it was invisible. Fine for walking, not so much when riding on the bus; on the bus, she'd move it to her hoodie.

On the way downtown, she stopped and sent a Facebook message to Odin: she was on her way to L.A. Shay made the bus with ten minutes to spare.

Hollywood.

6

Harmon rolled into the Singular parking lot and dumped the dusty Mercedes ML550 in a reserved parking spot that wasn't reserved for him; he had a reserved spot, but just didn't care. The truck was equipped with the off-road package, with brush bars front and back and a winch. A Day-Glo orange circle, four feet across, was hand-painted on the roof, the better to be seen by search planes should Harmon get hung up in the desert.

Nobody would mess with the truck, in its misappropriated parking spot, because anyone at Singular who was important enough to have a reserved spot would recognize the truck as belonging to Harmon. Nobody messed with Harmon.

A tall man who dressed in jeans and cowboy boots, Harmon had a desert-weathered face and a streak of brilliant white teeth when he smiled, which he did, and often. He wore aviator glasses with mirrored lenses. People who'd known him for years had never seen his eyes.

Around the company, it was understood that he'd been a Special

Forces sergeant in Afghanistan and had served with Sync, who had been with the Central Intelligence Agency. Not much was known about their relationship, except that it was close.

It was also known that Harmon spent much of his free time in Arizona and New Mexico, scouting the desert for Indian archaeological sites, which he would document with photographs and then report to the relevant university or state archaeological departments. Why he did that was not known.

Inside the Singular building, a pleasant-looking woman in a security guard's uniform checked him through the glass doors at the end of the lobby. Harmon gave her one of his smiles and said, "Thank you, Melissa," and she said, "You're welcome, Mr. Harmon."

Melissa was in disguise. Her uniform looked like a standard security guard's, but she was no rent-a-cop: she'd spent four years as a Secret Service agent on the presidential protection detail. She had a long alcove below the countertop that contained both a .40-caliber Beretta handgun and a Heckler & Koch MP5 submachine gun. Should a visitor prove seriously unwelcome, she was more than prepared to deal with it.

Harmon walked past the elevators to the stairs and took them, two at a time, to the fifteenth floor. There were a few people on the security detail who could have done that without breathing hard— but they had prosthetic legs. Harmon was working with original equipment and he was forty-five years old. By the time he got to fifteen, his heart was pounding hard, but he'd made it without slowing down.

He went through the door at the top of the stairs and down the hallway, getting his breathing under control, then through the door into Sync's outer office. Sync's secretary nodded at him, pushed an intercom button, and said, "Harmon's here."

Two seconds later, Sync's office door popped open and Sync, with shirtsleeves rolled to the elbow and tie loose around his neck, said, "You're sweating through your shirt."

Harmon sniffed an armpit, shrugged, and followed him inside.

Sync's office was an austere glass box overlooking a man-made pond that shone dull gray in the California sun. Beyond the pond was a view toward the Pacific Ocean.

Sync took a seat behind his chrome desk, and Harmon settled into a chair opposite. At ease with the man who made everyone else around him jump, he swung his black lizard-skin boots up on the desktop and scanned its spare contents: one epically encrypted laptop, one hardwired phone, one Rubik's Cube, and one twenty-ounce bottle of the green slime Sync ingested like a chain-smoker.

Harmon, Singular's intelligence chief, didn't believe in nutritional elixirs or dietary deprivations. He liked his meat bloody, his potatoes fried, and his tequila with two licks of salt. What he believed was this: the edge was entirely mental. Name the time and manner of the contest, and he'd be the last man standing.

Sync said, "Tell me, but make it short."

"Still looking," Harmon said. "They're not making it easy."

Sync said, "It hurt when they hit us on YouTube, but if they crack those thumb drives, it'll be much worse."

"I know, I know, the baby monkey film," Harmon said. "Didn't like seeing that shit myself. But finding these kids is hard stuff. They don't have a base, they don't have a real organization, they apparently only use a credit card when they're leaving wherever they are . . . they know how to do this. They're just crazy, they're not stupid."

They talked for a couple of minutes until Sync's desk phone rang. He picked it up, listened for a moment, said, "Okay, I'll be there," and hung up. After another swig from his bottle, he looked at Harmon and said, "You know who Gerald Armie is?"

"I've heard of him, never seen him."

"He's five minutes out," Sync said. "Micah's about to reel him in and Jimmie'll be there. We could get five minutes with Micah now, to talk about the hunt."

"Okay with me," Harmon said.

Sync rolled his shirtsleeves down and pulled on a suit coat and tightened his necktie. As they walked out of Sync's office, Sync told his secretary to hold everything until he got back, and they took the stairs up one floor, to the top. Micah Cartwell was Singular's CEO; Imogene "Jimmie" Stewart, the company's chief in-house counsel.

Gerald Armie was the billionaire owner of a national chain of supermarkets headquartered in Oklahoma.

On sixteen, they walked down the hall to Cartwell's office. Classical music played faintly from speakers set along the hall, adding not only a touch of elegance to the floor but also obscuring what one person might say to another farther down the hall; conversations would not be easily overheard.

The furnishings on Sync's floor were expensive and well chosen, but basically functional. On the top floor, everything was richer.

Instead of wall-to-wall carpet, there were chestnut floors covered with handsome Turkish carpets, tasteful pieces of furniture in walnut, and English and Japanese antiques scattered here and there.

Stewart, the attorney, emerged from the next door down as they got to Cartwell's office. She was a tall, thin woman of forty who ran triathlons and wore hawkish black glasses, but then went soft with gauzy knee-length dresses. She nodded and said, "Gentlemen."

"I'm not entirely sure of that," Harmon said.

Stewart smiled and said, "I'm not either, Harmon, but I thought I'd give you the benefit of the doubt."

Sync asked, "Will Armie buy in?"

Stewart said, "I'd be shocked if he didn't, after the research that we've done. He does not want to go away."

Stewart led the way in. Cartwell's outer office was large and quiet, with soft gray wallpaper dotted with California impressionist paintings of the seacoast and mountains; the air was touched with the scent of pine. Two secretaries sat out in the open, both looking at computer screens; an executive assistant worked in her own small office at the far end, behind a glass window, and got up to meet them and take them to the inner sanctum.

Micah Cartwell was seated at a long table cluttered with paper, a few family keepsakes, and a big computer screen. Six more screens were sunk in the wall behind him, showing worldwide stock market activity and news feeds from the United States, Europe, and Asia. All had been muted.

When they came in, Cartwell stood and said, "Hey, team," then looked at his watch. "Armie's at the outer gate, we've only got five or six minutes."

"We won't need more than that," Sync said. "We haven't found the thumb drives or the dog, but Harmon's got some lines on the group that has them."

Cartwell said, "Let's sit down," and gestured to a group of couches and chairs near a window looking out on the Pacific. The day was clear, and they could see a rusty freighter headed toward San Francisco. When they were seated, Cartwell asked Harmon, "What kind of lines?"

"They're careful, but we found out that one of the people with them is a kid named Danny Davidson, just out of high school. We got lucky two days ago and found a charge slip on one of his parent's Visa cards for a prepaid phone he bought at a Best Buy. It specified the time of purchase, and from that, we were able to get to the phone, and the number. It's a cheap throwaway phone, not a smartphone, and doesn't have a GPS signal—the best we can do is track which cell tower his call originates at. They're in Southern California at the moment, in the Los Angeles area, moving between L.A. and San Diego. They've made occasional jumps as far away as Albuquerque, Phoenix, and down to Baja. They move every few days. The problem is, every cell tower will cover several hundred thousand people down there, because the population is so dense. When the kid makes a call, our team heads to the area, but there are so many people around that they're impossible to spot, and they may even be long gone."

"Are you tracking who gets the calls?" Cartwell asked.

"Of course. But he doesn't make many, and most of them are to friends up in Oregon, or his family, which doesn't help. We are building some predictive models."

"Explain that," Stewart said.

Harmon nodded. "When he makes a call, we can see the point

of origin. We look at where they've been, and where they go from each place we know they've been, and then we try to predict where they'll go next. Getting inside their thinking. The more moves we record, the better we get. Eventually, we'll have a team in the same cell tower range as the kid is. We'll film everything we can, looking at vans and SUVs and other multiperson vehicles. Sooner or later, we'll start getting duplicates, and then we'll know what they're driving."

"What about a vehicle tag?" Cartwell asked.

"Don't have one. If we could get one, we'd be good. We could put out a BOLO."

"What's a BOLO?" Stewart asked.

" 'Be on the lookout,' " Harmon said. "We could put one out in the name of the FBI and have the local cops looking for it. When they spot it, they respond to the FBI. The feds wouldn't know what they were talking about, but we have ways of monitoring that exchange. . . . We could be right on top of them."

"How long is this going to take? To find them?" Cartwell asked.

"Honestly? I don't know," Harmon said. "For a bunch of crazies, they've got good security procedures, just like they had good technique going into the lab. But we'll find them. If nothing else, the Davidson kid will call one of the people he's traveling with, and if that person has a smartphone, that'll be it. We'll be able to track them by GPS all day long."

"We need those drives," Cartwell said. "The quieter, the better, of course. We have no budget limit on this: spend what you need to."

He looked at his watch again, and as he did, an intercom on his desk chimed. He turned and said, "Yes?"

A voice said, "Mr. Armie is in the elevator."

"Thank you, Anna," Cartwell said. He turned to Harmon. "You'll have to excuse us, Harmon. Find those thieves."

Harmon stood up and asked, "Back door?"

Cartwell grinned at him and said, "That would be best. You're not exactly projecting our corporate image at the moment."

"More like 'Ride 'em, cowboy,'" Stewart said.

"I yam what I yam," Harmon said as he headed for the door. Behind him, the intercom chimed again and Anna said, "Mr. Armie's here."

The back door to Cartwell's office, which looked like a closet door, was down a stubby hallway that also led to Cartwell's private bathroom. Rather than opening into a closet, however, the door led to a long, narrow, thickly carpeted hallway that ran parallel to the main hallway and emerged in an obscure niche near the elevators. Thickly carpeted to kill the sound of footsteps, of somebody coming or going. A sneaky way in and out, in case it was needed.

Harmon went through the door, turned and closed it, then stopped and leaned back against the wall.

He couldn't hear the words being spoken inside the office, but he could hear that they were being spoken—a friendly rumble as people met, the words getting fainter as Cartwell, Stewart, and Sync walked with Armie back to the conversation area where he'd just been sitting.

When he was sure they were all seated, Harmon quietly cracked open the door he'd just come through. He'd been an intelligence agent most of his life. He'd learned the hard way that the more intelligence you have, the better off you are. The meeting lasted for half an hour, and Harmon never moved. When they finished and he heard them stirring, he eased the door shut and hurried down the hall to the exit. From there he took the stairs to his own office.

He wasn't in the office much, and it was simply furnished: a desk, a computer, a good leather chair, and several file cabinets that were actually camouflaged safes. The door lock was the best that money could buy, and the entire office was monitored with equipment that nobody else knew about.

Harmon leaned back in the chair and put his boots up on the desk.

He'd learned more than he'd expected. He'd known the overall outline of the project, but not some of the uglier details.

They were killing people.

He'd have to think about that.

The sun was coming up over the Hollywood Freeway when something made a snuffling noise next to Shay's head. She unzipped her bivy sack and peered out. A rat the size of a chicken was sniffing at her backpack, looking for her saltines. Odin liked rats. She didn't. She could handle a nice, clean caged rat, maybe with a little chill running down her spine, but a garbage-eating feral rat was something else.

"Scram!" she screamed. She thumped her constrained legs against the dirt like a grounded mermaid. The rat seemed to be thinking it over. "Seriously! Beat it!"

The rat ambled away.

Not what Odin would have done. There'd been a rat phase after the gecko phase, until the rats started multiplying like rats and the clueless foster mother that year—Mrs. Thurman?—finally caught on. She'd called the caseworker at midnight and demanded that the creepy kid, his sister, and the rats be out of there by morning.

Shay checked her watch: six o'clock. She'd been asleep for less than five hours.

She rolled over with a groan. She didn't want to get up, but a bunch of crows were squawking about food. Overhead, the drone of the morning traffic was picking up and a semitrailer driver leaned on his air horn.

She wriggled out of the bivy, giving up. The Hollywood Starbucks on Gower opened at six. If she hustled over there, she thought, she could get some decent private time in the bathroom to clean up. It was her third day in L.A. and her fourth without a shower.

She smelled bad. She smelled homeless.

A quarter-mile hike from her shrub below the freeway and Shay was back in the land of make-believe. The Starbucks she'd been using was directly across the street from Paramount Studios. Billboards loomed overhead, advertising summer blockbusters she couldn't afford to go to. In a couple of hours, movie executives in black BMWs, black Mercedeses, and black Range Rovers would be pulling into the studio ramp, and their browbeaten assistants would be racing into the coffee shop, cutting in line for their bosses' half-caf, no-foam, two-Splenda soy lattes.

The Starbucks day crew was led by the same guy as yesterday, an overcaffeinated middle-aged man with full-sleeve tattoos wearing a green apron. Same dumb grin as he checked her out all over again. Shay twiddled her fingers and smiled. Maybe he'd make her another mocha frap "on the house." She was hungry and had noted, the day before, that the scones were almost five hundred calories—a third of her daily food requirement, if worst came to worst.

"Hi, Tobias," she said, reading his name tag. "Can I have the restroom key?"

Locked inside the women's room, Shay pulled off the bedroll and backpack and rummaged for her toothbrush. Living, and typically vying for just one bathroom, with dozens of different girls in foster care had made her extremely efficient at pulling herself together—and also a bit resentful of all the attention paid to primping. Most days, she was just glad if there was still hot water left for a shower.

If there was a time suck in her routine, it was her hair—and that was nonnegotiable. She'd worn it to her waist since she was a little girl: straight, thick rust-red hair, identical to her mother's. It wasn't easy to get a brush through, and it was sort of a pain to wash, but when she looked in the mirror, there was always the private reminder that she'd once been someone's daughter.

There wasn't enough headroom under the Starbucks faucet to shampoo, so, same as the day before, she unsnarled her hair and smoothed it back into a scruffy ponytail. Double-checking that the door was locked, she pulled off her clothes, pumped the soap dispenser a dozen times to get a decent amount in the palm of her hand, and sudsed up. She rinsed and dried with paper towels. After pulling on underpants and a T-shirt that she'd dried out on a branch, she gave the overnight T-shirt and underpants a quick wash in the sink and stuffed them into a plastic bag to be dried later.

At least they were clean, and so was she—more or less. She'd have to do something soon about her jeans, and the grungy hoodie that still smelled of the Greyhound bus she'd taken down from Eugene.

And her hair . . .

Tobias was waiting for her with the frap. She thanked him as she unwrapped a straw, told him she had a boyfriend when he asked, and took a seat in the far corner to sip her breakfast and go online.

She dropped another Facebook message to Odin, telling him that she was in Los Angeles. Then she began looking for places where he might actually be. There were more animal rights groups in Hollywood than Shay could believe—everything from pit bull rescue specialists to seal enthusiasts. Somewhere in that matrix, she thought, the Storm people were probably talking to allies.

She began saving names and addresses to a separate file, but she was suddenly so sleepy again. . . . She closed the laptop and then, just for a moment, her eyes.

An hour later, a toddler in a stroller screamed for more juice, and Shay jerked awake and looked around, a little dazed. She'd slumped straight over onto the table like an actual homeless person. When she sat up, a woman with cornrows was giving her a hard stare from the next table.

"What?" Shay asked. She was feeling cranky, and the sleep taste in her mouth didn't help. "I fell asleep."

"Yeah, I saw," the woman said in a Mississippi Delta accent. She had a pile of papers on the table in front of her, and a red pen. "Late night?"

"A little," Shay said. She tightened the compression straps on her backpack and pulled it on.

The woman said, "Hang on a minute. I'm not the police."

"Wouldn't matter if you were. I'm not doing anything illegal," Shay said.

The woman pushed back in her chair. "You need a place to stay? Look, I'm Rashika Jones, I'm a youth psychologist for the county."

"Uh-huh," Shay said. She stepped toward the door. She knew the lingo: Jones decided which abused and neglected kids were a little messed up, and which ones were *really* messed up.

"Let me give you a list of shelters," Jones said. "There's a halfway decent one just a few blocks from here."

"Thanks, but no thanks," Shay said.

Shay walked away but Jones followed along, leaving her papers on the table. "You're too good-looking to last on the streets. A pimp will come along, act like your best friend. He'll hook you up to something, and that'll be the end of you. There are two hundred and fifty gangs in this city. More than two hundred murders last year—"

Shay stopped and looked her in the eye. "I appreciate your concern. But I'm fine."

Jones said, "You're tough and I appreciate that, but this ain't Kansas. One of my clients, a girl about your age, tougher than you, was stabbed last year. On the run for nine days, dead on the tenth."

"I'm sorry about that," Shay said, and pulled at the door handle.

"Don't live here without an address," Jones persisted. "Nothing good can come of it."

Shay hesitated, then dug in the front pocket of her jeans and pulled out the black business card from the Cat in the Hat. "You ever heard of this guy?"

Jones took the card in her red-lacquered fingernails. "Twist. Okay. He's different, but if that's your preference, you'd be safe there. You wouldn't have to deal with the likes of me."

"What does that mean?" Shay asked. *"There?"*

"He runs a hotel. Or a flophouse. Or a crash pad," Jones said. "Kids only. Rumor is, he was one of you, until he grew up and got rich. Where'd you get his card?"

Shay hesitated again. "He gave it to me," she said, and took back the card. "Anyway, I gotta run." She readjusted her backpack and went out the door.

"Go see Twist," Jones called to her back.

Shay twiddled her fingers over her shoulder.

Good-bye.

Hollywood, the place, was a letdown, especially during the day. Shay rarely went to the movies because she didn't have the money, but she hadn't grown up under a rock. Where were the celebrities, the red carpets, the paparazzi and limos? Okay, she'd seen a bunch of limos, and a strange piggy-looking car that she suspected was a Rolls-Royce.

By midmorning, she was elbow to elbow with hundreds of tourists on the hunt for famous faces. The Hollywood they were looking for didn't really exist for outsiders.

The stars worked on closed sets and lived behind gates in Beverly Hills or up one of the canyons. This Hollywood was mostly cheesy souvenir shops and fast-food restaurants. Eventually, the tourists would have to settle for a five-dollar Polaroid with one of the hustlers who dressed up as Spider-Man or Shrek.

Shay looked at the map she'd bought from a grumpy Snow White outside the TCL Chinese Theatre and learned that L.A.'s Hollywood neighborhood covers about eight square miles. The seal enthusiasts' storefront was two miles from the Starbucks where she'd had breakfast. She'd walked over and found the place, and a sign in the front window that said CLOSED. It looked like it had been closed since the millennium, with a layer of dust inside the window.

Finding Odin might take a while. And she'd been thinking about her camp beneath the freeway. Jones, the Child Protection lady, was right. Outdoors, on your own, was too dangerous; there were too many dodgy people around, and sooner or later, one of them would stumble over her.

She couldn't help Odin if she were dead.

Shay was worried that her cell phone could be tracked. She'd meant to get rid of it, but hadn't. Now, because she'd run from her foster parents' home, she was afraid to use it. She'd asked a couple girls on the street and been directed to one of the rare remaining pay phones in Hollywood, one that the locals casually referred to as the "drug phone."

She needed a hassle-free place to stay . . .

She called Twist on the drug phone. A boy answered.

"Yeah? Whatta ya want?"

Definitely a boy's high-pitched voice, not a man's, and someone who sounded like he didn't care one way or another what she wanted.

"Is, uh, Mr. Twist there?"

"He's around somewhere, but Twist don't talk on the telephone," the kid said. "So whatta ya want?"

"He gave me a card last night . . ."

"You're gonna have to come over," the boy said. "Where're you at?"

Shay looked at the street sign and told him.

"That's a couple miles," he said. "Walk over to Sunset. You know where Sunset is?"

"Yes . . ."

"Walk over to Sunset, take a left down to Wilcox, then when you get to Wilcox, take a right and walk down to Fountain. Take a left down Fountain about ten blocks, past the Tea Leaf. We're on the same side of the street, right at the corner. It's the pink building. There'll be some time-wasting slackers sitting on the porch, and maybe a couple of righteous skaters."

He gave her an address.

"Have you got a place I can stay?" Shay asked.

"Twist's card will get you in the door," the boy said. "If he's not too busy to talk to you, he might give you a room and tell you what the rules are. But it depends."

"On what?"

"On what he's doing. You can at least sit in the lobby."

She walked, looking at faces as she went. No Odin.

The walk wasn't bad, took her twenty-five minutes. She passed the Tea Leaf and saw an old pink stucco building.

The entrance to the hotel was up wide, cracked-concrete steps and through double glass doors smoky with dirt. A hole in the center of the glass in the left door looked like something made by a small-caliber bullet. A Band-Aid had been stuck on the inside of the glass to cover the hole.

Four boys were sitting on the steps, smoking. The day had gotten warmer and they were all in T-shirts, two in jeans, two in long, baggy cargo shorts. One had a well-used skateboard. They were thin and had the dry, overtanned faces of street kids.

Shay thought of the street woman she'd seen the day before,

flailing her arms and shouting at imaginary enemies. The woman had looked old, although other cues, like a healthy mop of hair, hinted that she probably wasn't even forty. Years of outside living had wrinkled her face until it resembled a prune. These kids were young, but already had a bit of that look.

She was about to start across the street when she saw the cop car rolling down Fountain toward the hotel. She instinctively stepped back and turned, shoulders hunched, to slink away.

Walk, not run. She was in a bad spot: there was really no place to run to . . .

Then the patrol car stopped in front of the hotel steps and two cops got out, looking annoyed. The cop on the driver's side opened the back door and pulled a kid out onto the sidewalk—not about her at all. The kid was cuffed and the cop was rough, banging him against the car.

The kid said, "Ooo, hit me again, Officer Friendly; it'll make you feel like a man."

One of the kids on the steps said, "Yeah, hit him again. He's a master criminal."

Shay winced: she'd always gone for a strategic meekness.

Now here was this kid, apparently enjoying himself. He was tall, long-haired, and maybe consciously cool in jeans and a pumpkin-orange shirt that said DON'T WORRY, BE HOPI.

The cop was pulling him around toward the building, but the kid caught Shay in the corner of his eye and did a double take, and with the double take, he gave her a whistle she'd normally ignore. But the audacity of this boy, coming on to her while in handcuffs, made her smile back at him.

"Cade!" someone shouted. "Shut up!"

• • •

Twist was there, on the top step outside the pink building, and came down to the street to meet the cops. Cade shut up.

Twist was wearing the same bowler hat and carrying the same cane he had the night before, but now Shay noticed a limp that she hadn't seen in the dark. She sidled toward them, hoping to catch Twist's eye, but Twist was focused on the boy.

"What'd he do?" he asked the cops.

"Apple store at the Glendale Galleria," said the cop who'd hauled the kid out of the car. He used a key to pop the handcuffs as he spoke. "Shut down their demos, then switched them to a porn flick that's probably still playing, 'cause the Geniuses can't figure out how he hacked in."

Twist nodded. "Thanks for bringing him over. I owe you."

The cop said, "Next time, we'll book his butt into the Twin Towers. No more favors for this one."

"Well, thanks again," Twist said. "I'm serious, I owe you."

The kid said to the cop, "Yeah, thanks for the ride, dude. Saved me the cab fare."

Twist sank a hand into the boy's arm and said, "Shut up."

The cop said to Cade, "Listen to Twist, smart-ass. And if I *wasn't* the dude, you'd be in jail." He nodded at Twist, and the two cops got back in the car.

Twist, Shay could see, was furious.

Cade Holt was sixteen, better than six feet tall, and loomed over Twist. He wore his lank brown hair long enough to tuck behind his ears.

Despite his size, what had seemed like a permanent insouciant grin flicked away when Twist leaned into him and said, "You jeopardize my work again, you're out. I'm trying to hijack a whole freakin' skyscraper and you bring in the cops? I don't need cops. If the sign doesn't go tonight, it doesn't go. You've got one hour."

"Jeez, dude, I'm good for it," Cade said, but Shay could see he was worried. "I was only having fun with the Mac fanboys."

Twist tapped him on the chest with the tip of the cane. "You brought the cops here. You know the rules."

Shay edged closer. Twist had yet to look at her. He climbed the steps to the glass doors, a deflated Cade trailing behind. At the top, Twist hesitated, turned to Shay with a frown, and asked, "Are you coming? Or are you gonna stand there like a lamppost?"

"I'm coming," she said.

The lobby of the Twist Hotel looked like a set from an old movie—wide, with creaky wooden floors, faded red plaster walls, big windows that looked out at nothing, with canvas drapes pulled back over bronze hooks. A massive wrought iron chandelier hung from the ceiling, but the light sockets were empty. The check-in desk had pigeonhole mailboxes behind it. Worn, mismatched furniture, couches and chairs and a few tables, were scattered across ragged Persian carpets. The place smelled of French fries and Big Macs, Cheetos, popcorn, and pizza, with an undertone of ancient cigar smoke, floor wax, and flaking plaster.

A dozen kids were lounging around, plugged into headphones, reading books, typing on laptops, or texting on cell phones. When Twist walked in, a couple of kids called, "Hey, Twist," and a young woman with white-bleached hair said, "Cassie walked last night."

Twist stopped. "She okay?"

"I don't know. Her old boyfriend found her. She was crying and everything, but she said she wanted to go with him."

"Got her number?"

"Yeah . . ."

"Give her a day or two, call her. If she's not okay, we'll go get her," Twist said.

"Thanks, Twist."

A pimply kid, his black hair sticking like straw from beneath a miner's hat with a headlamp, was sitting behind the check-in desk. As they walked up, he put down a skater magazine and asked, in the high-pitched voice that Shay recognized from the drug phone, "New tenant? Gonna check her in?"

"If she wants to," Twist said.

"Gonna check her out first," Cade said.

Twist said to Cade, "Shut up."

Cade turned to Shay—he'd recovered his insouciance—and said, "You don't get any sympathy around here. You work your fingers to the bone, and what do you get?"

"Bony fingers," Shay said. She looked at Twist. "What's the deal here?"

Twist leaned against the desk, stretched his gimpy leg out into the air, and asked, "Still got that knife?"

Shay cocked her head, but didn't answer.

"All right, stupid question," Twist said. He got back on both feet and reached over the desk. "It goes here."

He pulled open a drawer on the end of the check-in desk. Inside were a half-dozen pocketknives, three butcher knives, a martial arts baton, and two canisters of pepper spray.

Shay said, "Jeez. Nice place."

Twist shrugged. "The kids who show up here are survivors. Survivors carry protection. The deal is, while you're in my hotel—my house—you follow the rules."

"Which are?"

"They're pretty simple; you'll get a list. One is, no weapons beyond the lobby, and no guns at all. Another one is, nothing that brings the cops. No drugs, no alcohol. And you're required to pay. Sooner or later, you have to pay. Most people here have jobs. Do you have any skills?"

Of course she did, Shay thought. She could do all kinds of things. She just couldn't think of any that might apply to the hotel. "I guess," she said, uncertain. "I worked at a yogurt stand for a while."

"You ever do any burglary?" Cade asked.

"That's kinda personal," Shay said, putting a little snot in her tone.

Cade turned to Twist. "She's useless. I'll give her some training in my spare time."

Shay ignored that and asked Twist, "You're not some guy who exploits orphans, are you?"

"Cade has an endless line of bullshit," Twist said. He was drifting away from the check-in desk, leaving her there, but she tagged along.

He said, "We have a group meal here in the morning and in the evening. Food's okay, not great. I know because I eat it. In the middle, you eat what you got. You get a room with a roommate. Bathrooms are all down the hall. I don't know if there's a job in the kitchen, but if there is, you can work there until you find something better. That's about four hours a day—I pay California minimum wage."

Shay said, "Outside, you mentioned something about hijacking a skyscraper. Are you a writer?"

Twist stopped, interested. "You know about writers? Where'd you pick up the slang?"

"I knew a bunch of them around Eugene, a couple others from Portland," she said. Writers: graffiti artists.

"Yeah? You know Gary Keats?" Twist asked.

"I know him, but I never worked with him," Shay said. "He did street stencils for a tree-sitting action I did with my brother."

"That's what we need," Cade said, "a tree sitter."

Twist ignored him and said, "You climb?"

"Yes. That's how I got to know the Eugene writers. I'd help them get up to billboards, off the streets. Did a couple water towers. A lot of them, you know, the ladder doesn't start for twenty feet up. I'd get them up there."

Twist looked at her for a long time, maybe with a little skepticism, then asked, "If you had to get down off the roof of a building—like twelve stories—how would you do that?"

"Would there be anything to tie into at the top?" she asked.

"Like what?"

"Like anything that would take my weight," Shay said. "I'm around a hundred and ten."

Cade, now serious, said, "There's all kinds of stuff up there. Steel struts, door handles, chimneys . . ."

"Then it'd be a piece of cake," Shay said. "Twelve stories is around . . . a hundred and fifty feet. I could do it in thirty or forty seconds. If I had the gear. I don't have any gear with me."

"How much does the gear cost?" Twist asked.

"For a building like that . . . three hundred and fifty dollars. Maybe four hundred, if you couldn't get any deals," Shay said.

"I thought it'd be more," Twist said.

"The equipment is pretty simple, really, if all you have to do is get down," Shay said. "A harness, some carabiners, the rope. We're not going to be buying cams or anything."

"I don't know what *cams* are," Twist said.

"Climbing tool . . . based on the logarithmic spiral," Shay said.

"Huh?" said Twist.

"Don't worry about it," said Shay.

They'd stopped in the middle of a long, dark hallway that led to the back of the hotel; the walls were a beat-up dark brown wood, warped in places, that might have been elegant a hundred years earlier. Twist scratched his neck, looking at her seriously now. "If you did something like that, you wouldn't kill yourself? I don't want anybody to get hurt."

Shay said, "If you've got the gear, it'd be as safe as walking down the sidewalk. For me, anyway. Of course, I'd need to know exactly what you're doing. I won't help you rob a bank."

"Could you get the equipment in L.A.?" Twist asked. "Like, right now?"

"Sure, if I had the money. Gotta be REI stores around . . ."

"Santa Monica," Cade said.

"I'm still not interested unless I know exactly what you're doing," Shay said.

Twist looked at her for another minute, then said, "Come on upstairs."

"I told you she wasn't useless," Cade said.

Twist said, "Shut up," then, to Shay: "The knife. The knife goes in the drawer."

Shay was reluctant. She'd had the knife for more than a year and worried that she wouldn't see it again if she gave it up. It had been handmade from a carpenter's file, the previous owner had told her, ground to a wicked point and a scalpel edge, guaranteed not to be deflected by ribs or breastbone. She had to decide: she looked around at the kids in the lobby. They all looked mellow enough. She didn't sense the fear that she often felt in street kids.

She walked back to the front desk, slipped the knife out of its sheath, and, with the kid in the hard hat watching, dropped it in the drawer.

"That's a mean damn knife," the kid said, surprise and a bit of respect in his voice.

"Yes, it is," Shay said. "Keep an eye on it or I'll have to punish you."

The kid said, "Ooooo . . ." but flashed her his best grin.

At the back of the building, Twist, Shay, and Cade walked by double doors that were swung open to a loading dock.

Three kids used hand trucks to move commercial-sized packages of food—sacks of flour and potatoes, rice, ketchup—down a corridor into what must have been the kitchen. Shay could smell the food being cooked, and the usual stinks that surround a food operation: old potato peels, a hint of rotten eggs.

Past the open doors, they stepped into another hallway and were facing a freight elevator. Twist lifted one door by a canvas strap, pushed the bottom door down, and they stepped inside. He pulled the doors shut and pushed a button marked PH. Penthouse? The old machine groaned all the way to the top. Twist said, "Don't worry, perfectly safe, guaranteed by the state," and, halfway up, "I live here."

Cade propped himself against the elevator wall between Shay and Twist and asked, "So . . . you new to L.A.?"

"Never mind," Twist said.

"Hey, I was thinking I could show her around," Cade protested.

"I know what you were thinking," Twist said.

The top floor of the hotel was almost wide open, probably a hundred feet long and nearly as wide. One end was closed off with an interior wall: Twist's living quarters, Shay guessed.

The other three walls were cut through with small windows, once the windows of hotel rooms. The ceiling was supported by vertical steel pillars, which were painted a flat, industrial gray.

Part of the roof had been removed and replaced with a glass skylight. Five oversized easels and three paint-spattered office chairs were positioned under the skylight, along with a long wooden table covered with jars holding paintbrushes, tubes and buckets of paint, and all the other detritus of a professional painting studio. Four of the easels had paintings under way, odd, twisted, but mostly realistic images of people on the streets of L.A.

To the left, as they entered, several desks were covered with computers and imaging equipment, including Epson and Canon digital projectors and an old Kodak slide projector. A half dozen couches and easy chairs were scattered around the floor, as were three sixty-inch television screens, stereo equipment with oversized speakers. In a long, open space between the painting area and the computer equipment, a huge piece of gray canvas tarp, the kind used to make tents, was partly unrolled on the floor.

Twist, Shay realized, was an artist.

Not a graffiti artist, but the kind who sold his work in galleries.
Jones had told her that he was rich. . . .

A middle-aged Latino woman with a puffy face sat on one of the
couches, watching an *Oprah* rerun on a sixty-inch television screen.
She was wearing red stilettos and a pink housecoat over what appeared to be nothing else.

Twist said to her, "You can take off, Maru. I got the pose down,
or close enough." He took a couple of bills from his pocket and
passed them to her. She took them, said, "Good luck tonight," and
clip-clopped across the room to a mirrored dressing screen, her ill-
fitting shoes and thick ankles visible from the other side.

"We're making a political poster," Twist told Shay. "We're going
to hang it from the top of a building over the 110."

"What's the 110?" Shay asked.

"The freeway through downtown L.A., where the courthouse
is," Cade said.

Twist added, "We've got to go tonight. We've got the newspeople
ready, we've got a guy who'll let us inside, and he might be moving
to a new job. So we gotta go. We climb up the stairs to the roof and
hang the banner over the edge right after it gets light. The problem
is, the building maintenance guys'll tear it down in fifteen minutes.
If the news choppers show up, we'll get that exposure, but it'd be
nice if we could keep it up there longer—you know, so the rush-
hour drivers can see it. Which is where you come in. If I believe you
about the climbing."

"What's the poster?" Shay asked.

Twist walked over to the blank canvas and prodded the edge of
it with his foot.

"The new L.A. County prosecutor is this hot 'n' sexy publicity hound who's trying to drive out the Latino illegals any way she can," he said. "I've made a cartoon. . . ." Twist pointed at the canvas on the floor. "Digital Boy is supposed to be projecting it to scale so I can repaint it. It's complicated because we don't have enough room for a full projection, so we have to move the canvas under the projector."

Cade had sat down at a computer desk, and by looking over his shoulder, Shay could see an on-screen cartoon that had been divided into small chunks for projection.

The cartoon showed a nearly naked comic-book female villain with large, globular breasts, pointing a .45 automatic at the back of the head of a kneeling immigrant figure whose hands were clasped in prayer. The figure was only *nearly* naked because she was wearing red stilettos and a red Nazi armband dominated by a black swastika.

"A very good likeness, if I do say so myself," Twist said. "You have a problem with it? The politics?"

"No," Shay said. "There was a girl in my class who's lived here since she was two years old. She's not really Mexican, but they'll send her back if they catch her mother. She can't even speak Spanish."

"There you go," Twist said. "It's a disaster."

"So why do I have to come down off the roof?" Shay asked.

"It's the silliest thing, but we couldn't figure it out," Twist said. "We unroll the canvas down the side of the building and run for it. If we close the roof door from the inside, even if we lock it or chain it, they can use simple tools to reopen it—you know, a metal saw. If we could chain it up from the roof side, they couldn't get at it. I mean, they could get at it eventually, but it'll take a long time. But how do we lock it from the roof side and then get off the roof?"

Shay smiled. "Gotta go over the side."

"That's right," Twist said. "That's impossible for me. I get a nose-bleed looking out a second-story window. Byte Boy isn't any better."

"I'm some better," Cade said. "I don't get the nosebleed until I'm up four floors."

Twist said to Shay, "If I believe you about the climbing . . ."

"Get the equipment and I'll climb up and down your building right here," she said.

Twist studied her for another moment, then nodded. "Okay. Which means a trip to REI. I'm gonna put you in a room with a girl named Emily. One useful thing about Emily is that she has a truck. She'll take you where you need to go."

He turned back to Cade. "Cade, call Emily. Tell her to get up here."

Cade said, "One minute. I've got the first segment coming up. Get the shades." At the computer, Cade wasn't the kid he'd seemed to be in the street: he was focused, efficient, intent.

Twist walked over to one of the pillars, which had a series of switches mounted on a metal panel. He began throwing switches, and blackout shades rolled down the windows and across the sky-light. In less than a minute, the room was dark, except for the light from computer screens and the LEDs glowing on all the electronic equipment.

Cade tapped some computer keys and an overhead projector winked on, throwing one section of the cartoon onto the canvas.

"Let's drag the canvas," Twist said.

The canvas had been lightly marked into squares, and they moved it around until the projected fragment of cartoon precisely filled the upper-right square. Twist looked at it for a moment and made some minute adjustments. "That's not terrible," he said.

"Yeah, it's, like, perfect," Cade said.

Twist asked Shay, "What do you think?"

"Looks fine to me—except I would have made the armband black and the swastika red, instead of the other way around. That'd make the swastika pop more."

Twist said, "Huh," then walked over to the painting table and removed his bowler hat like a bullfighter flinging off his cape. It was the first time Shay had seen him bareheaded. His dark brown hair was combed back from his forehead in a slight pompadour and trimmed neatly around his ears and neck.

He picked up a jar full of new black Sharpies and, handing one to Shay, said, "You can help trace until Emily gets here. Cade, call Emily." Then he plucked out a pen for himself, dropped onto his hands and knees, and went to work.

Tracing the cartoon wasn't difficult, but the canvas was so large that it took time.

Cade had divided the original cartoon drawing into twenty-eight segments, then scaled them to perfectly fit the canvas when projected from the eighteen-foot ceiling. They'd trace one segment and then move the canvas and do another.

As they worked, Shay fended off casual-sounding questions from Cade about her background. She'd grown up in Eugene and been placed with foster parents when her mother died, she revealed, and little more. "I have one more year of school, but I can't do it there," she said.

"We can fix that," Twist said. "Cade can come with you."

Cade said, "Man . . . you know how I get along with schools."

"It gets easier the further along you go," Twist said. "Middle school is the toughest. High school is easier. College is even easier, and grad school, I'm told, is a walk in the park."

Twist stood and walked around the canvas, judging the transfer. "It's gonna work, if Adobe Boy hasn't messed something up; if it all fits."

"It'll fit," Cade said. "Though if you'd spend a few bucks on decent equipment, it'd be easier."

"Money, money, money," Twist said. He sat back down and said to Shay, "Cade doesn't look like it, but he's a little rich kid. He's used to the best equipment."

"Really," Shay said. She looked at Cade for a moment and then said, "I can see that. Probably belongs to a country club somewhere."

"Thrown out of six private schools," Twist said. "Been to summer school in London, Paris, Rome, Berlin . . . Madrid, I think."

"Four schools," Cade said. "And Istanbul."

"Ran from the last school. A military school, where they teach kids to march. Showed up here with ten thousand bucks' worth of computer and camera equipment in a stolen car."

"Excuse me?" Cade said. "That'd be a stolen Porsche 911 4S."

"I stand corrected," Twist said. Back to Shay: "We got the Porsche back to the owner, and Cade's been our computer guy ever since. He's almost competent."

"My brother's a computer guy," Shay said to Cade. "Kind of a genius, actually. You have any brothers or sisters?"

"Nada," Cade said. "My parents realized one was too many and sent me off to boarding school when I was six. The only person who missed me was the nanny they fired."

"Said his first word in Spanish," Twist said to Shay. "The nanny was Guatemalan."

"Yeah, I'm bilingual," Cade said. "Of course, the schools all wanted French and Latin and screw the Spanish . . ."

Twist said, "Aw, you're bringing a tear to my eye. Exiled to a resort for kids where they only taught you French . . ."

Cade lifted his head and said with a little chill in his voice, "You oughta quit now, Twist, because you're talking out of your ass. You don't know."

After a moment of silence, Twist nodded and said, "You're right."

"Dude," said Cade, and they continued working side by side, following the contours of the drawing with the Sharpies, throwing the pens into a garbage can when they ran out of ink.

They'd been working for forty-five minutes when the door opened and a chubby young woman with a severe black pageboy came in. She was wearing a frilly blouse open to show some cleavage, a short skirt, and white patent-leather boots. She was chewing gum.

"What's up?" she asked Twist.

Twist, still tracing, said, "Emily—this is Shay. She's your new roommate and she's helping us out. She needs to get to Santa Monica to buy equipment for tonight. We wanna borrow your truck."

"Sure, fifty cents a mile, no problem," Emily said.

"You can take it out of your room rent, which I'm increasing fifty cents an hour," Twist said.

"Like I said, I'm happy to provide the truck at no cost, 'cause you're a pal," Emily said.

Twist looked at Shay. "You can take off. This'll be done in ten minutes."

"That's okay," Shay said. "I'll stay until it's done."

Twist pitched an empty pen over his shoulder and said, "In case you didn't understand, I'm paying you to go get the equipment."

"Oh." She sat back on her heels.

Twist stood up and fished some bills out of his hip pocket. "Here's five hundred. I want to see some change."

As he handed it to her, Shay said, "Money, money, money," mimicking his comment to Cade. Cade snorted and Twist himself laughed.

"C'mon, roomie," Emily said, motioning Shay to her feet. "Time's money."

"Money, money, money," Cade said.

9

They walked out to the staircase, and as they pushed through the fire door, Emily's eyes cut toward Shay. She sniffed, and Shay caught it.

"I know," Shay said. "I need a shower."

"We've got time for a shower. I'll dig you up some clothes, and we can get rid of those."

Shay looked down at herself. "Get rid of them? What's wrong with them? I know I need to find a Laundromat. . . ."

Emily said, "You look like a lumberjack, sweetie. You see a forest outside?"

"It's the way I dress," Shay said.

"That can be fixed," Emily said. "You just have to concentrate."

Down the hall on the fifth floor. Unlike most of the rooms, 510 still had its original silver-plated numbers.

"Home, sweet home," Emily said with a grin.

She pushed the door open and Shay's heart sank. The room looked like the back end of a loaded U-Haul, stuffed almost floor to ceiling with . . . everything.

"It's the only suite on the floor, with this sitting area," Emily said with pride, despite the fact that there was no place to sit. "Wangled it out of Twist a few months ago 'cause, well, I needed the space for my business."

"Cool," said Shay in the most neutral voice she could muster. "What's your business?"

"I'm a picker. I go around to estate sales and flea markets and find stuff that's more valuable than it looks. I sell it to people who can sell it for even more. Antique shops and so on," Emily said. "The sucky economy means there are tons of great scores out there."

"That *is* cool," Shay said. "You're in business on your own?"

"Yup. Here, I'll show you my system for moving around."

Emily wheeled aside a Radio Flyer wagon plopped inside the door—she used it to haul her "scores" up and down the elevator, she said—and angled between two old dressers. With Shay wading in behind her, Emily reached up and spun a mirrored disco ball hung from a nail in the ceiling.

"I do it every time I come home—I say for good luck, but both my shrinks in junior high would probably blame the OCD. Or maybe it's the ADHD."

Shay smiled, and gave the ball another spin. "Same shrinks we had. Every foster kid had something wrong: obsessive-compulsive, attention deficit, serial killer, flesh-eating zombie narcissist klepto cutter disorder."

Emily laughed. "Whatta you got?"

"Something to do with authority figures."

Emily raised a palm. "Gimme five."

They swatted hands and hopscotched their way through the sitting area, past the purple velour couch—"There's a rumor that it belonged to this old singer, Prince, a long time ago," Emily said. "Not entirely, you know, confirmed." And past the beanbag chairs, a dozen boxes filled with old pots, clothes, and paintings. Emily dropped her purse on a table that held two stacked microwaves, a TV, and a box of hair-straightening irons.

"You wanna borrow anything, just ask," she said. "Don't get too attached 'cause everything's got a price. Oh, and not to be a bitch, but . . . you break it, you buy it."

"Thanks," said Shay. "I think."

Emily pulled open a second door, giving the impression that more stuff was spilling over from the other side. Shay peeked in and her face filled with pleasant surprise.

Neat as a pin, two twin beds pushed against opposite walls, crisp white sheets, a nightstand with nothing on it but a glow-green alarm clock.

Emily grinned. "Scared you, didn't I? Let me get you some soap and shampoo and shit."

"I'll just be a minute," Shay lied.

Shay got her shower in a surprisingly nice women's restroom with individual shower booths. She wasn't quick about it. With the sample-sized tubes of bodywash, shampoo, and conditioner fronted by Emily, she stood for ten minutes under the pouring hot water, getting really clean for the first time since she ran.

Her jeans were still questionable, but with a room, access to a decent laundry, and a shower . . . the place would work.

If only until she could find Odin.

Out of the shower she dressed in her lumberjack outfit, but when she got back to the room, she found Emily pawing through bags of clothes. "The used kind that you'd pay big bucks for down at the resale stores," Emily said. "Go get undressed. I'll pass you the stuff."

Emily passed her stuff for ten minutes, and Shay began to run out of patience. She had never followed fashion, and didn't care what she was wearing on the hunt for her brother. Emily came in with another dress and started wriggling it over Shay's head like a stylist. "Really, chica, if I had your assets, I wouldn't be tenting them in sweatshirts and mom jeans. I'd be working it."

" 'Working it'?"

"Yeah, you know. *It.*" Emily stepped back and looked at the dress. "Acceptable," she said.

"I don't think I can stand any more," Shay said.

"Give me five more minutes," Emily said. "I'm starting to see you now."

"You couldn't see me before?"

"Your Smokey the Bear thing threw me off. Try these on." She handed Shay a pair of sandals with heels like spikes.

Shay shook her head. "No. Nothing higher than an inch."

Emily looked at her impatiently. "You're not making this easy."

"You're killing me," Shay said.

But when Emily had gone again and she looked in the mirror on the back of the door, she thought, *Not bad.*

Emily came back with strappy one-inch sandals. They were acceptable.

"You're still not L.A., but at least . . . mmm . . . you're in Southern California. So let's go."

Emily carefully locked the door behind them, and Shay followed her down the stairs. They went around the corner to the hotel's tiny—and nearly empty—parking lot.

"This is it," Emily said. Her truck looked like a cross between a jeep and a fire engine: a red 1977 International Harvester Scout with a missing hardtop, which made it a convertible.

"It's ugly, but at least it's unreliable," Emily said as they got in. "You better do something with your hair, unless you really want that windblown look."

Shay was twisting her damp hair into a bun as they headed for a freeway when Emily shouted over the wind noise, "Not to be snoopy, but the way you were dressed—where *are* you from?"

"Oregon," Shay shouted back.

"Ah," Emily said, nodding as if that answered everything.

Semitrailer trucks, hot rods, pickups, limousines, and practical sedans being driven by little old ladies whipped by them on the Santa Monica Freeway. Emily's vintage truck screamed with pain every time the speedometer touched sixty.

As Emily laughed off a bald guy in a Maserati who was giving them the finger for slowing down his lane, Shay took in Emily's appearance, which was anything but lumberjack. She had flat-ironed chin-length hair tipped with electric blue, emerald-green eyes magnified by thick false lashes and brown winged eyeliner. Her small, pouty mouth was kept constantly peachy with a tube of Nars Orgasm gloss.

"How old are you?" Emily shouted over the traffic.

"Almost seventeen," Shay shouted back.

"I'm almost eighteen," Emily said. "How'd you meet Twist?"

"Uh, I just met him last night." She didn't mention the fight in the alley. Then, "What's he like?"

"He's like . . . Mother Teresa, if she were an outlaw biker with a big fat bank account and a taste for Hollywood starlets."

"Oh," Shay said.

The REI store was all the way across town, practically on the beach. They could have stayed on the freeway, but Emily wasn't feeling the love from her Scout's transmission, so they got off on Santa Monica Boulevard at what felt like a walking pace, getting to know each other.

Emily had dropped out of school after tenth grade but, at Twist's insistence, had gotten a GED and now was thinking about a business degree in college, but only "after a couple more years of this. I'm liking what I'm doing right now, but people I trust tell me that I'll burn out on it."

Shay wasn't sure about a GED: "I'd like to get back in a real school, and finish there."

"Hollywood High—that's your school," Emily said. "Probably the most famous high school in the country. I'll consult on your wardrobe."

"You know where I'd like to buy a complete wardrobe?" Shay asked.

"Where? Maybe Wasteland? We could run over . . ."

"There," Shay said, pointing.

The REI store.

After the confusing morning, the outdoors store on Santa Monica Boulevard felt and smelled familiar, and Shay took charge. She said to Emily quietly, "Stay behind me, look interested, but don't stop walking. I need to find a particular guy."

"What guy?"

"I don't know yet," Shay said. "I'll know him when I see him. I don't want to get the wrong clerk. They can stick on you like sandburs."

They wandered past the bikes, the camping gear, the kayaks and paddles, past a couple of racks of climbing gear, and checked out lug-sole boots. Emily found a bin of tights—for men. "Awesome," she muttered, fingering the material.

Then Shay spotted her guy. He was kneeling by a display rack, sorting and folding T-shirts on a messy shelf of sale merchandise. He was short, with heavy shoulders, long hair, a tanned face and arms, and a silver hoop earring. Shay moved in, with Emily a few steps behind, and said, "Hey."

He looked up, nodded. "Can I help you?"

"I need to find some climbing gear," Shay said. "You look like a climber."

He checked her out in her new used clothes and asked skeptically, "You're a climber?"

"I did Jacob's Nose in a day and a half, on lead the whole way," she said.

He stood up and said, "Uh, you don't look like . . ."

Shay was wearing an ivory-net top over a soft, flesh-colored camisole that looked like nothing at all, a pale blue skirt that came to midthigh, and the one-inch-high sandals that precisely matched the net top.

"My friend just did a makeover on me," Shay said, tipping her head at Emily. "An hour ago, she said I looked like a lumberjack—with pinecones in my hair."

"It's true," Emily said, giving her gum a vigorous snap. "Pinecones."

The guy still wasn't sure, and Shay could see it. She stuck out her hands, palms up. "Don't look at the clothes. Look at my hands."

He reached out and took her fingers, felt the calluses, and said, "Jacob's Nose, huh? What is that? 5.11?"

"More like 5.10, not terrible," Shay said, taking her hands back. "But it was sleeting most of the time."

He smiled now. "Okay. What're you looking for?"

"I'll be teaching some kids up around Big Bear," she said. "We're gonna use a top rope, but I left all my stuff in Oregon. So I need like a climbing harness, maybe a hundred and ten meters of PMI E-Z Bend eleven-millimeter static line . . . couple good rappel devices."

"Pretty much everything, then."

She said quickly, "Listen, I was hoping I could get sale stuff. I'm light on cash. If you're not having a sale for a while, I could wait. . . ."

"Looking for a deal—now I know you're a climber," the guy said. "My name is Jonah. Let's go over here. So what else have you done?"

Shay mentioned a few Oregon climbs she'd been to with her foster parents, including one that Jonah had done himself, though he'd gone a different, harder route up the same face.

He was still feeling her out, and she said, "You took the hard way. There's that overhang going up the left fork, I can't get over it yet. That knob hits me at my collarbone, and I can't get my foot on it without coming off."

He grunted and said, "That's tough. You need to work on your fingers, is the trick. You gotta hang, and do a one-handed pull-up, just a short one, just a grunt, then reach up about another eight inches, there's a better hold there, off to the right. You can't see it, you gotta feel around. When you can pull yourself up, you can get high enough to get your foot on that knob."

"That's what I can't do yet," Shay said. "Don't have the finger strength, the upper-body strength." Making him feel a little superior, a bit manly.

They went off on other details, standing by a rack of climbing equipment, while Emily appeared to be falling asleep on her feet. Jonah said, "Your friend doesn't climb."

Emily woke up enough to say, "Only in and out of a truck."

"Well, you got a truck, anyway," Jonah said. Satisfied with Shay's credentials, he picked up a brand-new hundred-dollar Black Diamond women's climbing harness and said, "This is a little shopworn. I can give it to you for half price . . ."

She got the harness, three descenders, two ascender devices, locking carabiners, and 110 meters of rope for three hundred dollars, including tax, the prices manipulated by Jonah to the amount Shay wanted to spend. He threw in a box of Power Putty so she could work on her finger and arm strength, an eight-dollar value for, um, nothing.

Shay shook his hand as they left the store and said, "Thanks for all this, Jonah. I'd like to climb with you sometime. If you have an email."

They exchanged emails, and out in the truck Emily said, "Man, if I could work a guy like that, I'd be rich."

"I didn't work him—he's a climber," Shay said defensively. "He was helping me out. Climbers stick together."

"You got five hundred dollars' worth of gear for three hundred," Emily countered. "You knew *exactly* what you were doing. If you were a short, ugly, male climber—or even a slightly overweight female with a terrific personality—you think he would have helped you out that much?"

Shay smiled at Emily, then said, "I don't know."

"I don't know, my large pink butt. There's no way," Emily said as she fired up the Scout. "But it's for a good cause, so you're forgiven." She looked at her watch. "We've got time to stop at one more shop on the way back. You made me think about Wasteland. I got an idea about a really fantastic climbing outfit for you. If we hurry . . ."

"Oh my God," Shay said.

10

No one who lived at the hotel had ever seen where Twist actually slept. The kids who worked the front desk said the man came and went at all hours, sometimes with Dum and Dee, sometimes not, sometimes with his art, sometimes with any number of beautiful women.

Now here Shay was, her first day at the hotel, climbing gear looped over her shoulder, standing behind Twist as he unhooked a key ring from his belt loop and inserted a key into the steel security door built into the studio's only interior wall.

Emily had begged Shay to memorize everything in Twist's bedroom so she could relay every weird and exotic detail. Emily was betting on a mahogany four-poster bed with mother-of-pearl inlays and sweeping silk canopies fit for a sultan.

Maybe that's what it was, but all Shay could see was an entry room six feet by ten, with a scuffed oak floor, a rug, a non-Twist landscape, and a daddy longlegs making its way up one of the cloud-white walls. An archway, draped with a beaded curtain, cut through one end wall, with an exterior window on the opposite one. Shay leaned toward the beaded curtain, maybe even craned her neck a little; all she could see was darkness.

Twist said, "The fire escape's over there." He was pointing at the window.

Of course it is, she thought. "You don't sleep here?"

"You see a bed?" said Twist. "C'mon, let's see what you got."

He walked over to the window, flipped a lock, and pushed it open. Shay pulled her climbing harness on and, carrying her rope, stepped through to the metal fire escape and felt it rattle beneath her weight. She was standing on the back side of the hotel, seven stories above the parking lot and the loading dock she'd seen earlier.

"You coming?" she asked Twist, who was standing a foot back from the door. "Or you going to stand there like a lamppost?"

"Acrophobic lamppost," he said. "If I remember right from the fire marshal, it's six steps to the roof, so go ahead and get set up. If you need any help, I'll send someone. Otherwise, I'll be waiting for you on the ground."

"Got it."

"One other thing—"

The Cat in the Hat looked at her, suddenly serious, and in his expression, Shay felt something almost . . . parental.

"Twist," she said, "I won't kill myself."

He gave her a small salute and turned to leave. "See you down there."

"Momentarily," Shay said to his back, then turned and climbed the fire escape. Stepping onto the roof, she startled some pigeons into flight. The birds landed a few feet farther along the roofline and went back to hunting and pecking their way through an insulating layer of white gravel. Tangles of old cable wires ran in all directions, and swarming yellow jackets moved in and out of a nest that was growing on the rim of a satellite dish. The whole roof smelled of hot tar.

Shay looked down and caught Emily's wave. Emily was only vaguely interested in the climbing; she was much more interested in the climbing outfit she'd styled for her from her ragbag, which was a turquoise tank and formfitting indigo-wash stretch jeans.

It was now six o'clock, and a scrim of smog on the horizon kept Shay from seeing the Pacific to the west.

On a clear day, Twist said, she should be able to see the Santa Monica Pier and the rugged Malibu coast beyond. To the southeast, much closer in, Shay got her first look at the downtown skyline and found it, for a city built on theatrics, pretty boring: a basic bar graph of ten or twelve rectangular skyscrapers and one standard-issue sports arena. Somewhere out there was the building they were targeting.

Somewhere out there was Odin.

Focus.

Shay looked around for an anchor and found one on a steel support leg for the building air conditioner. She wrapped one of her nylon tie straps around the steel leg, slipped the rope through the tie-strap loops, tested it for strength—the air conditioner it was supporting probably weighed five tons, so strength was not a problem. She tied into the rope, then carried it to the edge of the building and dropped it over.

On the ground, fifteen kids from the hotel, along with Dum and Dee, were looking up at her. She waved, and saw Twist emerge from the building. He turned to look up, and she smiled to herself: time to prove the girl from Oregon did have some useful skills.

Stepping boldly onto the parapet, Shay put her weight on the rope, turned away from the crowd, and stepped backward into air until first her right boot and then her left found their spots on the coarse stucco wall. Relaxing into her harness, she began "walking" down the wall.

Nice and easy, that was her plan. Don't scare Twist with Spider-Man speed, just take a leisurely stroll down his building. As she passed a window on the fifth floor, a girl watching TV locked eyes with her in shock; Shay waved as she descended out of view.

She was almost to the bottom when she glanced down and saw a scrum of boys waiting for her with raised arms. Twist had assigned spotters?

She swung right to avoid the intercept, but the boys moved with her, and suddenly one of them was pulling her down into his arms.

"Gotcha," the boy said, as though she needed rescuing. He was a tough-looking Latino kid, with a swirl of black ink peeking out from the collar of his T-shirt.

"Put me down!" Shay protested, and pushed against his hold on her rib cage. "C'mon, let go!" He set her down like he might plunk down a shovel, and she angrily backed away.

Twist limped over and said, "That was brilliant."

"What are these guys doing?" Shay snapped at him. "If I'd fallen, I would have hit them like a meteor. Did you think they were going to catch me?"

"Ah . . . I don't know what I was thinking," Twist said. "It just seemed like a good idea." He looked up the face of the building, then back to her. "But you're right. You came down fast."

"No, I came down slow, because I didn't want to scare you," Shay said. "I can come down fast if you want me to."

Twist nodded at her confidence. "Good. The building tonight is nearly twice as high. Does that make a difference?"

"It'll take longer to get down, but that's it. A rope's a rope. After you get thirty feet off the ground, height doesn't matter anymore. You fall, you die."

"That doesn't worry you?"

"No, because I know what I'm doing." Shay was pulling down the rope, and when the far end of it slipped free of the nylon loop on the roof, she said, "Watch it!"

The rope fell at their feet and she began gathering it in, looping it around her arm. When it was neatly tied, she asked, "We good?"

Twist laughed and then nodded. "We're good. By the way, meet Cruz—I'll let him apologize for plucking you out of the air like a beach ball. He's going with us tonight."

Cruz nodded at her, maybe annoyed at her reaction to his help. He had a thick wedge of glossy black hair and dark, unreadable eyes. He was standing next to Cade, shorter than Cade by a couple inches, but more muscular, with wide shoulders and square hips. He was dressed in a Dodgers shirt and neatly pressed jeans.

"I apologize for listening to Twist. That won't happen again," he said. A little smile now, and Twist didn't tell him to shut up.

Cade leaned toward Cruz, looking at Shay as she turned away from them, and muttered, *"Esta bien pechocha."*

Cruz said, *"Olé."*

Shay caught it, turned back, looked from one to the other, and said, "What did you say?"

Cade shrugged with mock innocence and translated: " 'The barn is painted red'?"

Shay said, "Careful," and walked away.

• • •

The demonstration done, the group trailed back into the building. In the lobby, the kid behind the desk said, "Hey—you in?"

"I'm rooming with Emily," Shay said.

"Don't sniff too hard, you'll get an antique up your nose," the kid said. He held up an index finger, meaning *Wait one,* dug in his desk, and came up with a sheet of paper. "The rules."

"The rules." She glanced at it, found a short list, like the Ten Commandments.

"Yeah. Violate the rules, and there is one penalty," the kid said. "You're out on your ass."

"Okay . . ."

"He's not kidding," Emily said.

Emily led the way to the interior stairs, and as they climbed them, she explained that at one time, the Twist Hotel Rules hung in the lobby, but the adults who wandered in—cops, social workers, city inspectors, insurance agents—couldn't handle the implications. Now newcomers got a flyer when they checked in.

Shay ran through the rules:

1. **No Guns (check knives at front desk)**
2. **No Sex**
3. **No Alcohol or Drugs (weed counts)**
4. **No Ringtones (vibrate or die)**
5. **No Smoking (except me, and I quit)**
6. **No Pets**
7. **No Outsiders**
8. **No Trespassing in My Studio**
9. **Nothing That Attracts the Cops**
10. **No Excuses**

As a foster kid, Shay understood them instantly: they were pure crowd control.

"We're lucky we can have the Internet," Emily said as they paused on a burgundy-carpeted landing. "Twist's afraid that it's turning us all into zombies and porn perverts and celebrity worshipers. In his dreams, we'd all be reading art history or knitting bottle warmers for Third World babies."

She had been living at the hotel for almost two years, Emily said as they headed up the stairs again.

"Can't even have a boyfriend, huh?" Shay said. She'd never had time for a serious boyfriend. There had been two possible candidates in Eugene. So much for that. . . .

"Depends on how you define *boyfriend*," Emily said. "I asked about the no-sex thing, and Twist said he didn't have anything against sex, but when you start allowing sex on the premises, the boys start fighting, the girls start feuding, and the whole place gets crazy. And if somebody is underage, it could bring in the cops. The same thing with drugs. It's crazy enough without that stuff. He says the one big basic rule is, nothing that makes the place crazier. If you do stuff that attracts the cops, like Cade did today, it makes the place crazier."

"Doesn't sound too bad," Shay said. "Actually, it makes sense."

"Well . . . until you fall in love. Real love," Emily said. "Then you might want to get together with somebody. If that happens . . . Twist will kick you out. He can be a mean little bastard. He just won't take the hassle."

"Why does he do it at all?" Shay asked.

Emily shrugged. "Supposedly, he was a street kid himself. That's pretty much the sum total of what anyone knows. Oh, and that he sells those paintings up in his studio for about a million dollars."

"A million dollars?"

"Okay. Not a million, but a lot," Emily said. "When he got rich, the story is, this place was a flophouse, and he bought it with the idea that he was going to build free studios for street artists. Instead, it got taken over by kids."

"Except that he still makes the rules," Shay said.

"Yup, and keeps the twins around to enforce 'em, if they need to."

The twins . . .

Shay had seen what they were capable of in a dark alley against a couple of knife-wielding thugs. She wasn't sure how she felt about running into them in a hallway on her way to brush her teeth. "So . . . are people around here afraid of them?"

"No, they're not bad guys, as far as I can tell," said Emily as they walked out on the fifth floor. "A little strange, but that's no big thing around here. I've never heard either of them talk. They're musicians. Trumpets, the Tweedle Brass. They're the house brass at the Bridge, this hot studio over in Glendale."

Shay shook her head. "Stranger and stranger," she said.

Emily stood up, stretched, and said, "Listen, I've got to work. I found three little paintings today, on copper, a Western artist. I paid eight dollars each. I've seen the painter's name before. I need to look him up."

When Emily had gone, Shay got her laptop and walked out to the Tea Leaf. She'd decided against using the hotel's Wi-Fi, because the address might be tracked.

She got an iced tea, took it to a table, went online, checked Odin's Facebook account, and found it empty. Went to her SEND page and dropped yet another note, telling Odin where she was. Why didn't he call her? Was Rachel isolating him?

What if he'd been hurt?

She turned away from that thought and spent some time considering Twist and his hotel. She Googled him and found six thousand entries under "Twist, artist," mostly copies and recopies of gallery schedules and show announcements. There were a few stories from newspapers and magazines about his social activism and his social style of painting. She found no indication of a first name—or, for that matter, a real last name.

Twist was apparently it.

Odd. Judging from the kids she'd seen around, and their independent attitudes, she thought Twist was probably all right. But definitely odd. When she'd exhausted the online Twist research, she packed up her laptop and headed back to the hotel. As she was crossing the lobby, having nodded to the desk kid, she spotted Catherine, the woman who ran the kitchen. "Twist said you might have a job for me?"

"There's already a waiting list," Catherine said. "But it's Twist's call. I'll ask him. Give me a couple minutes."

Shay dropped into one of the beat-up overstuffed lobby chairs to wait. Cruz came through the door carrying a bundle of six long boxes bound together with tape. He looked around, took off his sunglasses, walked over, put the bundle down. The bundle hit with a thunk—it was heavy. "You ready for the big show?"

"I will be," she said. "I'm waiting to see if I've got a kitchen job."

He grimaced and dropped into the next chair. "If you gotta do it, you gotta do it. I did. It's bad. You always smell like a stewed tomato. Even when they're not stewing tomatoes."

"What do you do now?" Shay asked.

"Twist found me a job on a golf course. Five in the morning until eight," Cruz said. "I cut the greens, mow the fairways. Then I go to school. One more year."

"I don't know about golf," Shay said.

Cruz said, "Neither do I—I know about cutting greens and mowing fairways. Seems weird, chasing a little white ball around, but a lot of rich people do it. Movie stars and stuff, and they take it seriously."

She waited for Cruz to ask where she was from, but he never asked, nor did he ask why she was on the street. Hotel etiquette? She wasn't sure. He did say that he'd seen a sign for part-time help wanted in a car wash, but she shook her head and said, "I'd rather do the kitchen."

"Gonna smell like a tomato," he said.

"Better than smelling like a radiator," she said.

Catherine came back, nodded to Cruz, and said to Shay, "I talked to Twist. He said you'll be working up in the belfry, so you don't need the kitchen."

"The belfry?"

"His studio," she said.

"Am I supposed to go up?"

Catherine shrugged. "He didn't say. Anyway, you're not in the kitchen."

She left and Cruz said, "Come on, I'll take you up. I do his heavy lifting." He patted the bundles of boxes. "Fifty pounds of canvas rolls from Artist & Craftsman."

Twist's studio was buzzing. Cade and a serious-looking woman whom Shay hadn't met were on their hands and knees, painting the huge canvas with house-painting brushes. They were both wearing paper coveralls. Twist worked at a side table, mixing paint in plastic buckets.

Another woman, older, gray-haired, used a five-inch needle to sew a sleeve in the top edge of the canvas. The sleeve would take two wooden rods that would support the canvas off the side of a building, like a flag hung vertically.

Four big fans stood around the edges of the canvas, blowing air across it.

As Shay and Cruz came in, Twist looked up from the paint table and said, "Ah. Cruz and Shay. Good. We can use more painters. There are coveralls in that box."

The cartoon looked like a panel from an early comic book, in harsh, bright colors—yellow, blue, red, black, and white. The outlines that they'd drawn that morning were all labeled with the color they would be. Cade and the woman working with him had finished about a quarter of the visible canvas.

Cruz and Shay found paper painter's coveralls that were more or less the right size—the choices were medium and extra-large—got brushes from Twist, and went to work.

The woman introduced herself as Lou and said, "I'm Twist's executive officer." She had a soft accent that Shay later found out was Ethiopian.

Twist said, "Lou runs the place. I tell her what I need done, and she figures out how to do it without pissing off any more people than necessary."

"Which ain't easy," Cade chipped in.

The paint, Twist said as they worked, was cheap, but still cost more than a thousand dollars. "We want the coat of paint to be thin, but we want complete coverage. Don't slop it on. Thin coats. Thin."

And he was fussy about the technique: "I have a reputation to uphold." To Cade: "Slow down, slow down. Make smooth strokes. Smooth . . . Look at Lou."

Lou said, "How can it affect your reputation? This is anonymous."

"Anonymous, but everyone will know," Cruz said.

They were a well-coordinated crew, familiar and friendly with each other, Shay realized.

Shay was working with a pail of yellow paint, blocking the outline of the cartoon woman's body. After a while, Cruz said to Shay, "You're pretty good at this."

Cade: "You *are* pretty good."

Twist: "Cruz, Cade. Just paint. Okay?"

"Just trying to be friendly," Cade said.

"I know what you're trying to be," Twist said. "Do it on your own time."

Shay smiled to herself and kept painting.

It was almost midnight when they finished. Twist said, "Not as bad as it could have been."

"There's a spot," Shay said. She pointed to one of the center panels.

"Damn it," Twist said. "Cade, can you reach in there?"

Cade stretched across one wet panel to reach into the center, with Cruz holding his belt in the back. Cade managed to dab at a white spot showing through a blue layer.

"Got it," Cade said. He exhaled, as though done with heavy labor, and said to Twist, "Pay up."

Twist said, "Yeah, yeah."

He walked around the painting. The paint they'd used was thinned acrylic. With the fans playing across it, the paint had dried within minutes of being applied. Because the painting was so large, they'd had to roll one edge as soon as it was dry. They'd never seen the entire painted panel, all at once.

Twist said, "Is the Nazi armband big enough? We want that to really jump off the canvas."

"With bosoms like that, you think anybody is going to look at the armband?" Lou asked.

Shay had noticed that Twist had changed the colors on the armband, which was now black with a red swastika, as she'd suggested.

Twist shook his head. "Without seeing the whole thing, it's hard to judge the impact."

Cade: "Look at this." He went to the computer and punched a bunch of keys. Twist's cartoon, Photoshopped over an image of the target building, popped up on the screen.

Lou whistled. "If it looks like that in real life, she's really gonna be annoyed. I better check the hotel permits, in case she sics the health department on us."

Shay: "Who is she again?"

"Ann Banks—the district attorney," Twist said with a grin. "Man, this is good work, if I do say so myself."

Cade said, "So pay up. C'mon. I want to spend the money before the cops come."

Twist went off to the back room and Cruz asked Shay, "What are you doing next?"

Cade, before Shay could answer: "Probably sleeping, since we move out at three o'clock."

Lou: "Not a bad idea if you're planning to jump off a building on the end of a rope."

Twist came back with an envelope full of cash and began passing it out. To Shay, he said, "Two hours doing the outlines, three hours getting the climbing gear, an hour, more or less, going up and down the building, four hours here, ten hours total, at eight dollars an hour. That's a total of eighty." He counted out eight ten-dollar bills and handed them to her.

"Thank you," she said. Then, "Oh!" She dug into her hip pocket and pulled out a wad of bills. "We got some deals. Here's your change—two hundred dollars."

Twist's eyebrows went up. "Change? That's a whole new concept."

He paid off Cade and Cruz, told Shay that Lou was on a regular salary, and put the rest of the money in his pocket. He said, "We move at three a.m. Do not be late. Now everybody go away. I've got to think."

Emily was in bed dozing, a three-year-old copy of *Cosmopolitan* folded over her chest, when Shay returned. Shay said, "I'm going to have to pay you for the clothes a little at a time." She handed the girl fifty dollars: "Okay?"

"You have enough to live on?"

"For a few days," Shay said. "I think I have a job with Twist, but I'm not sure. Nobody tells you anything."

Emily said she got up at first light. "I go to flea markets all over the L.A. Basin. If you want the good stuff, you've got to move early."

They turned the lights off and talked for a while. Emily was upfront about her life: her father, she said, abandoned her mother when Emily was less than a year old. She'd never known him, and had no inclination to find him.

Her mother had had drug and boyfriend problems, and still did. "She's only thirty-four—she feels more like a sister than a mother, especially since she wouldn't know good advice if it bit her on the leg. Her idea of good advice is to stay away from wine in cans."

That made Shay smile, but she felt a touch of sadness at the same time. She didn't talk about herself, not to Emily or anybody. All she said was that her parents had been killed in accidents, and that she and a brother had lived with their grandmother until she died.

"We wound up with Child Protection—that's when I was nine and my brother was ten."

"Brutal," Emily said.

"Yeah. I try not to think about the past too much," Shay said. "We've been in Social Services for so long it almost feels normal."

Emily was quiet for a moment. Then, "At least your foster parents taught you a skill. How many people can climb up and down buildings?"

"That's right," said Shay. "Less than a week in L.A., and I've already got a gig."

Eventually, they drifted off to sleep, and an odd peace seeped into Shay's subconscious: she was safe, among friends. She could sleep without worrying about it. . . .

So she was startled when, two hours in, the phone alarm vibrated against her chest. She was wearing a man's shirt, a loan from Emily, with the phone in a breast pocket. She killed the vibration, swiveled her feet to the floor, and dressed in the dark. She found her comb and toothbrush, and made a five-minute bathroom run. Back in the room, moving as quietly as she could, she picked up her pack with the climbing gear.

Emily said in the dark, "Be careful, Shay. Do good."

11

The group was meeting in the lobby, where a half-dozen sleep-deprived kids were still working the Net with their laptops. *Like an addiction,* Shay thought. Everyone arrived within a minute or so, and Twist, the last one down, said, "I had to go back up for the key. Let's get the stuff off the dock."

Twist drove a three-year-old black Range Rover that had never been washed by anything but rain. The large roll of painted canvas went in the back, along with two heavy bags of chains. The wooden support rods were tied to the roof.

One of the long pieces of chain, Twist told Shay, would be used to lock the door to the roof. Several short pieces would weight the bottom edge of the banner, to hold it flat down the side of the building. "You'll see when we get there."

There were four of them: Twist, Cade, Cruz, and Shay. They took the 101 Freeway east out of Hollywood. More than a few motorists were taking advantage of the light traffic and speeding along at a hundred miles an hour or more. Twist drove a steady sixty-five: "The last thing we need is a speeding stop," he said. "Remember that when you're planning your next crime."

They passed the exit to Dodger Stadium, shifted onto the 110 North, and continued to the cluster of buildings that made up the Los Angeles downtown area.

The route was complicated, but Twist knew exactly where he was going: he took an off-ramp, switched down a series of poorly lit streets, and pulled into a parking lot that lay almost under the freeway, next to a short white building that smelled like baking bread.

"Nice and dark," Cade said as they unloaded the truck. The predawn air was cool, a break from the hot days and warm evenings.

"Won't be for long," Twist said, looking at his watch.

"I just hope your guy is here," Cruz said. Cruz was carrying the massive canvas. Although the poster canvas was lighter, yard for yard, than the artist canvas Twist used for his studio paintings, there was so much of it that the roll forced Cruz into a painful stoop after he got it up onto his shoulders.

Cade carried the heavier of the two chain bags, and Twist carried the lighter one with his free hand. Shay handled her climbing gear and the two support rods—the rods were long and awkward, but not especially heavy.

The limp and the cane didn't seem to slow Twist down. He led the way over a three-foot concrete wall at the end of the parking lot, then down a dirt path and along a hurricane fence that separated the bottom of the freeway from the private land on the other side. The warm odor of baking bread had gone away, to be replaced with the stink of a wet basement.

Their target was the Secox Building, a green-glass-and-steel box that virtually hung over the freeway. They'd walked the length of a couple of football fields, Shay thought, when Twist turned and led them across a narrow service driveway toward the back of the target building. As they got close, he took out his cell phone and made a call.

Shay muttered, "I thought he didn't believe in cell phones."

Cade whispered back, "Only for the cause."

Shay suddenly thought of Odin, and the raid on the animal lab that had put him on the run. *This is the same thing,* she thought: sneaking into a building in the middle of the night, doing what felt right, but with the possibility that everything could go wrong. She was amazed at how easily she'd been recruited into the whole scheme. She really didn't have time to go to jail, get sent back to Oregon, and make her way to California all over again.

A door popped open in the side of the building and a Latino man in a Nike tracksuit was looking out at them. He looked nervous, but said, "Hey, man," in a thoroughly L.A. accent, slapped hands with Twist, and led the way up.

Twelve floors.

"There's gotta be a better way," Cade groaned. "There's this device called an elevator . . ."

"Three of them," Twist said. "With devices called security cameras."

Cruz had to stop halfway for a breather. Twist offered to help him carry the canvas, but the narrow stairway was too awkward for that. Cruz said he was okay, he'd caught women who were heavier than that. Shay said, "Hey, am not," and after a minute, they started up again.

The stairway ended at a locked steel door. The Latino man pulled a key out of his pocket, opened the door, gave the key to Twist, and said, "I'm outta here. Good luck." He headed back down the stairs.

The roof door opened out of a concrete-block shed, little more than a box sitting in the center of the roof. To one side were a series of metal structures, ten or twelve feet high, that housed heating and cooling equipment. After they came out onto the roof in a light breeze, Twist led them to the space between the shed and the air-conditioning units.

"Our biggest problem is that somebody in one of the other buildings might see us and call the cops," he said quietly.

Shay looked around: their building was one of the shortest in the area—thousands of windows looked down on them, although only a few were lit, and she couldn't see anybody in those. In the space between the metal boxes and the shed, they were relatively hidden.

Cruz said, "We've got an hour before the sun comes up."

It took half an hour to assemble the banner. The poles went in the top sleeve and were linked together with a piece of pipe and two bolts to make one long, stiff rod. Six lengths of rope were tied to the poles through holes in the sleeve. They'd been premeasured so they could be tied to ventilation ducts coming out of the roof. Six short lengths of chain, from Twist's bag, had to be attached to the bottom of the banner to weigh it down and keep it from flapping if the wind kicked up.

The assembly would have been simple enough—in a lighted room. On the dark roof, it was more complicated. Twist had a flashlight, but was reluctant to use it—flashlights looked too burglarlike.

By the time they finished, light was leaking over the San Gabriel Mountains to the east, and the city was waking up. Traffic was heavier, and more windows were being lit with every passing moment.

When the banner was ready to go, Cade shook a long length of remaining chain out of the bag, and Twist dragged it over to the concrete-block shed that protected the roof door.

"Here's the way this works," he told Shay. He dragged the chain in a loop around the entire shed, then fed it through the steel handle on the door. "All you do is feed the chain through the handle here, then padlock it."

He took a fist-sized padlock out of his pocket and slipped it through the two end links of the chain. "That'll keep them from opening the door from the inside. The door is steel, so they'll have to get some heavy gear up here to knock it down. Or knock down a wall. Or hire a chopper to land on the roof. Whatever they do, it'll take a while to figure out and then get it done. Hours, maybe. The longer the banner is up, the better for us."

Shay walked over to one of the cooling units, looked at the metal stand that supported it, kicked it, looped one of her nylon tie-ins around it, threaded her rope through the tie-in, and threw her weight against it as hard as she could. Nothing budged. She yanked it twice more, and was satisfied. "I'm ready," she said. "Where do I go when I get down?"

"We'll be waiting for you," Twist said. He looked at the light coming over the mountains, and his watch. "Fifteen minutes, and we go." He dipped into his pocket and pulled out a wad of red bandannas, the kind cowboys wore around their necks.

And anarchists wore over their faces.

"Masks, everyone," Twist said.

They should have gone in fifteen minutes, but didn't go for almost twenty-five. Twist was pacing in the space between the heating and cooling boxes and the shed, muttering to himself.

Cade said, "Man, it's getting pretty light . . ."

"Can't go yet. . . . Can't go," Twist said.

"Gotta go soon," Cruz said. "Everything's lighting up."

Everything was: the buildings around them were coming alive. Twist looked at his watch and said, "We might have to go without them."

At that instant, they heard the first of the news helicopters. "There they are," Twist said. "Let's do it."

Moving as quickly as they could, the guys ran the bundle of canvas out onto the parapet at the edge of the roof, where it loomed like a long, thick snake—a freshly fed anaconda, maybe. The poles along the top edge of the banner were already tied to the support ropes back to the ventilation ducts.

Twist got on his phone and made a call. He said to Shay, "They don't know exactly where the action is going to be. They just know it's on the 110."

He turned away, put a finger in his other ear, and began talking into the phone. Then he clicked it shut and said to Shay, "You're sure about this? About going down the building? About not landing on your head?"

Shay could feel the tension in her stomach, but also a warm, uncoiling excitement. She grinned at him as she knotted her long hair into a bun and said, "I'm good."

He studied her for a moment, then said, "Nothing we do would be worth you getting killed. Or hurt. Nothing."

"Don't chicken out on me, Twist. You got me all hot to do this."

"All right, all right," he said. "Let's go."

She went to get tied into her rope while Twist, Cruz, and Cade moved to the edge of the building. Twist called, "Everybody lift . . .

everybody stand clear of the poles. Don't get your feet tangled up, or you'll go over the side with the banner. Careful, careful . . . Goddammit, Cade, watch your hands. . . ."

As they were doing that, a helicopter came thrashing down the 110, just at eye level, stopped, hovered, and Shay could see a cameraman in the door. A half mile behind the first chopper, a second one was moving in.

Twist shouted, "Wait, wait. We got another camera coming. . . . Wait, here comes another. . . . On the count of three . . . everybody. One! Two! Three!"

They dropped the banner, and the support ropes snapped tight against the poles that held the banner straight. Twist shouted, "Let's go! Let's go!"

Cade, Cruz, and Twist ran for the roof door, where Shay was ready to lock it behind them. Cruz stopped and told her, "You've got guts," and Twist pushed him forward and asked her once more, "You're sure?" and she said, "Yes!" and pushed him after Cruz, and suddenly Cade's hand was on her wrist, and he pulled her into his chest and said, "I'm putting something in your pocket for protection," and he slid something past her harness and into her back pocket.

Shay stared up at him, feeling his rapid heartbeat through her shirt, and asked, "What am I protecting?"

He let go of her wrist and kissed her forehead through his mask. "It's to protect *you*. Go!"

He went through the door, leaving Shay alone on the roof. Quick now: she pulled the chain through the door handle and snapped the lock into the chain. The helicopters were louder than thunder now. The air got choppy, and when she turned, there were four machines looming overhead, with television call letters painted on their sides.

She pushed the red handkerchief a bit farther up her nose, checked the tension on her rope, and stepped onto the parapet. She stretched, back arched and hands over her head, and almost laughed with the pure over-the-top rush. She turned, took a breath, and started down the side of the building, her toes bouncing off the reflective glass.

And saw below her a fold in the banner.

Something had happened during the drop, and one edge had folded across the cartoon—the edge with the woman's arm and the Nazi armband. She dropped down for a closer look, aware of the beat of the helicopter blades close behind her.

Two of the weighting chains, she saw, had somehow become entangled when the banner unfurled down the building. She dropped farther, until she was just below the level of the problem spot, and began to pendulum back and forth across the green glass of the building, her knotted hair falling loose.

The sound of the choppers was ferocious, but she didn't have time to look. On her third run across, she managed to grab the entangled chain, saw it was simply looped across the other, and flicked it clear.

The banner dropped open. She looked down and saw Twist, Cade, and Cruz on the ground. Twist was shouting at her, but she couldn't hear what he was saying. She kicked off the face of the building as hard as she could and dropped the rest of the way in a half-dozen big jumps.

When she hit the ground, hard, she freed the rope and began pulling on one end. How long had they been? Three minutes? Maybe.

Cruz was coiling up the accumulating rope and shouted, "Faster,

faster," and finally the rope fell free down the building and Cruz coiled the last of it, and then they were running, down under the freeway where the chopper cameras couldn't follow, along the chain-link fence, until they were at the SUV.

They could hear sirens now. The cops were close, but up above, on the freeway, Shay thought.

They threw the rope in the back of the Range Rover and Twist said to Shay, "You almost gave me a heart attack. If you ever . . ."

"What?"

He shook his head and pulled off his mask. "Nothing. I just . . . nothing."

She climbed inside with Cruz and Cade, Twist cranked the ignition, and they were gone.

Lou was waiting on the loading dock behind the hotel with Catherine, the kitchen supervisor. As they got out of the truck, Lou stepped over and said, "You're not going to believe it!"

"Good or bad?" said Twist.

Lou nodded at Shay. "She's coast to coast. You can't turn on the TV without seeing her swinging across the building."

Catherine said, laughing, "When she kicks out that Nazi armband . . . Oh my God . . ."

Shay felt everyone's sudden stare, and her face flushed.

"Did they get the banner down yet?" Cruz asked.

"It was still up five minutes ago," Lou said. "I don't think the building manager's in any hurry to get it down, either. They had him on Channel 5. He said he was outraged—outraged!—but he was laughing up his sleeve."

"Let's find a TV," Twist said.

• • •

They hurried up to the studio floor, where the big television screens were, and caught video of the banner unfurling on the first channel they looked at—all in high-res, close-ups of the masked faces above the banner, then the three men disappearing through the door and Shay locking the chain through the door handle.

Then Shay standing on the parapet, stretching, a flock of helicopters upon her.

"What're you doing, yoga? Or jerking me around? You're so damn high up," Twist said. "I'm getting sick to my stomach looking at the TV."

Shay watched herself bounce down the side of the building, the turquoise top flashing across the face of the banner, her long red hair coming loose, flying behind the mask, as she swung back and forth, reaching for the tangled chains. Twist closed his eyes like he couldn't watch, though he was peeking through his fingers, and shouted, "Look at you! Jeez, look at you . . ."

Shay cleared the banner and it dropped, and the cameras got a shot of Shay swinging across the Nazi armband, and then she dropped like a rock down the rest of the building.

The news cameras got them fleeing under the 110, then cut back to the banner, and then, later, to a shot of several cops walking up to the building and staring up at the bare white cartoon breasts of the district attorney—laughing at it.

Twist collapsed on a couch, a broad smile on his scarred face, and said, "This is the most fantastic action in the history of Los Angeles. People, an extra five dollars for everybody."

They laughed at that, and Cruz clicked through the channels, one click, two, three, and there she was again, swinging across the building. Shay flushed and thought, *Who is that girl? Twenty-four hours earlier, she had a rat in her face. Now she's famous, whoever she is. Doesn't feel like anybody I know, though. . . .*

Some people knew.

Checking her email at a Starbucks later in the day, she'd find a note from Jonah, the climber from REI: "That was so cool. Take me on your next climb, I'm begging you."

In San Francisco, West was walking along the street licking a pistachio ice cream cone and caught the image on a television set in the window of a stockbrokerage. When Shay's hair came loose, he couldn't believe it and stood frozen, the cone forgotten.

He said aloud, to nobody, "Really? Really, Shay?"

12

After the initial excitement died down, Shay went back to her room, found a note from Emily that said "Unbelievable—talk to you this afternoon." She'd seen the video.

Shay'd had only a few restless hours of sleep the night before, and the cumulative weariness from her trip down from Eugene, plus the excitement of the morning's action, got on top of her. With Emily gone and the room quiet, she stretched out on her bed, fully clothed, and immediately fell asleep.

When she woke, it was almost noon. She felt good, still a little sleepy; she felt a knot against her hip and dug into her back pocket. She found a flat black stone the size of a quarter, but oval, and remembered Cade's gift on the roof. She turned the stone in her hand: it was black as midnight, but with a white line running through it, slightly off-center.

For good luck? Shay didn't believe in luck, really, or in omens. She believed in mathematics and hard work—but the stone was interesting and had a nice feel to it. She rolled off the bed and put it back in her pocket. If there *was* any such thing as luck, she could use some.

She cleaned up, got her laptop, and headed out. On the way down the stairs and in the lobby, people nodded at her, lifted hands, said, "Hey," and "Great video," and "So cool," and she again felt the buzz of it all.

Shay had spent a good part of her life being shuffled between temporary parents who didn't much care about her. The sudden attention felt strange. And not bad.

She walked out to another coffee shop, bought a cup of coffee and a yesterday's scone for half price, and went online.

Nothing at the Facebook page. Where was he? Odin had sometimes left her eight or ten messages *a day*.

She went to Google News, typed in "animal rights" and "Eugene activists," and found nothing new. There were references to the YouTube video that Storm had released after the raid, with the horrifying monkey shots, along with Singular's public relations counterattack. And she found dozens of iPhone shots of college kids rounding up mice and rats for money. Then at the bottom of Google's main news page, she saw a thumbnail photo of a girl on a rope.

She clicked on a link from a Los Angeles TV station and found the video: she'd already seen it five or six times, but she watched it once more, then read the short attached story.

The action was attributed to a local artist known as Twist, who'd been involved in other actions calling attention to the problems of street people and illegal immigrants. As for the district attorney, she had no comment, the station said. A "source close to her" said she was disgusted by the sexism displayed in the action, and that she'd asked the Los Angeles Police Department to investigate the possibility of a hate crime related to the Nazi armband.

A police spokeswoman, who happened to be Latina, said they'd get right on it. The tone of the comment suggested that they wouldn't get right on it, because they had better things to do. The banner itself had finally been taken down at ten o'clock in the morning.

Amazing that it lasted that long, Shay thought; Twist had hoped for seven o'clock. Maybe there was something about Los Angeles that appreciated any kind of free entertainment. Shay went back to her list of animal rights groups in Hollywood.

She'd found several references to a group called HARC, for Hollywood Animal Rights Conference. Pronounced HARK, one story said. From the news reports, HARC seemed politically similar to Storm, and the reports were recent. . . .

Going to a map, she found that she was two miles away from the HARC address. Shay had never had a parent to drive her places, and only rarely had had access to a bicycle, so she walked everywhere; two miles was nothing. She packed up and started walking.

If HARC was as radical as the news stories suggested, they might well be in touch with Storm. On the other hand, Shay had learned from her tree-sitting days that the politics among animal rights and other environmental groups were complicated, often fractured, and occasionally bitter. If she walked in HARC's door and asked for Storm, they might call the police.

Better, she thought, if she found a place where she could watch the front door. She knew several faces associated with Storm, from past news reports. If she saw one of them coming or going, she could intercept him or her on the sidewalk. Maybe even see Odin. It was a long shot, she admitted to herself, but better than running through crowds of clubbers at midnight and being chased by pimps.

She was standing at a streetlight when a guy in cargo pants and a T-shirt took a long look at her and said something to his girlfriend and the girlfriend looked, and then they drifted over. "Are you the girl, you know, who came down the building?"

Shay, shocked, said, "Uh . . . ," and tried to think of something coherent, but the other girl said, "You are! That was so cool. That was just so fabulous!"

Shay, still fumbling, asked, "How did you know?"

The girl's boyfriend said, "Hair."

Halfway to the HARC office, she walked past a truck parked in front of an apartment house: DOS HERMANOS MOVING. Three Mexican men were carrying a couch up a ramp into the truck, and one of them glanced at Shay and said something in Spanish.

The other two men paused to look at her, then put the end of the couch down, and one of the men clapped his hands, applauding, and the other two joined in. A fourth man appeared at the door and called *"Qué?"* at those in the truck. They shouted something back, and then the fourth man called after her—she was thirty feet down the block by then—*"Gracias, gracias,"* and joined in the applause.

Shay moved along, thinking, *Jeez. Everybody knows.* Eyes were all over her. Were they watching in Eugene? Was somebody talking to Child Protection, and was her social worker calling Los Angeles?

Turning a corner, she found herself outside a frame shop, looking at a collection of mirrors. She regretted not changing out of the turquoise tank—it was like a signature saying, *Yeah, it's me.* She took a moment to pull her hair back into a ponytail, then dug into her pack, found a baseball cap and her last semi-clean Eugene flannel shirt, put them both on, and checked herself again.

There. Video Girl was gone.

HARC had a second-floor office in a building on a block full of pawnshops and used-clothing places—not used clothing of the kind Emily collected, but worn Levis for two dollars, good for covering your body. Shay walked by on the opposite side of the street, tried not to gawk, and decided not to go up.

A Laundromat sat on a corner, and she found that from a row of chairs in the window, she could see the doorway leading to the HARC office. Shay spotted a FREE WI-FI FOR CUSTOMERS sign, purchased a single-wash box of detergent from the laundry lady to get the password, and opened her laptop. Ninety minutes later, she'd seen only two people coming or going through HARC's door. She hadn't recognized either of them, or anyone else on the street.

Still nothing on the Facebook page.

Has to be a better way to do this, she thought.

As she was about to leave, a man stepped out of a doorway down the street, on the same side that HARC was on. He walked a bit, then paused and took out his phone. There was something about him—his athletic body, his well-cut suit, his short, military-style hair—that reminded her of Cherry and West.

She watched as he held the phone to his ear for a minute or two, all the while watching the HARC entrance and not once speaking into the mouthpiece. He was faking the call, she decided, doing surveillance on the animal rights group, same as herself.

Then a young bearded man walked out of the HARC office, a courier bag over his shoulder. The man on the telephone followed, and Shay picked up an odd rolling motion in the way he moved. That was it, she thought. His legs.

He had the same prostheses as West. Good, but not perfect. The Singular people were watching HARC. In fact, the way the man walked out on the street, it was as if he had known the bearded man was coming out. Were the HARC offices bugged?

Her fingers flew to the laptop, out to Facebook, and she left another message for Odin:

Singular is watching the office of Hollywood Animal Rights Conference. Office may be bugged. Don't go there.

She closed down the page and headed back to the Twist Hotel, more worried than ever about Odin. She thought about the Singular watcher back at the HARC offices. How many were there? Were they everywhere?

She never saw the man who followed a block behind her in khaki slacks, a wrinkled blue guayabera shirt, and window-glass spectacles. He didn't need real glasses, because he was almost physically perfect, except for the bionic arm.

She got back to the hotel at dinnertime, and the kid in the miner's helmet said, "Hey! Twist has been looking for you. He wants you to go up."

• • •

Twist was in his studio with five other people, four men and a woman, all adults, plus Cade. When Shay walked in, Twist said, "Ah, here she is. Finally. Where've you been?"

"Laundromat. What's up?"

"We got a hell of a kick out of this morning's action," Twist said. He was wearing a cheery red blazer, the usual brown bowler hat, and a satisfied grin. "These are friends of mine," he added. "David, he's my dealer, and Joey, he does PR for David. Hernando is a photographer, Logan does makeup and hair and clothes, and Adelmo does political strategy."

"We need a poster of you in your mask, on a rope, making a fist," Adelmo said, making a clenched fist to demonstrate. "We need to have it on the street tomorrow. Stark, clean colors. At the bottom: SOLIDARITY! Half the posters in English, half in Spanish: SOLIDARIDAD!"

Shay frowned. "I'm going back to that building?"

"No, no," the photographer said. He pointed at the wall behind her, where a long roll of seamless paper had been hung. "We'll shoot you here, against the seamless. Put a fan on you to blow your hair out, like you're swinging. Once we get the shot, we'll Photoshop you over a photo of Twist's banner. We'll make a bunch of photo repros for the street, and Twist will produce an exclusive silk screen based on the photo to sell to rich people."

Adelmo said to the others, "You know what I'm thinking? T-shirts. We've got to copyright the image . . ."

"I don't know," Shay said. "I'm not really that political."

"Don't be a child," Twist said. "This might all seem very L.A. to you—"

"Yeah, it does seem that way," she snapped.

He rode over her. "But it's serious business. We made a dent in the illegal immigrant debate this morning. We need to keep the momentum going."

"You do, more than me. I'm not here for this—and to tell you the truth, I'm not sure a bunch of posters is going to make much difference in a fight that's been going on for years."

Joey had moved in close and Shay felt his eyes on her like a magnifying glass on a bug. "Make you into a movie star," he muttered.

"I don't want to be a movie star," Shay said.

"We need to talk," Twist said. To the others: "Give us two minutes."

He led her over to the far corner of the studio.

"You don't have to be a movie star," Twist said. "But this, you've got to do. You're not playing in a sandbox anymore."

"I don't want to be a jerk—you've given me a lot of help, Twist. But the attention—that's *not* helping me. I've already given away more than I wanted."

Twist looked at her for a long moment, then asked, "Is that why you've gone back to the lumberjack look?"

"Maybe," she said.

"So you're not so much a runaway as running."

It was like he'd seen right through her, and it put her off-balance. She didn't want him to probe any further—if he learned she was chasing a group of radical activists, and that the police were chasing them too, well, he might just kick her out of his hotel.

"What if I don't show your face?" Twist said.

Shay thought it over for a moment. "I can live with that."

"Good, done." And, with a half-inch grin, "I'm gonna have to make inquiries."

"Don't," she said.

• • •

Then she did it, removing the flannel shirt, changing into her climbing gear and cowboy mask, swinging on her rope across the seamless paper, her hair blowing in the fake breeze from the fan, back and forth, fifty times. Logan worked on her hair with a tease comb and gel, and Hernando operated a Nikon digital camera and a bank of strobes behind silky white light boxes until they got a shot that Joey and Twist agreed was almost perfect.

"We'll never get better than almost," Twist said, looking up at the monitor where the shot was displayed. Then, to Cade, "Cut it out, let's see it on the banner."

Cade went to work on the computer, with Joey looking over his shoulder, while David and Twist helped Shay get off the wall and retrieve her rope and gear.

Adelmo said, "We'll need five thousand handbills. We can get them out tomorrow if I can move the image to the printer before six."

"I can do that," Cade said from the computer. "If the master can get me the final version."

David said to Twist, "We'll want another thousand on good heavy paper, photo repros, we can wholesale them to L.A. Bookster for thirty-five bucks each, and they'll get fifty from the college kids. Then we need ten oversized silk screens. A little obvious touchup on each one of them, with a brush, to give them individuality. Signed on the screen *and* with the brush."

"I thought this was supposed to be all anonymous," Shay said.

"Screw anonymous," David said. "Everybody knows—and signed, we'll get twenty-five grand each over the next couple of weeks. I can peddle them all over the Hollywood Hills and Malibu. If we could have them in two days, that'd be good."

Shay ran the numbers in her head: *More than a quarter-million dollars? For this?*

Out loud, she asked, "What's my cut?"

Twist, startled, looked at her, then grinned. "Artists' models usually get a flat fee. Thirty dollars an hour. In this case, though—"

Logan said from behind them, "She's not an artist's model. She's talent. Talent gets way more."

"Whoa, whoa, whoa," said David, shifting into dealer mode. "Let's not go that way."

Twist said, "I'll give you ten percent of what I get. You'll get it under the table, in cash, tax-free. If I'm lucky, I'll get a bit less than two hundred thousand, after David takes out his piece, and the expenses—the paper and paint and paying these guys, and paying street kids to put up the leaflets. The feds and state will get nearly half of that. I'll clear maybe a hundred, and you'll get ten. If we're lucky."

"No luck in it," David said. "You get me the screens, I'll get you the cash."

Ten thousand dollars was outlandish, Shay thought. For an hour's work? She could live on that for a year. "Deal," she said.

"What do I get?" Cade asked.

"Shut up," said Twist.

Cade said, "Look."

A photo popped up on a monitor: Shay swinging across the face of the banner, one fist held up in a "power" pose.

They all looked for a minute, and Twist said, "Still needs a lot of work." Then: "Listen up: We're not gonna sit on our asses feeling all smug about all this. We gotta get moving on our next action. It's gonna be big."

Cade shook his head, unable to repress an eye roll. "Bigger than this?"

"Yeah—a lot bigger. Hollywood big," said Twist. "Now, everybody, out! Everybody except Cade. Go. Go. I've got a lot of work to do."

Shay was lucky to catch the tail end of dinner, which she ate feeling like the center of attention at a table full of kids who wanted to talk about climbing, and about Twist's art and the immigrant campaign. Later, back in the room, Emily told her about finding two rare pots in Echo Park, and Shay told Emily about the posters.

"Things are moving for us," Emily said, excitement in her voice. "We're gonna do good, Shay."

13

Two days at the Twist Hotel, and life had changed in a hurry.

Then it all slowed down.

Shay helped get the leaflets, posters, and silk screens out, and for the next week monitored her computer through a coffee shop's Wi-Fi. Nothing happened. She didn't bother to go back to HARC—Singular was hanging around there, and if Odin was checking their Facebook page, he'd been warned. She watched a couple other animal rights groups but saw nothing, and stopped expecting she might. Maybe he'd already left Hollywood . . . and she'd be buying a bus ticket to somewhere else. She'd have to wait for Odin to contact her.

Eventually, she relaxed a little. Enough that she never noticed the changing rotation of athletic men ambling along, always just a half block and a few people behind her.

• • •

She worked four hours a day for Twist in the belfry. Twist, she learned, did three basic kinds of art. One was an intricate realism that he called, half jokingly, reportage, with a French turn to the name: RAY-POR-TAHJ. That was done on canvas with oils, and he might work on each piece for a month or more. He also did cityscapes in a similar style, without the politics. Those, she learned, sold like hotcakes. The reportage also sold well, but a lot of it went for modest prices to museums—Twist wanted to be in the museums, he admitted, so he did what he had to to make a deal.

His other art was purely political, derived from Mexican frescoes and wall art from the 1930s and '40s. These were huge and cartoonlike, often thirty feet long and ten feet high, and went out to interested schools and political organizations for free. That's where he needed help from Shay.

Twist began to teach her about mixing color. "I need so much paint that I can use the help. I'll make a sample of what I need, and then you have to match it exactly, in whatever quantity I need. I mean *exactly*! When I get a cartoon done, I need you to transfer it. Cade and Lou can help, but you'll be my main man, if you can keep up."

On her seventh day at the hotel, she made it down to breakfast, spoke briefly to Twist, who'd cut in line behind her, about the day's schedule, then carried her tray to her usual group, Emily and two other girls she'd started eating with.

They talked about this and that, including an analysis of what *cute* meant when applied to men, and then a couple of guys went by with trays and Shay heard one of them say, ". . . whales on the beach. I guess there are a whole bunch of them. They're gonna die."

Shay's forehead wrinkled. *Whales?* She turned in her chair to where the two guys were about to sit down and called, "Excuse me. Did you say something about whales?"

The guy who'd been talking about them nodded and said, "Yeah, there's been a beaching, up in Ventura. It's a real circus."

"Where's Ventura? Is it far?"

The two guys looked at each other, and one said, "What? An hour or so?"

Emily broke in: "I saw a story about that on the lobby TV. I think they said twenty-seven of them. Why?"

Shay forgot about breakfast and reached out and gripped Emily's wrist. "We gotta go. I'll pay you."

"What's the big deal?" Emily asked.

"My brother will be there," Shay said, still holding the other girl's wrist. "He's the reason I'm in L.A. I can't explain right now, but if he's within two hundred miles, he'll be there."

Emily stood up. "I could use some beach time."

"I gotta tell Twist," Shay said. "I'm supposed to be working this morning."

Shay took the glacially slow freight elevator up to Twist's loft. In the week she'd been at the hotel, she'd let slip bits and pieces about her pursuit of Odin. She hadn't told anyone about the raid at the lab, but had implied that her brother was socially awkward and had left his foster home—run away—because of personality conflicts. She'd worried that he wouldn't make it on his own in a city as rough as Los Angeles, and so had come to find him.

In the studio, she found Twist talking with Cade and Cruz. Twist caught her intensity: "What happened?"

"I can't work this morning," Shay blurted. "I'll give you four hours free tomorrow. I gotta go to Ventura."

"There's nothing *in* Ventura," Twist said. "Believe me, I've been there."

"There are twenty-seven whales on the beach," she said. "My brother will be there, if there's any way he can."

Twist said, "I really need—"

"Whales, dude," Cade said.

"I'll need six free hours," Twist said, "time and a half, since I'll have to do your four hours this morning."

"I'm gone," Shay said, and started toward the door, and Cruz said, "Me too," and Cade said, "Save the whales? Hey, wait up."

Emily knew the beach and pushed the truck to a record sixty-five miles an hour, and with almost no traffic going out of town and a shortcut over to the beach below Oxnard, she got them there just after nine o'clock.

None of them were prepared for the horror that lay strewn for a quarter mile across the sand.

Or the noise.

Twenty-two clicking and blowhole-gasping sperm whales were pitched across the beach like a freeway pileup. Ranging in length from fourteen to forty feet, they'd come ashore in the middle of the night, at high tide, for reasons none of them could speak. Another five were already dead.

Someone had gone through the motion of stringing yellow police tape between two sheriff's trucks, which were parked like parentheses around the stranded animals, but there was no containing the growing chaos on an easily accessed public shore.

Emily wedged the Scout into a too-small parking space. For a few seconds, parked there above the dunes on the Pacific Coast Highway, the brownish-black humps glistening in the morning light almost looked lovely, like a natural wonder that four teens might have stopped to see.

The spooky sounds of distress carried up on the breeze betrayed the illusion.

"They can be saved, can't they?" Cruz asked.

"Not without a tsunami-sized tide to float their boats," said Cade, scrolling through web pages on his phone. "The Zoological Society of London says your average beached whale starts having kidney failure within an hour, so you might as well just shoot it and get it over with."

"They do not say to *shoot it!*" Emily protested.

Cade showed them the article. "For you more sensitive types, the word they use is *euthanize.*"

"A gray whale got pushed back to sea at Devil's Elbow State Park in Oregon and lived," said Shay. "My brother was there, and told me about it."

Shay, Emily, Cade, and Cruz ran for the beach, absorbed in the chaotic streams of volunteers and spectators. It was half carnival, half emergency rescue. Functional outdoor clothes and hats and gum boots mixed with beer coolers, beach umbrellas, kids, and dogs.

Media crews jockeyed for the best live shots, though there seemed to be enough whales for everyone to claim an "exclusive." Overhead, news choppers buzzed the shore for aerial footage, sometimes dipping so low the propellers kicked up gusts and swirls of sand. "Help! Over here!" a guy in a Greenpeace vest shouted.

Emily broke Shay's concentration as she scanned the beach for Odin and said, with a tug, "C'mon!"

They crossed the beach to the nearest whale, a mother who was nearly dead from dehydration, and beside her, a young daughter.

"What do we do?" Emily asked.

"Keep them wet—hope the tide will carry them back out," the Greenpeace guy said, and handed each of them a bucket.

Emily and Cade joined the crew helping an orphaned male, while Shay and Cruz teamed up to help the mother and baby. For some reason, the mother kept raising her tail fluke and slamming it against the ground with such force that Shay and Cruz felt their legs wobble with the impact.

"Why does she keep doing that?" Cruz asked. "She's wasting energy."

"I don't know," Shay said.

They'd been throwing buckets of seawater on her and her eighteen-foot baby girl for an hour when Shay picked out a pattern.

"I don't know what it means," she told Cruz, "but listen. The next time the baby makes two long clicks, and then three short noises that sound more like pings, the mom's gonna slam her tail."

The baby lay with her flat forehead lodged against the mother's right flank so that together they formed a T. The angle was such that the mother, unable to twist around in the sand—unable to twist around for the first time in her life—could not see her dying child.

Ninety seconds later, the baby clicked and pinged, and the mother slammed her tail.

"You're right," Cruz said. "They're talking."

Shay decided it meant: *Hang on.*

• • •

Twice, Shay left her post to chase down phantoms.

"Odin! Stop!" she shouted at the tall, slim backside of someone in khaki shorts and sandals. She got close enough to tag a shoulder. The brown-haired stranger turned around with eyes that weren't blue like their mother's and a chin that wasn't dimpled like their father's and said, "Excuse me?"

The stranger was a middle-aged woman.

Suddenly Odin was everywhere . . . and nowhere.

Everyone working to save the whales—marine biologists, local environmentalists, animal lovers, even a few homeless campers— understood that defeat was inescapable, and the desire to comfort the doomed creatures was palpable.

Emily and Cade were working three whales over from Shay and Cruz, draping wet sheets on the orphaned male. At one point, Emily collapsed on the sand with frustration and began weeping. Cade shouted at her, got her on her feet, and they began dousing the baby again. One of the lead Greenpeace volunteers felt the baby stood a chance, that he might be light enough and near enough to the water to be pushed out with the tide.

And meanwhile, the carnival rolled on.

Single-engine planes towed advertising signs along the beach, including one for a new sports drink. Two minor celebrity chicks from a reality TV show arrived in their bikinis to help pitch in . . . more or less.

The governor, who had a mansion in L.A., showed up in a wet suit.

• • •

By noon, postmortems on half a dozen whales were under way. Scientists passed around boxes of latex gloves and a few wore fishing waders against the blood and gore. More yellow tape was staked around the open-air dissections, but there was nothing to stop dozens of spectators with cameras from standing on the edges and documenting every slice. Two scientists cut into one of the dead whales and carved out her heart. The video was on YouTube within the hour.

The tide came in, but it was too late for Shay's whales. The young mother had continued thumping her tail fluke all morning in seeming reply to her daughter's clicks, but for more than an hour now, the baby had been silent.

And when life finally left the baby, they all knew. They continued pitching buckets until a veterinarian who'd come up from SeaWorld in San Diego made it official. Time of death: 12:30 p.m. Shay sank to her knees and cursed; a moment later the veterinarian sank down beside her and started to cry. Cruz stood by, his face grim; no tears. He continued to pour water on the deteriorating mother.

A few minutes later, they helped Emily, Cade, and six other volunteers wedge and wiggle and roll the surviving baby male out into the surf. It went under, then tried to swim, then started to roll, and they steadied it, holding it upright. It seemed to know that they were trying to help, but when they freed it, it slowly turned, as though it were going to try to swim back to its dead mother, still on the beach.

They turned it again, shouting at each other, groaning with its weight, and kept it turned out to sea.

They took it deeper, and finally its flukes began working and the baby nosed out into deeper water.

Four helicopters were overhead, filming them: Emily, burned pink despite all the sunblock, said, "We're all TV stars now. Oh God, this is awful . . ."

Shay joined another team of volunteers working on a juvenile whale. An hour later, it died.

"I'm so sorry," she whispered. This time, she didn't collapse on her knees or curse; there was too much death all around. One by one, the whales were going, nothing anyone could do anymore to stop it. She put down her bucket and told the others she'd be back after a short break.

Twenty minutes later, Cade walked up to where Shay was sitting alone on a beach boulder. He handed her a bottle of water and noticed she was rubbing the stone he'd given her on the roof. He asked how she was doing.

She shrugged.

He nudged her over so he could sit too. "I'm sorry this didn't work out."

Shay opened the bottle, took a long, moody drink, and said, "I never believed they were going to make it anyhow."

"Huh," said Cade. "I sort of figured you for one of those optimistic, sunshiny types."

"Sunshiny?"

Cade said, "Yeah, I don't know where that came from."

Shay allowed herself a small smile. She hadn't been sure she liked Cade before, with his cocky, braggart style. Today, he'd been different.

"I'm more the chance-of-rain type," she said, and continued working the small black stone between her thumb and forefingers. "Oregon, remember?"

Cade, nodding, paused her hand with his own and said, "You're going to polish the spirit line right off the thing."

Shay looked down, unaware that she'd even taken the stone with the odd white stripe from her pocket. "*Spirit line?* I've never heard of that. What's it mean?"

"Supposedly, it connects the natural world—plants, animals, people, you, me, the whales—with the supernatural one," said Cade, and she gave him a squint, unsure whether he was being sincere or a smart-ass.

"I'm serious," he said, and told her a story about going to school for a while in New Mexico and meeting a man from the Hopi tribe, and about receiving the stone himself as a gift right before he took off.

"If someone gave it to you, I shouldn't keep it," Shay said, and pressed the stone against his palm. Then she heard it. She craned her head around. "Did someone just yell at me?"

"Not that I heard," said Cade. "Maybe a whale? There's still a couple of them making noises."

Shay heard her name again and this time she was sure. She stood up and looked toward the bluff and there he was, waving at her.

"Odin!"

14

Shay sprinted across the beach, veering around volunteers headed back to their cars, and saw Odin stumbling down the bluff towing . . . a dog? She called, "Odin!" but her voice was lost to the surf.

Here came her brother, trailed by a big gray dog thuggishly outfitted in an eye patch and wire muzzle. Shay had only a second to wonder about that before she and Odin collided.

"I knew you'd come," Shay said, and wrapped him in her arms. "Did you just get here? The situation's so bad—"

The dog jammed itself between them, ramming its caged jaws into Shay's bare thigh. She lurched backward and tumbled into the sand.

"Did he just try to bite me?" she asked as the dog loomed over her. Odin reeled in the slack on the dog's heavy choke chain.

"It's okay, boy, she's my sister," Odin said in a voice that seemed deeper—older—than the last time they'd spoken.

His voice wasn't the only thing that had changed, Shay thought as she got back on her feet. He'd cut his shaggy brown hair short and gelled it—unbelievable. His pale complexion was gone too, as if he'd shed it like a snakeskin, and in its place was a deep tropical tan. He wore fashionable sunglasses of the sort they could never afford in foster care and gingery whiskers that aged him out of high school.

"Sit!" Odin said to the dog. He said it again, "Sit!" and again, "Sit!" and finally, finally, the dog dropped back on its haunches. Its one-eyed focus remained on Shay, and it released a whispery growl through clenched teeth.

"You ran away and got a bad dog?"

"He was locked up in a cage with nothing, Shay," he said, reaching down to give the dog a scratch between the ears. "They must have tortured him bad, he's so down on people. I wish he didn't have to wear the muzzle. It wasn't my idea, he was already wearing it, but since he really *is* a biter—and you can't blame him—we can't take it off. He even eats and drinks with it."

Odin's words were coming at warp speed, the way they always did when he was worked up about animals. "They must have been experimenting on his eye 'cause it was patched and bloody, and even though he was doped up, he was telling me with his good eye, *Get me outta here,* so I put down the rat to help him out a window, but then, dammit, I forgot the rat—"

"He's not from the research lab?" Shay clasped her head as though it might spin off. "Odin! Don't tell me he's from the lab?"

"The poor rat," he continued, as if she hadn't spoken. "They'd cut off three of her feet, she only had one foot left, what good is one—"

"Do you understand how much trouble you're in?" Shay asked. "That dog has to be microchipped. Stealing a research animal is probably a felony; you'll go to prison."

"Definitely chipped," Odin agreed. "That's why Rachel says I can't take him to a vet. Something's wrong with him. He started falling down last week like he was drunk. It's happened twice since we got here and started looking for you—"

"That too! Why didn't you answer me on Facebook?"

"You realize, as of six o'clock this morning, you had 1.7 million hits on YouTube? Radical action, though next time, I'd wear a ski mask, and definitely tuck in your hair, it's pretty much a dead giveaway—"

Shay stopped him with a raised hand. "Stay on point."

Odin looked over his shoulder, as though checking for faces, looking for threats. "I wanted to contact you as soon as I saw the video, but the situation wasn't safe. Then, when we heard about the whales this morning, I thought, *Shay will go there because she'll expect me to go there.* Didn't even need your text to know that. I drove so fast it's a miracle we didn't have the cops all over us."

"If you got stopped by cops and they checked your license—"

Odin dug through his cargo shorts and pulled out a California license with his face, but a new name—Dario?—a different birth date, and an address in Van Nuys. "Rachel said I should say I was twenty-one."

"A fake license? God . . . Rachel pisses me off," Shay said. "She's made you do so much stupid crap!"

"Rachel hasn't made me do anything, Shay. I do what I need to. I made this excellent license, and I inserted it in the DMV records, and I made the excellent security card that got everyone inside the lab because *I* decided to. Okay?"

"Yeah! You're a big freakin' genius, breaking the law to get a fake ID. That's, like, ninth grade! Odin, they're using you," Shay said.

"And I'm using her! Did that ever occur to you?" Odin asked.

"She gets what she wants and I get what I want. I'm not just talking about sex, though that's . . . pretty good. Okay? Get it?"

"C'mon, Odin, jeez," she answered. "You're a good-looking guy, you don't have to—"

"I have a neurobiological disorder characterized by poor social skills, odd speech patterns, inflexible obsessions, and sensory sensitivity to odors and high-pitched sounds," he said, starting to flail his arms at her.

"Stop! You're right, I'm sorry." If she didn't stop pushing, he might run off again.

"You never fully get it, Shay, you're neurotypical—"

She grabbed him by the shoulders and said it again: "Stop. I know your history. But you gotta tell me what's going on now. Please."

He nodded, looked around again, down the line of dead whales and gawking tourists and worn-out whale rescuers, lowered his voice to nearly a whisper. "Singular's not doing Parkinson's research, Shay. It's a cover. Singular's running a top-secret program: they're experimenting with robotics and neural nets and nerve regrowth and biomechanical links. They've killed thousands of animals to do that; they'll kill thousands more. But that's not enough. They need people to work with. They need living humans for—"

"Whoa, whoa," said Shay. "Slow down. Back up. Singular—isn't that just a medical company? You're talking like they're a cult."

"They're a company and a cult and they've got connections with the military and with politicians," Odin said. "I'm still decoding their computer files."

"Odin!" Her voice went up an octave, and the dog stood up as if taking sides and fixed its large yellow eye on her again. "You took their computers?"

"Easy, boy," Odin said, and held the dog back. "Just one computer, and some thumb drives with their backup files. Decoding them has been problematic since we've had to keep moving. I've cracked one so far. Once we've got them all, we'll dump them on the Internet. There was this one baby monkey, she's so traumatized she bangs her head against the wall nonstop and all this blood comes spraying out . . ." Odin choked up.

"You're only going to make the situation worse," Shay said. "If they get you for stealing their files, you could go to prison for years."

"Whose side are you on?" Odin snapped. "What they're doing is probably illegal, and completely sick—"

"I'm on your side, Odin," Shay said. "That's the only side I've got. But you're scaring me. Why do you have to keep moving? Who's chasing you?"

Odin looked away evasively, something he was lousy at. The dog grunted and suddenly collapsed on its belly.

"See what I mean?" said Odin. "You have to help me."

"How? I'm not a vet, what do you expect me to do?"

Odin's eyes came back to her. "I don't know, but Rachel doesn't care about him. And you're good at helping me."

The dog's head was turned on its right side, the patched eye pressed into the sand. The seeing eye darted watchfully between brother and sister, and Shay found herself feeling sorry for the animal.

"Does he need water?" she asked, and picked up the bottle she'd dropped when he'd tried to bite. "Actually, can he even drink water with that thing on his face?"

"Yeah, he pokes his tongue through the spokes," said Odin. "He'll only eat or drink when there's nobody around. We have to leave the room to get him to eat or else he'd starve."

"What's the patch all about?"

"Don't know, but we decided it was better to leave it alone. He's had some other stuff done, too. I'll show you, but he doesn't like having his head touched much, either."

Odin reassured the dog in a gentle voice as he eased a hand into the thick gray fur behind the right ear. He felt around for something, then parted the hair and peeled back a flap of skin to reveal a hinged metal plate, about an inch square, set into the dog's skull.

"My God," Shay said with a shudder.

"Heinous, huh?" said Odin, and as he laid the flap back down, she noticed it was inscribed with a tiny red tattoo: x-5. "So far, I can't say what it's for," Odin continued. "Maybe it's explained in the files . . . speaking of which . . ."

He looked around, then reached into the pocket of his cargo shorts and pulled out a Ziploc bag full of thumb drives, stepped close, and said, "Hide these."

"Are these them?" she asked, looking at the drives clustered inside the bag.

"Stick them in your shorts."

He said it so urgently that she thrust them into a deep pocket.

"They're the files from Singular—that's why they're after us, why they keep coming. These are copies; all of them but one are still encrypted. Now listen: the files are double encrypted. They automatically encrypt all their files, and probably store them somewhere up in the cloud. I don't know where. But then they made these backups, and they saved them onto special thumb drives, which encrypts them all over again. I can copy them—but all I can see is gobbledygook. The thumb drives have their own passwords, up to thirty-two characters, although not all the passwords are thirty-two. When you get a password, the drive itself decrypts the first level.

Then you have direct access to the second-level encrypted files. They kept the second-level decryption software on a computer that we stole, and the red drive in that bag is the copy of the encryption software. You can use it to decrypt the second level after you crack the passwords. I've cracked one of them. I wrote the number '1' on the side of it in silver ink. Look at that one first. Rachel and Ethan don't know I made these copies, I decided not to tell them everything, not yet at least—"

"Odin—" A woman, screaming.

They both turned and looked up to see a slender figure at the top of the bluff, pointing down the beach.

"They're here. Odin! Odin! They're here! Singular, they're here!"

"Rachel?" Shay squinted at the other woman.

"Yeah," said Odin, looking to where his girlfriend was pointing. "Ah, shit. I gotta go," he said, and pulled the dog back onto its feet. "But I gotta tell you—"

"What's happening?" asked Shay.

"Listen," Odin said urgently. "Look at the file I cracked. There's a note to you—"

Rachel came skidding and sliding down the dirt bluff and latched on to Odin's arm. "Give her the dog. Hurry up! Give him to her!"

"Give him to me?" Shay stepped back.

Odin shook his head. "I think I've changed my mind."

"That's why we're here!" Rachel shrieked.

Shay looked back and forth between them. "You're here to give me a stolen dog?"

Rachel tried to pry the leash from Odin's hand, and the dog snarled at her: he didn't like Rachel, not at all.

"Dammit, Odin!" Rachel said as she stepped back. "If you get caught—and you will, the dog's too crippled to run—who's going to decode the files?" She looked anxiously up the beach. "We gotta run. We gotta run right now!"

She was staring, frightened, openmouthed: Shay looked that way and saw a man in a gray running suit closing in like a cheetah. In three or four seconds, the man covered another fifty yards. People were watching up and down the beach as he sprinted across the sand faster than any human should be able to run.

Odin closed his eyes as if he didn't want to see what he was about to do.

"Here," he said, and thrust the dog's leash at Shay.

She took it, but said, "I can't keep him."

The man running down the beach was almost on top of them, but then thirty yards out, he slowed to a jog, and then to a walk. Rachel yanked Odin toward the bluff, but Shay held his other arm, pulling him back: she had recognized the runner.

West.

"Shay, Odin . . . slow down, take it easy." He got closer. "Odin, all we want to do is talk. We need to take the dog back with us. And you have some more of our property—"

Rachel had stepped behind Odin, as though seeking shelter; West was looking at Odin, and Odin and Shay were looking at West, not at Rachel, when her hand cleared the bag with the Taser.

West almost had time to say *Don't* before she pulled the trigger. The Taser element hit him in the chest and he howled and went down and Shay shouted, "What'd you do?"

Rachel had Odin's arm and said, "Run, run, there's gotta be more of them . . ."

Odin shouted at Shay, "Don't let them get you," and then he and Rachel were scrambling up the bluff. The dog pulled frantically after Odin, but Shay held him. The dog started yipping, calling to Odin to come back.

And at her feet, West was shaking and thrashing on the sand, one arm bent back behind him, and he cried to Shay, "Help me, help me . . ."

Shay looked after Odin and thought, *I can't lose him.*

She said "I'm sorry" to West and then began scrambling up the bluff; the dog was ahead of her on the leash, going after Odin, but tumbled back twice, as though it couldn't keep its feet. When they finally got to the top, she saw Odin running up the coastal freeway, trailing Rachel by about two hundred feet.

Shay thought she still might be able to catch them and started running, but a white delivery van suddenly pulled alongside her brother, pacing him, and a door slid open. Two men leapt out, trapped Odin between them, pinned his arms, and threw him in the van. The van was moving before the door closed.

Shay screamed for her brother, and though there was no possibility that Rachel had heard her, the young woman turned, saw that Odin was no longer behind her, stopped, did a little jig, moved back and forth, searching for him, as if expecting to see him come out from behind a car, and when he didn't . . . turned and kept running.

Shay screamed again, "Odin!" but she was screaming at nothing but a highway. With the ocean rumbling behind her, it was unlikely that anybody heard.

She looked wildly around for any kind of help, but there was nobody to help.

And she thought: *West.*

• • •

She skidded back down the bluff, the dog at first resisting, but then tumbling behind her, falling as much as running. Cade was coming up, and he looked at the fallen man, then at Shay. "What'd you do?"

"I didn't do anything. Take the dog," she said. "Hide. Hide him."

"I don't do dogs, really—"

She grabbed a handful of his shirt and pulled on it. "It's my brother's dog! Get him to the truck! But be careful, he bites. He's sick."

"How come he looks like Hannibal Lecter?"

"Because he bites. Go! Go!"

Cade took hold of the leash, frightened a bit by her intensity, and got the dog moving. Shay squatted next to West.

"How bad is it?" she asked.

"Ah, God, it's pretty . . . it's bad. You've got to do something for me . . ."

"What?"

"That Taser blew my legs, but the nerve connections are still firing," he groaned. "On my back, just below my waistband, just pull up my shirt. There's a port there. You have to unscrew the lid, I can't reach it very well . . . ah, God, this hurts, the circuits are going crazy."

"Yeah, right," Shay said.

"Shay—please!"

He was in agony, she thought, his face twisted against the pain. He rolled away from her and she hesitated, then pulled up his jacket and pulled his shirt out from his pants. When he rolled farther, she saw the port: a brown plastic circle set into living flesh, with a recessed groove that might take the edge of a quarter like a screwdriver. It reminded her of the port in the dog.

"I see it," she said.

"Push hard on it with your thumb, turn it counterclockwise. It'll start to unscrew."

"What'd you do with my brother?"

"I didn't do anything . . . please, Shay. Please!"

"What'd you do with my brother?"

His legs began to spasm in a kind of running movement, and he groaned again.

"They're just going to talk to him. They need to get some property back from him . . . and that dog. Just give up the dog and give . . . ahhhhh . . ."

"Hold still," she said. She pushed on the port and twisted, but her thumb slipped on the slick surface; she pushed harder, and the disk slowly turned, then began to go faster. After three turns, it popped loose, but was held to his body by a needle-thin strip of shiny, flexible metal.

"It's open. Now what?"

"Inside, there's a card. Push on it. Like a card in a digital camera."

She did that, and the card popped loose, and West's face relaxed, and his legs stopped twitching. "Ah, jeez. That was bad. Thank you. Thank you." He took the card from her, slipped it into a jacket pocket.

"Can they fix your legs?" Shay asked.

"Oh, yeah. I've got some blown boards." He used his arms to push into a semi-upright position, his legs splayed out on the sand. "I guess the pointy-headed geniuses never asked what would happen if somebody laid a few thousand volts on one of their experiments," West said. "Anyway, I owe you, though you're a goddamned hard bargainer."

"Why don't you pay me off by telling me what that lab is really doing? Why is it killing all those animals? Odin told me that you're killing thousands of rats and monkeys. If it's all okay, why do you lie about what it does?"

"Your brother is not entirely objective," West said. "We have humane protocols in place." Then he looked past her and said, "We'll talk about it some other time. But now . . . let's not."

She turned and saw another runner coming up—Cherry. She stood up and backed away. Cade and the dog were nowhere in sight. Cherry knelt beside West and asked, "How's the equipment?"

"Tased me, bro," West said. "Blew my circuits. I got nothin'. Shay helped me out, pulled my card. The dog is gone—she gave it to some kid and he ran off."

Shay said, "I know you're not the police. Whatever you told the social worker, you're not the police or the FBI or anything else. What makes you think you can snatch people off the street? That's kidnapping."

"You know why," West insisted. "Your brother stole information that can save lives, let people walk again."

"Yeah, right, but that's not all you're up to, is it?"

The comment caught the two men off guard and they looked at each other, then West shrugged and said, "She sorta thinks we're lying."

Cherry said, "Yeah, whatever, we gotta go—look at the crowd."

West looked around. His sprint down the beach and the tasing had drawn spectators, and the number was increasing.

The other man said, "Give me an arm."

West put an arm up, and Cherry stooped and rolled West into a fireman's carry on his shoulders, lifting him effortlessly, as if West were light as a feather. He nodded at Shay and said, "We'll be seeing you, little sister."

And West, dangling off the man's shoulders, said, "You're really a hard-ass. I didn't see that coming." But he grinned at her.

Then Cherry jogged back down the beach toward one of the less steep parts of the bluff. Shay watched them go, and though Cherry wasn't fast, he never slowed down, either, not even as he was climbing. In its own way, it was as impressive as West's speed. Shay wondered what they'd done to him that he could carry two hundred pounds at a jog up a slope and out of sight.

Shay clambered up the slope. She had no hope of seeing Odin, but far down the beach, she saw Cade angling toward the truck, trailed slowly by a reluctant lump of gray fur.

15

She had to do something—she stood there, trembling, unbelieving, as all the main actors in the drama disappeared. She turned around in a circle, then around again, as if she might pluck an explanation out of the sky or the ocean, find somebody to explain it to her. She'd come a thousand miles to find her brother, only to talk to him for five minutes? Then to witness his kidnapping?

What to do? If she called the police, they'd want explanations. As far as the authorities were concerned, at least those in Eugene, it was *Odin* who was the criminal. This was all surreal, but she was living through it.

She was working through that, turning, looking up and down the beach, when her phone rang. Thinking that it might somehow be Odin, she looked at the screen and saw UNKNOWN.

"Hello?"

A woman's voice: "You know me, we just met. Don't say my name. Don't say any key words. Do you know where our . . . fellow . . . went?"

Rachel. Key words that a dark intelligence agency might be listening for—*Odin, whales, Rachel, Shay, kidnap, van, police, FBI,* a combination of those.

"How'd you get this number?"

"Our fellow gave it to me, for emergencies only. Is he with you?"

"No. He was taken . . . by them. I saw it. I don't know what to do."

"Don't call who you'd normally call," Rachel said quickly, and Shay realized she meant the police. "Please. That would bring even more trouble for everybody. We'll work on it from this end."

"How?" Shay said. "I need more information—"

"Stay with this line. I'll call you if we find out anything."

Then Rachel hung up.

Shay looked at her phone, then pushed it into her pocket and jogged down the beach to where the truck was parked. Cade, Cruz, and Emily were already there, Emily looking doubtfully at the dog, which had been loaded into the truck, behind the backseat.

"What just happened?" Cade asked. "Who were those guys? That one guy was running like a . . . like a . . . like I don't know what. Like an alien."

"He almost is," Shay said. "He has prosthetic legs. He lost his real legs in Afghanistan."

"How do you know that?" Cade asked. "What are you doing, you and your brother?"

Shay waved off the question. "I'll explain it . . . sometime. Not now. But we've really got to go. This dog—my brother rescued it, and I think the abusers want it back. We've got to get out of here."

Cruz said, "Dog doesn't look so good."

The dog picked up on the word *dog*, lifted his head, and snarled at him.

"I'm looking at that yellow eye," said Emily. "It's like old amber."

"Lobo have a name?" Cruz asked.

"I think it's X," Shay said, and when she said it, the dog turned its yellow eye on her. "That's it. He recognized it."

Emily put a sunburnt arm around Shay's shoulders and said, "Let's go. Are we taking X to the hotel?"

"Yes," Shay said. "I gotta keep the dog. Look, when we get back, I'll get my stuff out of the room."

"Slow down," Cade said. "I'm calling the question: how many in favor of sneaking in Scooby?"

Three hands went up, but Shay protested. "Twist has been too nice to me. I don't want to lie," she said. "I'll camp out. At least until Odin shows up."

Emily shook her head. "If you leave, you camp out. If Twist finds the dog, you camp out. So why not wait until Twist finds the dog? Something good might happen."

"That's not been my experience," Shay said, but her resistance was thin; she wanted to stay at the hotel. She didn't want to think about finding another place.

The dog slept most of the way back to Hollywood, and seemed to have regained strength by the time Emily pulled into the hotel parking lot. Shay dropped the tailgate and grabbed hold of the leash as the dog jumped down to the ground; he stumbled, but quickly recovered, looked around, and made a whuffing noise through his nose. They'd planned to take him through an emergency exit in the lobby behind the staircase. The door was locked from the outside, and Emily ran in through the lobby to open it.

She didn't know that the exit had a silent alarm, which flashed at the front desk. Montrel, the kid on desk duty, hurried over to the emergency exit as soon as the light winked at him. Emily saw him coming just as Shay, Cruz, and Cade came through the door with the dog trailing behind.

"Where's Twist? We thought we saw him heading out here, we need to talk—" Emily said, improvising as she tried to block his view.

"Out with some actress you'd recognize," Montrel said, puffs of his Afro billowing out from the requisite miner's hat as he peered past her. "Or parts of her. She's played a pole dancer in, like, five different movies."

"Living the dream," said Emily. "Probably trained at Juilliard and did Shakespeare in the Park. But you know, the number of decent speaking parts for women in Hollywood . . ."

Shay, Cade, and Cruz were veering off toward the service elevator in a clump, the dog on their far side. But Montrel wasn't blind.

"Hey! Whatchu got there?" he asked, switching on his headlamp.

They kept going. "Nothing," Shay lied over her shoulder.

"Well, Nothing's got a tail, and Twist don't allow no tails."

Cruz turned back and handled it. "The dog's hurt, Montrel, we're just trying to take care of it for a couple of days. You sound like the *policía*."

Montrel recoiled. "Damn, I do, don't I?"

"That's cool, we all go a little power mad sometimes," said Cruz. "But Shay's gonna go up to her room."

"Yeah, well . . . make sure nobody gets bit." Montrel turned the headlamp off.

· · ·

Inside the room, Shay led the dog to her bedside and said, "Lie down."

The dog looked at her with curiosity, but made no move to lie down. "Sit," she said. "Sit." Nothing.

She sat on the bed herself, and the dog sat down, still watching. "Try lying down," Emily said.

Shay put a pillow against the head of the bed and lay down, and what followed was a several-minute stare-down before the dog simply dropped onto his belly. His sharp yellow eye looked away from her and took in the surroundings, and his erect ears were cocked to catch any unexpected noise.

"Wait—I got something this boy is gonna love," Emily said, and she darted into the outer room, dug through a chest full of junk, and came up with an old porcelain dog bowl that said DOG. She found a bottle of water by the bed, filled the bowl, and shoved it toward the dog.

The dog ignored it.

"Now what?" Shay asked.

Emily didn't know. They sat without talking, and finally Emily said, "Screw this, I need a shower." She gathered up her beauty supplies and headed out. With Emily gone and the room suddenly silent, Shay could hear the dog's breathing, like he had emphysema or something. She looked up, feeling his eye on her like a burden.

"I'm sorry you don't feel well," she said.

The dog maintained his hard stare. Shay wasn't ready to let go of first impressions, but now that they were alone, she considered him more closely: wolfish, but in reality, not nearly as large as a wolf, maybe eighty pounds. And not entirely gray, either: white socks on his front paws, a white shield on his chest, a Y of black like Magic Marker over either eye and down his nose. Shay suspected he was a German shepherd mix, or something crossed with one of those smiley-faced sled dogs, though this dog, when he wasn't baring his teeth with ferocity, had a face so brooding it felt almost human.

"You got another name?" she asked quietly. "Is X okay?"

Still staring . . .

"Yeah, it's no fun being an unknown value," she said. The dog didn't react; apparently he didn't know algebra.

She stood up and stretched her sore arms and back, rolled some noisy cracks out of her neck. She hadn't noticed his tail in much detail, either, and stepped around to see that it was long enough to curl around his hips and tipped with white fur.

"Ever felt happy enough to wag that thing?" she asked him quietly.

The dog dropped his chin on his white paws and let out a sigh, like he was thinking. After a while, he closed his eye, and Shay, dropping back on the bed, just let him be.

Later that night, after she'd showered, and when she was sure Emily was asleep, Shay looked at the thumb drives. She picked through them for the one that had the numeral 1 written on the side in silver ink. She plugged it into her laptop. The first thing that popped up was a password box, subdivided into small squares for letters or numbers or symbols, with instructions that said:

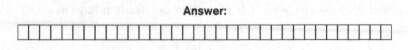

You always had a problem managing the rook ISH.

Answer:

Beneath the box was a warning:

After three unsuccessful tries, the drive will be destroyed.

A problem managing the rook ISH? Ever since they got their first laptops, Odin had loved sending his sister messages that took a password to unlock. A password generated from a kooky-sounding clue. It was a hedge against any of their foster parents reading their emails, and Odin, non-neurotypical guy that he was, had concocted some real brain twisters.

Shay counted thirty-four squares and groaned. A problem with the rook ISH? She didn't have days to work out a puzzle—her brother was in trouble.

Shay lay down on the bed to think about possibilities. She guessed that *rook* might refer to chess—they'd both belonged to a junior high chess club—but what the heck did *ISH* stand for? They'd never really played that much chess together anyway, so what problem with a rook was he . . .

She crossed into sleep, without even a minute or two of fighting it. After the whales and Odin and the dog, biology simply called time.

Much later, she woke to a quiet slurping sound. She could hear Emily snoring lightly on the other side of the nightstand.

She sat up to locate the dog and the noise stopped. It took a moment for her eyes to focus, but then she saw him in the glow of the night-light, his tongue poked through the wire muzzle; he'd been lapping from the bowl, and now was looking at her with an expression Shay recognized as pure guilt. She'd lived with foster parents who made you feel guilty about eating their groceries, and that's how X looked.

Shay slipped out of bed and approached the dog cautiously, whispering so as not to wake her roommate. "It's okay, boy. You can have as much water as you want. It's free."

He had to be hungry too. She'd have to spend time trolling the Internet for advice on feeding a dog since she'd never had one. Emily kept an assortment of snacks in the closet, but gummy bears or Cocoa Puffs probably weren't wise food choices for a dog any more than they were for a human. Peanut butter—she still had some left, and some saltines.

As Shay uncrinkled the wax bag, Emily stirred, mumbled something that sounded like "Will you take a quarter?" and fell back into sleep. Meanwhile, the dog went down with a thunk, seemingly out of gas, though he was rapt when Shay started buttering crackers with a plastic knife.

"Here, these are for you," she said, and placed a pile by his nose.

The dog stared at her, unmoving. She stared back at him for a while, then remembered what Odin had said on the beach, that the dog only ever seemed to eat and drink when he was left alone.

Shay climbed back into bed and pretended to go to sleep. Even fake-snored a bit. After a few minutes, she peeked with one eye and saw that the food was uneaten and he was watching her.

At five o'clock, she woke to find the dog still watching her. Every last bit of the crackers and peanut butter was gone.

It was a start, she thought. "You need a walk?"

• • •

The dog had no trouble walking down the stairs. They went out the back through the kitchen; the breakfast crew came on at five-thirty. Shay found a brick to block the self-locking door that led to the loading dock, and then led the dog around the parking lot until he pooped.

Going back up was another problem.

X made the first two steps up the loading dock, but then fell back on his haunches and looked at her as if to say, *I'm just too tired.*

She hadn't had much experience with dogs and didn't quite know what to do. She gave his leash a tug and tried pleading, and he stood and made the last three steps. The freight elevator was generally considered to be off-limits to everyone but people going to Twist's loft, but she had little choice: the dog could hardly walk by the time they got to the stairs, and was too heavy for her to carry up four flights.

She called the elevator and then urged him inside, where he flopped to the floor, and they rode up to five. From there, it took two minutes to walk ten rooms down the hall; she whispered, "X, come on, come on. People are getting up . . ."

When X got back in the bedroom, he lay down and closed his eye. Shay watched him for a moment as Emily quietly snored in the other bed. Everybody was asleep—and Shay lay back down and, a minute later, was gone as well.

By eight, they were all up again. Emily was dressed and out the door; there was an estate sale of a *Star Trek* set designer rumored to have kept one of everything, from a pair of Spock's ears to one of Captain Kirk's many identical command chairs.

Shay, meanwhile, needed to get to a supermarket and see about buying actual dog food. Maybe he just needed some better nutrition? Hope against hope. He was awake and alert, but wasn't yet standing. She left him some more peanut butter crackers.

It would be X's first time alone in the room, and she wasn't sure that it wouldn't be destroyed when she came back. She decided to pen him inside the bedroom.

"Don't chew the legs off the bed," she said as she closed the door.

The supermarket was a twenty-minute walk. Shay used the time to work on the thumb drive's password. Supposedly, the files on the drive were filled with horrible and inhumane things being done to animals, but Shay's only interest in discovering the password was to learn who had forced her brother into the van. If Odin didn't surface again soon—either directly or through Rachel—she saw no choice but to contact West. And/or the police.

An hour later, back at the hotel with a twenty-pound sack of organic dog food recommended by a clerk, she unlocked the door to her room and found X sitting on the other side.

"Hey! How'd you get out of the bedroom?"

Shay called out for Emily, but Emily hadn't returned. She walked back to the bedroom, half expecting the door to be knocked off its hinges. It was merely open, as if the dog had pushed it open just enough to let himself out.

"Weird," she said to herself. "Guess I didn't shut it tight."

With the dog watching her, Shay filled another one of Emily's pottery bowls with too much food, and freshened his water.

"All right," she said. "You didn't trash the place, so I'm not going to lock you up. But be good. I've gotta go to work."

He watched her all the way out the door.

• • •

Shay mixed paint, washed brushes, and bagged up disposable rags that Twist used by the hundreds. "Today," he said, "I'm going to show you how to stretch and prep canvases. There's only one acceptable way to do this—"

"Your way," Shay said.

"I was going to say *perfectly,* but now that I think about it, those are the same thing," Twist said.

He showed her how to do it; it wasn't rocket science, but like ironing the seams straight in a pair of pants, it was trickier than it looked. She spent four hours at it—in the first hour, she got ninety-five percent of it; another three percent in the next hour; one percent in the third hour; and in the fourth hour, she felt like she was going backward.

"You're doing fine," Twist assured her. "Stretching canvas is a pain in the ass, and I will be happy to unload it on you. Next we talk about how to apply a ground. People call it gesso, but it's not, it's an acrylic dispersion . . ."

When the morning's work was done, she went back to the room to check on the dog. Emily was there, and they talked about Shay's new job, and Emily said, "I'd bet my truck he's training you to be his assistant."

"He is not," said Shay, embarrassed at the teacher's-pet tone in Emily's voice. But now she was curious. "Has he ever had one?"

Emily put a finger on one cheek, which she did when she was miming that a thought process was going on, then said, "Not for a long time. He had this one girl who left right after I got here, almost two years ago."

"Why'd she leave?"

"She went to Harvard," Emily said.

"Seriously?" Shay said, impressed.

"No. Sorry. I don't know. She moved in with her boyfriend, I think. I mean, some of us do eventually check out."

X watched them talk, but still wouldn't take any food or water. Emily went back out the door on another mission, and Shay spent an hour trying to crack the password code. Nothing worked. She didn't need to grind on it, she thought, she needed to *contemplate* it.

Restless, she walked out to a Starbucks and went online to Facebook, and found nothing. Where was he? Where could he be? Rachel said she would call when there was news, but could Odin even find *her* again?

Still restless but feeling that the computer wouldn't help, she drifted back to the hotel. She didn't want to sit alone with a sick dog, and so took the elevator back to Twist's studio. The steel outer door to the studio was half open, classical music with a lot of anxious violins coming from the other side. Shay knocked and then pushed through.

Twist was working on one of his smaller landscapes and turned, frowning, as she walked in. "Why are you back here?"

"I owe you six hours."

"Huh," he said, not pleased. "One thing: work, but don't talk. Can you do that?"

"I dunno. I could try."

He led her to the far wall, where three huge canvases, big as billboards, had been leaning for the last week.

"We'll be putting on three coats of gesso, the same stuff you were putting on the small canvases, with a light sanding in between," he said. "When I say *we,* I mean *you.*"

The first two coats would be white, the last coat a steel gray. "I'll show you how to mix that when we get there. Right now, we focus on the white stuff."

He opened the first pail, and she found the gesso had the consistency of a runny pudding. "I like to add a little water," he said. "Maybe a few teaspoons per quart. It's ready when it dribbles off your spoon like cream," he said, demonstrating. "Voilà."

He handed her a house-painting brush and nodded at an aluminum ladder that could get someone onto a second-story roof. "You'll need that eventually, but we start right in the middle and brush out to the sides and the top and the bottom."

The plan was for Shay to lay the first coat on all three canvases. The next time she came, she'd give each canvas a light sanding and repeat the painting process on her own until the job was finished.

"Got it? Now paint; don't talk."

"Can I ask you one thing?"

"Just one."

"How'd you get them in here?"

"We made them in here," he said. "Fifty yards of raw Belgian linen, two staple guns—one will always jam—and stretcher frames made to my exact specifications by Dum, who is good with a chop saw."

"But how . . ."

"Ah-ah. Only one question. Now shut up."

Shay said, "This isn't a question, it's a statement: If you don't let me ask one more question, I'll be mumbling all afternoon."

Twist looked at her for a long moment, not in a funny way, then asked, "Do you ever lose?"

"No. Now, how are you going to get them out?"

He pointed at the skylight. "That opens. We lift them up there with a block and tackle, and lower them down the side of the building. When I say *we,* I mean *other people.* Guys who move pianos."

"Ah. No more questions. Sir." The *sir* was as insolent as if she'd said *dumb-ass.*

With occasional monitoring from Twist, Shay started putting down the first coat on the first canvas. He gave her a few tips, then let her go, moving to a drawing table at the far end of the room. She got into the painting, into the rhythm of it, and began thinking about the whole Odin/dog problem. She didn't see Twist step back toward her until he said, "Hey, Shay. Don't have to work it that much. Just get it on, smooth as you can. You don't have to force it."

"Right," said Shay, almost surprised to see she'd been painting at all. Freaky, how a part of the mind can run on autopilot while some other part wanders off into the past or future.

She put her focus back on her brushstrokes, left to right.

"Shay!"

Emily plowed through the studio door, her complexion drained white as the gesso. Twist was at the drawing table and looked up. Shay, working through her third can, knew it had to be about the dog.

"Problem," Emily said, and pulled Shay in close for confidentiality, though whispering wasn't her strong suit.

"The dog just had a seizure."

Shay sagged. Odin hadn't said anything about seizures. X was getting worse. "Is he all right?"

"Unclear. It lasted about a minute, then I texted Cruz to come watch him so I could come get you."

16

As Shay was bursting into Twist's studio, Sync, Harmon, and Thorne were meeting at Singular headquarters four hundred miles to the north. Sync got right to it. "What does the little shit know?"

Thorne said, "He knows it ain't about Parkinson's. That we're not up in Eugene building a cure."

"Any hint where the drives are now?" Sync asked.

Harmon shook his head. "Nope."

"Are there copies out there?"

"Don't know yet," Harmon said.

"Does the Remby kid know who we are?"

"Meanies," Harmon said.

"Harmon," Sync said sharply.

Time to pay a little lip service to rank. "Look," Harmon said, "the kid's a little funny in the head. Excitable. Had a meltdown when we showed him video of Thorne's monkey roundup, and the unfortunate exterminations that had to be done on account of him and his misguided friends. So ... give him a few hours to think about it."

Sync leaned over the desk and an artery pulsed in his cheek. A facial tic Harmon had seen any number of times in Afghanistan, and which tended to presage a loss of composure.

Sync said, "You're pushing hard." Not a question.

Thorne rubbed his palms together. "We're not running a bucket yet, if that's what you're asking. But we could. The capability is there."

Harmon: "I don't think—"

Sync stood up angrily and slapped the desktop. "If we don't get some answers soon, I'll waterboard the kid myself."

The tension was broken by Sync's desk phone.

He checked the caller ID, then picked up the receiver and asked, "What?"

He listened and said, "Cut everybody else out and then put it on P54A. Okay, good. I'm gonna watch it right now. Find West, tell him to come up here."

Sync hung up and said, "We're looking at media outtakes from the beach where the whales were grounded. The imaging guys were pulling all the stuff out of the sky. They ran ID tags on the different faces in the crowd after they got a positive ID on the Rembys . . ."

"Let's see it," Harmon said.

Sync picked up a remote and pointed it at the curtains, and they rolled across the windows. Another click and the lights went down and a sixty-inch flat-screen lit up on the wall behind Sync's desk.

Some symbols flickered in a corner, then a digital clockface came up and the video began and they were looking at the beach. A pale orange circle appeared, surrounding a girl who was throwing water on a whale, and a caption came up: SHAY REMBY.

There wasn't continuous coverage of the girl because the media wasn't interested in her; she was just another body throwing water. They watched as she flicked from one passing view to the next, as the whales began to die, as a baby whale got pushed off the beach.

They watched for another five minutes, and then Sync's secretary beeped him on the intercom. "Mr. West is here."

"Send him in," Sync said, and quickly to Harmon and Thorne, "He doesn't know we still have Remby. Let's keep it that way."

There was a knock, and West rolled through the door in a wheelchair. Sync stopped the video and said, "We're looking at the tapes from the beach."

Thorne added, "That was a nice piece of work, by the way, finding the sister."

West nodded and said, "Thanks." He knew Thorne by sight, but not exactly what he did.

Sync turned back to the video screen and said, "Watch with us."

They watched Shay Remby on one piece of video and then on another, in changing image sizes and orientations—sometimes the media cameras were north of her, sometimes south, sometimes looking down from the bluff above the beach.

Then her brother appeared. He was shown walking down the bluff, his image surrounded by a green circle. Another caption came up: ODIN REMBY. Then a pale red circle around another woman: RACHEL WHARTON.

"There's that damn dog," Sync said, showing a bit of excitement.

The screen split into two images, one following Odin Remby, the big gray dog, and Rachel Wharton, the other following Shay Remby.

The two digital clockfaces under the videos showed the same time. They saw, but couldn't hear, Odin Remby shouting something and, on the other half of the split screen, Shay Remby turning and then the brother and sister running toward each other.

Thirty seconds later, Odin and Shay collided, the muzzled dog lunging between them, and a third screen split came up and they watched as West dashed after them.

"Man, you were moving fast," Thorne said to West. "You gotta watch it, you were giving it away—"

"Okay under the circumstances," Sync said.

They watched as West approached, and then as Rachel Wharton gunned him down.

"Tasered you," Sync said to West. "Nice shot."

"That's the first thing I thought," West said. "After I stopped screaming."

They saw Shay Remby pass the dog's leash to an unidentified man, who left with the dog. Another split screen followed the dog in a long shot, while the first one remained with Shay Remby and West. West said, "She killed the power for me. I've explained the exotic world of fuse technology to the wizards downstairs so I won't have to go through that again."

"Watch the dog, watch the dog," Sync said.

The man with the dog was hurrying down the beach, and the dog stumbled a couple of times. Simultaneously, they saw Cherry pick up West and carry him out of the picture, which stayed with Remby, who climbed the bluff and stood looking for a moment, then hurried off in the same direction the man and dog had.

They lost the man with the dog until another newsclip caught

• • •

West rolled out of the room, and the door closed behind him.

Harmon asked, "So—I thought the dog was another lab animal. Is there more?"

Sync: "I won't bore you with the details. Let's just say that even a test monkey needs a test monkey. Janes had just wired a new round of neurons into the dog when the crazies broke in. Idiot that he was—and is—about security, he'd had a real breakthrough on the neural integration front. We need to watch that process, that's why we need the dog. And we don't need anybody else getting curious about it."

"So what are we doing?" Thorne asked.

"Well, we need the dog, and we need to find the leadership group. Odin Remby should be able to help us with that," Sync said, "one way or another."

On the video screen, the picture had frozen on an image of Shay Remby.

"Silly girl," Sync said.

"Not really, and we need to keep that in mind," Harmon said. "Could we rerun the last minute or so of the dog pictures?"

Sync said, "Sure," and reran the video. They watched the young man and the dog moving down the beach and saw the dog stumble once, and then again, and Harmon said, "That's what I thought—Lassie seems to be dragging."

Sync said, "No," but watched the segment again, and suddenly buzzed his secretary. "Get Dr. Janes on the phone, now," he said.

"This is more trouble?" Harmon asked.

Sync took a swig of his green drink as if to steady himself. "Let's just say the dog, as high-tech as he now is, has basic maintenance needs, or we lose him."

"Shit."

"Janes said we had at least another week—"

The artery in Sync's cheek fluttered, and in the next second, he was hurling the only thing he could find on his uncluttered desk: the Rubik's Cube bounced off the window.

"Harmon. Thorne. Find Wharton and get the goddamn dog."

17

Twist pushed open the door with his cane and went inside, trailed by Shay. The dog lay in the space between the beds, too weak to lift his head or shift his eye toward the cane's clacking approach. Emily and Cruz backed away.

If Twist was angry about the rule breaking, there was no reading it in his face. Shay hung back in the doorway as he bent to the muzzled animal and pressed two fingers to the femoral artery on his inner thigh. He counted the dog's pulse against his steel Rolex, then made all three teens jump with a two-fingered whistle.

The dog didn't blink.

Twist yanked a patchwork quilt off Emily's bed and tossed it to Shay. "He's in shock, keep him warm. We don't have a lot of time."

Twist drove south on Alvarado Street in a hurry, dodging cars and trucks and jumping lights, past MacArthur Park, an urban mishmash of noisy geese, mothers pushing strollers, homeless campers, food carts, counterfeit ID vendors, uniformed schoolchildren, and drug-dealing gangbangers.

The dog was sprawled in the back of Twist's Range Rover, the canvases and climbing gear removed in case X had another seizure. Where exactly they were going, Twist hadn't explained. After stepping outside the room to make a private call, he'd said, "Shay, I'll get one of the twins to carry the dog to my truck. You're coming with me. Emily, Cruz, we'll talk when I get back."

Twist shifted lanes, blowing past a Volkswagen, and veered off Alvarado to park on a side street. Shay opened the passenger door and considered the possibilities: On one corner, a twenty-four-hour bail-bond business, neon sign flashing in the window. And across from it, a small storefront with its security gate pulled shut. Beyond the grimy bars, Shay could make out a plaster cast of a dark-skinned Virgin Mary surrounded by half a dozen sun-melted candles and the word BOTANICA painted on the window glass.

"The one on the left," Twist said, and opened the rear hatch.

Dum carried the limp dog like a sheep, one arm around its chest, the other around its hind legs, no struggle from the animal, no sign he was even aware of being carried. Twist stuck his cane through the storefront bars and pressed a doorbell.

"What is this place?" Shay asked.

"Your basic everyday drugstore except for the religion, mysticism, voodoo, and wishful thinking thrown in with it," Twist said.

A small, wrinkled woman in a traditional huipil top and black polyester pants unlocked a deadbolt on the interior door, then rolled back the gate just enough to allow them inside. A gray braid hung down her back.

"Hola, señora," Twist said with a respectful tip of his bowler.

Shay's nose twitched at the stew of odors: patchouli incense, seared meat, dirty diapers, cleaning fluids heavy on the bleach.

The old woman took a peek at the dog in Dum's arms, then turned on her yellow flip-flops, crooked a finger at them to follow. A parrot in a cage hanging from a rafter started to squawk. Twist motioned for Shay to go ahead of him, the room too crammed with floor-to-ceiling shelves for anything but single file.

Snaking through the narrow aisles, Shay marveled at the variety of things a person could buy here: pharmaceuticals with Spanish labels; bundles of dried herbs poking out of Coca-Cola bottles; religious statues; Dodgers baseball caps and gardening gloves; pastel skulls made out of sugar; incense sticks and aromatic oils that promised to cure various habits and addictions; candles that promised to attract love and money; brand-name toothpastes and shampoos; a bin of wire-sprung mousetraps, three for a dollar.

Arriving at what seemed to be the back of the store, the old woman knocked twice on a blue-painted door. An inset panel the size of a hand swung open, and someone in silver aviators peered out.

"Amigo," came the low voice.

"Dr. Girard," said Twist.

It was a whole different world behind the blue door. Bright fluorescent lights, white-tiled walls, a jar of disposable thermometers and a box of plastic gloves sitting on a stainless-steel sink like a trough. The slender, middle-aged Girard wore a serious expression, belted jeans, a tan pullover, and a stethoscope around his neck.

"Please," he said, and motioned for Dum to place the dog on

a large metal exam table draped in sanitary paper. Then, *"Gracias, Rosita."*

The old woman's cue to leave the room. Twist gestured at Dum to clear out too, and he went, closing the blue door behind them.

Shay peeled back the quilt and realized, at the same moment as the doctor, that the dog wasn't breathing. Twist hooked her by the arm to move her out of the way, and the doctor, unable to find a heartbeat through his stethoscope, started cardiopulmonary resuscitation.

For the next minute, he pumped his laced hands into the dog's chest no differently from the way Shay had learned on a mannequin in health class. But the animal wasn't reviving and the doctor said he needed to add oxygen. He puzzled over the mechanics of mouth-to-mouth, then glanced up at Shay.

"Can the muzzle come off? Is he dangerous?"

"I don't know," she sputtered, "he's not mine."

The doctor looked at the dog for a moment, then went to a drawer where he found a plastic mask, attached it to the coupling on a hand-sized oxygen tank, wrapped the mask around the muzzle as well as he could, and turned on the oxygen.

Nothing happened; they could all feel it, death roiling around them like smoke.

The doctor watched for a minute, then went to another drawer, brought out a syringe with a five-inch needle, took a bottle out of another drawer, and sucked a clear fluid into the syringe. Bending over the dog, he used one front leg as a lever and half rolled it, then felt through the dog's fur for the breastbone and, in one sharp movement, punched the needle into the heart.

Twist flinched and said, "Ouch."

"Adrenaline," the doctor said. "Sometimes it restarts things."

The doctor began pumping the dog's chest again—Shay's own heart thumping wildly—and somewhere between the forty-fourth and forty-seventh count, the dog's eye popped open.

"Look! He's alive," she said.

"Like Frankenstein said about his monster," Twist said.

The dog shifted his head toward Shay's voice, and she broke away from Twist to stroke his head. The doctor straightened, then said, "We're not out of the woods yet."

Shay whispered "Good boy" in the dog's ear and then, for the first time, took a look around the room and realized it was a clinic for humans, not for animals.

"You're not a veterinarian?"

"I'm not," he said in lightly accented English. Shay thought he might be French. "But Twist asked if I might help a young lady with an emergency and, mmm, special circumstances."

Shay looked back at Twist, who merely shrugged and opened up a metal folding chair to sit down. She checked the room again—it felt like a real medical clinic, but it also felt . . . covert?

"What kind of doctor are you?"

The man smiled in a way that suggested things were complicated. He said, not evasively, "An unlicensed one, in California."

"Dr. Girard's a healer, period," said Twist. "I'd trust him to take out my appendix right here, right now."

Girard asked, looking amused, "Didn't you tell me you had your appendix out as a child?"

Twist shrugged and Shay interjected, "Is X going to be all right?"

"Let me take a closer look," Girard said.

"Please," she said.

• • •

"I'd like to examine his eyes. Can you tell me about the patch?"

Shay shook her head. "I was told he was wearing it when he was found . . . by someone I know."

"All right. Well, let's see what's under there—he's been coopera-tive so far."

The doctor tried lifting off the dirty patch, but the medical tape wasn't like anything he'd worked with before, the seal like rubber cement. Shay said the dog had been wearing the patch for at least a month, and the doctor said, "Unusual."

Twist said, "I'd like to buy stock in that tape."

Girard gave up on removing the entire patch and picked up a scalpel to slice through the gauze. The dog jerked his head away, but the doctor's hand was steady, and with a slice up the middle, he parted the gauze like drapes to reveal a new surprise: the right eye wasn't a yellow match for the other, but a pale and watery blue. The pupil was a thick black hyphen that didn't contract with the light.

Girard trimmed the gauze away to the edge of the tape, then held up a finger and moved it inward and outward to test whether the eye could focus, and though the reaction time was slow, it could. He picked up a scope and leaned in to examine the eyeball through the lens.

"My God," he said almost instantly.

"What?" asked Twist.

Girard went silent as he continued examining the eye from every possible angle. More than a minute passed before he finally looked up and said, "This isn't just any dog." He turned a dubious eye on Shay. "Exactly where'd this dog come from?"

"I don't know," she lied. "I was just told some people were abusing him and, somehow, he got rescued."

Twist pushed out of his chair. "What's the problem, G?"

The doctor wasn't ready to say. "I'd like to take some X-rays before we talk about that."

It had been more than an hour since Girard had ushered them out of the room to wait on the other side of the blue door. Shay mostly paced the store's aisles to distract herself, while Twist took a pocket notebook out of his corduroy jacket, turned it sideways, and sketched.

He was sitting on an old church pew, periodically glancing up at the chatty bilingual parrot—"*Lunes,* Monday, *Martes,* Tuesday"— when Shay finally slumped down beside him.

After a while, Twist said, "I had a dog once."

"You did?" Seven days at the hotel, assisting him in the studio, and beyond the observable facts—rich painter who dabbled in guerrilla art and disarmed the occasional knife-wielding hoodlum— Twist had yet to share anything personal.

"When I was eleven, a mutt I found roped to a tree. Took her water and school lunches for a week. Figured someone would come back for her, but they never did."

"So . . . you got to keep her?"

Something in Twist's expression seemed to regret the subject. He tucked his pencil behind an ear, tore out the page he'd been working on, and put away the notebook.

"Couldn't keep a dog where I was staying," he said.

Where I was staying . . . Shay remembered the rumors that Twist had been a foster kid. She herself was a master of euphemism when it came to hiding her living arrangements from classmates. Various aunts and uncles were always dropping her off at school in the morning or signing permission slips while her parents were out of the country on "business."

Shay probed further—was he staying in an apartment?—but Twist was done being personal.

"Let's not overshare," he said, then handed her the sketch: a frustrated parrot opening its wings through the bars of a cage.

Suddenly, from the bird, *"Adiós,* good-bye." Girard stuck his head through the door and said, "Come in here."

The dog's artificial blue eye was like something plucked from the future.

A half-dozen X-rays of the dog's head and body hung on a viewing panel for Twist and Shay to see for themselves. On the back of the eyeball, the image clearly showed a clump of tiny, complex electronic chips, a small black disk the size of three stacked quarters, and a web of wires threading into the animal's brain. More wires led out of his neck further into his body, parallel to his spine, until they actually entered the spinal column just above the dog's back legs. And those two legs themselves—they weren't bone, they were metal, with what appeared to be a miniaturized computer control complex, half the size of an iPhone, buried in the body cavity.

"I can't tell you what the mechanisms do, except in a general way," the doctor said. "I will tell you this dog belonged to someone—or something—with access to new and very expensive science."

Twist squinted at him. "You're saying this dog's got a better health plan than I do?"

"I'm saying this dog's probably *practice* for people," Girard said. "This wiring . . . this is remarkable." He tapped the X-ray of the computer complex in the body cavity. "This apparently controls the back legs. You can see that the natural muscles are attached to the metallic components—don't ask me how. A radical new medical glue? I don't know. The wiring disappears into the spinal column . . . here. I think they've somehow managed to merge natural nerves and these wires—if they are wires—so the dog's brain actually controls these legs in a natural manner."

"A lab rat?"

Girard nodded. "I'm thinking government. And something else, here. . . ." He pointed to the black disk at the back of the skull. Shay realized it was probably connected to the plate her brother had shown her.

"There's a metal plate behind the right ear. I thought about trying to open it, but there's no obvious latch, and the dog wasn't cooperating. Maybe with anesthesia, but there's a serious risk with putting him under, given his weakened state. So again, I can only hypothesize . . . the disk might possibly be a battery. What it controls, I don't know. . . . This work, I tell you—the technique is marvelous. . . ."

Twist pivoted to Shay, who was carefully screwing her own eyes into the floor.

"Hey," he said, "is there something you want to tell us? How 'bout ten seconds to compose something with free will, after that, we'll just go ahead and beat it out of you?"

Shay bit down on her lip, trapped. Ten seconds of testy silence, a crack of Twist's cane against the floor, and then:

"The dog was taken from a laboratory in Oregon," she said. "They were doing experiments on him and some activists freed a bunch of animals that were being tortured. One of the guys got carried away and took the dog."

"The Parkinson's lab in Eugene," said Girard. "I heard about that."

"It's not for Parkinson's," Shay said a little too quickly.

"Oh yeah?" said Twist. "Tell us more."

Shay clammed up again.

"Were you there?" Twist pushed. "Is that why you're here? You took this dog?"

"No. I didn't take the dog, and I wasn't there. I didn't even know about the dog until yesterday. The people that were—they know the real situation. C'mon. Wiring a dog up like this? Does that seem like legit research to you?"

"It could be," Girard said.

Twist didn't say anything for a moment, just held his focus on her, studying her, Shay looking back at him with the sensation she was being X-rayed herself.

"It's the truth," she said.

Twist turned away and looked at his friend.

"Is this fake eye causing the seizures?"

"I don't know, and frankly, I'm not sure it matters. His white cell count is low, his liver enzymes are high, his heart's barely pumping blood."

"Are you saying—"

"Yes. I don't think I'm going to be able to help."

Shay stepped forward, anguish in her voice. "You have to do something. The person who found him—okay, it was my brother—I don't know where he is right now. He might not be around for a while, it's his dog. Please . . ."

Girard shook his head. "We can try antiseizure medicine and

sedatives to make him more comfortable, but there's no cure for congestive heart failure. Animal or human. I'm sorry."

Shay put a hand on the dog's neck and hung her head.

"How long?" she asked.

"I'm not a vet, but . . . a few days. Maybe a week, at the outside."

In the Range Rover on the way back to the hotel, Shay told Twist the rest of the truth, so far as she knew it. She told him about West, and his extraordinary legs, and how they'd short-circuited like a firecracker on the beach; about meeting her brother, who'd given her a sack of encrypted thumb drives stolen during the raid in Eugene; about the dog; and about the van, and the men from Singular who'd snatched Odin off the beach road.

"They kidnapped him. They are not the government, they are not the police. They're an out-of-control corporation, and nobody knows what they're doing. But my brother is a good person. The best person I know. He's smart—that's why they took him. He was figuring them out."

"I don't know what to make of the guy with the legs or what you think you saw with that van and your brother, but you could go to jail for having this dog," Twist said. "And maybe those thumb drives."

"So I'll go to jail. I don't want to drag you into it—I'll pack up my stuff as soon as we get back." She reached back over the seat to check the dog; she felt his warm breath on her hand, but it seemed weak, too soft.

"No hurry," Twist said. "We need to think about this, and I need those canvases done by six tomorrow night."

Shay: "You're serious? We can stay?"

"For now, but no bragging about cyber-dog. If that news goes viral, your new sworn enemy—me—won't think twice about ratting you out to the cops. I ain't doing time for dognapping."

"Not a word," Shay promised.

The dog was still woozy from the sedatives the next morning. Shay guided him slowly to the studio, settled him on a bed of blankets, and got busy on the canvases. Her laptop was nearby so she could check her email every half hour or so, and her phone was in her shirt pocket so she could monitor any texts that came in. She'd messaged Odin—wherever he was—about the dog's deteriorating condition before they'd left the botanica because both she and Twist suspected that Girard was being optimistic when he'd said the dog might last a week.

Six hours of work passed, with the dog barely stirring. The small appetite he'd had before the seizures was now gone altogether; he showed no interest in a cheeseburger that Emily brought up from the kitchen.

As Shay applied another layer of gesso to the canvases, her mind kept circling back to her encounter with West on the beach.

He'd credited the Eugene lab with his robotic legs, with making him whole after Afghanistan. A soldier, maybe even a hero for losing his legs in the name of freedom. Not a bad guy, right?

The strange mechanical thing she'd pulled out of his back . . . a power source of some sort for the circuitry that maneuvered his legs. Did the plate behind the dog's ear function in a similar way? The port through West's flesh was round and capped, while the dog's was linear and came up empty on Girard's X-ray. . . .

Shay looked down again at the unmoving animal. He appeared

to be sleeping, but she couldn't be sure from such a distance and climbed down to check his breathing.

Still alive, but not by much.

Her hand crept around to his ear, and she pulled up the flap of skin that covered the plate. The dog didn't move. She gently probed around the plate. The dog twitched, and then lay still again.

It must be an access port, but how did it work? It shouldn't be something complicated, if they'd needed access to it. She bent over the dog, got her eye two inches away from the plate, and saw on its top a tiny dome no bigger than the head of a pin, and easy to miss. Easier to feel, in fact, than see.

She tried pushing it with her finger, but her finger was too big, and too soft. She stood up, went over to one of Twist's worktables, and found a dental pick he occasionally used for carving the surface of a painting.

Back with the dog, she bent over, placed the sharp point against the dome, and pressed, first gently and then more firmly, and then felt a faint but definite click. She lifted the pick away and the plate popped up, just a fraction of an inch. She slipped the point of the pick under it and pulled it upward.

Inside was a rectangular port. She knew that rectangle: "Thunderbolt," she said aloud.

A standard computer connection. More critically, she thought, a Thunderbolt connection could feed up to nine watts of power into a target device. That black disk in the dog's head: Could it be a battery, as Girard had suggested? A power supply for the electronics that fed into his brain?

She took out her cell phone and called Twist. He answered on the third ring, and she asked, "Where are you?"

"Kitchen. Trying to hustle a little food out of—"

"Do you know where you can get a Thunderbolt line? Like a line out to a hard drive?"

He chewed on something for a moment—a carrot, maybe—then said, "Yeah, there are a few of them around."

"Get a line and get up to the studio. Right now. Right now!"

"Hey. Calm down, I'm—"

"RIGHT NOW," Shay shouted.

Twist showed up five minutes later carrying the Thunderbolt cable. He said, "I was—"

"Shut up," Shay said. Twist cocked his head and looked at her. He wasn't used to taking preemptory orders in his own studio.

"Please," she added.

"What do you want me to do?"

"Plug your Mac in," she said. "Use that extension cord, and get over here as close as you can to the dog."

Twist shrugged and moved to do it. "What's the plan?" he asked as he started unwinding the coil of extension cord.

Shay was bent over the dog. "I found a Thunderbolt port. I think that the electronics in his brain are powered off a battery—that round black thing we saw on the X-ray. He's weak because his brain isn't working. They've done something to him that means he needs auxiliary power."

"You're going to plug him in? Isn't that taking a serious risk?"

Shay looked up and said, "Yes. But he's dying. He's getting worse every hour. If he dies because I plug him in, he's no worse off than if he dies because I didn't."

Twist plugged the Mac laptop into the extension cord and the

Thunderbolt line into the Mac as he thought it over. "What if they pull some other amount of current?"

"Why would they do that?" Shay asked. "It's a standard port. You'd just use a standard setup instead of a special one. If the black object is a battery, that means the Thunderbolt doesn't power the electronics directly, it just recharges that battery."

"It's your call," Twist said.

Shay nodded, took the end of the Thunderbolt cable, bent over the dog, hesitated, then plugged it into the port behind the dog's ear.

Nothing happened.

"Could take a while," she said tentatively. She wasn't sure why she did it, but for the first time, she unbuckled the muzzle strap and pulled the cage off X's head.

Then they sat and watched, and five minutes after they plugged the dog in, Twist reached out and put his fingers on the femoral artery, just as he had the first time.

He tipped his head and Shay asked, "What?"

"It may be wishful thinking . . . but it feels stronger to me. Steadier. Like somebody plugged in a pacemaker."

Another ten minutes. Twist walked back and forth from a half-finished painting to the dog, watching both Shay and the animal.

Fifteen more minutes, and the dog lifted his head off the cushion and his yellow eye fluttered open. He stared up at Shay, who was stroking his neck.

"It's working," Twist said. "He seems almost alert . . ."

Another ten minutes, and the dog's mechanical eye popped open. The blue was different from before—not faint and watery, but a deep, dark navy. For several moments, the dog's gaze stayed locked on hers, and then his tongue slipped out of his mouth and he licked her wrist once, twice.

Shay felt a lump in her throat, and Twist, tapping his paintbrush against his hand, said:

"I think you got yourself a dog."

18

She had herself a dog.

The dog's recovery was remarkable. Over the next two days, X ate everything Shay fed him. He showed some careful pleasure when he encountered Emily, Cruz, Cade, or Twist, but he was Shay's dog, never more than a few feet from her. Shay went online and read through how-to sites about feeding and handling and exercising a dog.

In the meantime, Twist put up an announcement in the lobby that said:

THE NO-PETS POLICY IS REAFFIRMED.
WE ARE NOT ABLE TO ALLOW PETS FOR REASONS OF
SAFETY AND SANITATION, AND BECAUSE THE CITY MIGHT
GIVE US A HARD TIME. I AM MAKING ONE EXCEPTION TO
THE RULE: SHAY REMBY'S DOG, X, IS ALLOWED IN THE
BUILDING AS HE IS NOT A PET. HE IS WORKING FOR ME

AS A MODEL AND AS A WATCH DOG, AND ALSO BECAUSE I
SAY SO, AND I'M THE BOSS HERE.

After that went up, Shay no longer had to sneak X in and out of
the hotel.

In some ways, the Twist Hotel was like a big high school, easy-
going most of the time, but sometimes not. There were always kids
in the halls, talking, laughing, arguing, coming and going. And gos-
siping.

A number of them thought it unfair that Shay was allowed to
keep a dog when they weren't even allowed to keep a goldfish, and
they talked about that, and suggested that maybe there was something going on between Shay and Twist. But there was enough "Hey,
you want to live here?" back talk that the gossipers finally gave up,
and X was in.

The posters of the immigration action went out, and Twist told Shay
that his dealer had sold all of them in a single day.

"We're today's fad," he said as they mixed paint in the studio.
"You can't be a liberal young actor in Hollywood and not have one
in your front entry. I'll get you the cash next week, I think. It takes
a while for everything to clear."

"Is money always this easy?" Shay asked.

"Let's not overshare," Twist said, grinning, and handed her a
bucket of gesso.

The next morning after breakfast, Shay was sitting on the building's
steps with X because X liked to go outside and exercise his nose. A

man was walking toward them on the sidewalk, a muscled-up guy with a shaved head, in khakis and a minty golf shirt and oversized Ray-Bans. He took Shay in and said, "How you doin', sweetheart?"

He had big white teeth, like Little Red Riding Hood's wolf.

Shay said "Fine" with the kind of dismissive tone that usually moved people along.

"Fine? That's all you got for me?"

"That's all I got," she said.

"I'll tell you what . . ." He stepped closer, not too close, but close enough to create pressure.

X stood up, but not fully up; his hind legs were bunched beneath him like springs, and he looked at the man's throat and snarled. The snarl was more than just a warning; it was a death threat.

The man, backing away, said, "That dog jumps me, we'll be in court."

Shay had a hold on X's collar, a bit unnerved by his protectiveness but not letting the man know that. "My dog jumps you, I'll be in court," she said. "You won't be."

The man looked at her face, then at the dog, made a decision, and moved along. And Shay thought he moved . . . like a man from Singular. Was she becoming paranoid? Maybe. Shay stroked X between the ears and said, "Good boy."

He licked her chin once, and they went back to people-watching, and sniffing.

Shay worked on the password for the thumb drive. Twist still wasn't sure there was any point in trying to unlock the contents—and he privately doubted that her brother had been kidnapped—but he did recommend bringing Cade into her confidence.

Cade was fascinated.

"You always had a problem managing the rook ISH."

Staring at Shay's laptop screen up in Twist's studio, he reread the pop-up riddle Odin had linked to the thirty-four-letter password box. She'd already shown him what she'd found when she'd turned to Google for ideas: how when you typed in "ISH," you'd come up with a lot of business stuff—there was an International Shiphold-ing Corporation with the stock symbol ISH—and dictionaries that defined the suffix -ish, as in girlish or boyish, and there were an im-probable number of people named Ish, as either a first or last name.

Cade said, "There's also ish, like when you see something nasty. You know, like people eating octopus sushi."

"Oh, ish," Shay said.

"Exactly. But from what you've told me about your brother, it's gotta be something you could figure out, but nobody else could. Thirty-four letters and numbers and symbols . . . that's a heck of a password. But with that many letters, if you just get one word right, you'd have the whole idea."

"Maybe," she said.

"You said you guys played chess."

"Sure, but we weren't serious about it."

"What was your problem with the rook?"

"I don't know. We had this book on chess openings at school, and we learned a few, but we were just kids."

They were sitting shoulder to shoulder on the couch in the stu-dio, the dog at their feet. Cade added, "It's got to be something from your past life, right? Did you know somebody called Rook, or something like rook? Something that rhymes with rook? Or how about a castle, a rook is supposed to be a castle, right?"

"When we were really little, my folks took us to Disneyland and we saw the castle, but that can't be it. It says 'managing the rook.' I never had anything to do with managing a castle. Or anyone named Castle. Or anybody who rhymed with *rook*. . . ."

They heard the ancient elevator start.

"Aw, shoot," Cade said. "The boss arrives."

She could feel his disappointment: he'd wanted to talk. And she hadn't minded.

The elevator stopped and X stood up, a streak of hair rising on his back. The door split open noisily, Twist pulling on the canvas strap. Seeing the three of them, he said, "Howdy."

X wuffed a hello, let his tongue slip out and the hair on his back lay down again.

"Cade's helping me break the code," Shay said, and patted the laptop. Closing the cover, she got up, and X, already seeming to anticipate her moves, headed for the elevator. "We'll work on this again," she told Cade. "Remember: you always had a problem managing the rook ISH."

"I'll be thinking about it all night," he said to her back.

Shay got inside the elevator with X and returned a smile as she reached for the strap and heaved the door shut.

Late that night, Shay woke, groped for her phone, and looked at the time: 4:15. She could hear Emily's deep breathing from the other side of the room.

You always had a problem managing the rook ISH . . .

Odin had always enjoyed teasing his younger sister, making up puzzles that had simple answers when you finally saw them, but were sometimes impossible to see. Not because he didn't give you enough information, but because you couldn't see what was right in front of your nose. The obvious problem was, she didn't understand *rook,* and she didn't understand *ISH.*

She'd nearly gone back to sleep when her brain opened the puzzle for her. *Rook ISH?* How about *rookish?* Sort of like a rook. A rook was like a crow, like all those big black birds.

Like a raven, she thought. Like Poe's "The Raven."

She'd memorized "The Raven" in ninth-grade English class. She'd had trouble managing one line, because she didn't know the words, and she didn't know how to pronounce them, and even the English teacher hadn't been certain about it.

Quaff, oh quaff this kind nepenthe . . .

Was it pronounced like KWAFF, rhyming with *laugh,* or like KWOFF, rhyming with *cough?* How about *nepenthe?* Was it NA-PEN-THAY? Or NE-PENTH? NE-PEN-THEE?

She still didn't really know, but she lay in the dark and counted the letters, spaces, and punctuation on her fingers. Thirty-four. Exactly.

Shay smiled in the dark. The dog heard her moving, she heard him stir, and when she looked toward the foot of the bed, she could see in the near dark his gray-black face turned toward her.

She whispered "Shhh" and dropped her feet to the floor. She pulled on a pair of jeans and, trailed by X, carried her laptop and her sneakers through the other room, quietly turned the lock, and slipped into the hallway and locked the door behind her. She put on her shoes, then decided to head up to Twist's studio rather than down to the lobby with its night owls. She needed the privacy.

The studio was dark, except for the ever-present red, orange, green, and white LEDs glowing on various bits of electronic equipment. The door to Twist's private rooms was shut. She took a seat on a couch, turned on her computer, used the light from the screen to plug in the thumb drive, and brought it up.

| Q | u | a | f | f | , | | o | h | | q | u | a | f | f | | t | h | i | s | | k | i | n | d | | n | e | p | e | n | t | h | e |

Thirty-four letters, spaces, and punctuation marks.

She checked that she'd spelled it all correctly, pressed ENTER, and got back an immediate response.

Fail. You have two remaining chances.

The thirty-four-letter box came up again. She smiled at that, and typed in: "No, I don't."

That part was a private code they'd developed to fight intrusions by snoopy foster parents. They knew each other's log-in passwords, and Odin had developed a second step that they'd both always know, but nobody else would. Even if somebody typed in the correct password, the fail message would appear. If you didn't know the proper response—if you tried to type in another password—the system would lock up. If you typed in the proper response, which was *No, I don't,* it would let you in.

She pressed ENTER.

The first thing up was a note from Odin:

So you're in. This is the only drive I was able to crack. All of them are protected with heavy encryption, but the red thumb drive has the encryption/decryption software on it.

They're also protected with passwords. The passwords are tough, but not impossible. The head scientist at the EDT Lab in Eugene is Lawrence Janes. He was born in 1962 and his wife was born in 1964. His

children were born in 1995 and 1997. The password for this drive was LJ1962MJ64S95M97. His wife's name is (or was, I think they might have gotten divorced) Marjorie (MJ) and his son is named Stephen (S) and his daughter is named Mary (M). I haven't figured out the others, but you're better at social reverse engineering than I am, so maybe you can.

If you can't, think about this. There should be a list of passwords somewhere, because these are too complicated to simply remember . . . but then, Janes is really really smart, so maybe he does (just remember). But I think there's a list. It's not on his computer, so I figure it's in a safe on his cell phone. If someone could get his cell phone, we might be able to get the list.

Anyway, in this drive, in Folder 7, get a load of Files 12 and 17. Actually, look at all of them, and be prepared to freak out. But 12 and 17 . . . these should hang them, if we can figure out a way to make them public and believable. In the 12 video, look at that uniformed guy in the background. What kind of uniform is it? Who is he? Who does he work for?

Don't do anything with this until I say it's okay. We're working on a strategy to bring them down, and if you pull the trigger too soon, it may screw us up. Don't let Rachel or anyone else from Storm know that I gave this to you. I'm not sure how far they can be trusted, and I need a backup plan. Take care. Wipe this note now.

The studio was full of paper, and Shay got a piece from a scratch pad and wrote down the Janeses' names and birth dates and stuck it in her pocket.

She erased Odin's note, then opened Folder 7, File 12, which had no further protection. As soon as she selected it, an MP4 file came up and began to run a video apparently made with an ordinary camera. The point of view never changed, and it showed an Asian man sitting in a chair, wearing what looked like a prison uniform, in front of some kind of electronic console. He was shown in profile, and the back of his head was covered with what looked like a dull silver bowl. There appeared to be a number of electronic ports in the bowl, and a half-dozen thin cables led from the console to the ports.

The man simply sat in the chair as the camera watched him, and then, without prompting, he began to speak. Shay thought he was speaking an Asian language, but then, after a few seconds, realized that it was English—but English so heavily accented that it was hard to tell, at first, exactly what he was saying.

After a minute or two, she began to sort out the accent, and started the video over. The Asian man said, "My name is Robert G. Morris of St. Louis, Missouri. My wife's name is Angela Agnes Morris, and we live at 22955 LaFontaine Street. My children's names are Robert, Michael, and Joy. . . ."

The Asian man's face was immobile as he spoke, except for his lower jaw and lips. Although the camera showed a close view of him, he never seemed to move his eyes. He continued to describe his life with his family, including a dog named Danver.

The recitation was extremely detailed, and went on for ten minutes. During that time, the torso and arm of a man could occasionally be seen in the background—no face, just the body and one arm, but the man was dressed in a military uniform. Not an American uniform; Shay didn't know what kind it was, but it had a foreign feel to it.

When the man came to the end of a description of his job at a St. Louis post office, he abruptly shut up, and the video ended.

As Shay sat staring at the frozen screen, X got to his feet with a snort. She stepped on his leash to hold him and saw Twist peering out from the doorway of his living quarters. He was barefoot, wearing a pair of jeans and a T-shirt, and had bad bed hair.

"What are you doing?" he asked.

"Looking at a video."

"You cracked it?"

"Yes."

"What is it?"

She restarted the video, and they watched the man in the chair as he recited his name and the names of his family members. When that video ended, Twist, who'd been peering over her shoulder, sat down and asked, "What the hell?"

"I don't know. That's only the first item."

Shay backed up to the menu to open File 17. Another video came up, this one of a man on an operating table, who was shaking uncontrollably. An offscreen man's voice said, in a clipped English accent, "This is now the fourth time we've encountered this reaction, and we no longer believe that it is subject specific. Once the reaction begins, it is not controllable except with the largest doses of opiates. In the first subject, the reaction was allowed to continue until termination. In the second and third, the large doses ended the reaction, but the subjects were no longer useful and had to be discarded. We will try a different technique with this subject, with a different mix of suppressive techniques, but we now suspect that the fault may lie with the applied current level in the microtaps . . ."

He went on with more science-speak, but Twist had put his hands to the sides of his face, as if he were holding his head together. When the video ended, he said, "Jesus Christ. Shay, they're killing them. That's what he was talking about. They're human lab rats. That first guy . . . they made him into . . . I don't know. Into somebody else."

The remaining videos were more technical and less graphic, but still terrible in their own cold, scientific way, showing implantation techniques and experiments, and with more talk of discarded subjects.

When it was done, Twist said, "Go back to the first one again."

They did, and Twist took out a pen and jotted down the subject's name and other information on a piece of scrap paper. When he had everything, Twist said, "Let's see if we can find him."

It took three seconds on Google, and the search came back with several hundred returns on Robert G. Morris of St. Louis, Missouri. Morris was an American aid worker with a Christian food program. He'd gone missing a year earlier in China, not far from the North Korean border, and friends thought he might have tried to cross to assess the North Korean hunger situation. He was now assumed to be dead. The dozens of photos of the man—he was a pink-cheeked blond—looked nothing like the Asian man on the video.

"What'd they do to him?" Twist asked. "What in God's name are they doing?"

"Twist. They have my brother. These people have Odin. . . ."

19

Odin knew he was in terrible trouble.

He was in a cold room: four walls of concrete blocks, penetrated by a rectangular window on one side—an observation window, he believed, though it was mirrored so he couldn't see through it—and a steel door with a small silvered window on the other. There were steel grilles along the top edges of the two otherwise blank walls, and from a couple of them poured a screaming stereophonic noise that seemed to be made up of fingernails scraping down a black-board, a metal garbage can beaten with a pipe, and the howling of a wounded monkey.

He had a small rag rug, but no other furniture; the toilet was a cracked porcelain bowl in a corner. He was dressed in the clothes he'd been wearing when he was kidnapped, a cotton shirt and shorts. They'd taken away his shoes, and he was so cold that sleep would have been impossible even without the noise.

He didn't know where he was.

He'd been thrown inside the van after they snatched him off the highway, blindfolded with a hood, cuffed, and placed in a box, probably for concealment. He'd fought the box in spasms of fear and anxiety, trying to kick it, trying to push it with his shoulders, trying to press against it hard enough to open even a crack, but it was too strong.

Eventually, exhausted, he gave up, and his claustrophobic mind crawled into a tiny shell and tried to protect itself. He'd been so panicked that he hadn't been able to keep track of the turns the van had made, but still it hadn't made a U-turn: it had gone more or less in the direction in which they'd started—that is, north.

Nor was he able to keep track of the time. He'd never worn a watch, and they'd taken his phone away from him immediately. But the travel time, he thought, was substantial—several hours.

When they took him out of the van, he was outside for a minute, then in a dark corridor with raw cement floors. He could see just a line of the floor beneath the edge of the hood, which fell to his chest. So he'd been hours in the van, but arrived there on the same day. Six hours, or seven.

There'd been no possibility of escape: the men who'd taken him were larger, stronger, and faster than he was. He'd tried to ask questions, but nobody had bothered even to acknowledge him—not even to tell him to shut up.

He'd been locked in the small room, but they hadn't removed the hood or the cuffs. He'd walked around the perimeter, trying to figure out the terrain; it was, he thought, about eight by ten feet, and made of concrete block. He eventually walked across the rug, and settled uncomfortably onto it.

He hadn't been there long before the door opened again, and two men came into the room and lifted him to his feet. They led him out of the room and down a corridor to another room, where they pushed him into an office-style chair, then used some cargo tie-downs to bind him to it.

One of the men finally spoke. "This is what you did."

The hood was pulled off his head, and he found himself inside an office of some kind, with a desk, a computer screen, some file cabinets, and, on one wall, directly in front of him, a television, with perhaps a forty-inch screen.

"I didn't do anything . . ."

And the pictures started. People running around in a parking lot and across a lawn, scooping up mice and rats. There were shots of monkeys with the tops of their heads removed.

The lab they'd raided in Eugene.

"The lab animals were no good anymore. They had to be destroyed."

The videos shifted to something that must have been a crematorium, but instead of dead animals, tubfuls of live mice were shoveled into a roaring fire. Some bounced off the front of the furnace and landed on the floor, and the videos showed people scurrying around capturing them with nets, then throwing them, in ones and twos, into the fire.

Odin started to weep.

Then came the monkeys. They were euthanized with killing injections before they were fed to the fire . . .

He tried closing his eyes, but a man's muscular hand squeezed the sides of his jaws and the man shouted, "Watch what you did, watch what you did!" and his eyes opened despite himself.

"Where is Storm? Where'd they go? They have to be stopped, if you want to stop the animal slaughter."

Odin shook his head and screamed at the television.

· · ·

Some time later, the hood was put back on his head and he was taken back to the small room. "Think about it," the man said, and the metal door slammed behind him.

He was in the room for a long time, but didn't know exactly how long. He managed to sleep—and dreamed about the videos. Sleep, he realized, was worse than staying awake. And would be, until the dreams stopped.

When the long time had passed, the man came back and asked, "Did you think about it?"

Odin wept again: he would not give up his friends. These people who burned living animals—they hadn't had to do that. It wasn't he and his friends who'd done it.

"All right," said the man. "This is your own fault. Remember that. Your own fault."

They took him out of the prison room and into something that smelled like a shower. He was thrust into what felt like a plastic-covered dental chair.

"We're going to show you something. A demonstration. We're going to demonstrate to you why, when somebody comes to ask you questions, you should answer."

A rope was thrown around his torso and he was tied into the chair; another rope was fastened around his legs, and the chair was tipped back.

The hood was pulled away and then a wet towel slapped over his entire face. He hadn't seen the man who'd spoken to him—all he'd seen was hands and the towel.

And they began pouring cold water over the towel. The water soaked his face and mouth, and when he had to breath, it flooded into his throat and caused him to begin gagging. He swallowed some of the water, and then was seized by the realization that they were drowning him. He tried to kick, but couldn't. Tried to scream, tried to beg, but couldn't get out anything but muffled grunts.

The water seemed to keep coming forever, and then, as he was about to die, he thought, it suddenly stopped and he was upright again, the water spewing out of his throat and down the front of his shirt.

The end of the wet towel was lifted just enough that he could breathe.

The man said, "Pretty bad, isn't it? But you know what? Anybody can take it once. The question is, how many times can you take it before you go stark raving insane?"

The chair was tipped back again and the towel pulled tight and the water came again and he choked and struggled and tried to scream, felt the rope cutting into his chest and arms, and as he was about to pass out or die, suddenly . . . he was back upright again, vomiting water down his chest.

He screamed, "Don't don't don't don't . . . !"

The man said, "You can take it two times. You might be able to take it five. Can you take it six? I don't know. Why don't we find out?"

They tipped him back a third time. But this time, a little, rational corner of his mind said, *They don't want to kill you. They won't let you drown.*

The combination of his claustrophobia and fear of water pushed his back against the wall. *Okay,* he thought, *do it.*

He inhaled. In case he was wrong, he said good-bye to Shay in his thoughts, and he then sucked the water straight down into his lungs.

Everything went dim after a few seconds, but he felt his body being moved, and moved violently, but it all seemed at a great distance. He heard two men and then maybe three shouting, but he couldn't make sense of the words. . . . He felt his legs being lifted in the air, his head dangling, and wondered if they were hanging him by his feet.

Then it all came rushing back, and he was vomiting and spewing water, and great heavy hands were beating him on the back, and somebody was shouting, "You little shit, you little shit . . ."

After a while, when he was breathing again, the hood went back over his face and they half walked, half carried him to the room where he was now confined.

The man who'd almost drowned him had said only one more thing: "We'll be back."

Odin thought, *I'll do it again.* It was a tiny spark, but it was there. He could fight them.

They'd left him on the cold floor, the hood loose around his face. He'd managed to get it off by dragging his forehead across the rug, and found himself in the concrete room. A mirrored window, a steel door, a few vents.

And from the walls, the screaming stereophonic noise began again.

20

Shay and Twist couldn't stay away from the videos. Couldn't stop talking about them. Eventually, Shay went back to the room and managed to sleep. When she got up, late in the afternoon still tired, she found herself at loose ends. There was nobody that she really wanted to talk to with the videos running through her mind.

And Odin. The memories of him as a child. A kid so obsessed with animals that he'd crashed his computer's hard drive downloading thousands of articles and photos from *National Geographic*'s website . . .

She went back to the studio, did a little unpaid cleaning up, and worked for a bit on the large canvases. Finally Twist, who'd spoken hardly a word to her, said, "Get out of here. Go see a movie. Go do something else."

"What am I gonna do?" Shay asked.

"It's not just you anymore," Twist said. "It's *we*. What are *we* going to do? And I don't know. But for right now, get out of here."

She left the studio with X and headed back to the room. She'd get cleaned up, she thought, and go out to a coffee shop and get a little private online time. And X could use the walk.

As she did that, two boys and a girl were sitting on the hotel's front steps smoking, talking music, cars, and celebrities, and about a girl they all knew who the week before had gotten on an elevator at the Getty Museum and Brad Pitt had been inside, and he'd said hello to her and seemed pretty cool. They stopped talking when five vehicles—four SUVs and a white delivery van—swung to the curb. There was a military precision to it, like the president was dropping by.

Then the men got out, and it was exactly like the Secret Service had arrived. They weren't all big, but they were neatly dressed and in good shape, like soldiers disguised as golf pros, all in wraparound shades, pressed khakis, polo shirts.

And black gloves.

One of the boys later told Twist that when the doors rolled back on the van, he saw what looked like a cage inside, a big one with steel bars, like you might use for a gorilla.

"Or a person," the kid said. "If you're running a torture chamber."

Two of the men broke off and went around the building, out of sight, two more stood on the sidewalk in front, watching the street, and the other five went straight up the steps, never taking a glance at the smokers.

A tenth man the smokers never noticed pretended to doze at a bus stop across the street. He was dressed in shabby street clothes and had a proprietary hand on a grocery cart filled with blankets, aluminum cans—and a hidden high-res camera. He'd been making movies of everyone who lived at the hotel, and had confirmed that the targets were both in the building.

The man stirred and readjusted a woolly green blanket across his lap—and as he did, the toes of his boots poked out from beneath the blanket.

Shiny lizard-skin boots, the kind real cowboys wore.

When the five men hit the lobby, the room was filled with kids. They were waiting for dinner and everyone was around, poking at computers or plugged into headphones, or just talking. The five intruders spread out quickly, peering into faces, speaking only to each other through discreet mouth- and earpieces.

A man in a peach-colored shirt approached Trina, a long-haired girl in low-slung yoga pants who was propped against a bookcase, madly texting. She flicked him a look, used to blowing off leering, age-inappropriate men, and said, "What?"

The man studied her face with no subtlety whatsoever, and the silence and dark glasses struck her as rude.

"Seriously," she said, still texting. "Stop it."

He nodded and walked away.

Rory Ames was on duty at the front desk and talking to another kid when he noticed the stranger in Trina's airspace and the other strangers sifting through the room like vultures. He switched on his headlamp, because he sensed something bad was about to happen, and he thought he should do something, even if it was stupid. He grabbed the house cell phone and pressed Twist's number on the speed dial.

A man with cropped blond hair and a lavender shirt—Thorne—locked in on Rory and snapped, "Hang up."

Rory held the ringing phone away from his multipierced ear. "And you are?"

The man shook his head to that. "Where's the dog?"

Rory mulled over the question for a moment, but came up baffled. "The dog? You guys lost a dog?"

"The dog and the girl," the man pinged back. "We know they're here. Which room?"

The dog and the girl . . . Shay and the big gray mutt? Rory had only seen the animal in passing once or twice, but had heard how Shay had rescued it from somewhere, and that it was now living in Shay and Emily's room.

"No dogs allowed here," he said. He started to back away from the desk and heard Twist's voice through the receiver, annoyed enough for both he and the man to hear. "Yeah. What is it? Hello?"

"I'm gonna have to ask the boss," Rory said to the lavender shirt, and then to Twist: "Yeah, Twist, man, there's some guys here, they're—"

Thorne, fast as light, ripped the phone from Rory's grip as the kid screamed, "We're being hit, we're being hit," a line he got from an old movie.

Twist had his face in a mist of sawdust. He'd painted a four-by-eight street scene on a sheet of plywood to be hung outside a school, but the painting wasn't working, and a painting that didn't work never left the studio in one piece. He was using a table saw to cut it to scrap.

He was thinking about nothing at all, except keeping his fingers out of the spinning blade, when Rory called. The phone was on the table's edge, beside his hat. He couldn't hear the ringer over the whir, but the white rectangle lit up and LOBBY flashed on the screen.

The list of people who had Twist's number wasn't long, and the number of calls he actually answered was next to none, but one interruption he never ignored was a call from the kids who worked the front desk. He warned all new desk hires to measure their need to bug him against this simple equation: if the building's on fire and the fire department can't be reached, and you can't put out the fire yourself because the fire extinguisher malfunctions and you're too stupid to find another solution—call. In other words, it'd better be an emergency bordering on cataclysm.

He switched off the saw and picked up the phone: "Yeah. What is it? Hello?"

Thorne stepped between four boys who'd been killing each other on an Xbox but had stood up because of Rory's sudden screeched warning. He turned his face to his mouthpiece, which was attached to his shirt collar: "Let's go up."

At once, the five men cut through the lobby like sharks and assembled at the central staircase to the rooms. The kids in the lobby—most of them—were on their feet now, uncertain, watching. Thorne waved the others up the staircase and had started after them when Rory caught up.

"Stop!" he blurted from two stairs behind, and in reaching for the man's arm, he hooked a slim case dangling off Thorne's right shoulder. Rory felt a barrel through the nylon: rifle? Dangerous waters: he tried to backpedal down the stairs, but the man spun with fury and seized him by the collar. "You little asshole," he said, their faces an inch apart, "I oughta shoot you along with the damn dog."

"Gun!" Rory screamed.

Thorne cuffed him across the face and knocked Rory back down the stairs into the lobby, a gusher of blood spurting from his nose, and threw the phone after him. Rory landed like a rag, limp, as though he were dead. Two of the kids in the lobby started screaming, and the man disappeared up the stairs.

Briana Murphy and Cherise Porter shut the door on their second-floor room and were talking about Cherise's possibly cheating boyfriend as they turned down the burgundy-carpeted stairs and ran into the phalanx of men coming up.

"Shay Remby's room?" asked a man in a yellow golf shirt. The girls traded looks, confused about what they were dealing with, but experienced at stonewalling. They shook their heads.

"The girl with the dog," said the one in the peach shirt, while two other men in pastel colors stepped above and behind them, boxing them in.

They were girls who had grown up on gang blocks and didn't scare easily, who knew their way around a juvenile courthouse and, as the saying went, knew their rights.

"You LAPD?" Cherise asked.

"I don't talk unless I'm Miranda'ed," said Briana.

The man in yellow produced a thin, mean smile, grabbed Cherise by the throat, and lifted her onto her tiptoes one-handed. "Give me the room or I squeeze."

Cherise made a strangling sound as Briana tried to kick him in the leg, but the man easily dodged that, and another man grabbed the second girl by her hair and lifted, then grabbed her upper arm and twisted, and the two girls knew then that these weren't cops. These were something far worse, more like the gangs, but in better shirts.

"Gimme the number or I'll pull your arms out of their sockets," the peach shirt said, his face two inches from Briana's. She squealed with pain, and the man wrenched her arm higher and twisted until she said, "Fifth floor, fifth floor! I don't know the number."

The men let go instantly, the girls no longer relevant to anything, and stormed the stairs.

Rory Ames was a twitchy kid who'd arrived at the hotel seven months earlier with a split lip that had taken stitches to close and a tendency not to look anyone in the eye. He'd gone to work in the kitchen and done well there, always on time, always ready to do the worst stuff. Twist had decided to put him on desk duty, and the routine social contact seemed to raise his confidence.

Now: *We're being hit?*

Trumpet music floated in through the open window: one of the twins was practicing on the fire escape outside their room, a floor below. Sometimes Twist inched out onto his own landing to listen, hating the height but loving the music. When the twins were out there together, really jamming, the steel grille beneath him pulsed with the sound.

Nothing but garbled noise on the phone. Twist said, "Rory? What did you—" and heard an angry male voice shout something about "the damn dog," and then Rory screamed, "Gun!"

Twist dropped the phone and ran to the window and shouted, "Dum! Dee!"

Shay had gotten her laptop but then had dropped onto her bed, thinking about what she'd seen on Odin's thumb drive. One possibility: contact West through the Facebook account he'd given her, BlackWallpaper. Would it be possible to negotiate?

Another question: what was her responsibility to the victims of Singular—people she didn't even know?

On paper, Shay didn't know West from a stranger on the street, and yet, in their first brief, strained encounter in Eugene and in their second harrowing, surreal encounter on the beach, she'd felt, literally felt in her stomach, a vibration between them. Something that didn't feel dangerous, though by Odin's account, West was the enemy. He was Singular.

She thought about the fact that some people—Twist was one—could manipulate you simply because they knew more about how to do that than you knew about how to resist. She didn't think she was so easily manipulated, but then, she'd been pulled into Twist's action over the 110 when she hadn't known him for more than a few minutes.

X was lying on the floor, and she leaned off the bed and ruffled the fur along his spine. He turned his head and his yellow eye fixed on her while the blue one stared off in the opposite direction.

• • •

"Should we call 911?" Trina asked the crowd of teens crouched over Rory. His eyes were closed and someone asked, "Is he dead?" and someone else said, "Who are they?"

Rory blew bloody bubbles through his nose and tried to sit up, and one of the kids helped him as he blew more blood down his shirt. A kid named Jaxon, tall and lean from the street, who'd seen any number of broken and bloody noses, said, "He's okay . . ." and then, "Those guys aren't cops. We gotta take those guys."

As he said it, the two men who'd been stationed out front came up the steps and walked into the lobby, pointedly blocking the doors, and one of the teens on the Xbox, a big kid, took a run at them, and the guy on the left batted him like a fly and sent the big kid crashing into a table.

Jaxon screamed, "Get those guys!"

The kids swarmed the pair, and though they fought like men who'd been trained in hand-to-hand combat, there were twenty-five street kids on them and they went down, and the kids ripped at their hair and faces and bent their arms back and a girl built like an elf ripped a metal lamp off a table and screamed, "Give me room," and smashed one of the men in the head and he groaned facedown in the ragged carpet.

Rory, now thinking more clearly, shouted, "They're here for Shay and the dog—get Twist," and groped for the key latched to his belt. "Get the knives too. They got a gun."

One of the two men the kids had taken down managed to crawl out the door as the kids tore off, and he spoke something into his mouthpiece.

Cruz noticed one of the two men stationed at the rear of the hotel as he unloaded art supplies from Twist's Range Rover. Didn't matter that it was a middle-aged white guy dressed like a banker on vacation—a lookout was a lookout, and this guy's eyes were radar behind his shades, just as obviously as any cholo from East L.A.

Cruz started toward the loading dock with a bolt of canvas under each arm and feigned an interest in the trumpet music coming from above. Looking up, he thought, *Doesn't feel like a cop.* The undercovers he was used to seeing generally tried to dress "street." A spy from the district attorney's office, maybe? He'd alert Twist as soon as he got up to the studio.

All at once, the guy was on the move, and then a second guy— same clothes, same gang—was racing across the back of the hotel from the other side, and the three of them practically smashed into each other at the base of the dock.

"What's up?" Cruz said, but the men pushed past him, up the stairs, and through the fire door into the kitchen. Overhead, he heard Twist shouting.

Twist finally broke through the trumpet noise, calling down to Dee: "Guys with guns, coming through the lobby, looking for Shay and the dog. Don't know if she's in her room, but get down on five, and be careful! Be careful!"

He plunged back through the studio, and Cade, who'd been working at the bank of computers, came running at him.

"She's in her room, Twist—"

Twist was already in the lead, moving as fast as he could, but his bad leg was a drag. "Stay here!" he hollered at Cade's back. "Hold up!"

Cade snagged a pair of scissors off a table and was out the door and down the back stairwell.

• • •

Jaxon inserted Rory's key and yanked the drawer open and the kids piled on the desk, arming themselves with pocketknives, screwdrivers, a fish scaler, an eighteen-inch piece of rebar . . .

The men led by Thorne were mounting the stairs two at a time, headed for five. No sign yet of the girl or the dog.

The two lookouts from the rear of the hotel powered through the lobby, one of them swatting away a couple of boys that came at them with knives, while the other grabbed the man who'd been hit with the lamp and carried him out the door.

Cruz followed the screams to the lobby, and a girl with a screwdriver went running by and said, "They're on five!" and he said, "Who?" and she went up the staircase and called down over the banister, "The guys who want to kill Shay!"

Shay heard what sounded like shouting from the hallway, but it was muffled, and it wasn't the first time she'd heard shouting from the hallway. Then X got to his feet and pointed his nose toward the commotion, like a hunting dog, and bared his teeth.

Shay thought about the muzzle but said, "Hey, pretty boy. Easy, it's okay."

X growled, *Wrong about that.*

Someone banged on the door, which was locked. She got off the bed, and X started with her toward the front room.

"No. You stay," she said, and closed him inside the bedroom. She turned back into the jumbled living area, cut around a rack of clothing, and stumbled on a skateboard. "Just a sec! I'm coming!"

At that moment, the banging stopped and the door exploded off its frame.

Two men were there, and she knew them instantly by type—Singulars. She tried to turn and one man caught her hair, shouting, "Got her, got her. . . ."

The man yanked her close, pulling her head back, and she cried out in pain, but there was no easing up, just more shouting, "Where's the dog, where's the—"

He didn't finish, because he didn't have to: the bedroom door swung open and the dog was right there, airborne for ten or twelve feet, bared teeth leading the way. He leapt right past Shay's shoulder and sank his inch-long fangs in the man's face, and the man howled in agony and went down, and the dog ripped his face and then turned in a whirling motion and went for the second man, clamping first on a metal-and-plastic leg, recognizing it for what it was, and then virtually climbing the man's body to go for his throat. The man hit the dog in the chest and the dog came off for just a second, but then, recovering with phenomenal speed, was back at the man's face.

The man caught the animal by the throat and X twisted to get away, but the man had his collar.

Shay hit him on the back of the head with the only thing she could reach, a blue-and-white china pot, which shattered like an egg, but the man went down and—just for one instant—the dog's yellow eye caught hers, and the dog seemed to be saying, *Thanks for that*.

Then there were more men coming through the door, and the first man, whose face had been ripped open, was back on his feet, thrashing through all of Emily's junk, trying to get at Shay or the dog, and howling like a wounded animal all at the same time.

One of the new men—Thorne—had a gun, but he pointed it at the dog and Shay threw a snow globe at his head and he ducked and came back up with the gun.

Cade took the stairs two and three at a time, plunging down the two flights and around the landings, and burst into the hallway on five to find a dozen hotel kids, both male and female, swarming two men in golf shirts and black gloves and one of the girls was screaming, "The gloves are weighted, they got lead in their knuckles," and one boy was crawling out of the mass of people, blood running from his nose and mouth.

The fight had pushed the two strangers away from Shay's room, and Cade sprinted around all the fighters, getting to the broken-down door and seeing more men inside just as Cruz arrived from the other side, and Cade saw him now and shouted, "Shay's inside!" and Cruz thrust past him and went in first.

And Cruz went down, tripped up by the mass of Emily's junk, and Cade, just behind him, saw a man with one hand on Shay's neck, and on the other side of the room, X in a swirling fight with another man, who was screaming in pain as the dog ripped at his face and arms while Thorne aimed a short rifle at the dog.

Cade jumped over Cruz and came down two feet behind the man wrestling with Shay, and he swung the art scissors at the man's shoulder and felt the blades penetrate and the man screamed and turned, and Thorne turned and the barrel swung toward Cade's head and he tried to duck and the gun went off with a sharp crack and Cade saw something flash past his eye and then Cruz, coming off the floor, put one arm under the gunman's crotch and another at the back of his neck and lifted him clear of the floor and then overhead and smashed him down into a prized Louis Vuitton trunk Emily had collected, and Cade saw another flash and then the man he'd stabbed raised his good arm and backhanded him, and Cade, feeling as though he'd been hit by a dumbbell, went down into the junk.

One of the gloved men at the door pushed through and screamed, "Get out, abort, get out, get out," and Thorne got up off the crushed trunk and looked around for his dropped gun, and Cruz went after him again until the gloved man thumped him once on the back of the head and Cruz went down. Thorne found his weapon and the two men pushed back through the broken door, where more kids were flooding the floor.

All of that in twenty seconds.

The three men from the room joined the two in the hall, all of them bloodied, one man's face terribly ripped by the dog, another bleeding from Cade's stab wound, his arm useless, and together they fought their way to the main stairs and then down the stairs, the kids pushing behind them. In the confined area of the stairs, the kids, who'd been winning the fight through sheer numbers, couldn't compete with the weighted gloves and the attackers' training, and the five men pushed around and down and around and down and into the lobby.

And then Dee and Twist came down the back stairs, too late for the fight on five, and Dee, swinging his weighted bat at one of the attackers, connected with the man's forearm but the man took it with no sign of pain and swung back at Dee's face with the same weighted hand, and Dee went down.

Twist came in with his cane but the men lurched away toward the door, with the kids running at them, slashing with knives and rebar and pieces of furniture, and another kid went down, and Twist, realizing that the men were trying to get out of the building and that they were empty-handed, began shouting, "Let them go, let them go, let them go. . . ."

From the doorway, a huddle of kids watched as the injured men were loaded into the four SUVs, and meanwhile, from across the street, the homeless man in the cowboy boots jogged over, beeped a remote key at the white van with the empty cage, and climbed behind the wheel.

And the motorcade, led by the van, sped away.

The dog stood over Shay, guarding her against any more violence. Cade and Cruz were on either side of Emily's crushed trunk, struggling to get upright.

Cruz got to Shay first and asked, "Are you all right?"

She was on her back, her eyes open and her lids fluttering, and the dog whimpered next to Cruz's face and Cruz said, "She's all right, X, she's tough," and Cruz cupped a bloody hand to her cheek and said it again in a voice that caught with emotion, "She's tough."

Shay touched the top of her head. "I think he ripped my scalp off."

At the sound of her voice, the dog nosed Cruz out of the way.

"X," she cried, and pulled the dog into her chest. "I saw you open the door! Cruz—he opened the door with his paws to come help me, I saw him."

Cruz leaned back in and said, "Taught yourself a trick, huh? I knew you were smart."

X licked Shay's face, and she saw that he was injured, too. The dewclaw on his right forepaw had been snapped off, leaving a bloody divot.

Cade, his cheekbone bleeding, came around her other side and repeated the question, "Are you all right?"

"Cade, your cheek—"

"It's not too bad," he said, and to Cruz, "You okay?"

"I hurt," Cruz said, pressing a hand to his rib cage. "Those guys, the guy I hit, his arm felt like metal . . . like he was a robot."

Shay sat up at that, with Cade and Cruz each taking an elbow. Her mind swirled with thoughts of West and his metal legs, and of Cherry and his unusual strength.

"Gotta stop the blood," Cruz said as he examined X's inside ankle where the claw had been. He looked around, picked up a sock, and pressed it to the wound. "A couple minutes of pressure, I think we'll be okay."

"At least he didn't get stuck with this," said Cade, and held out what looked like a hypodermic needle with a yellow tail.

"What is it?" Shay asked.

"Tranquilizer dart. Should be at least one more around here somewhere, 'cause the guy with the gun got off two that I saw. Which means, whoever they were, they wanted X, and they weren't expecting him to go willingly."

Shay said, "It was them—the guys who took Odin. The same guys, they're these . . ." She got to her feet, shaking with the realization. The dog nosed at her leg and she stroked his forehead and said, "I won't let them take you."

"Who?" said Cruz. "You know those guys?"

In the hallway, people were crying and shouting for help.

"We better get downstairs," Cade said. "People are hurt. Some of them are hurt bad."

21

Harmon usually took care to be casual with Sync; it was a way to demonstrate their equality, or at least a sign of camaraderie. Not this time. He was squatting in a hospital emergency room in the stink of disinfectant and blood, on the phone with his boss, still angry about what had happened at the hotel.

Angry with himself, and with Thorne.

"Our fault," he said. He didn't excuse mistakes made by others, or by himself. "We saw kids, we just didn't see what *kind* of kids. It was a complete hornet's nest: going in there was like going into an al-Qaeda hotel. They had knives, scissors, and clubs, and there were twenty or thirty of them, and they knew how to use that stuff. Vance was stabbed twice in the back, in the kidneys, we'll be lucky if he's working in a month. Dennit's face is pudding from that damn robo-dog, they're calling in a plastic surgeon. Kyle has a concussion and a bad stab wound in the shoulder, and Carter has a broken arm, Thorne sprained a knee. Christ, they're all cut up, stabbed, slashed. . . . We're lucky nobody was killed. We won't be going back in there, not without armor and a lot more men."

Harmon had been at the hospital for two hours seeing that the entry team was properly cared for; six of them had injuries that needed urgent medical attention.

"Forget the hotel," Sync said. "We won't be going back there—we'd have to hurt somebody too bad. Do you know if they're talking to the police?"

"Apparently not. This artist, Twist, takes kids off the street. A lot of them, probably most of them, have criminal backgrounds. They stay away from the cops."

"That's one for us," Sync said. "What about the artist? He there?"

"Missed the main event. Thorne saw him on the staircase when they were backing out. Guy's on a cane, a gimp—"

"So we made a mistake," Sync broke in. He picked up a yellow pencil and rolled it between his palms. "Maybe we'll have another shot at the dog on the street."

"There's a problem there. The professors said the dog should be dead by now, or so weak it couldn't walk. That dog was like a hurricane, from what the entry team tells me. When Dennit did the brush-by yesterday, he said the dog looked sharp. So it's been recharged—the girl must have figured it out. Trying to take it on the street might be like trying to capture a leopard."

A nurse came out from behind a curtained bed, glanced at Harmon, saw that he wasn't one of the injured, and jogged away.

"Dammit, the problem is spreading out on us," Sync said. "It's like an oil slick—if you don't get on top of it immediately, you wind up all over TV and people are calling you criminals."

"What about her brother? What are we doing?"

were there in golf shirts and khaki slacks and hoods with nothing but eyeholes so he couldn't see their faces. They picked him up, pulled the hood back over his face, walked him to another room, and sat him in a chair.

The man who'd called him a "little shit"—Odin thought he was the same one, from his voice—said, "Okay, we're going to ask you a question. If you answer it correctly, we won't hurt you. If you don't answer it correctly, we will hurt you. Do you understand?"

Odin said nothing.

"The question is this: Where is Storm? Where are they now?"

Odin thought, *They would have moved by now. They would have moved as soon as they realized he'd been picked up.* He said haltingly, "We're camping at a state park by San Diego."

The man said, "Good. What state park?"

"I think it was Palomar Mountain."

"You think?"

"It was Palomar something. I think Palomar Mountain."

"How long had you been there?"

"A week, about, we move around. We were down in Baja on the beach before we came back north. . . ."

"The woman who was with you at the whale beach. What is her name?"

Rachel. They'd seen her, but they don't know her name. Odin said, "Gretchen. Park. Gretchen Park. She's my—"

WHAM! He thought he'd been struck by lightning, and the pain was unbelievable, flashing through the base of his neck and radiating through his body. His body spasmed so hard that he almost tipped the chair over.

The man's mouth seemed to be only an inch from Odin's right

ear when he said, "How did you like that, you little shit? You know what that was? That was the same kind of gun that you zapped the guard with up in Eugene. How'd you like it? Now: we know what her name is. We want you to say it."

Odin took the risk:

"Really, her name is—"

WHAM!

Sync watched through the observation window; one of Thorne's men stood next to him. The interrogator hit Odin with the Taser, then hit him again.

Sync said, "I was wrong. He is a tough little rat."

"We've got to find a different wedge," the man beside him said. "He doesn't have normal reactions. . . . Let's go back to the water. We know the water scares him . . ."

"But the other day . . ."

"Slightly different technique."

They watched as the interrogator waterboarded Odin again, and then again, but this time using a lot less water. "This way," Thorne's man said, "you get most of the sensation of drowning, but not the reality of it. He could breathe in a little water, but not much, and then we empty him out and start over."

And that's what they did. They knew his girlfriend's name was Rachel, but he never gave it up. He insisted, crying, weeping, that it was Gretchen. At one point, Sync called the interrogator out of the room and they conferred about the name. "He may be unable to give it up. Or maybe she's using a fake name with him, and he really does think it's Gretchen," the interrogator said. "He's getting weak. I want to move to the thumb drives."

"I hate to go there without breaking him first," Sync said. "Because I think he knows the girl's first name. But try it: ask him about the drives."

That question finally seemed to open the boy up.

"I've been trying to crack them," Odin said. He was weeping, and his body shook with fear and cold and despair. "I can't. I just can't. They're encrypted. I can see all the garbage, but I can't break it. I don't even know why you want them—"

"Where are the drives?"

"Gretchen has them. And Ethan." Odin had thought about it: he'd give up one name that was correct. That might convince them he was telling the truth about the other things. Besides, he thought Ethan was a jerk.

"What do you think?" Sync asked.

"I don't know," the other man said. "I think he was lying about some of it, but the drives are encrypted, just like he said."

"Double encrypted, actually." Sync rubbed his lower lip with his index finger, then nodded and rapped on the glass of the observation window. The interrogator came out and Sync said, "Put him back in the room. Give him food and water, put in a cot and a blanket. We'll let him think about it for a while longer. Oh—and hit him one more time with the Taser. We want him to think about that too."

22

It never felt like a victory.

At the Twist Hotel, the aftermath of the raid was confusion, anger, and pain: five boys and one girl had to be taken to the hospital, three for broken bones, two with concussions, the girl for stitches to her lower lip. Dee's nose was practically rammed inside his head. Despite the chaos in the building, no police ever showed up—nobody called them.

Twist rang the fire bell four times, which meant there was a mandatory meeting in the lobby, and when all the kids had jammed into it, he stood on the check-in desk and gave a speech.

"One of our residents was the target of this attack. We don't know exactly why, but we've got some ideas. We don't want to talk to the cops, because . . . well, you know why. There are quite a few of us who *can't* talk to the cops, and we don't want them sticking their noses in here. Even though we don't know *exactly* why we were attacked, we know *who* they are—a big, greedy corporation run by a bunch of assholes. We'll take care of this problem ourselves, like we always have. But I'll tell you this, you fought like warriors for each other. Those guys marched in here like a bunch of fascist thugs and they left like a bunch of frightened chickens. You guys did that. I can't tell you how proud I am."

And, at the end: "Hey, knives back in the drawer. And before we do that—Rory. Let's have a round of applause for Rory, who held it together for us."

Twist pulled Rory up onto the desk, and he got a roaring round of applause, something that had never happened before in his life; he was embarrassed, but not unhappy, and the guys in the crowd were slapping him on the back, and the girls were giving him hugs.

Shay, X, Cade, Cruz, and Emily—Emily had been delivering a dresser when the attack occurred—were standing together listening, and when Twist jumped down off the desk, cane first, he walked over to them and said, "Up in the studio."

They all rode up in the elevator, not speaking, but when they got to the studio, Twist turned to Shay, someone's blood on his brow, and said, "These people deserve to know everything—the dog, your brother, the videos."

They all looked at her, even X. She looked back and thought, *I've only known them for a few days, but they're the best friends I've ever had.*

"All right," she said.

She told them the whole story, starting with the attack on the lab in Eugene, about meeting West and Cherry, her search for her brother and finding him at the beach, where she'd gotten the dog and the stolen thumb drives, about seeing Odin getting shoved into a van, about the X-ray that showed the dog's wired brain and hind legs, about just hours earlier unlocking the disturbing videos made by the mysterious Singular Corporation, and:

"What happened here—the attackers had to be Singular. I'm so sorry about everything. X and I will go."

"Go where? Don't make me tired," Twist said.

"If I stay, I'd be putting everyone in jeopardy—"

"No one runs anyone out of my hotel, except me," Twist said, and thumped his chest. "Get over that right now. You got it?"

Shay had forgotten what not being abandoned by an adult felt like. She caught Emily's thumbs-up, and the nods from Cruz and Cade, and the cocked ears of her dog, and said, "Yes. Thank you."

"Good," said Twist, running his hands through his disheveled pompadour. "Now show them the videos."

Shay reentered the poetry password, went to Folder 7, and opened File 12. Twist pulled a chair up to the computer table and sat down beside Shay while the other three teens hunched around the screen.

"When you understand the accent," Shay said, "I'll start it over."

Emily understood right away, the other two in a minute. Shay started the video again, and they all watched the long recitation in silence. When the man finished and the video froze, Twist inhaled deeply and asked Emily, Cade, and Cruz, "What do you think?"

"I'm afraid to say," Emily said. "You'll think I'm crazy."

"Then I'll tell you what I think," Cade said. "I don't think those were his memories. I think those memories had been transferred to him. In those clothes, he looks like a prisoner who was being used in an experiment. I don't know what country. You saw that man in the background? He was wearing a uniform. We might be able to look it up."

He stopped talking and Shay asked, "Do you think it might be faked for some reason? The whole video?"

"It didn't look faked to me. It had a kind of laboratory realness to it," Cade said.

Twist nodded. "I'd already seen it, and I couldn't forget it. I kept coming back to that uniform—if it was a fake, something somebody put together for the hell of it or as a joke, they wouldn't have a guy in a strange uniform get caught at random moments. . . . That's just too real."

"Okay," Shay said. "Here's another."

She showed them the video with the shaking man and said, "Listen to the . . . whatever he is. The lab guy. The scientist."

When it was done, they all looked at each other, and Cruz said, "They're killing people. They're using them like lab animals."

Again, they all looked at each other, and they all nodded.

"Tell me more about this West guy," Twist said. "You said you had a way to contact him. Do you think you could negotiate for your brother? To get him back?"

"I don't know," Shay said. "West doesn't seem like a bad guy—but how can I be sure?"

"One problem with getting Odin back," Cade said. He turned to Shay. "I don't want to bum anybody out, but as the Nazis would say, 'He knows too much.' They might have . . . killed him."

"I don't want to hear that," Shay snapped. "I won't stop looking for him. If I've got to burn Singular down, I'll find a way to do it."

Twist: "Whoa, whoa, whoa . . ."

Shay crossed her arms, and didn't take it back.

Cade said: "Something else. Maybe we should give these videos to the FBI or somebody—we could do it anonymously, maybe. But if we do, and the FBI starts investigating Singular, then they might try to get rid of the evidence. Like . . . Odin."

"You seem pretty anxious to kill off my brother," Shay said with a cold streak in her voice.

Cade came back with an equally cold tone: "Listen. I'm just laying out the logic. I don't want anybody to be dead, but if we're going to do anything, we need to think through it, and figure out what the consequences will be. If we try to sic the cops on Singular, one consequence might be that they get rid of the evidence before we can prove anything."

Twist nodded and said to Shay, "Listen to him—because he's right."

Shay touched Cade's arm, a small apology, and said, "Then we find a way to negotiate. We get Odin back, *then* we burn the place down."

Twist rubbed his chin. "I think we need to open a line of communication. You said you had a way to contact West—a secure way?"

"That's right . . . or at least that's what West said."

"So you tell West, 'I got the thumb drives, I don't know what's on them, but free Odin and you can have them back.' "

"You saw what was on the drive," Cade protested. "We're just going to let that go?"

Twist turned to Cade with mock weariness. "If Odin could copy the drives, I'd assume that my computer staff could figure a way to do the same thing."

Cruz was checking X's dewclaw. The dog had been tracking blood, but the bleeding had now stopped. He gave X a forehead scratch. He asked Twist, "You mean double-cross them?"

"That's what I mean," Twist said.

"I hate always being the practical one," Emily said. "How about not double-crossing them? How about if we call them up, say, 'Give us Odin and we'll give you the drives and you'll never hear from us again, as long as you don't mess with us anymore'?"

"And pretend we didn't see what we just saw?" asked Cade.

"Do you read the headlines?" Emily persisted. "Right now, right this second, somewhere in the world, a hundred women are being raped, a hundred children are being abused or are starving to death, a hundred men are being murdered, and maybe, maybe, it's a lot more than that. Just this second. We can't do anything about it. Nothing. There's nothing we can do, because that's just the way the world is right now. This is just another example. We could walk away, and get on with our lives."

After a moment of silence, Twist asked, "If you could make a difference, don't you think you should?"

"I don't know," Emily said. "I don't have enough information. One thing I do know, for sure, is that Shay is a friend, and her brother is in big trouble, and we might be able to get him back. That's what we should do. Get him back, worry later about saving the world."

Cruz said, "I don't know about saving the world, either, but I do know that Singular came into our house and attacked our friends, and hurt them, and they need to pay."

"I think some of them might have been soldiers, the way they were organized," said Cade. "At military school, we had these former army guys around for training. They looked like those guys— the guys who taught guns and bayonets."

Twist was up and pacing. "All right. Try this. I don't want to risk the hotel, so I think we should move out, at least for a while. Shay could open a link to this West guy, and talk to his bosses. First off, tell them that we're out of the hotel, that nobody in the hotel knows where we are."

"I could do that," Shay said.

"Then we see if we can get a trade. If we can get a trade, we do that—and then we talk about it. Maybe we double-cross them. Maybe we think hard about what Emily has said."

Cade: "When you say, 'We're out of the hotel,' who's *we*?"

"You, me, Shay, and X. Emily and Cruz stay here, and they're our contacts here in the hotel. They both have access to vehicles—Cruz, you've been talking about getting a decent used truck. I'll give you some cash tonight. If we need to be moved around, or to have food brought in, you handle that. Shay, X, Cade, and I are going to hide out until we see if we can pull off the trade. If they need persuading, I've got an idea for a Hollywood stunt that'll whack them upside their heads."

"You might need a fighter," Cruz protested. "I should go with you. If those guys come after Shay again, and the dog—"

"We might need a fighter here," Twist said. "We will definitely need somebody to go back and forth between the hotel and hideout."

"Where are you going to go?" Cruz asked.

"I gotta make a call," Twist said. "If the place I'm thinking of is workable, we won't be uncomfortable."

They all looked at each other and finally Emily said, "It's a plan. Those guys . . . I have a bad feeling that a bunch of street kids won't be able to take them a second time."

"Not without somebody else on our side, like the FBI," Twist said. "Those are the kinds of options we have to explore. We have to be old grown-ups now. Talk to the right people—if there are any right people."

"What if there aren't?" Shay asked.

"Well . . . then, I guess, the five of us—excuse me, hound, the six of us—take on the world."

23

Shay had almost nothing, so packing took ten minutes. She got it all in her backpack and in a canvas tote bag that Emily gave her for X's food, and she rode the elevator with X and Emily back up to the studio.

Twist already had a bag of clothing ready to go, and he was jamming art supplies into a valise. Cade's computer was gone, along with all the attached equipment.

Twist: "You ready?"

Shay nodded.

"Back in a second. . . ." Twist disappeared into his room and returned a moment later and handed her a wad of cash. "Two thousand," he said. "That's the first of the payments due on the posters. I owe you another eight thousand or so, but you'll have to wait."

"I can wait," she said. "This is the most money I've ever touched at one time."

"You may need it. Everybody needs to carry cash. Until this gets straightened out, credit cards are forbidden."

"I've never had a credit card," Shay said.

"Good. Also, shut down your cell phone. I'll ask Cade, but we might need to pull the batteries out of them too."

Shay peeled off several hundred dollars and handed it to Emily. "Gets us square for all the clothes and the damaged stuff in your room."

Emily put up her hands, refusing the money. "You might need it, and I'm okay. You're still my roommate."

Cade came in, carrying a green army-style duffel bag and a big computer briefcase. "I'm all set."

Twist asked him about the cell phones, and Cade agreed that they should pull the batteries. "When we need to use them, we'll move away from wherever we're staying, put the batteries back in, talk, and then pull the batteries again."

"Sounds inconvenient," Emily said.

"We'll get prepaid phones, like the dope dealers use," Twist said. "We'll use those to stay in touch with people we trust. Not smartphones—just phones we can talk with, without any GPS features."

"Maybe a couple of phones apiece," Cade said.

"Good thought," Twist said.

Shay asked, "Where are we going?"

"Show you when we get there," Twist said. He looked at his watch: 10:00 p.m., and they still had a couple of stops to make. "Let's go. Cruz is waiting."

"I'll meet you. I gotta stop in the lobby," Shay said.

Twist: "What for?"

Shay: "My knife."

• • •

They loaded everything into the back of Twist's Range Rover, and then Twist spent a few minutes talking with Lou and Catherine about the hotel. He told them to call 911 if the hotel came under attack again. "Tell the kids if those thugs come back, to run for it. Just get out. If they come back, they'll be ready for anything we could fight them with." He told them to leave the knife drawer locked.

Emily pulled Shay into an embrace. "You'll be back," she said with all the confidence she could muster. "Your brother can live here too."

Shay nodded, then suddenly thought of something. "What time is it?" she asked.

Emily checked her watch. "Almost ten-thirty. Why?"

"Because in ninety minutes my big brother turns eighteen."

Cruz drove, with Twist in the passenger seat, Cade, X, and Shay in the second row.

"First stop is the Avenues," Twist said.

"I don't know what that is," Shay said.

Cruz looked at her in the rearview mirror. "It's where I grew up. I called a couple of friends. They're going to make sure nobody is following us. I mean, maybe they could follow us in a helicopter, but they won't be behind us on the street. Or ahead of us."

"Helicopter isn't likely. Maybe a bug on the car," Cade said.

"I got that covered," Cruz said.

The Avenues was an area northeast of the Los Angeles downtown. Shay couldn't see much of it because of the dark; she knew they were on the 110, because they drove past the building she'd swung down. Five minutes north of downtown, they got off the freeway and headed into a neighborhood of small houses and lots of chain-link fences.

Cruz knew where he was going, and after taking a half-dozen turns, he pulled into a driveway and then under a carport. Cruz said to Twist, "Fifty bucks."

Twist dug the money out and gave it to him, and Cruz said, "Just hang here," and he got out of the truck as another man came out of a one-story house with bars on every window and door. Cruz and the man hugged, and then the man got something that looked like a broomstick with a long electrical wire trailing out the back, plugged it in, and began crawling around the truck.

Three minutes later, he was back on his feet. He and Cruz spoke for another minute, then Cruz handed him the cash and waved at Twist, telling him to get out of the truck.

Twist got out, spoke to Cruz and the other man briefly, then climbed into the driver's seat and said, "No bugs."

"Who was that guy?" Cade asked.

"Cruz says he's the neighborhood cleaner. Sometimes the cops put trackers on people's cars," Twist said, and backed out of the driveway. "He has a little business, spotting them and taking them off."

"Cruz . . . ," Shay said. He was standing in the headlights, watching them go. Their eyes hooked up, and she felt her heart lurch.

"He'll get a ride back to the hotel," Twist said. "Tomorrow he's going to buy a truck, so we'll have a backup, if we need it."

"Where are we going now?" Shay asked.

"A twenty-four-hour Walmart to buy telephones," Twist said. "There's one on the other side of I-10. And then, Malibu, here we come."

"Malibu?" She'd heard of it. Everybody had. "Isn't that for movie stars?"

"Exactly," Twist said.

The Walmart was a twenty-minute stop. Then they rolled across the city on a welter of surface streets and freeways, and finally down a long slope to the Pacific Coast Highway.

Shay hadn't been to the L.A. waterfront—the whales had come ashore farther north—and she hadn't known what to expect. What she hadn't expected was that the famed, star-studded beach town of Malibu, at least after dark, would look like a bunch of elbow-to-elbow shacks with garage doors inches from the highway.

Twist said he'd been to the house they would be staying at a few times, but a lot of the places looked the same. He used one of the new phones to call ahead, and when he got to about the right place, he slowed down, looking for an open garage door and a mailbox shaped like a porpoise.

"There," Cade said, pointing.

"That's it," Twist said. He signaled the turn, then cut across oncoming traffic and into the lighted garage. A man was standing on a set of steps at the back of the garage, and as soon as they were in, the garage door came down. They got out next to a black sports car—Shay didn't recognize the model, but it looked exotic and expensive—and a customized candy-apple-red Ducati motorcycle that Cade did recognize: "Sweet. A Monster 1200."

The man stepped up to them with a snarly grin.

"On the run, eh?" he said with a hint of an Irish accent, and bumped fists with Twist.

"Sean. Thank you."

"Come on in, I'll show you how to operate the place." He looked at X. "Nice dog."

X growled at him, and Shay said, "Easy."

The house had a glass-walled living room overlooking the ocean, with a museum-quality Twist cityscape on one wall. A galley kitchen was on the street-side wall, along with a library filled with art books and a glass case protecting a collection of old Zippo cigarette lighters, most of them with military insignias. There were three bedrooms on a second floor and a circular staircase that went to the roof, where there was a deck with folded beach umbrellas.

Sean took them through it with the unthinking nonchalance of a man who'd been rich for a while. He was of average height or a little shorter than that, and handsome: a movie star, in fact, with blond hair combed straight back, blue eyes, a square chin, too-perfect teeth. Shay recognized him from movies she'd seen on TV—real, theater-style movies, not TV movies—in which Sean usually played a bad guy, or the lead star's sidekick. He got killed a lot.

He and Twist spent a minute or so catching up as they walked through the house. To Shay, Sean said, "I know you. You're the girl who came down the building." He took her hand, and turning to Twist, he said, "That *was* you."

"Yeah, that was us," Twist said.

Sean nodded at Shay, impressed. "That also makes you the masked girl in the artsy-fartsy poster too, huh?"

Shay felt herself flush at the attention: he was *so* good-looking. At the same time, it made her angry. She said to Twist, "I guess we know why they hit the hotel—my picture is everywhere, and everyone knows you did it."

Twist grimaced. "Yeah . . . yeah."

Sean got serious: "This is real trouble?"

"We haven't done anything—but we've got a bad-ass corporation after us," Twist said. "We're gonna talk to the feds and so on, but for the time being, we need to lie low."

Sean nodded. "Not that you should trust the feds any farther than you could spit a rat."

"There's that," Twist said.

"Well, you know what I think," Sean said. He gestured toward the front room. "Stay as long as you want. . . . Well, stay as long as you want until December, anyway. My mother will be here from December through March."

He and Twist talked for a few minutes about the art world, and about film, and then Sean looked at his watch and said, "I've got to get out to Burbank. So you're good?"

"We're good," Twist said. "Thanks again."

When he was gone, Shay asked Twist, "How do you know him? How'd you get to be friends?"

"Art world stuff," Twist said. They were in the library, and Twist was looking at the cigarette lighters. "We connected over politics, this and that."

"He's shorter than he looks in the movies," Cade said. "He's Irish, huh? How'd he get here?"

"Not Irish. Not Sean. His real name is Bill. Not William—just Bill. He sounds Irish. He picked up the accent in acting school and decided it was his thing. He's Culver City High, Pasadena

Community College. Like that. He's a pretty good actor. And he has a good eye for art."

"I'll tell you what," Cade said, looking out a bay window at the ocean. "This is my idea of a hideout. If we could get some pizza in here . . ."

Twist walked into the compact kitchen, opened the freezer door on the refrigerator, and looked inside. "You want pepperoni? Or you wanna go vegetarian?"

They went for the pepperoni, and while it cooked, they probed the house, X staying beside Shay. There was an ocean-facing bedroom with a private bath for each of them, crisp white sheets that a housekeeper normally laundered—Twist told Sean he'd pay her normal salary for her to stay away—and French doors that opened onto balconies with eight-million-dollar views.

Shay dumped her backpack on the four-poster bed in the middle room and was drawn immediately to the balcony by the crashing waves. They were invisible in the dark, but the noise of them came at her like rolling thunder.

Leaning against the teak railing, she closed her eyes and let the roar and reverse take the edge off her worry. When she opened them again, she saw X sitting with his nose through the railing and his eyes closed, as hers had been, sucking in the new odors of the seascape. The spell was broken when Cade yelled, "Pizza!"

She headed back downstairs to the kitchen, X at her heels. Twist was pulling three bottles of Pepsi out of the refrigerator, and Cade was setting up his laptop on a small drop-down desk.

"Are we safe to use it here?" Shay asked over Cade's shoulder.

"For general browsing, yes, but I wouldn't make contact with anyone on email or Facebook. We should use open systems, up in the city, for that. We've got to be careful."

"We've got to be crazy paranoid," Twist said. "Let's go to higher ground and discuss."

Cade lowered his voice. "You think this place is bugged?"

Twist cracked a smile. "No, dummy. I want to eat my supper under the stars. C'mon."

They went out a side door on the second floor and climbed the circular staircase to the rooftop patio. From three pillowy loungers they dragged to the patio's front edge, they could see ships' lights out on the water, headed into the Port of Long Beach, and a constant string of passenger jets taking off and landing at Los Angeles International.

The shoreline ran directly east and west from where they were, then curled around to the bluffs of Santa Monica and the carnival rides on the Santa Monica Pier. They passed on lighting the patio's tiki candles, preferring to look up at the clear night sky and stars that seemed much closer and sharper than they ever had in Hollywood.

Shay picked the pepperoni off her pizza, fed it to X, and asked, "What do we do first?"

Twist said, "Two things. In the morning, I'm going to contact a friend in the LAPD, a very discreet friend. I'll tell her a bit about the attack on the hotel, see what she can find out about Singular that Cade hasn't been able to find on the Web. Also ask her to find out what police in Eugene know about the raid, about the kids on the run, whether they know any names. Then we'll know if the cops are really looking for Odin.

"Meanwhile, Shay, you reach out to West. Tell him we're out of the hotel, we've got a new hiding place—the dog too—so there's no point in sending the goon squad back in."

"We can't send it from here," Cade said. "We go up the coast, or maybe south somewhere. . . ."

"Orange County," Twist said. "You could get online at South Coast Plaza."

Cade said, "Yeah, that'd be good."

Twist said to Shay, "That's a ginormous shopping mall down there. Tens of thousands of people going through every day. Even if they knew you were there, they couldn't find you."

"Fine, wherever," Shay said. "I need to talk to West as soon as I can."

"Hand me another slice," Twist said to Cade. When he got it, he said, "I think we tell them almost the truth. That your brother cracked the files. We don't say 'one file,' or that we can't crack the others. If they give us your brother back, we give them the drives, wash our hands, and walk away. Tell them that we're not interested in their lab, even if Odin is—and we've got the files, not Odin."

Cade said, "We should give them a deadline for producing Odin. Tell them that if he doesn't show up, we post the files on the Web one by one."

"We'll need to specify a way for Odin to get in touch with us," Shay said.

Twist said, "Here's what I learned from watching movies. The big problem is the swap—the money for the kidnap victim, the drives for Odin, or whatever. We show up in some dark place, and they just grab us."

"I must have watched better movies," Shay said. "We say we want to see him on the steps of the federal courthouse, by himself, taking a picture of himself with his own cell phone, so we know he's free. If that doesn't happen, we'll assume he's still being held captive."

"Still not a hundred percent," Cade said. "Somebody could be across the street with a rifle. . . ."

"That's a fantasy," Twist said. "They're not going to shoot him down in the middle of L.A."

"And I think it should all be on me," Shay said. "I think the message should say 'I will do this' and 'I will do that.' To make it look like I'm strictly on my own again."

Cade and Twist both thought for a moment, then they simultaneously nodded. "That's probably the best way to go," Twist said.

"You tell them that you're not in the hotel, and not going back until this is all over with—gotta remember that," Cade said.

They wound up writing a script for it. When they were satisfied, Twist asked Shay, "You're really good in math, right?"

"Yes."

"All kinds of math?"

"All kinds of math at my level—not all kinds of math," she said.

"What about probability?"

"Probability is not so hard. I know probability," Shay said.

"What are the chances they'll buy all this?" Twist asked.

"Twist, that's not how . . ." She was going to say that's not how probability works—you need at least a few numbers, you need an understanding of the situation, which they didn't have. She trailed off, and looked up at the stars, and nobody said anything for a moment, and then she said, "Not fifty-fifty. They might be *scared* to give him up. They've done so many crimes."

Twist nodded as he stood up, stretched, leaned on his cane. "It's nearly two. We need to get some sleep."

"Wait a sec," Cade said, staring out over the ocean. "I've been thinking—about what they're doing. The name *Singular.* The dog with the implants, the guys with the robot legs. They're trying to get to the *Singularity*—"

Twist: "Where's that?"

"It's not a place, it's an idea about how men and machines are going to merge in the future. There's a lot of geek talk about it," Cade said.

"Of course there is—that's what geeks talk about," Twist said. "That's all Arnold Schwarzenegger makes movies about . . ."

"Shut up, Twist," Shay said. "Cade—tell us."

Cade said, "It's complicated, but one piece of it is that some people, even some scientists, think there'll come a point where you can download people's minds into a computer. Like a huge thumb drive. If you could do that, and if your robotics were really good, you could build an artificial man with the brain of a real, living person. That means . . . well, you could replicate the brain whenever you needed to. And that means you could live forever."

Twist: "Really?"

"No reason you couldn't live forever, if you had the technology," Cade said. "I think these guys are not only researching the Singularity, I think they're trying to get there. They'll have to figure out how to splice brains to storage units to do that. I bet they'd kill a lot of brains doing the research."

"Jesus." Twist dropped back into his chair. It was a whacked-out theory, but it fit the evidence they had so far. . . .

They sat in silence for a few moments while, down below, an occasional walker went by on the beach. One called up to them, "Insomnia bites, huh?" and then ambled on, not needing a response.

Finally Twist said, "Immortality. I'll tell you what, there are lots of people in this world, rich and powerful people, who'd be first in line. Who'd do anything to get there. Billionaires, politicians, generals, cops. We could be in deep trouble, folks. Deep trouble."

Shay: "No one who helped take Odin will live forever. I guarantee you that."

24

Dogfight.

Shay jerked awake before seven and rolled to her feet, shocked out of bed by the barking. She'd left the French doors open overnight, and now found X on the balcony, going bark for bark with a sea lion on the beach below.

"Okay, this is weird," she muttered. Sea air swept in: the smell of salt and seaweed. X looked up at her, as though he expected to be congratulated for defending the balcony. Down below, a shiny black male glared up at them while a harem of tawny females sunned themselves on a rocky outcropping. Marking territory?

X had actually shown restraint, she thought: with his robo-charged hind legs, he might have leapt off the deck and attacked the sea lion, and that wouldn't have ended well. She'd have to keep the doors shut when she slept; she was still learning what it meant to own this dog. . . .

Shay stretched and yawned and X licked her hand. "Play nice," she said. She shut the doors and headed for the shower. She hadn't gotten a lot of sleep, but things were finally moving. She felt alert and anxious to get down to Orange County to contact West.

Into the shower, out of it, dressed in eight minutes. Twist was already downstairs, drinking coffee.

When Shay came in, he said, "Hey" and "I'm talking to Catherine and Lou." He was on one of the clean phones and he pressed the SPEAKER button, and Catherine came up. "Things will be fine until they notice that you're gone. We need to see your face here. Lou and I can do everything, but we need your authority."

"I didn't know I had any authority," Twist said.

"Please—stop with the false modesty. We're sitting on a volcano of street kids, and you're the cork. When will you be back?"

"Tell you what," Twist said. "I'll sneak back when I can to show my face. Any trouble?"

"No. Dum spent the whole night working the streets and the buildings for a mile around, and he couldn't find anything."

"How's Dee?" Shay asked.

"On drugs," Lou said. "He has huge black eyes. His nose is in a splint. They were worried that it would mess up his chops, how his trumpet sounds. But now they think he'll be okay. Won't know for sure until he heals."

"Jeez, I might have wrecked his career," Shay moaned.

Twist shook his head. "Guy's got a nose like Play-Doh. Docs have patty-caked it back into shape before, believe me."

They talked for a couple more minutes about hotel operations and moving money to pay for food. Shay watched Twist, who was clearly glad to be reconnected with the hotel, even if only by phone.

He was wearing a faded Pearl Jam T-shirt, jeans, and his motorcycle boots. When Twist clicked off the phone, she said, "I still feel bad about all the people that got hurt. If it weren't for me and X . . ."

Twist, looking past her, said, "Morning, sunshine."

Cade dragged up to the breakfast counter like a zombie, albeit one with a ripped bare chest, trendy surf shorts, and a rakish case of bed head.

"I don't need this time of day," he said. To Shay: "I heard the dog come down in the night. I gave him some fresh water, but he still won't take treats from anyone except you."

Twist handed Cade a mug and a box of sugar.

"Thanks, man," Cade said, and made himself what looked to Shay like a cup of sugar with a spoonful of coffee. Twist took a set of keys out of his pocket and jingled them at Shay.

"You drive, right?"

Shay nodded. "Yes. My foster parents made us get our licenses the second we turned sixteen. That way, we could take turns driving all night to these climbs they wanted to go to. We'd drive to Idaho and back on the weekend."

"Okay. You'll drive my car to South Coast Plaza, and Cade'll follow behind on Sean's Ducati to make certain no one's tracking you."

"Makes sense." Cade showed no discernible reaction to the part about driving a customized sixty-thousand-dollar motorcycle instead of, say, taking the bus.

"Wait," said Shay with a suspicious squint at Cade. "Are you sure you know how to drive one of those things?"

Twist broke in: "We mentioned that Cade grew up a snotty rich kid, didn't we?"

Cade rolled his eyes.

"More fun facts about young Mr. Holt," said Twist. "Holt Sr.

kept a fleet of Italian cars and bikes that would make a Saudi prince weep."

Cade shrugged.

"I believe you stole your first cycle from the collection when you were thirteen, am I remembering that right?"

Cade said, "Twist, man, it's too early in the morning. . . ."

"You're right, this is serious," Twist said. "You watch her like you've never watched a girl before."

Cade met Shay's eyes. "I'll watch her."

They watched each other. For the next hour, Shay kept checking the rearview mirror and shuddering. Everyone drove too fast, speed limits apparently being optional on California freeways, and over and over, the boy in the tiger-striped helmet would slide through gaps between the speeding cars.

Twice, Shay shouted into the mirror, "Don't do that!" and X, sitting upright in the passenger seat, whirled around, wondering what he'd done wrong. "Not you, boy, sorry," she'd say, and reach over to stroke his neck. Periodically, Cade would roar up beside her, hovering at eighty miles an hour, then peel off and lose himself in another lane.

The Range Rover's GPS got her to the right exit ramp, and from there, Shay hardly needed guidance. She just fell into the parade of vehicles aimed at the area's most luxurious shopping center.

They had a plan for where she should park if Cade wasn't behind her when she arrived, but he was, and so she turned into the first lot and found a space. Cade parked nearby, unstrapped his computer bag from the back of the bike, and walked over. Shay rolled down the window.

"No sign of tails," he said.

"You shouldn't drive so fast."

"Says the girl who jumps off buildings. Moving right along, I got you something. Don't tell Twist," he said, and handed her a turquoise jewelry box with a white silk ribbon from Tiffany & Co.

Shay squinted at him. "Open, please," he said.

She untied the ribbon and lifted off the cover, and smiled curiously as she picked out a laminated card on a loop of chain featuring a shot of X under the heading OFFICIAL GUIDE DOG IN TRAINING FOR THE AMERICAN GUIDE DOG ASSOCIATION.

"What's this for?"

"You wanna take him into the mall, right?"

"So you made him a fake ID?"

"I didn't have time to sew him a fake guide dog vest."

"What a great idea . . . I think."

"Put it around his neck, and let's find out."

But they didn't have to.

There were plenty of open Internet connections outside the shopping center, and so they decided not to press their luck with the dog. Instead, they sat on a bench outside a Barnes & Noble, and Shay sent a query to BlackWallpaper.

You there, BlackWallpaper? The dog and I went into hiding last night, so there's no point going back to the hotel and hurting any more kids.

They watched the screen for a reply, looking away only to politely tell at least a dozen dog lovers that they were sorry, no one could pet the dog when he was "in training."

Ten minutes in, they refreshed the screen, and West was live:

Same name, G+.

They went to Google+, and found another note:

You can't edit Facebook, all you can do is delete big blocks. You can edit this. The company may know BlackWallpaper, so I'll bring them here. Go to GandyDancer on Google+ and we can talk there. As soon as you acknowledge, I'll destroy this message.

"Do you really trust this guy?" Cade asked, watching the screen.

"Enough to talk," Shay said. "Maybe we should move to another location in case he can't be trusted and they've got a way to track us that we don't understand yet."

"Right." They acknowledged West's message with:

OK. Privacy concern on my end, back in ten minutes.

Cade decided they should leave the shopping center entirely, on the ultra-paranoid chance that West had figured out the bookstore's IP address and was sending in a fresh band of thugs. Shay and X got back in the Range Rover and Cade on the Ducati and they picked a coffee shop six blocks farther south.

The Wi-Fi was strong in the parking lot, and Shay opened the computer on the front seat to find West waiting. Cade got in back and followed the conversation over her shoulder. . . .

[WEST] You there? I'm confused. What do you mean—hurt any more kids?

[SHAY] C'mon.

[WEST] I really don't know what you're talking about.

[SHAY] Eight or nine guys with weighted gloves, punching out a bunch of teenagers who have NOTHING to do with any of this, and shooting tranquilizer darts at the dog? Six kids went to the hospital.

[WEST] I swear I didn't know. Are you all right?

[SHAY] Where's Odin?

[WEST] I assumed he was with you or the group he's running with.

[SHAY] How could he be? You guys kidnapped him at the beach.

[WEST] Shay . . . we're not holding your brother against his will.

[SHAY] You guys shoved him into that van.

[WEST] The van was driven by a couple of my colleagues who had to handle things on their own when Cherry and I left—thanks again for pulling the card. Our instructions were to locate Odin Remby and question him about things he stole from us. We hoped to convince him to help us find the senior members of Storm in exchange for legal immunity. Whether that discussion took place in the van for privacy's sake, I can't say, because I was down. If there had been cause to hold him, the police would have been brought in.

[SHAY] Odin would have contacted me by now. To let me know he's all right.

[WEST] That concerns me. But your brother is involved with some very dangerous people.

[SHAY] So are you. You work for a company that tortures people and animals.

[WEST] Shay, we aren't the only medical company that works with animals. Many government-funded labs work with animals. And we don't work with people.

[SHAY] Now you're lying. I'm going.

[WEST] Wait. You've lost me again. You still there?

[SHAY] I'm sending a file.

Shay found a file with a screen grab taken from File 12 and sent it.

They waited a moment, then:

[WEST] A photo of an Asian guy with a bowl on his head? What's the relevance?

[SHAY] Look closer. It's not a bowl, it's some kind of electronic plate, just like with the monkeys at the lab. This is from Dr. Janes's research. A screen grab from a pretty freaky video in Folder 7, File 12.

[WEST] Jesus, Shay, are you saying you have the stolen thumb drives?

[SHAY] Tell your boss I'm putting the video on the Web if my brother doesn't contact me in the next 24 hours. I want Odin to take photos of himself standing on the federal courthouse steps by himself and then call me, to prove to me he's free. If you do this, I will leave the drives for you at a place that's safe for both of us, and I will walk away. You know that I'm not an animal rights radical. I will do this. All I want: Odin for the thumb drives.

[WEST] You need to walk away right now. If you try to smear Singular with whatever it is I've been looking at here, you'll go to jail too. Those thumb drives were stolen in a violent attack on a legitimate laboratory.

[SHAY] Not by me, and I can prove it. Tell your boss that I've seen File 17 too. Disgusting.

[WEST] Don't do anything until I get back to you. I'll talk to the people I work with, see if they have a handle on where your brother and the rest of Storm are right now, find a way to assure you that wherever Odin is, it's not with us.

[SHAY] So you'll give them my message now.

[WEST] Today. Right now. I'm going to edit this message and transfer it to BlackWallpaper. Watch both that site and this one for contacts. Don't tell anyone else about GandyDancer.

[SHAY] The 24-hour clock starts when I say bye.

[WEST] Be careful.

[SHAY] Bye.

25

The Star Hideout Motel was two long blocks from the beach in Oceanside, a tough, sprawling town roughly halfway between the Twist Hotel in Hollywood and the Mexican border.

Oceanside was known for servicing the huge U.S. Marine Corps base at Camp Pendleton. Oceanside motels were not expensive, and the Star Hideout had never been a hideout for stars, though now, unknowingly, it had become the hideout for the four fugitive members of Storm.

The group had moved there after Odin disappeared, afraid that he'd give up their hideout in Hollywood. They'd deliberately chosen it at random—none of them had any connection to the place—and because of the town's easy access to major highways north, south, and east. Their presence would be lost, they hoped, among the hundreds of short-term visitors associated with the marine base.

The Star Hideout was standard old motel: it smelled like

yesterday's French fries and damp carpets. A fat white man who shaved every third day was usually at the front desk reading a newspaper, always in the same slightly yellowed V-necked white T-shirt that showed matted gray chest hair in the V. When he wasn't there, his wife was—a thin, nervous woman with goggle eyes who looked like an ostrich. They lived in the back.

Although the motel was two stories tall, there was no elevator. Instead, there were three sets of stairs—one at each end of the building, and one going up from the lobby. Ethan, James, and Danny shared two interconnected rooms on the first floor. Rachel had taken the smallest room in the motel, a tiny cube at the far north end of the second floor.

At the front of the motel was a circular drive. In the oval formed by the driveway, the owners had planted a jungle of short palms—not because they looked exotic, but because they were low maintenance.

That decision had caused the FBI some difficulties, because they couldn't see into the lobby. They'd seen all four of the Storm members individually, when they went to breakfast, but not all at once, or in the same place.

Storm had been spotted by two of Harmon's agents, who'd finally nailed down a phone call. The Singular people had determined that the Storm members were in two first-floor rooms, but Sync had vetoed a raid. For one thing, half their operators were laid up from the aborted raid at the Twist Hotel. For another, the motel was full of marines, and if trouble started, they might well be on the wrong end of it, or might not be able to get out before the police arrived.

Better to do it straight up, he'd told Harmon. They'd called the FBI, which had a complaint from the U.S. attorney's office in Eugene.

Harmon drove down from Los Angeles to watch the raid. Before he left L.A., he'd gotten together a handful of DARPA thumb drives filled with encrypted but harmless research files.

Neither the Singular operators nor the FBI agents had told the motel owners that a raid might be coming because they might give it away, so the motel owners hadn't told them that the young woman who'd arrived with Storm had taken a different room, a third one.

Harmon was there with his two agents who'd spotted the phone calls. They were all, including the FBI, based across the street at Mary's Marina Motel.

"We won't get anything more," the lead FBI agent told Harmon. The agent's name was Recca. "We could get a warrant for a bug, but that would take time. We can take them right now, based on the Eugene warrant and our visual ID."

Harmon nodded. "It's your call. We're just here to help. From our perspective, the key is getting back those thumb drives—there's a lot of high-cost research in there. Not having access to it would cost us a fortune and a half."

"Okay. I'm sending the team in."

"Take it easy," Harmon said. "Don't get any of your guys hurt."

"We're taking all the precautions—armor, the whole works," Recca said. "We'll go in with a key, so they won't know we're coming until we're on top of them."

Rachel would have been caught if she hadn't gone back to her room. She'd grown increasingly tired of the three men, and increasingly frightened of the people she imagined were pursuing them.

Odin had simply disappeared. He'd been running up the highway behind her at the whale beach, and then . . . he was gone. She hadn't seen where, but he'd never turned up, and his sister had said he'd been kidnapped. Rachel tended to believe that, but wasn't absolutely certain of it. Everything was so confused.

If he'd been taken by Singular, then Singular probably knew everything: their real names, their histories, where and how they hid, phone numbers, where they got their money.

Everything.

Ethan called her paranoid. He'd never liked Odin, though he'd found him useful. He also thought him weak, and thought he'd probably just freaked and run.

The three men—now behaving like the college boys they should have been—had spent the last few days playing video games, watching movies, and, when they were not doing that, arguing about what they should do next.

Since the computer geek's disappearance, the effort to crack the lab files had stopped: they could no more decrypt a file than throw a hundred-mile-an-hour fastball.

They had only one van, and James and Danny thought they should leave for somewhere else entirely—New Orleans had been mentioned. Wait for things to cool off and maybe find another computer guy to work on the thumb drives. Ethan and Rachel wanted to stay in California, or at least the Southwest. Nothing had been de-cided, and now the three men were sprawled on the bed and floor of one of the rooms on the first floor, watching *Iron Man 2,* hooting at the explosions, eating vegan BBQ corn chips, and swilling Red Bull.

Rachel had gotten disgusted and walked out and headed up the stairs to her room. She had just gotten there when she glanced out the window and saw a man across the street in what looked like a fat suit . . . carrying a gun, and wearing a black helmet.

An entry team: she'd seen them on the nightly news, all armored, hitting the houses of dope dealers and terrorists. She had no doubt what was about to happen.

She said, "Oh, shit," and with no thought for the three men—they were done, there was no way out for them—she grabbed her laptop and charging cord, jammed them in her backpack, looked around wildly for anything else she couldn't leave. Odin's pack and laptop. And the hard drive: Odin had taken the hard drive out of Lawrence Janes's office computer and rigged it so he could control it from his own laptop. She picked it up, shoved it in her purse.

That took ten seconds.

At the door, she paused for another second, frightened, but thought that if they were already there, she was done anyway. She opened it, and the hallway was empty. She ran down the back stairs, then peeked around the corner at the front of the motel just in time to see four armored men in dark jackets jogging up the driveway, and more men across the street in dark blue FBI jackets.

Four SWAT men, she thought, *one for each of us.*

The men disappeared into the motel, and then . . . nothing. She heard nothing at all: no screaming, no orders.

She turned and ran to the back of the motel, scrambled over a wooden fence to the property behind it—a Korean barbecue restaurant—and then around the restaurant and across the street, where a bus had just pulled to the curb.

Ten seconds later she was on the bus. She paid and took a seat at the back, rode it for five blocks, trying to think.

Trying to think . . .

She had her money, her fake ID, her iPad and laptop and cell phone, though the phone would have to go. She took it out of her purse, opened the back, and pulled out the battery. She'd throw it in a trash can as soon as she could.

She had no clothes, no makeup, but she could get those at any mall. They'd been living on cash, and she'd carried most of it for the group: she had almost three thousand dollars with her.

She rode the bus for three or four minutes, then realized that she was approaching the Oceanside Transit Center. There, she looked for the first train leaving, she didn't care which. The first one appeared to be a Sprinter. She took a minute to look at the system map, saw that it went to Cal State–San Marcos, and bought a ticket.

If she could make it there . . .

Once on the campus, how would they be able to find a particular girl whose description was "dark hair, wearing a backpack"?

Answer: with great difficulty.

At San Marcos, she thought, she'd have time to figure out her next move.

The first FBI man looked like a tourist, in cargo shorts and a T-shirt and flip-flops. He said, "Hey, there," to the fat man at the desk, and the man nodded, and the FBI agent cheerfully pulled out his ID and explained the situation.

"I had no idea," the fat man said.

The agent got keys to the rooms, checked the hallway for their precise location, then used a walkie-talkie to call in the entry team.

The entry team crossed the street, followed by four FBI agents in black nylon jackets and then the three men from Singular, who stayed well back. Two tourists and their four-year-old kid, who had walked in behind the first man, were told to sit in the lobby until they could be cleared.

Two minutes after the entry team moved into the motel, and one minute after Rachel climbed the fence in back, and five seconds after she got on the bus, the key man slipped the room key into the lock, nodded to the door man, turned the key, and heard it click.

The door man turned the knob and banged the door open, and then they were inside, the four of them all in black with shotguns, right on top of the three men who'd been watching the bang-bang on *Iron Man 2* and suddenly were overwhelmed by the men in armor with guns, for-real guns, who were screaming, "Lay down, lay down. . . . Show me your hands, your hands. . . ."

And Ethan screamed, "No, no, no . . ."

The agents handcuffed them, sat them on the beds, the lead agent, Recca, shouting, "Where's Rachel, where's Rachel?"

Ethan said, "Don't know, she was just here."

James said, "Maybe she went for another coffee. . . ."

Two of the agents hustled out of the room and down to the front desk, and one asked the fat man, "Do you have a coffee place . . . a room?"

The fat man pointed at a coffee urn on a side table, with Styrofoam cups.

The fed said, "The girl who was with them. Did she have another room?"

"What girl? There are a bunch of girls here," the fat man said, looking frightened.

The fed said, "I'll be right back."

He ran back to the room and said to Recca, "I need the mug shot of the girl."

Recca gave him an eight-by-ten color photo, and the agent ran back to the front desk and showed it to the fat man.

"I've seen her," he said. "I gotta call my wife. She'll know the room."

Instead, the agent ran the man back to his living quarters. His wife looked at the photo, frowned, and said, "Two-forty. She's in two-forty."

The agent got the key from the front desk, got the entry team. At just about the time Rachel climbed aboard the Sprinter train, the feds went through her door and found a few pieces of clothing and a modest collection of cosmetics around the bathroom sink—and a window that looked out at the street they'd just crossed to raid the motel.

"She's running," Recca said. "I think she looked out the window and saw us coming. We need to get to the cab companies, the bus lines. . . ."

"She could be on foot, or maybe she *is* getting coffee," the agent said. "Maybe we ought to cruise a few blocks around, see if we can spot her."

"Do it," Recca said. "Don't take too long. If you don't find her, get on the cab companies."

Between the bunch of them, they came up with a search plan, but by then it was too late. Rachel was halfway to San Marcos before they made the first call to a cab company. And she'd never taken a cab.

Putting together the search for Rachel had taken time. When Recca got back to the first floor, he found the three Storm men still sitting on the bed. They'd asked for lawyers and shut up.

Harmon and the other two Singular agents were in the room next door with another of the FBI agents, looking at a laptop. Recca went over and asked, "What's this?"

"Just checking the thumb drives to make sure you got the right ones," Harmon said. He gestured at a line of drives sitting on top of a desk. "We brought Lanny along so you'd know everything is on the up-and-up. These are the thumb drives."

"You're sure?"

"Nearly. They were encrypted. We're just putting in the encryption codes, and as soon as they start to decrypt, then we'll know for sure," Harmon said.

"We have to take those with us," Recca said. "Somebody higher up will have to release them to you."

"We knew that," Harmon said. He pulled a thumb drive out of the USB slot on the laptop and said, "That's the last of them. We're done. You can have them."

The feds gathered up the drives, sealed them in an evidence bag.

Outside the room, Recca said to the other agent, "Don't ever do that again. Don't let civilians handle the evidence."

The agent nodded. "Sorry about that. I was right there. And we'd been talking about checking them."

"Yeah, no harm done," Recca said. "Just don't do it again."

Inside the room, after the door was closed, Harmon dug in his pockets and pulled out the thumb drives.

"Slick," said one of the Singular operators. "I was watching and I never saw you make a switch."

"Just old magic show stuff," Harmon said. He got on his phone, and when Sync picked up, he said, "It's done. We're gold."

Sync said, "Aw, sweetheart."

As he said *sweetheart,* Shay was on Google+ with West, typing *Bye.*

26

West was at his apartment a few miles from Singular headquarters. When he got off-line with Shay, he called Harmon's office and was told by the group secretary that Harmon was not in, and wouldn't be until evening. "Gotta put me through to his cell," West said.

"Can't. He's involved in something . . . complicated."

"It's pretty critical."

"If it's critical enough, go upstairs," she said. "Call Sync."

One thing about Singular, West thought, was very different from the military: it was efficient, and everybody, right down to the secretaries and the janitors, knew how to make decisions. He called Sync's secretary. "I need to see the man," he told her. "I tried to call Harmon, but he's out of town."

Sync's secretary said, "He's really stacked up. If it's critical, I can squeeze you in between a couple of appointments."

"Tell him it's so critical that I'm making a note of the time right now, so there are no questions later about when I called."

She said, "Just a minute," and West heard her put the phone down on the desk. A minute later, she came back and said, "He'll be available for five or six minutes, right on the hour. Get here at five minutes of."

"Thanks. See you then."

Elementary ass covering was what it was, West admitted to himself. He spent a minute editing the GandyDancer text and inserting it into BlackWallpaper. He kicked back at his desk and thought about what Shay Remby had told him.

West had been hired as an investigator-researcher, doing corporate intelligence work. He looked at other companies doing biomechanical research—the cynical might call it corporate espionage—and also investigated the frequent attempts of hackers to break into the Singular databases. He had a vested interest in this company. When they had hired him, they'd told him they wanted him both as an investigator and as a research subject—and replaced his clunky army-grade prostheses with million-dollar robotic legs, the ultimate fringe benefit.

But as an investigator, he was a naturally curious man, and a man who, without even thinking about it, could soak up information from others. Like the people he worked with. He was aware that Sync ran several different groups of what might be called security personnel—just as the military did. Harmon's team, which included himself and Cherry and a dozen more men and women, were essentially detectives and researchers.

Others were like security guards, providing physical security for the offices and labs.

And over the months he'd been with the company, he'd become

aware of another group, one that was almost invisible, run by Thorne. He didn't know exactly what they did, but they had a paramilitary feel—guys with guns who weren't afraid to use them. He'd known the type in Afghanistan, knew how they behaved, what they looked like. From time to time, he'd seen people like that around the building.

He didn't know where they were based, but it wasn't at Singular headquarters. If there actually had been a raid on that hotel, as Shay had said, if people had been hurt, then it was probably that group. If Odin had been snatched off the beach and taken away, again, it would be that group.

If West had found Odin, he would have done about what he'd told Shay he would: given the kid a hard time and probably, at the end of the interview, called the local police or even the FBI. He would have identified Odin as one of the raiders who wrecked the Oregon lab, and then he would have let the law take over.

Now West found himself conflicted. He'd been looking at life as a badly crippled human being. Singular had given him that life back. In some ways, his new legs were better than the originals, though he would have preferred the old ones, of course.

He would, he thought, risk his life for the company, if that for some reason should become necessary.

He wouldn't kill for it.

He broke out of the pensive state and checked his watch: time to go. He printed out the conversation with Shay, including the screen grab of the man with the wired-up brain. He folded the papers once, and walked down to his car.

• • •

At Singular headquarters, he checked in past the good-looking but vaguely frightening woman at the front desk and took an elevator to Sync's floor.

Sync's secretary looked up as he came though the door. "Right on time. His conference is just breaking up."

A minute later, a smiling, affable Sync herded three suits into the outer office, shook hands with them, and walked to the outer door with them. When he came back, the affability was gone. "You say it's critical?"

"Yes. I can't reach Harmon, but you need to know this."

"Come on in," Sync said.

As the door shut behind them, West took the printout from his pocket and said, "When I talked to Shay Remby back in Eugene, I set up a link with her. I told her if she ever needed to get in touch, for any reason, she could go to a Facebook or a G+ page called BlackWallpaper. This came in today."

He handed the printout to Sync, who read it as he sank into the chair behind the desk. When he finished reading it for the first time, he muttered something unintelligible, and read it again.

"God . . . bless me," he said finally. "They figured out how to copy the drives. I'll tell you what, this is the last thing I wanted to hear—but it's good work. You've got to keep this link alive. We need to talk with her."

"She says we have her brother . . ."

Sync waved him off. "That's not your area," he said.

West did an instant translation: *Yes, we have her brother. Keep your nose out of it.* He decided on prudence and nodded once; he'd sort out later whether he meant it.

Sync was up now, pacing in a tight loop behind his desk, cyclonic thoughts coalescing into crisis-management mode. "You've got to get back to her. Can you do that?"

"Yes. BlackWallpaper on G+ and Facebook. They're secure—I clean them out every time I use them."

"Then tell her that we need to talk. Keep her talking, keep her negotiating."

"But . . . there's a twenty-four-hour window."

"Anything you can do to find her," Sync said. "Anything. Look: this is the most serious problem we have in the company right now. There are things in those files that would really hurt us if they got out. Competitive stuff. And some really bad PR, if it were to get out without a proper explanation. That image you saw, that's bullshit, but if people started to pry . . ."

"I can look. I can try to run down the IP address she's sending from."

"Do all of that. I'll have to check with Cartwell, but I'll put this out there: you can earn yourself a bonus, the biggest bonus that you've ever seen, if you can give us a hard link to her. I mean, you want a Porsche? No problem. Find her, okay?" Sync looked at his watch again. "I need to move this information along. You start looking, and I've got another meeting."

Sync walked West out of his office, and as West headed for the outer door, he said to his secretary, "Get me Harmon. Like, now. In the next one minute. And then Thorne."

The sixty-three-mile drive back to Malibu cost Shay and Cade two hours. The problem wasn't on the first fifty miles of inland freeway—traffic flow was the typical ten miles over the speed limit—but the instant they turned onto the Pacific Coast Highway, aka Malibu's Main Street, they were crawling like babies.

Twenty-seven coastal miles of "scenic beauty," according to the road signs and tourist maps, but in practical terms, Sean's house lay in the sweet spot near the Malibu Pier. Cade occasionally walked the Ducati over the last mile to stay in time with Shay.

"Sean! Sean! Sean!"

The Range Rover and the Ducati pulled into the driveway, and as they waited for the garage door to lift, a huddle of autograph seekers rushed the motorbike. Cade, his face hidden behind the helmet's smoky mask, waved Shay forward, then took the notebooks and Sharpies being thrust at him and signed. With a couple of revs of the engine for effect, he saluted the fans and vanished behind the closing door.

"Wow! He's even hotter than I imagined!"

"And taller!"

"Way taller!"

"Hey, wait a sec. . . . Who's Cade?"

Twist was limp-pacing the length of the living room, hands clasped behind his back, cane propped against a potted palm. "Not good, my little chickadees, not good. . . ."

"What's happened?" Shay asked as X heeled beside her and Cade removed his helmet.

"My lady at LAPD just told me the 'alleged incident' at the hotel never happened. I asked her to do some checking around for us on Singular. She called this guy she knows at the FBI, told him a bit about the raid, and an hour later, some higher-up federal is screaming at her to back off. He warns her that if a 'halfway house for juvenile delinquents,' as he called it, tries to claim this upstanding organization brutalized them in any way, they'd better lawyer up 'cause Singular will sue them into their graves."

"They're kidnappers," Shay protested.

"The cops aren't going to march into Singular headquarters with-out serious evidence," Twist said. "They'd need a search warrant—"

Cade pushed the laptop at Shay and said, "He's back."

Message delivered. Give me time to sort things out. Don't do any-thing stupid.

"Can your connection there be traced to here?" Twist asked quickly.

"Not as long as we don't respond," Cade said.

Shay looked up from the screen. "He's not saying they don't have my brother anymore, is he? They still have him, don't they?"

Cade looked at her and nodded. "I think so. And I think maybe . . . he really didn't know."

Twist picked up his cane and pointed it at Cade. "Where are we on the clock?"

"Three hours, thirty-eight minutes," Cade said.

"All right, we need to be ready to pull the trigger on our threat," said Twist. "Cruz is on his way over with a load of supplies we'll need to pull this thing off. It's too windy to set up our workshop on the deck, so let's push the furniture to the walls, roll up that rug. Move that Zuniga bronze peasant, and take it easy—it's worth about two hundred K."

Shay and Cade exchanged confused looks.

"Supplies for what?" Cade asked. "I thought we were uploading the decrypted files onto a website?"

Twist rolled his cane between his palms and frowned. "Think about it, Cyber Boy. There's about a trillion videos on the Web. How will we get people to watch ours? We have to get it out there fast—we don't know what's happening to Odin."

"It's the major challenge," Cade agreed, "driving traffic. . . ."

"The action I'm proposing will create a traffic jam," Twist said with a beatific smile. "What we did with the district attorney—that was like hanging a flyer on a telephone pole compared to the scale of this thing."

"I hear five-to-ten calling us, no parole," said Cade.

"Shut up," said Shay. To Twist: "Tell us."

Twist raised a hand. "If we do this—get millions of people to look at a website that we set up and that shows Singular doing this brain stuff—there'll be a lot of pressure on us. By which I mean *you,* Shay. You're the one who Singular knows."

"If we can get Odin back, I don't care," she said.

Twist pointed Shay and Cade to the couch and started pacing again, his mind sewing up loose threads.

"I started doing the logistics on it years ago, waiting for the right cause," he began. "I was on the brink of using it in the next couple of weeks against the DA, to really put the spotlight on immigrant injustice."

"C'mon, man," Cade said, "spill—"

Twist directed Cade to move over and perched himself next to Shay. "You know the Hollywood sign?" he asked her.

"Sure," she said. "It was one of the first things I saw when I got here."

"It's the first thing everyone sees when they come to Hollywood. It was definitely the first thing I saw, that I remember, from when I was a kid," Twist said. "Nine letters forty-five feet tall, four hundred and fifty feet across . . . How many stories is forty-five feet, by the way?"

Shay scrutinized him. "You're serious?"

"I am."

Cade was already nodding in approval. "So what's the website we're driving the traffic to?"

"They're killing brains," Twist said. "What do you think about Mindkill? It's available."

West went down to his small office and, when he got there, stared out his window at the parking lot.

The company was kidnapping kids? And why was Sync so shaken by the photo of the man in the skullcap if it was bullshit? That wasn't the reaction of a man who was worried about a trade secret getting out—that was the reaction of someone who was worried about going to jail.

Cherry wasn't there to talk to—he was in Cincinnati, looking into a hacker who'd made repeated runs at the company's computers. Even if he had been there, West wasn't sure he'd have talked to his partner: Cherry wasn't the type to question authority. He would do what he was told.

He said aloud to the parking lot, "What are we doing? What am I doing?"

West had a bad four hours working through the implications of what he'd learned, but he also put the time to use by tracking the IP addresses Shay had been using, as he'd told Sync he would. Anything critical, he decided, he'd delete—but when he tracked them down, he found that they all came from open public Wi-Fi sites, and that she'd been moving around Orange County. Giving that information to Sync couldn't hurt, because it would increase his own credibility while not really helping to locate Shay.

At the end of the day, he sent a note to Harmon with a copy to Sync detailing the network addresses. Out of the office, he drove to his apartment, made himself a microwave dinner, forced himself to take a brief nap, watched part of a Giants-Dodgers baseball game, and, at ten o'clock, drove back to the office.

When he was in the military, he'd learned a lesson about secrets and security. Plans were always guarded, but anytime the military was planning anything, the guys in logistics knew it first, even if they didn't know the details. Cars and trucks and airplanes had to be counted, allocated, moved into place, and prepped. So many boxes of rations had to be located and delivered. Key people had to be warned not to take leave, or had to be called back from leave. Even without the specific knowledge of what was going to happen, you could always tell that *something* was. All of this, outside the circle of high security.

On the fourth floor of the Singular building, a man named Robert Johnston had a messy little office that he ran with the help of Rose and Carmen, two cranky, officious, efficient women. They paid expense accounts, bought airline tickets, rented cars, scheduled maintenance, purchased office supplies ranging from printer paper to toilet paper, and did general troubleshooting for the company. If somebody plugged up a toilet and you needed a plumber in a hurry, you'd call Bob or Rose or Carmen.

Singular headquarters, unlike the labs, didn't have internal surveillance cameras—Cherry had suggested privately that the company might not want an outside agency, like the FBI, to subpoena the tapes to see who was coming and going.

In any case, the company had good perimeter security, but once inside, you were inside. All the floors had lobbies at the elevators and stairways, and the doors leading into the building from the lobbies were locked at night—but locks were not really a problem for West.

At the building, he parked and checked in through the guard at the entrance. Not the frightening woman, but a sharp-eyed man of the same variety. Pleasant, but heavily armed.

"Working late tonight, Mr. West?"

"Not for long," West said. "I just wanted to sneak home and catch the first game of the Giants-Dodgers. Now I've got to pay for it."

"Ah, the Giants. I keep my fingers crossed."

"Gotta keep more than your fingers crossed—got to keep everything crossed," West joked as he carded himself through the front door.

Past the first set of doors, he took the elevator up to his floor, carded his way through that door, and walked down to his office. There, he turned on his lights and computer, signed on, and brought up an old file to give the impression he was working. Then he called Johnston's office and let the phone ring. Nobody home.

He sat for a few minutes, gathering courage, then pushed his desk aside, revealing a lockbox in the floor. He used a key to open it and took out an electric lock rake and a sealed plastic clamshell box containing an unused hard drive.

In a typical lock, the teeth in a key move a set of pins to various heights inside the lock, which allows the lock cylinder to be turned. A rake flips the pins up and down at a rapid rate, and eventually the alignment will be just right and the cylinder will turn.

The hard drive—because nobody kept paper files anymore.

West put the rake, the hard drive, and a computer cable in a Nordstrom shopping bag with a roll of duct tape, a pair of latex gloves, and a flashlight, opened his door just a crack, and listened.

Nothing: the floor was quiet, as it always was late in the evening. He walked down the hall to the back of the building, pushed open the door to the fire stairs, taped the lock, and went down two floors.

And listened. Listening was about the most important thing you could do in a burglary. He heard nothing, and before he could get cold feet, he put on the gloves, took the rake out of the bag, slipped the pick arm into the lock, put sideways pressure on the lock, and pulled the trigger.

The rake chattered for a moment, and the lock turned. He pulled open the door and listened, taped the lock, then slipped through and padded down the hall to Johnston's office.

A moment later, he was inside. He shut the door and left the light off because it might be seen around the edges of the door. Navigating with the flashlight, he walked past the assistants' desks to Johnston's cubbyhole. The door was locked, but the rake took care of that.

Inside, he touched the RETURN key on the computer, and the computer screen came up, asking for a password.

He could work his way around that, given a few minutes, but a password would be handy. If Rose and Carmen were like all the other assistants in the world . . .

He went back to their desks, put the end of the flashlight in his mouth, and pulled at the center drawer on Rose's desk. Locked. He opened it with the rake and began pulling out drawers. He spent three or four minutes at it, but found nothing that looked like a password.

He moved to Carmen's desk, which was also locked, but before he used the rake, he noticed that Carmen had an old-fashioned Rolodex. Was it possible?

He quickly thumbed through the cards, starting from the back, and, as luck would have it, he didn't find the password until he got to the second card from the front.

Three passwords: 19BarstowDr23, 56Susie120, and 1025USB.

He copied them down, returned to Johnston's office, and entered the first one, and Johnston's computer opened up. After that, it was a matter of waiting as the computer copied ten megabytes of files onto West's hard drive.

While that was going on, he sat quietly on the floor in the outer office with his back against the wall: if somebody came down the hall, he might feel it before he heard it.

Nobody came.

When the copy job was done, West returned the computer to its original state, unplugged the hard drive and placed it in the shopping bag, used the rake to relock Johnston's door and Rose's desk, moved to the door, and listened.

When he was satisfied he was alone, he stepped into the hallway, pulled the door shut, walked down the hall to the fire stairs, stripped the tape off the lock—he could have gotten into the stairway by pushing the lock bar on the inside of the door, but lock bars make noise. By taping the lock, he could go through silently.

From there, he climbed back to his floor, stripped the tape off the top lock, and ambled down to his office. Light-footed: as though a boulder had been taken off his shoulders. He put the hard drive in his pocket, and the lock rake back in his floor safe. Then he headed back downstairs, checked out through the guard, and drove to his apartment.

All of Johnston's files used standard Microsoft Office programs—Outlook, Excel, and Word, for the most part. The problem wasn't so much seeing the files as trying to figure out what he wanted to look at. A complete review would take days, and he didn't have the time.

West began by scanning subject headings, and after a few minutes, he came upon a folder titled "Facilities—Maintenance and Repair," with subfolders by location. He jotted down the name and continued reviewing. He found one for expense reports, and another for rations. Why would a company need rations? He could think of one reason: if they needed to feed troops . . . or prisoners.

When he was finished with the first quick review of the subject headings, he went back to the rations folder and found that food was being shipped from a Costco warehouse in Sacramento to one facility, also in Sacramento. And the invoices were signed by Thorne. He noted the address, which he'd never seen before. As an investigator for the company, he'd assumed that he knew all the different labs and offices; he'd been wrong.

He then turned to the facilities folders. The subfolder for the Sacramento address was slim, but contained one valuable document: a copy of the city's building permit for the construction of the building, which had been granted seven years earlier. The permit included a file of plans, and the basement looked a lot like what you'd expect with secure strong rooms.

Or cells.

He called up the Sacramento address on Google Maps, in satellite view. The Singular building was at the far southwestern edge of what appeared to be an industrial park on the south side of the city. He looked at it for a few moments, then did a directions search and found out that by the best route, he was 120 miles away—two hours or so.

He looked at his watch: after eleven o'clock already. If he left immediately, he couldn't be there until after one o'clock in the morning. Would they be doing anything that late at night? If the place were some kind of prison, and if they were trying hard to avoid notice . . . maybe.

He printed out the satellite view of the site, changed into a dark jacket, black jeans, and boots, walked down to his car, and set off for Sacramento.

27

Earlier that day, Twist, Cade, and Shay took delivery of what Twist called "essential supplies" for the action at the Hollywood sign. Twist had been planning a Hollywood sign action since he was a teenager.

Visible from virtually all parts of Los Angeles, the sign was an American cultural icon, and if one were a subversive political street artist looking for instant global notoriety, it was the perfect sign to hijack. Back then, he hadn't had a clue what he was going to say to the world, but when the subject came to him, 450 linear feet of corrugated metal was where he was going to post it.

The sign was just below the top of Mount Lee, a seventeen-hundred-foot peak inside a rugged urban park two miles north of Hollywood Boulevard. The first time Twist had hiked up to it, he'd been a ninth-grade dropout not yet walking with a cane, not yet afraid of heights. Also, by then he was not much surprised by anything—but he could still conjure up the awe he'd felt as he'd come around the last blind bend and found himself staring up the *H*'s back side.

It was an irresistible temptation, climbing the thing, and so he waited out the park's ten o'clock closing and got busy: over a flimsy chain-link fence, down the thirty-foot slope to the letters, and up a maintenance ladder at the back of the first *O*. He took a seat in the crescent and spent the night watching L.A. twinkle.

"That was a more innocent time," he said as Shay, Cade, and Cruz unloaded supplies from Cruz's new used pickup. "You could still hike several different trails up to a viewing area at the back of the sign. Then somebody decided that wasn't good enough, or the lawyers got to them, or something. Now it's razor wire on a beefed-up fence, security cameras, and NO TRESPASSING signs. There's also a live twenty-four-hour webcam."

"The sign isn't lighted," said Shay, remembering the night she'd slept at the bottom of the mountain. She was hauling a thirty-pound pack of plastic sheets into the house. "What can a camera see after dark?"

"Not much," Twist said, rolling a compact generator through the door. "The video quality is poor, and there's not much city light way up there. Which is why, with good planning, a couple of roadblocks to slow down police, and fast footwork, I'm projecting a sixty percent chance we'll get away with it."

"Sixty percent?" Cade asked, not liking the odds. He was carrying a spool of heavy braided wire. "What'd you pull that number out of?"

"You had to ask," Shay said.

• • •

They had a lot to do and only a day to get it done.

The only way to drive up to the Hollywood sign was on a restricted-access road used by police, park rangers, and fire trucks. Everyone else was supposed to get a city permit, including film crews.

Dum and Dee became a film crew.

Twist had cultivated a source inside the division in charge of sign access and already had a permit in hand, acquired for the now-canceled publicity attack on the district attorney. The twins would haul all the needed equipment up the mountain and position it.

Cade grinned and said, "You can do anything in this town if you say you're making a movie."

"That is correct," said Twist. "You can make a living by counting on that. A lot of people do."

Late that day, Cruz was unpacking a climbing harness and Cade was sorting through strings of LED Christmas lights when Twist came in, trailed by a short, potbellied man named Roy, who wore brown work pants and a T-shirt that failed to reach his belt. Roy said, "I'm not going to ask any questions, and I don't want you guys to tell me anything. I'm just here to do the electronics."

"That's what we all say," Cade said.

Roy stepped over to look at the Christmas lights, then chuckled. "Gonna be interesting, whatever it is."

Shay looked at Twist, a question in her eyes, and he said, "Roy is good. He's been involved in actions before—besides, nobody will ever know."

"Even I don't want to know," Roy said. He asked Cade a question about a big pile of plastic sheets, and Shay nodded at Cruz's harness. "Let's go try it," she said.

Cruz had stopped at REI and been outfitted by Jonah, the climber who'd helped Shay. Emily phoned ahead to make sure Shay's not-secret admirer was working and blabbed that this time around, a rich artist was picking up the tab so go ahead and load up the shopping cart with the good stuff.

"I hope you're a quick study—your life sort of depends on it," Shay said as she and Cruz stepped out onto the first-floor deck; the house was elevated on a bluff. They had one evening and one morning to take Cruz from beginner to semi-Sherpa.

Cruz stepped through the leg loops of his new harness and positioned the belt low on his pelvis.

"Uh, no, climbers don't do hip-hop," Shay said, and gestured at his waist. "Up, above the belly button."

Cruz pulled the belt up, but it still hung loose, and the various slide buckles befuddled him. Shay reached in and cinched the strap tight in two places and Cruz feigned a choking noise.

She glanced up at him, serious. "This part's important: double back the strap for extra hold," she said, rewinding the end through the buckle. "Do the same thing with your leg buckles."

Cruz got busy while Shay clipped a steel carabiner to one of Cruz's gear loops.

"Jonah gave you an auto-lock," she said, and stood back. "Won't accidentally release and send you high-diving off a letter. No fear of heights, right?"

"No fear of anything," Cruz said. Shay raised an eyebrow and he said, "Okay, maybe *mi madre* the first time I got inked."

It was as personal as Cruz had been with her, and she was curious. "Your mother still around? I mean, here in L.A.?"

Cruz shook his head. "Nah. She moved back to Mexico a couple years ago with my baby sister."

"So then . . . you lived with your dad?"

Cruz fiddled with the carabiner, not looking at her, and Shay said, "Hey, sorry, it's none of my business."

He was silent a little longer, then: "We all got stories, right?"

"True," said Shay.

Cruz leaned back against the teak rail and glanced over his shoulder at the waves. The sun had set, and the beach had cleared of everyone except a few locals walking their dogs. X was lying at the edge of the deck, nose between his paws, keeping track of them.

"My mom had to leave after my brother got killed," he said without emotion. "Gang stuff, lots of cops and lawyers involved. Anyway, she wasn't legal. When the case got dropped, they told her she had to go. My sister—she was too little to not be with a mother. I moved in with some people, some other stuff happened, and eventually . . . Twist."

Shay was quiet and leaned back against the rail beside him. Finally she said, "I'm sorry about your brother."

"I'm sorry about yours," Cruz said. He bent for the bag and pulled out a coil of rope. "Am I ready for lesson two?"

Shay looked him over for a moment, then patted her thigh to attract X's attention.

"Come," she said to the dog. And to Cruz: "You too. Let's go up a deck."

Shay had looked at Internet photographs of the Hollywood sign letters and decided they would tie into the top bars for safety while walking across the brace bars, which were a few feet lower. They needed to work on balance.

She pulled her harness on over her jeans, stepped out onto her bedroom deck, and startled Cruz by hopping up onto the banister. Six inches wide, thirty feet to the sand—a decent stand-in for honing balance, building confidence, and testing reflexes.

"Be my anchor," she said, and tossed him the free end of her rope. She double-checked the figure-eight knot she'd used to tie into her harness, then took an amble around the three-sided railing. It was nearly dark now, and she'd decided to leave the deck lights out to both simulate the conditions they'd be facing at the sign and keep beach walkers from looking up and freaking out at a couple of reckless kids.

She did a pirouette and came back toward him, moving along the railing on the inner edges of her boots, then the outer edges, and finally, up on her toes. "It's about focus as much as anything," she said, and spun away again to demonstrate.

"That's gotta be easier than it looks," Cruz said, his grip secure on her rope as his gaze followed her every step.

"Actually, it probably is," Shay said, and jumped back onto the deck. "Your turn."

Cruz tied himself into the harness and handed her the free end to be his anchor, but she had a second thought about that. "Untie again, and give me your rope for a sec," she said. As he did, she added, "I'll be right back."

Shay took the circular staircase to the roof terrace and started hunting around for something to tie the rope into. She settled on the brick chimney, used a sling and a carabiner to tie on the top end, and pitched the other end over the side. Then she went back down to Cruz, plucked the rope out of the air, and clipped it to his harness.

"If you fall off the rail, you'll find yourself dangling like a fish on a pole, but you won't fall. Trust me."

"I trust you," Cruz said, and hoisted himself up onto the rail. "As much as I trust anyone."

It wasn't exactly climbing, what they were doing up on the banister, but the way Cruz balanced along the narrow beam of wood felt like something he was a natural at, and Shay was impressed. She asked him several times to look down, to see if the height made him uneasy, and was relieved when he showed no fear. Over the next ten minutes, he held his focus, worked it.

She almost felt bad about what she was going to do.

Cruz was up on his toes, a crinkle between his eyes as he concentrated on his footwork. He glanced at her and smiled, then was back at it, starting to corner the rail, when Shay stepped forward, reached her hands up against his stomach, and pushed.

Cruz said, "Oh . . . shit" as he left the banister, and in the next second, his back arched against the harness as the nylon rope took the shock of his weight. And there he was, dangling above the sand.

"I had to do it," Shay said, leaning over the rail, talking to the top of his head.

"Not feeling the trust right now, Shay," Cruz said.

"Yeah—but now you trust the rope, right?"

Twist came out, chewing on a carrot stick.

"You might be hanging with the wrong crowd," he said to Cruz;

he'd come up for a look after seeing Cruz, from the knees down, swaying outside the first-floor French doors.

"I'm laughing inside," Cruz said as he began to clamber back up to the balcony.

Cade, who'd come out behind Twist, said, "*I'm* laughing on the outside." He held his ribs and said, "Ho, ho, ho."

Shay asked Twist, "How are the lighting panels coming?"

"We're getting there. If nobody calls about Odin, we'll be ready by tomorrow afternoon . . . if we decide we're really going to do it."

"If you need somebody to pull that trigger," Shay said, "I'll pull it."

28

As Shay was finishing her lesson with Cruz, West was driving toward Sacramento. By the time he got there, it was after one o'clock in the morning.

The Singular site was in an industrial park that included several recycling businesses and two junkyards, as well as a couple of light-electrics assembly plants, two or three different metal-supply businesses, and a building gutted by fire but left standing.

There was a lot of scrubby, vacant land, and that was how he eventually found the Singular building—it was in the industrial park, but separated from everything else. He could see a half-dozen cars in the parking lot; lights burned all around the perimeter of the building, and he suspected that there were cameras behind the lights.

The burnt-out building, though, would provide cover. He drove through the area a last time, picking his spots, and eventually left his car with a hundred others in the parking lot of an assembly plant.

When he'd parked, he watched and listened, and then got his pack, crossed a road into the vacant land on the other side, and cut across to the burnt building, thinking about snakes the whole time he did it. Of course, if a snake struck at him, it was in for a surprise when its fangs hit titanium; but snakes still scared him.

There was enough ambient light to navigate, but not enough to see details in the burnt building. He moved around it until he got to the side facing the Singular plant, then climbed up in an open window and, risking the flashlight, shined it down into the building.

He was above a concrete floor, most of which was covered with collapsed roofing panels. He carefully hopped down into a clear patch and shined the light around. Halfway down the building, maybe a hundred feet away, he saw the remnants of a concrete stairway. He picked his way down to it, walking carefully through the rubble; there was more rubble on the stairs, but he managed to get up to the second floor, and a window looking out at the left front corner of the Singular building.

His eye was caught by a ramp that was not visible from ground level. The ramp came off a parking lot on the side of the building and went down to a circular pad at the basement level. From where he was, he could see a line of two double doors and a single human-sized door looking out at the circular pad, which was just large enough for small trucks.

Interesting.

The stairway behind him went up to a third floor, but he didn't need to get higher. He picked a few boards off the steps going up, clearing a space big enough to sit down. He put his pack beside him, took out the binoculars, a wool army blanket, a ham-and-cheese sandwich still wrapped in cellophane from the convenience store where he'd bought it, two cans of Diet Pepsi, and earbuds for his iPhone.

The key to a successful surveillance, he'd learned, was warmth, food, drink, a convenient place to pee, and a few decent tunes that nobody else could hear. He wrapped himself in the blanket, plugged in his earbuds, and brought up a Jay Z album.

Over the next three hours, and a couple more albums, three trucks stopped at the building, unloaded boxes, and left. West had begun to think about leaving—he didn't want to be anywhere near the area when the sun came up—when a fourth truck rolled through the parking lot and down onto the Singular ramp.

A man came out of the building, and one got out of the truck. They talked a minute, then popped a side panel on the truck and the driver climbed inside. A moment later, he pulled a human being out of the truck. West was too far away to pick up every detail, even with the image-stabilizing Canon binoculars.

He could see that the person was a woman, maybe a girl, and that her wrists were cuffed behind her back and her ankles shackled, and that there was something weird—something mechanical—on her head.

"Sonofabitch," he muttered as they pulled her inside.

Now he was frightened. He'd seen something he shouldn't have, something protected by people who had guns and were willing to use them. He eased out of the burnt building into the growing daylight, hurried back to his car, and drove west, back toward the Bay Area. He was scheduled to be at work in an hour and a half, but could fake his way around that: he needed some sleep. He took a quick shower, pulled down the blackout shades in the bedroom windows, twisted and turned for half an hour, thinking about the woman in chains, then fell into a restless slumber.

He woke to the sound of his cell phone buzzing at him. He picked it up and looked at the screen: Singular calling.

"West," he said.

"This is Harmon. Sync filled me in. We have a couple of people over here working on a response. We need you here to edit. You know, put it in your own words."

"Just sitting here staring at my computer," West said. "I'll be in as quick as I can."

He was *quick,* and ten minutes later he walked into Singular head-quarters and went straight up to Harmon's office. Harmon wasn't there, and the group secretary sent him to a conference room on the next floor up. He found Harmon and a couple of suits working over a computer. Harmon said "Morning" when West walked in, and then said, "Take a look at this."

"What're we doing?" West asked.

"We're trying to slow them down. If we slow them down just a little, we can find them and take the drives back. They can't do much without the thumb drives."

West nodded, bent over the computer. "Let's see what I'm say-ing. . . ." He read through the message and said, "It sounds pretty white, you know. Kinda uptight. No offense."

"No offense taken," Harmon said. "Fix it."

West nudged one of the suits out of the computer chair, sat down, looked at the proposed message for a minute or so, then began rewriting it. When he finished, one of the suits said, "Not that much different."

Harmon read it once, then again, then smiled at West and clapped him on the shoulder. "You *are* a smart guy. We gotta talk more. It's not any different, but it's got a different feel. Sounds like you."

"So now what?" West asked.

Harmon shrugged and said, "Push the SEND button."

At the Malibu house, everyone was up early.

They still had to make two letters to finish their sign, and Cade was uploading video to the new website—the man shaking on the operating table—placing it in a restricted cache until they were ready to launch.

There was always the possibility that Odin would be released and none of it would be needed.

Shay mentioned that a couple of times over scrambled eggs cooked competently by Cruz. Nobody disagreed with her, but finally Twist said, "I don't think we can count on Odin being turned loose. If they really did kidnap him and turned him loose, he could testify against them, and people would go to prison. I don't think these people want to be looked at."

"Only *if* he could identify who took him," Shay said. "It seems to me, if you were going to kidnap somebody in broad daylight, you'd be careful about being identified. These people are professionals."

"Kicked their asses at the hotel," Cruz said. "Not so professional then."

"You think we'd kick their asses if they came back? With thirty guys and armor?" Twist asked. "Listen to Shay. They're pros, and we're not. They underestimated what they were going to run into, but they wouldn't make that mistake again."

After breakfast, they rolled out a sheet of the plastic they were using to make the letters, agreed that it was too early to work, and went for a walk on the beach, the dog chasing wavelets down to the waterline, then retreating when the next wave came in.

Shay had been checking BlackWallpaper and GandyDancer every few minutes, and at ten o'clock, fifteen minutes after they got back to the house, BlackWallpaper posted:

I've talked to a couple of the top people at Singular and they absolutely swear that they do not have Odin. Three men in the surveillance van stopped him, and they all drove to Kimberley's Magic Burgers in Oxnard, where they conducted an interview, but your brother refused to cooperate. I'm told there was an argument: our people wanted to call the police, but Odin said he'd file a kidnapping complaint against them, and in the end, they let him walk away. (Your bro has got some balls.) He was last seen entering the Oxnard Transit Center. (See the photo—it was taken by the surveillance guys.) Anyway, you can see he's talking on a cell phone. We believe that you have that cell phone number. If you call it, we can trace it, and we will tell you where he is. But you'd have to give us the number, and we're not sure you'd trust us with it. (I can't tell you how the trace would be done.) Be assured that this company does NOT (and did not) kidnap anyone. The CEO of Singular has ordered his researchers to trace the origin of the photo you sent us, but several imaging experts at Adobe (who we called in for an emergency consult, which wasn't cheap, believe me) say it was shot on film and transferred to video, and there's a belief that it was taken from a sixties or seventies horror film shot in Hong Kong. He says that if you post that clip on the Internet and claim it is a Singular experiment, you will look very foolish. To tell you the truth, the big guys are running out of patience with you, your brother, and Storm. You may not know it, but several members of Storm who were part of the attack on the lab in Eugene were arrested in Orange County yesterday and are now cooperating with the authorities. You can confirm it with the FBI, there is a statement on their website. That's how we handle all these cases: we bring in the feds and we sue. So, Shay, we can't meet your demand, because we don't know where your brother is. Please think about it before you take your next action, as you are opening yourself to severe criminal liability.

I wasn't lying about taking care of my sister, and I don't want to see you get hurt, either, because you seem like a great kid who's had a rough ride. So talk to me, okay?

"Well, that's just complete, utter—" Shay stopped speaking when she rolled down to the photo. It was in color, and it was Odin all right, on his phone, his hair gelled in its new style, walking into the Oxnard Transit Center.

"Is it him?" Twist asked.

"Yes," she said, transfixed. "Why hasn't he contacted me? He'd contact me after what happened at the beach, I'm sure of it."

Cade leaned in over her shoulder to study the details. Twist bent in too and asked, "Is it Photoshopped?"

"Can't tell yet," said Cade, scanning for some giveaway, like an incorrect date or time stamp in the background. "I'd need to do a more serious analysis."

"Analyze the hell out of it," said Twist.

Shay: "You think I should call Odin?"

"He's never answered before," Cade said. "Why would he answer now? And if you call, maybe it's *your* phone that they're looking for."

"Should I answer West?" Shay asked.

"And say what?" Twist said. "I think we wait, keep working on the last two letters, make a decision tonight."

They'd been working for an hour when Cade gave up on the photograph. "If they made a composite somehow, they did a heck of a job. Something doesn't feel right about the shadows I see, but I can't put my finger on what's wrong. If anything's wrong. I might have been looking at it too long. You start to imagine stuff after a while."

They'd gotten one of the *L*'s done when Shay made one of her semi-compulsive checks of BlackWallpaper to see if anything new had come in. Nothing had, but there was a note on GandyDancer.

"Oh my God," she blurted, and Twist, Cade, and Cruz came to look.

Ignore the note I sent this morning. That was written and dictated by the security people here. They are tearing up the world looking for you and those thumb drives. I think I found the place where Odin is being held, a prisonlike facility in Sacramento. It looks bad. There seems to be more than one prisoner too—I may have seen an experimental subject, looked like a young woman. From the way they were talking this morning, they will not give Odin back to you. I think you have to go with your action, whatever it is. I can't promise that you'll get your brother back, but it might help.

When those three men from Storm were arrested by the FBI yesterday, there were Singular agents on the scene, and I think they recovered all of the other thumb drives. Yours are the last ones out there. If the FBI is cooperating with Singular, I don't know who else we could talk to, to enter the prison legally. I know you don't have much reason to trust me, but I think we need to meet, and very soon—tonight, tomorrow night. I can't get out in the daytime.

Shay: "A prison? Twist, are they torturing my brother?"

Twist put a hand on Shay's shoulder, then turned away from her, rubbing his forehead with his fingers. He turned back and said, "If they are really, really smart, they sent that first message to set you up, and the second one to pull you in."

Cruz shook his head. "No. I think he's straight."

Twist said, "Tell me why."

"Because he tells us to go with the action, and no matter what, Singular wouldn't want the action. The second thing is, if it's a trap, it's too easy to avoid. If they're professionals, they'd know that. They'd be trying something more complicated than 'Let's meet,' and then leaving it up to us."

Twist: "That's not entirely convincing. Telling us to go with the action might mean they think they can handle it. At the same time, it makes us believe that West is being straight with us."

Shay: "But you know what? I get an answer to him, tell him that I'll meet him. Me. Like a scared teenager. Set up a meeting in a place where they can't hide anybody. Then Cruz and Twist actually meet him . . . and you guys make an evaluation. Be lie detectors—figure out if he's lying to us."

Cruz nodded. "There'd be no reason for them to try to grab us. You're the one they want."

"Except that grabbing you would give them a bigger hammer over me," Shay said.

Twist said, "We could handle a meeting, I think. We just have to be smart about it—we need to talk it over some more."

Given Singular's official response, Shay knew they wouldn't hear from Odin, and they didn't.

They finished the last of the preparations for the sign action shortly after noon, and at two o'clock, Dum and Dee, the "movie crew," showed up in a van to pick up all the gear. Shay gasped when she saw Dee: his face was one large bruise.

She went to him and asked, "Are you okay?"

He nodded and managed a thin-lipped smile, but he looked like he hurt, and she gave him a long, tight hug. When she backed away, he waved his arms, almost like Odin, and said in a high-pitched voice, "I'm . . . okay."

The first words she'd ever heard him say. She turned to look at Twist, who shook his head and said, "One hug and he makes a speech. Hard to believe."

Dum and Dee had scouted Mount Lee and picked out a site where they could stash the equipment. They put "Hollywood sign" in Google Maps and zoomed in on the mountain. The satellite view showed the dirt trails leading up the hill like a spider's web, and individual clumps of brush.

"Not many people walk directly up the face of Mount Lee, though there's actually a couple of old trails," Twist said, tapping the map on his computer screen. "Most hikers come up the back road to the TV tower. That's how Dum and Dee will get in, except they'll be driving. They'll wrap all the gear in a couple of tarps and leave it in the bush here. Off to the left of the letter *H*"—he tapped the screen again—"which is inside the fence. The fence is only along the road, above the sign. You'll walk up from the bottom, where there is no fence."

"How steep is that? Going up?" Shay asked.

"It's steep, but it's not climbing like you know it. You can walk up. But it'll be dark. You'll need your headlamps. Keep them on the red light, it'll be enough to see."

• • •

After Dum and Dee left, they were all restless, feeling cooped up, on edge about what they were going to do that night. Cade and Cruz decided to check out a commotion on the beach involving a couple of big video cameras, a wedge of paparazzi, and three young women in bikinis romping along the water's edge. Shay and Twist got Diet Cokes and climbed up to the rooftop deck.

They talked about West, about the depth of his obligation to Singular for his legs. She told Twist about the college professor who had tried to extort sex from West's sister, and West's reaction—running the professor out of the country.

That made Twist smile, and he said, "I'd probably like the guy . . . but I still can't trust him."

Shay said, "Okay," and the conversation drifted for a while, and they talked about Eugene, where Twist had never been, and the street culture there, and the kids at the hotel.

Finally Shay said, "You know, you have all these worries and questions about West. I've sort of wondered about *you*. Some of the same questions. Actually, even more questions. I know why West was working for this company, why there's loyalty there, but I don't understand what you're doing at all."

"You're saying you don't trust me?"

Shay said, "That's not it. I just have questions."

Twist said, "I answer only a limited number of questions. I'm pretty private."

"Except, of course, you've got about seventy runaways who you're involved with, which is pretty unprivate," Shay said.

"I rent them space," he said. "Like I told you on the first day, sooner or later, you have to pay."

"That's not true," Shay said. "I haven't been there long, and I've already met at least ten kids who've never been able to pay anything, and never will be able to."

"Give me their names, I'll kick them out."

"You know their names, and you won't kick them out," Shay said. "I understand, just from the rumors about you, that you spent some time on the street yourself, and now you're rich, so you decide, *Okay, I'll help out.* A lot of rich people do something like that. Maybe not so hands-on. . . . But why have you gotten involved with *me,* and my problems? You're not required to save me—but here you are."

"What's this thing you've got about sharing stories?"

"I don't want to know that your mom didn't nurse you long enough; I just want to know why you're doing this."

After a long time, Twist said, "Because a lot of what's happened is my fault. I needed to use you, for my immigration action, and I did. You made that about a hundred times better than it would have been. Then you were famous, and Singular was able to track you. Because they could track you, they found your brother and they took him. My fault."

"Not entirely your fault," Shay said. "I could have said no."

"Really? You're on the street and you're desperately looking for your brother, and a guy offers you a safe place to stay and some money for one easy job? I don't think you could've said no. Now it's come to this."

"Okay, it's all your fault," Shay said with a forgiving grin.

"Aside from that, I hate what these guys are doing," Twist said. "Experimenting on people? Discarding them. . . . And what are do-gooders for if they don't take on assholes like Singular? As far as your brother goes, I think they ought to give him a friggin' medal."

Shay nodded and said, "Thank you. I'd like to know how you got this way, but if it's private. . . ."

"You know what I always say."

"I do," Shay said, and together they intoned, "Let's not over-share."

Cade and Cruz came back, amused by the sighting of a movie star who'd been arrested for impaired driving the week before—*impaired* meaning by both alcohol and a variety of illegal drugs—and was apparently trying to reinflate her healthy All-American Girl image by splashing around in the surf with two carefully chosen girlfriends, carefully chosen to be slightly less attractive.

The rest of the afternoon and early evening featured a series of what-ifs: What if they were seen going up the hill? What if somebody else was at the sign? What if something happened and Twist couldn't pick them up after they fled the sign site? What if a police helicopter came before they could light the letters?

Nobody said it, but everybody thought it: what if the action was futile because Odin was already dead?

Late in the afternoon, Dum called and said that the equipment had been delivered and was waiting in the designated bush.

"He said all that?" Shay asked.

Twist said, "Actually, what he said was 'Done.' "

"Remember the sequence, everything is packed in sequence," Twist said about six times. "As soon as you get there, get to the equipment bundles."

He ran through the rest of the action until Shay waved him off. "We got it, Twist. We got it."

320

get close, it'll look like high-voltage lightning is shooting through the brush under the sign. The cops won't mess with it until they can get a specialist electrician up to look at it . . . or until the gas runs out on the generator."

The second problem was how to keep the police away from the sign long enough for Shay, Cade, and Cruz to get the letters up and working. Twist had an answer for that too. The road to the top was blocked with a locked steel gate at night. Twist would drive to the gate and simply add his own lock—a heavy chain with a massive padlock designed to defeat bolt cutters.

"Simple, but effective," Cade said.

"Like I said, I've been thinking about this action for years," Twist said. "I just hadn't thought of anything I really, really needed to say."

As Shay, Cruz, and Cade climbed the hill, Twist found a place to park in an affluent neighborhood where the Range Rover would feel at home. Shay would call when they were ready to start lifting the letters, and then he'd go up the hill with his gate chain.

Everything was on the clock. They had a maximum of forty-five minutes to climb up to the sign, thirty-five to forty minutes to scale the nine letters, secure the plastic sheeting, set up the lightning boxes, and, with fifteen minutes left before L.A.'s eleven o'clock news, flip the switch on the generator—

And run.

The climb was a tough one: Mount Lee was a mountain, but a mountain of rough dirt with embedded rock fragments. They could walk, mostly, but at a few washouts, they had to go to all fours.

X turned out to be a gift: he was visible in the red light and moved slowly ahead on his leash, picking out a route. He seemed to sense where they wanted to go, and he sniffed at the air and turned and watched and led the way up.

The night was warm, and they were all sweating in their long sleeves and long pants. They stopped twice to drink from their water bottles, looking down at Hollywood below them, the lights stretching away across the Los Angeles Basin, with an inky spot below and to the west: the Hollywood Reservoir. Lavender, sage, and eucalyptus scented the air. There was little traffic noise; they could hear a couple of horses whinnying back and forth at a stable half a mile away.

They had one encounter on the way up: the ghostly flash of a coyote pack cutting across their path. X had had their scent almost from the beginning of the climb, and when they were within ten yards, he growled a warning, pointing with his nose, throwing a glance back at Shay, then looking forward again.

Shay risked a quick flash with the white LEDs and caught the yellow eyes of the coyotes, like road-sign warning reflectors. They pulled back and paused, three thin, flea-bitten things that looked more curious than menacing. Young coyotes, maybe siblings, with patchy, gray-brown fur and large, cartoonish ears.

X lurched toward them, restrained by his leash, the low rumble in his throat not a fight call, but a warning. The coyotes looked him over for a second, then moved away in the dark. Shay went back to the red light.

"Well done," Shay whispered to X, and ruffled his neck.

"Thirty-four minutes," Cade whispered from behind.

They picked up the pace.

• • •

They weren't talking much by the time they got to the sign. The trip up the hill had been tough, and if not for the gloves and long-sleeve shirts and jeans, the brush would have torn them up. Twice they'd hit pitches so steep that all of them slid back down the trail, grabbing bushes and protruding rocks just to stay upright.

They finally saw the pale, white-painted *D* looming overhead, and Shay whispered, "Before we get too close, let's take a minute to get our heads together."

They found a shelf in the dirt, six feet long and a couple of feet wide, sat down, and looked out over the city. "Pretty," Cade said. "Be cool to come up here with a camera."

A moment later, Cruz said, "It's so quiet."

"And that's good," Shay said. "Listen . . ."

They listened, and Cruz said, "I don't hear anything."

"So it's time to go," said Shay. "Not a word now. Turn the headlamps off."

For a sign as huge as it was, HOLLYWOOD looked almost fragile in the night. They crossed behind the *D,* then walked across the hillside to the bush where the equipment packs were hidden. There were lights at the top of the hill, at the TV or radio tower or whatever it was, but they saw nobody. Moving slowly in their dark clothes, they were all but invisible.

They'd talked all afternoon about possible problems with finding the equipment, but they'd looked at the Google Earth photos for so long and talked so much about angles off the *H* that they went directly to it. The bundles of gear were well to the side, where they wouldn't be found by casual intruders. Cruz and Cade pulled them out as carefully as they could, while Shay looked up in the dark for the security cameras that were mounted at the tops of the letters. She whispered, "I don't think anyone knows we're here yet."

"The longer, the better," Cruz whispered.

"Okay. Keep moving slowly, and stay in the shadows and behind the brush as much as we can," Shay said. "We need to change the plan: Cruz and I will help take the letter bundles and the equipment out to the sign to get the heavy work done. I don't think they'll see us until we start climbing."

The whole setup went so well that Shay could hardly believe it. They pulled the packs apart and made sure that each of their LED-lighted letters was placed beneath the correct HOLLYWOOD letter. With all the gear in position, Shay took out one of the clean phones and texted Twist: "Ready to climb. See any problems?"

A moment later, an answer flashed on her screen: "Nothing. Will lock gate. Close to schedule. Go."

Shay took a deep breath and said to Cruz, "Think about your feet. Use your hands to balance. Be sure you're tied in, don't be afraid to fall, but stay up any way you can."

"I will."

She turned to Cade and said, "Since we've got the letters in place, you've got more time. Don't hurry with the lightning boxes and all those glass rods. Be cool. Take your time. Get it right."

He nodded.

"And remember," she said to both of them, "the worst thing that could happen is if one of us gets hurt. We'd have to give ourselves up. I don't know what would happen then."

"You guys be careful," Cade whispered. "And, Shay—take this."

"We've got a permit. Tell the police to look at the permit. We're shooting a couple night scenes here for Disney."

There was a moment of silence, then: "You've got a permit?"

"Yes. With Disney," Cade repeated. "Tell the cops to look for a Disney permit. Just take a minute to check. They don't want to mess with Disney."

"All right. I'll be back."

Shay had frozen on the ladder, but then heard what sounded like the man walking away, on gravel. She hurried to the top, clipped her cable to the sign, and threaded the lift line through the carabiner and climbed down.

She got to the bottom and could see Cruz moving across the top of the *W,* their last letter. He fumbled with the clip, got the cable tight, then moved slowly to the middle of the letter and threaded the lift line through. That done, he moved back to the ladder and climbed down.

"Harder than I thought," he said, slapping his hands together.

"I think that guy's gone," Shay said. "Let's start lifting."

They went to the *H,* where Cade was already lifting the plastic sheets with embedded lights up the face of the letter.

"I got all the electrical stuff hooked up, except the connections at the bottoms of the letters," he said. He was breathing hard: he'd been running back and forth across the hillside, snaking wires through the brush. He'd had to reposition the generator, and the thing was heavy. "You guys lift the letters and tie them off, I'll start connecting cable."

The loudspeaker was back:

"ATTENTION. TRESPASSING IS A MISDEMEANOR PUNISHABLE BY A HEAVY FINE AND A JAIL SENTENCE. MOVE AWAY FROM THE SIGN IMMEDIATELY. IF YOU

DON'T MOVE AWAY FROM THE SIGN, YOU WILL BE ARRESTED."

The blaring voice went on for a while, but Shay stopped paying attention.

The two of them worked together, across the face of the Hollywood sign, hoisting each letter into place by pulling on the lift lines. After making sure each sheet was straight, they tied off the lift lines on the scaffolding. The work was hard, because of the brush tangling up everything, and the sheets were heavy.

They'd gotten to the *W*, with Cade hooking up the plug-ins at the bottom of each sheet, then taping them to make sure the connections wouldn't break loose. They'd started lifting the *W* when the support cable popped loose at the top of the letter and the sheet slid sideways and then hung there, folded across the left side of the *W*.

"Ah, damn, I knew I did that too fast," Cruz said, looking up at the dangling sheet. "I gotta go back up."

Shay said, "I'll go—I'm a little quicker. You guys get the other sheets up."

She ran around behind the sign to the ladder and went up. At the top, she tied in and walked across the support to the left side, where the cable had held. She got hold of it, but when she tried to pull it across the top of the letter, the weight of the dangling sheet was too much.

Cade and Cruz had just finished hauling up the last of the other letters. She called down, "You guys have to lower the sheet to give me some slack cable to work with."

"Got it," Cade called.

"Make sure it's straight when you lift it back up."

"We got it, Mom," Cade said.

• • •

Seconds later, she heard the sheet starting to slide back down, and then the cable went slack. She took the cable in her hand and edged across the top of the sign and clipped the other end in place.

"Pull," she called.

Cruz and Cade heaved on the line, and the cable popped loose again.

"Wait, wait," she called. They gave her some slack, and she looked at the clip at the end of the cable. It was twisted—bad metal. She pulled the cable tight again, then wrapped it around the bar. That was strong enough, but she couldn't bend the cable enough to tie it. What to do? She reached back to her ponytail, stripped off the leather tie she'd used to bind it, and tied down the cable to the bar as best as she could.

"Pull again," she called down.

Cade and Cruz hauled on the lift line and pulled the letter sheet to the top of the *W.* Shay brushed the loose hair out of her eyes, checked the leather tie: it looked solid.

At that moment, the man from the station came back. Shay didn't hear him until he called, "Hey, on the sign," and Shay, still holding on to the top of the *W,* reflexively turned to look toward him. She was blinded by a flash that might have been lightning, but wasn't.

"What are you doing?" she screamed, and X howled in support.

Another flash, and he said, "For my Facebook page. The cops are coming. There isn't any permit."

"They just looked in the wrong place," Cade shouted. "Tell the cops they're messing with Disney. Did you tell them Disney?"

"They said they didn't care if you're the president, you can't climb the sign. I'll tell you what, you guys are in deep shit."

And the loudspeaker started again: "ATTENTION. THE LOS ANGELES POLICE ARE ON THE WAY. REMAIN WHERE YOU ARE. REMAIN WHERE YOU ARE AND AWAIT THE ARRIVAL OF POLICE."

Shay, still blinking away the after-flash, found her way to the ladder, unclipped, and started down. Cade, from the other side, said, "We're good."

Shay called back, "One minute."

Cruz: "I got the dog."

Shay: "I'm down."

Cade: "I'm gonna fire this mother up."

Shay: "Do it. DO IT."

Several hundred feet below, Twist turned left on Beachwood Drive toward the mountain. He'd chained up the access gate without a problem, and now was moving back to the pickup area.

Talking to himself. What had he been thinking, sending a bunch of teenagers up the mountain like that? If somebody had asked him to do the same thing as a teenager, he would have done it, but that was different—

At that moment, the sign blinked on:

MINDKILL.NET

"Holy cats," Twist said aloud, peering through the Range Rover's high windshield. The hill looked like it was on fire . . . with letters.

Cade had yanked on the starter cord and the Honda generator caught the first time. There may have been one instant of delay— they weren't sure, but it seemed that way—and then suddenly the whole array flashed on, the brilliant letters reaching out toward the city, the lightning boxes flashing through the weeds under the sign like crazy, high-voltage, arm-length electric sparks.

The lights were so brilliant that Shay couldn't help herself and began laughing. It wasn't just that the lights were brilliant, they were totally, ludicrously, outrageously brilliant.

Shay now had X's leash and they all crossed in front of the sign, the guy at the top of the hill shouting, "Who are you guys? Who are you guys?"

Shay shouted back, "Snow White. I'm here with Stinky and Sparky, the electric dwarves."

They got to the *D,* and the path that led down the hill. Cade said, "Cruz is Stinky, right?"

They all started laughing again, a little hysteria in the mix, and they went over the side of the mountain.

The trip down the hill was a lot faster than the trip up, but it still took twenty minutes, with X again leading. Cade fell twice on steeper sections, cursing as he slid into the brush off the trail. The second time, he was unable to stop himself, but Cruz grabbed his shirt collar, which ripped, but held.

"Hurt?"

"No. I keep landing on my ass," Cade said.

Up above, the loudspeaker began spewing more threats, but they couldn't make out exactly what they were.

Then the first news helicopter showed up, hovering over the hillside, and turned to take video of the sign.

• • •

At the bottom of the hill, they slid down the last dirt patch and saw the Range Rover pull out from the curb. People were standing in the backyard of the house next to the dirt patch, looking up the hill. They saw Cade, Cruz, Shay, and the dog, and somebody called, "You guys do that?"

"Do what?" Shay called.

Then they were piling into the SUV.

Twist said over his shoulder as they pulled away, "Singular's gotta deal with us now."

30

Twist had the truck bucketing down to the base of the mountain, worried that the police might be prowling the streets. They got flashes of the sign as they went, a good shot as they turned off Beachwood onto Franklin Avenue and then took a left onto Gower and drove under the Hollywood Freeway. There, Twist slowed, then pulled to the side of the road.

"What are we doing?" Cade asked.

"I don't know what you're doing, but I'm going to get out and look—like those guys," Twist said. Farther along Gower, people were standing in the street, looking up at the mountain, heedless of the traffic trying to thread past them. Shay snapped X's leash on his collar, and they hopped out and looked up at the sign.

MINDKILL.NET

The sign dominated the darkness like nothing else in Los Angeles.

"You gotta admit, it catches the eye," Cade said to Twist, prodding him with an elbow.

Twist said nothing for a moment, just looked. Then he turned to the group and said, "I've been dreaming about this for fifteen years, but I had no idea. I was thinking about hanging a banner across it or something, but this"—he threw his hands out—"oh, baby."

Cruz: "It *is* good."

Twist began to laugh, the way the three of them had up on the hill, with a little note of hysteria. He shouted it this time: *"Oh, baby."*

Back in the Range Rover, they turned right on Sunset Boulevard and took it to Santa Monica, then down the bluff to the Pacific Coast Highway and around to Malibu.

They were waiting at a stoplight when Twist took a call from Lou. He looked at the face of the phone and muttered, "Something's happened at the hotel. She's not supposed to call."

He clicked on the answer bar and said, "Yeah?"

He listened for a moment, then frowned and turned quickly to Shay, then said, "Okay, thanks, Lou. We'll check as soon as we get back."

He clocked off and asked Shay as they started rolling again, "Somebody took your picture up there?"

"Oh, God, that guy," Shay said. "We just thought he was a fool. He flashed me right in the eyes."

"Yeah, well, he's apparently peddled the picture to every TV station in Los Angeles. Full color. Your hair was all over the place—they all know it's the same girl who climbed down the building on the 110."

"Ah, jeez."

" 'Girl on a Wire.' That's what they're calling you," Twist said. "It's the kind of publicity that you can't buy."

"I'm not looking for publicity," Shay said.

"I know, but you got it. You're a publicity magnet," Twist said. "That creates some problems. Everybody who's anybody knows that the girl on the 110 was working with the artist Twist. So you know who they'll be looking for?"

"The artist Twist," Cade said.

"Since we're coming and going in the artist Twist's car, we've left ourselves open," Twist said. "We've got to get some more no-questions-asked transportation. Cruz's truck is too tight for all of us and a dog."

"I know a guy," Cruz said. "He's not cheap."

"Same place you got the truck?"

"No, that was legitimate. We need something with plates that won't get registered right away."

"Cost isn't a problem," Twist said. "I mean, there are limits. . . ."

"Get you a Camry for five or six thousand, if you don't mind that funny sound coming from the tranny," Cruz said. "You'd get ten thousand miles out of it before you needed to do something. Car is totally invisible."

"Set it up," Twist said.

Back in Malibu, they went to the oversized television and turned it on. The local news was over—they clicked around and eventually found an aerial shot of the sign on a cable channel, with completely irrelevant commentary by the big-haired anchorman.

"Let's try the Channel Two website," Twist suggested. Sean had the television hooked to his Wi-Fi system so he could play Web-based games. Cade brought his computer up, went out on the Web, found the site, found the link to the "Girl on a Wire" story, and clicked it.

The anchorwoman popped up and said, "A few minutes ago, another astonishing political action began in Hollywood, and the Hollywood sign has taken on a new look. Jason Billings reports. Jason?"

Jason Billings, the reporter, was standing on Gower, where they'd been an hour earlier, with the sign aglow above and behind him. He said, "Jennifer, one of the biggest crowds in recent Hollywood memory is out here on Gower tonight, looking up at a political action attributed to the Los Angeles artist Twist. As you can see, he has—if it is him—lit up the Hollywood sign with a new sign that says MINDKILL.NET, apparently an effort to drive traffic to the artist's website."

As Billings spoke, the view switched from the street to a helicopter shot, and Twist cried, "Oh . . . that's . . . that's . . . *not bad.*"

Billings said, "Paul Jordan, a technician at a transmission tower on Mount Lee, saw the group before they turned the sign on and took a picture of one of the activists, believed to be the same red-haired young woman who took part in the pro-immigrant action on the 110 last week."

The photograph of Shay flashed up on the screen, and Shay said, "Oh . . . shit."

To give Jordan credit, it was a great shot: well lit, well focused, well framed. He'd caught Shay hanging off the back of the sign, her feet braced against the support bar, her body cantilevered out toward the camera. Her head was half turned toward the lens, so Jordan had caught her in profile, with her hair swirling out behind her. If you'd seen the girl on the rope coming down the building over the 110, you'd have no doubt that the girl on the wire was the same one.

Billings said, "We went out to the website, Jennifer, and found a video of a man who appears to be undergoing a medical experiment. The text with the video claims that a company called Singular, based in San Francisco, is doing mind-control experiments using human beings. A Singular laboratory in Eugene, Oregon, was attacked by a radical animal rights group last month."

Billings went on for a while about the raid and said, "This latest link apparently ties the artist Twist to that attack."

"Don't like that," Twist said.

Billings: "Up at the Hollywood sign, police say that some kind of electrical generator is shooting high-voltage lightning strikes along the bottom of the sign, keeping police from turning the sign off until they can get electrical experts on the scene. . . ."

"Wonder if it's still up?" Cruz asked.

Cade to Twist: "I wonder if we're going to jail?"

Twist: "You think Singular wants a big televised trial? I don't think so."

Sync was having one of his least favorite nightmares: the one where he was holed up in a cave somewhere in Afghanistan, looking down at a muddy road on which an armored personnel carrier was approaching. He had a French LRAC F1 rocket launcher, and boxes and boxes of rockets. Unfortunately, the rockets were for launchers made by the U.S., by the Israelis, by the Russians, and even by the Swedes. The APC was closing in, and Sync was rattling through the enormous pile of unusable rockets, looking for just one that would fit the French launcher, and at the same time, fully aware of the heavy machine gun that poked out of the APC and seemed to track his very thoughts—

The phone went off, and his heart nearly stopped. He sat up, frightened, said, "Jesus," ran one hand over the top of his head, then looked for the phone.

Harmon.

"Yes? Harmon?"

"We've got what you might call . . . a nightmare."

"What? A what?"

"That kid—Shay Remby. She really stuck us. She put one of the videos online, but that's not the worst of it. You've got to go to L.A.'s Channel Two. . . . Let me give you the website. . . ."

Sync, wearing sleeping shorts and a camouflage T-shirt, crouched over his computer, looking openmouthed at the sight of the Hollywood sign's new message: MINDKILL.NET. He put his hands to his temples as the television station ran the video of the man on the operating table. "Oh, no. Oh, no. No."

He watched it three times, then called Harmon back. "I've seen it. Remby's got to be with this artist, the Twist guy. Get his driver's license, his plates, get a BOLO going—tell them just to tag him, but we don't want a stop. We've got to make sure we can get at Remby."

"We're doing all that," Harmon said. "We're already looking at his credit cards, but he doesn't use them much."

"Gotta find them, gotta find them," Sync said. "You do that, I'll do damage control. Gotta try to kill the website."

"I'm gonna wake up West," Harmon said. "Tell him to get a message to Remby, see if he can buy some time."

"Do that. We've got to go on the offensive here. You find that artist. Remby will be close."

• • •

Shay, Twist, Cruz, and Cade stayed up late, hyped on adrenaline; they found the coverage on the other L.A. stations and then watched as the story went national and began rolling through the cable networks.

Lou called again and spoke to Twist. "The cops came by, asked if you were home. I told them you were out of town, I didn't know for sure where, but I thought New York. Also, your dealer called. He wanted to know what the hell this was all about, and he thinks you should push your prices by fifty percent."

"Aw, man . . ."

Before going to bed, they talked about whether they should contact West that night, or wait until morning, to tell the Singular people that more would be coming if Odin wasn't freed.

"We've only got the video of the guy who thinks he's from St. Louis," Cade said. "The rest of the files are mostly just words. We need to crack more of the thumb drives."

"I'm working on it," Shay said. "It took Odin a month to crack the first password. It shouldn't take me that long to get the next one, but it'll take *some* time. Especially when we're running around like this. I need time to think and do some research."

"Don't have a lot of time," Cade said.

"We don't know if Singular even knows about the action yet," Twist said. "It's two in the morning. Let's get some sleep, and then reach out to West as soon as we get up."

They spent a restless night—Shay got up at four o'clock, pulled on her jeans, and, trailed by X, thought she'd get a Diet Coke and look at the television for a while. When she got to the living room, she found Cruz sitting on the couch eating microwave popcorn and looking at a muted TV.

"Anything good?" she asked, her voice quiet.

"I've seen you about twenty times, hanging off the back of the sign," he said. "Somebody said that they've turned the sign off, but I haven't heard anything more."

Shay got her Coke and came back to the couch, twisting the cap off, and asked, "How long was it up?"

"I heard it was down about a half hour ago, so . . . maybe until three o'clock?"

"That's more than Twist expected."

Shay put her feet up on a smoked-glass coffee table and watched the muted TV as Cruz cycled through a hundred channels; they found several stations showing the MINDKILL sign, and almost all of them ran the video from the website.

"Anything from West, you think?"

Shay got her computer and checked, but there was nothing new. She went to the Mindkill website and looked at the visitor counter: 621,255. Twist's plan for pulling in eyeballs had worked.

"Maybe someone out there will recognize the guy they cut up and killed," Cruz said.

Shay hadn't considered that. "Jeez, that would be awful. I'd hate for someone to see a friend suffering like that. Oh, God . . ."

"Better to know the truth than not," Cruz said, and continued cycling through the channels. Shay decided she didn't want to think about it, and closed her computer. She yawned and said, "I'm going to bed."

She was back up at seven-thirty, groggy but unable to sleep. She checked the Facebook pages for West, but again, there was nothing new. She got cleaned up, and when she went down to the living room and kitchen, she found Twist making pancakes, and not well. She elbowed him out of the way. "I was the breakfast cook twice a week. Let me tell you: you don't start by turning the burners onto nuclear. You want *low* heat. . . ."

She made pancakes, and everybody ate, and Twist said, "Cruz said you checked West last night."

"I checked again this morning."

"We're all over the news," Twist said. "Singular's going to make a statement at nine o'clock."

"What can they say?"

"Quite a bit," Twist said. "But we'll see."

"Are you worried?" Cade asked.

"A little—but not too," Twist said. "We knew they'd have to say something."

"What about contacting West?" Shay asked.

Twist said, "Let's wait until after the press conference. See what we're dealing with."

Micah Cartwell, the Singular CEO, decided that Sync would handle the press conference. "You've got the military background," he said. "And we'll be talking military. There'll be a lot of questions, and you know the answers."

"I think we need somebody softer—" Sync began.

"No, actually, we need somebody authoritative," Cartwell said. "You're the man. You get Danville and Richie with you . . . how's Richie's arm? Is that fixed?"

"Fixed a week ago," Harmon said. "At least it was. . . ."

"Can he do that juggling act?" Cartwell asked.

"I'll check."

Sync's secretary came to the door. "Mr. West is here."

"Send him in," Sync said.

West stepped in, and Sync said, "We've got a statement for you to transmit to Shay Remby. You have to rewrite it, and put it in your own words."

"Are we going to mention her brother?" West asked.

"We have to," Sync said. He handed West a sheet of paper. "It's all in the statement. They'll be looking at this BlackWallpaper site as soon as our press conference begins. So get it ready, and when you see the conference start, send it."

"I will," West said. He understood he was being dismissed, and turned to leave. Just outside the door, in the secretary's office, he stopped and patted his pockets. Always nice to hear what is said after you leave the room. . . .

Cartwell asked, "The Remby kid is secure?"

"Yeah, but we're going to have to come up with a permanent solution," Sync said.

West dug his cell phone out of his suit coat pocket and smiled at the secretary. "Thought I'd lost it. Almost stopped my heart."

"I know what you mean," she said as he went by her desk. "If I lost my iPhone, my life would be over."

The press conference was carried live on CNN and on the websites of a couple of San Francisco stations, but got nothing like the immediate coverage that the Hollywood action had gotten.

That would change.

The press conference began with a statement from a man described as a Singular vice president, Stephen N. Creighton. He was a tall man with closely cropped silver hair, wearing a suit that was nice, but not too nice.

"Our medical start-up company has been profoundly disturbed by a political attack by a radical group from Los Angeles that put out a fraudulent film, probably produced by the group itself, to charge us with ridiculous mind-control claims. This is apparently the same group that did millions of dollars in damage at one of our laboratory facilities in Eugene, Oregon, a month ago . . ."

"Fraudulent film," Twist sneered. "Explain that to the guy lying on a table with half his brain scooped out."

"Or to the guy whose memories are in someone else's skull," Cade said.

Sync was talking about the work being done by Singular: ". . . apparently because some of our proprietary work leaked out to these people, who are nothing more than Luddites, opposed to any kind of progress. Especially progress that might aid members and former members of the military, or work that does not lead to their supposed agrarian paradise, where we'd all be out on motor-free, electricity-free farms with our hoes. But that's not the world the rest of us live in. I want to introduce you to a man—Danville, where are you? I want to get former army staff sergeant George Danville, who fought with the legendary Delta Company troops in Somalia, Iraq, and Afghanistan, up here on the stage."

The camera turned—the cameraman may have been prompted ahead of time—and the man called Danville jogged across the small auditorium, but instead of climbing the stairs, he vaulted onto the stage, rolled neatly to his feet, and stood smiling next to Sync.

"Do you news folks really want to know the kind of work these radicals are trashing? Well, George here has something to show you. Are you wearing those funky trousers, George?"

"Yes, I am, Steve," Danville said, leaning toward the microphone.

"Then do your thing," Sync said.

Danville, who was facing the cameras and the small crowd of reporters, reached behind himself and pulled with a tearing sound—Velcro being pulled apart.

"Oh no," Shay said.

Twist looked at her. "What?"

She pointed at the screen.

Danville pulled off his pants by separating Velcro attachments down the side seams and stepped out of them to stand there in a modest pair of paisley boxer shorts, to giggles from some of the women in the crowd.

"Good-looking guy, huh?" Sync asked. And to Danville: "Show them how flexible you are, George."

George nodded and, standing on one foot, bent his other leg forward from the knee. The giggles turned to gasps.

Sync intoned into the mike, "George lost both of his legs in Afghanistan, almost to the hip. These legs are entirely synthetic." He reached under the rostrum he was standing at and tossed Danville a jump rope. "Do something with this, George."

Danville unbent his knee and did a series of jump rope maneuvers that a trained man with natural legs would have trouble with.

"This is what we're doing at Singular," Sync said. "Some of the things that have been said about us—the mind-control business—touch upon what we're really doing. George's mind controls these legs. We have worked out nerve-to-electronics grafting techniques that, along with physical therapy and rigorous training, have given him his legs back."

He turned to Danville and said, "If you're not too modest, George, why don't you hop down off the stage and show your legs to the ladies—and gentlemen."

Danville jumped off the stage, landed flat on his feet, and smiled at the cameras.

Sync said, "Did I mention that he can run the hundred-yard dash in world-record time? But leaving that, I want to say that when these radicals trash our labs, what they do is take legs away from thousands of disabled people around the world. George is impressive; but he's also hugely expensive. We know this stuff works, but we need to drive down the cost by a factor of a hundred, or two hundred—his legs, which are custom-made, circuit by circuit, and fitted using our surgical nerve-splicing technique, cost more than ten million dollars each. If we can just do the research, we think we can drive the cost down to perhaps a hundred thousand each, or even fifty thousand. That still sounds like a lot, but it's doable for many, many people. If we're allowed to proceed with this research. I emphasize that all of the research we do is inspected, cleared, and approved by the United States government. These radicals, these criminals . . ."

Cruz said, "We're screwed."

Cade said, "This guy . . ."

"This guy has just shown us that he can talk with us," Twist said.

"He's shown us that they've got teeth, which we already knew. He's just keeping the conversation going—we'll talk back too."

"How?" Shay asked. "I mean, look at this. . . ."

Sync had introduced another man by tossing three red balls to him. The man had caught them in the air and begun juggling—and his artificial arm and hand, which were sheathed in black carbon fiber, never missed a beat.

"We're going to get your brother back," Twist said. "They can make all the robotic arms and legs they want, but kidnapping is still a major crime, and cutting up living brains is a capital crime."

The press conference lasted a half hour, with excited questions from the reporters—they'd at least lost the reporters, Shay thought. As they watched, the video of Danville and the juggler began spreading across the networks. The Hollywood sign action was getting a lot of attention; the Singular press conference might have been getting more.

At ten o'clock, Twist turned away from the TV and asked, "Anything from West?"

She went to BlackWallpaper and found a new note:

Singular wants you to know that we do not have your brother. As we told you earlier, several members of Storm were arrested near San Diego by the FBI. We also understand that one of them, a woman named Rachel Wharton, managed to escape. Our contact with the FBI believes that Wharton drove north to Los Angeles, where she met with at least one and possibly more fugitive members of Storm, and then continued north, and may now be in the Lake Tahoe area. Your brother may be with Wharton. That's all we have. Oh, one other thing: your brother left a notebook in the van that dropped him off. It's been examined, and

there's nothing in it that pertains to us. If you want to get together and claim it, I'll be in L.A. tomorrow on other business. I expect you saw our press conference. This is the work we are doing, Shay. Please don't do more damage to it.

And on GandyDancer:

Ignore the stuff at BlackWallpaper, although the Wharton part is true. The notebook thing is bullshit, it's a setup to grab you. The statement was dictated by the security chief, Stephen N. Creighton, who you probably saw on television giving the company's reply to your action. The security people here believe you're traveling with an artist named Twist, and they have his license plate number, his credit cards, and other information. If you are with him, then you are at risk. We must meet, in the Sacramento area, as soon as possible, if we want to free Odin. I am now certain that he's being held by the company. We should meet late tonight, if possible. Erase this.

"How far to Sacramento?" Shay asked.

"Six hours, straight up I-5," Twist said. "We should stick here for a while, just monitoring things, and I've got to make some calls. If we leave after the rush this evening, we'll be there by one o'clock in the morning."

"We've got to go," Shay said.

They were still uncertain about West, but his warning about Twist couldn't be ignored.

"We need to get that second car," Twist told Cruz. "Call your friend now."

As Cruz did that, Shay, Cade, and Twist talked about how to reply to the message from Singular.

"They won't believe us if we *totally* buy everything they say," Cade said. "Maybe they'll believe it if we sound like we *sorta* buy it. We should tell them that we're checking with people we know and will get back to them tomorrow. But a couple of new video threats would help."

"We only have the one other video so far," Shay said.

"They don't know that," Twist said. "You're a teenager—haven't you heard of lying?"

"But . . ."

"We don't tell them what's in the file," Twist said. "We just tell them that if we decide they have Odin, we'll release another file, and we'll keep releasing them until we see Odin."

Cruz came back and said they had a choice of four used vehicles, two Camrys, one Corolla, and a Ford Focus, all guaranteed for ten to twenty thousand miles.

"This guy doesn't have to register the transfer for thirty days, so it won't show up under your name until then, and nobody could track it," he said. "If we return it with no damage in less than thirty days, they'll buy it back at half price and tear up the transfer papers. Oh yeah—they want cash."

Before leaving, the four of them worked out responses to both BlackWallpaper, directed at Singular, and GandyDancer, directed at West alone.

They told BlackWallpaper that they were checking with people they knew—they didn't specify who—about Rachel's whereabouts, and whether Odin might be with her. They said that if they couldn't find Rachel, or Odin, they would release another video.

About the response to West, Twist said, "We have one remaining clean telephone. Do we give him the number?"

Cade said, "If we answer a call, they might be able to trace our location."

"If he's really on our side, and I think he is . . . I feel like he is . . . it might be useful to have somebody on the inside who could call us," Shay said.

Cruz: "We can always get more phones."

They all looked at each other, then Twist said, "I agree with Shay. Let's give him a number."

• • •

Shay wanted to get out of the house, to somewhere she could go online and work on breaking into the Singular thumb drives; Cruz suggested the Malibu Country Mart, but she couldn't go as Girl on a Wire.

Twist found a big, stylish, floppy black hat probably belonging to one of Sean's girlfriends in a closet, and with her hair pinned up, the hat, and the sunglasses, Twist said Shay looked like a minor starlet pretending to avoid the paparazzi.

They'd take no chances with posting their messages. Cruz and Cade would drive Shay, X, and Twist to the Malibu shopping center, where Twist would get money at the bank and Shay could go online. Once they got the money, Cade and Cruz would drive Cruz's truck into Santa Monica, thirteen miles to the east, go to the public library, get online, and send the two messages to BlackWallpaper and GandyDancer. Then they'd drive over to East L.A. in the truck and buy the second car.

At the shopping center, Twist got the money and gave it to Cade and Cruz, who took off. Twist walked with Shay to a coffee shop, where they both had espressos, and Twist said, "I'm gonna walk back to the house. Quite a few people out here know me. Probably be best to stay out of sight."

"You should try a new hat," Shay said, and he tipped his bowler at her and moved along. She took an outside table, opened her laptop, went online, and resumed sifting through articles by and about Dr. Lawrence Janes for password clues.

West had been checking BlackWallpaper on his laptop and Gandy-Dancer on a Windows 8 slate that he hoped Singular didn't know about—its signal was routed through AT&T cell phone service rather than the company's Wi-Fi. When Shay's answer came in on BlackWallpaper, he immediately checked GandyDancer and found she'd sent a phone number. He saved the number to an encrypted file on his phone and wiped the GandyDancer message.

He carried the laptop up to Harmon's office and showed him the BlackWallpaper exchange.

"Good work," Harmon said. "That probably gets us at least twenty-four hours. We'll find her before then. I'll pass this on to Sync, and you keep watching that site."

"I think I'll do some deeper research on this Twist character and see what pops up."

"Can't hurt," Harmon agreed.

West didn't care much about Twist, but gave the research a good half hour, saving the most interesting stuff to a Word document in case he needed to show it to somebody.

Then he fired up his laptop, plugged in the hard drive he'd copied at the logistics office, and began harvesting names, job descriptions, and expense account notes. The expense account notes told him what people were doing—what they were buying, where they were going.

In an hour, he'd isolated most of what he identified as the company's combat arm—it was called "operations"—which reported to Thorne, who reported directly to Sync. Thorne had spent a lot of time in Sacramento, where the Singular prison was. According to the records, he had at least a dozen men and women working for him there, none of whom West recognized.

West knew little about Thorne, and had never figured out the Singular bureaucracy—questions were discouraged—but as he worked through the hard drive, it became apparent that Thorne was Harmon's bureaucratic equal. West knew all of the guys in intelligence, though they mostly worked separately or in pairs. Kicking back in his chair, he thought about the division of labor between the intelligence arm and operations: Harmon would find Shay. Thorne would grab her. He'd better stick close to Harmon.

He composed a note to Shay and posted it on GandyDancer:

This is critical. I need to keep talking to the top people here so I know what's going on. Send me a note on BlackWallpaper every couple of hours, so I have a reason to go talk with them. They are hunting you and believe they will find you. I say again, we need to meet tonight near Sacramento. We have to talk.

Shay got the note from West as she sat at the shopping center doing her password research. She sketched out a reply on her laptop, then called Twist and told him about West's request.

"I've written a note that we could send him, but I think we should find a place to send it that's not close to here," she said.

"I'll call the guys over in East L.A. That ought to do it," Twist said. "What do you want to tell them?"

West carried the note up to Harmon's office and showed it to him.

West: Our friends up north haven't seen or heard from Rachel or Odin. We think you're stalling for time. Give us a better location on where you think they are, or we'll drop another video on you. Tell your boss that we really don't want to fight. We just want Odin, and to go back to Eugene, and never hear from you again.

"You know, we really do think this Rachel chick is headed back north," Harmon said. "Those guys the feds busted say she didn't have any more of the thumb drives, so we don't much care where she's at. Let me talk to Sync. Maybe we could tell them that we're sending you out to find her and you'll know something in a day or two. She seems to have a certain rapport with you."

"Whatever you want," West said. And: "I've been looking into this guy Twist. Never had any contact with animal rights people, not that I can find. He's mostly involved with street kids and immigrant rights, all of it inside the city of Los Angeles. He operates that shelter for kids—I think Shay must have recruited him there. She might have wound up there by accident."

"Bad accident for us," Harmon said. "But it happens. That's the way of the world—all the critical stuff blows up because of accident, error, and stupidity."

"I'll have that tattooed on my chest," West said.

Harmon laughed and said, "Upside down, so you can read it in the shower."

Shay was still on her laptop at the shopping center when two notes came in.

BlackWallpaper:

Shay—the company has authorized me to go over to the Tahoe area to see if I can find Rachel myself. We have the names of a few animal rights activists in that area, and she may be with them. We don't really much care about her as long as she doesn't attack any more of our labs, so we haven't been trying to find her. If I find her, I will let you know immediately. Please don't hurt us before you hear from me.

The truth came in on GandyDancer:

I'm not going anywhere. Answer the BlackWallpaper note in a couple of hours. Something provocative. Erase this.

Shay thought about that and composed a new note. Twist called a few minutes later and asked, "Where are you?"

She'd just packed up her laptop and left the shopping center. "Walking back to the house with X."

"Did you hear from West?"

She told him about the last messages, and about her proposed new one—that they would extend the deadline until noon the next day.

"I'll call Cade and tell him to stop at a Wi-Fi place and send it," Twist said.

As Shay was walking back to the house, Harmon took a call from one of his agents in L.A.: "This Twist—we think he's been talking to a woman who runs his hotel. She called somebody last night and the phone was answered on Gower, which looks right up at that Hollywood sign. An hour ago, she was talking to the same number in Malibu. We got the location, checked it out. A half hour ago, a guy walked out on a deck at that location, and it's him."

"Excellent. Keep watching it," Harmon said. "Look for the girl and that son-of-a-bitch dog."

Five minutes later, West took the BlackWallpaper message up to Harmon's office, but Harmon wasn't there. The group secretary said, "He went running up to Sync's office."

"I got a message from this girl, they need to see it," West said.

"It doesn't matter," the secretary said. "They spotted the guy she's with, they're moving in on them. In Malibu, I—" She realized what she'd just said, the security breach. She stopped and put a hand to her mouth.

West's heart sank, but he played it cool, as though he hadn't paid much attention to what she was saying. "Well, tell him to call me when he's got the time."

Out in the hallway, walking back to his office, he called up the encrypted phone number, hesitated, then punched it.

As Shay came through the door, Twist, cranked up, said, "I think we're all set to go north. I need a beer, I need a cigarette, I need my feet rubbed, and, man, we're operating."

"I thought you quit smoking?" Shay said. "And you'll have to find somebody else to rub your feet."

"I did quit. Ten years ago, but I still dream about it. And nobody ever rubbed my feet. Ever. I ask, and they say *eww.* Cade and Cruz will be here in a few minutes. They're going to stop and get a pizza."

A phone rang. An odd sound, not one of the phones they'd been using. Shay frowned, and stepped over to her backpack. "It's the number we gave West," she said.

Shay and Twist looked at each other for a moment, then Twist rapped his cane on the floor and said, "Answer it."

She answered it, punching up the speaker. "Yes?"

"Get out. They spotted your friend Twist and they're coming for you. They're already in Malibu. Get out now." He was gone.

Twist said, "C'mon," and they ran up the stairs that led to the roof. They went to the ocean side first and peeked over the edge, and Twist said, "There. The two guys. West's right: they're already here."

The two guys were ambling down the beach in knee-length

shorts and Tommy Bahama shirts, but they still looked like soldiers. "They're *those* guys, they're like West, we could never outrun them," Shay said. She felt a tickle of panic.

Twist said, "C'mon." He jogged across the deck to the front of the house, facing the highway. They leaned over a board railing, and Shay said: "That van. Two vans."

"I see them. And maybe that BMW." He turned to her, scratched his cheek.

"What are they gonna do?" Shay asked.

"What'd they do at the hotel?" Twist asked. "They knocked your door down. They'll grab you, throw you and the dog in the van, get out of here. C'mon. Let's move. Call Cade and tell them to stay away. . . ."

They ran down the stairs, and Shay punched in Cade's number. Twist was on his phone too and Shay asked, "Who are *you* calling?"

Twist looked at her and said flatly, "Oh my God, the house is on fire."

"What?"

The 911 operator came up and asked, "Is this an emergency?"

Twist shouted, "Oh my God, there's been some kind of an explosion. It smells really bad and there's fire all over the place, I think somebody had a meth lab, call the police, these houses are on fire."

"Sir, are you in danger?"

"Not me, it's three or four houses down. . . ."

He gave a nearby address east on the highway, toward Santa Monica.

The operator said, "Are you saying it's in Malibu?"

"Yes, yes, Malibu. On the ocean. Oh my God, it's like we're burning out the movie stars, oh my God, there's a burning man. . . ."

"Sir . . ."

Twist screamed, "I gotta go. I got a Rolls, I gotta get it out of the garage."

He hung up and then asked Shay, "Cade?"

At that instant, Cade answered and Shay said urgently, "Singular is here in Malibu. You and Cruz stay away, we'll call you."

She hung up and looked at the front door, expecting to see it explode inward. Twist had gone to a closet and dragged out a huge suitcase. "Get the guys' stuff from the bedrooms, throw it all in here. And all the computer stuff. Don't pack it, just throw it."

"Do we have time?"

They could hear sirens, and not far away. "They'll wait until they see what the sirens are about."

"Then what?"

"Then we run," he said. He had that odd, happy smile, like he'd had the night he, Dum, and Dee had broken the two thugs in the alley.

"Not a game, Twist," she said, and ran to the kitchen for her knife.

32

They hadn't been in the house long enough to really spread out. In two minutes, they'd packed up, dragged the suitcase out to the garage, and thrown it in the back of the Range Rover.

Shay climbed into the passenger seat; X, in the back, licked her ear.

Twist said, "They'll see us as soon as the garage door goes up, so hold on: I'm coming out of here in a hurry."

Lots of sirens now, and close by.

Twist: "You ready?"

"Let's go," Shay said. In the backseat, X turned to look out the rear window.

Twist pushed the button on the garage-door remote and the door started to lift. They were parked facing in, and Shay turned in her seat as Twist shifted into reverse, and she blurted, "Stop. Don't go."

Twist was looking in the rearview mirror. "Ah, crap. Outsmarted myself."

The arrival of fire engines, ambulances, and police cars a block away had created an instant traffic jam just feet from the garage door. Although the far lane was clear—and no cars were coming from the other direction, either—the near lane was blocked by a red Jaguar convertible driven by a young blonde, who was fixing her matching red lipstick in the sun visor mirror as the car idled.

"Give me a second, I'll ask her to move," Shay said. She jumped out of the car and ran out to the Jaguar.

"We've got an emergency," she called to the woman. "We've got to get out. Could you move over to the other lane?"

"No, I can't. Can't you see what's happening?" the woman said. "Everybody's got a problem."

"But . . ."

"There are fire engines and everything."

"We want to go the other way. . . ."

"Tough luck," the woman said, and dabbed at her lips in the mirror. "Now stop bothering me."

Shay glared at her for a moment, then went steaming back into the garage, where she'd seen a couple of baseball bats, a glove, and a ball. She grabbed a bat and went steaming back outside and said, "Now! You've got three seconds to get out of my way, or I start swinging. If Mr. Disney doesn't get to his doctor in the next five minutes, we will sue you and you'll spend the rest of your life driving a bicycle."

The woman's eyes had gone round and she said, "Wait, wait." Then: "Mr. Disney?"

"Move the fucking car!" Shay screamed.

"All right, I'm moving. . . ."

Shay ran back and jumped in the Range Rover with the bat, and Twist, when he saw the Jaguar moving, backed into the gap, then around into the outbound lane, then jammed it into drive and hit the gas.

"What'd you tell her?" Twist asked.

"That you were Walt Disney and we had to get Bambi to the vet," Shay said.

"Looks like Bambi's going to the vet in a convoy," Twist said. "They're right behind us."

Shay turned again: the BMW was fifty feet behind them, and the two vans were behind it. She could see faces through the BMW's windshield; nobody she recognized—two hard-looking men in sunglasses.

"What are we going to do?" Shay asked.

"Give them an automotive demonstration," Twist said. "Can you get X in your footwell? Push the seat all the way back."

"I think so. . . ."

She tugged the dog into the front seat—he was happy enough to join them, but less happy about dropping down into the footwell. X was large enough that there was barely room for Shay's legs around him.

"Keep him there," Twist said. "We've got a turn coming up, and then we're going up the hill, and then we're going to show these guys the difference between a genuine off-road vehicle and a Beemer, the Beemer basically being a good car for taking the dog to get washed. Let's hope they don't know that."

Twist looked a little different behind the wheel. "I didn't know you're a car guy," Shay said.

Twist laughed. "I'm not. I wouldn't know a Chevy from a John Deere. I got the free off-road school when I bought the car. Then I brought it back here in the hills a couple of times, just to try it out. I know this place. . . ."

They were going down the Pacific Coast Highway at a hundred miles an hour. The BMW was staying with them, though the two men that Shay could see in the car's front seats were looking grim. One was on a telephone. The vans had fallen back.

"Now hold on," Twist said.

They were approaching a narrow notch in the Malibu bluff. Twist braked hard and the BMW handled that without a problem, closing up to within a couple of car lengths, and then they were climbing the bluff. A sign flashed by: LATIGO CANYON ROAD. The BMW stayed with them up the blacktop road, staying close through the curves and humps, past narrow gated driveways and lush, overgrown yards.

Then it closed up until it was only a few feet behind them. "They might try to bump us," Twist said. Again, the happy smile.

They were coming onto a straightaway, and he jammed on the brakes while moving to the center of the road. The BMW handled that, too, but almost tapped the back bumper.

Twist accelerated again, the BMW staying farther back, and then they were over the top, and the world began to change around them from oceanside lush to near desert. "Vans are gone," Shay said. She'd braced her feet against the dashboard to give X more space in the footwell. "You're driving like a maniac."

"So's the other guy," Twist said. "Now shut up and let me concentrate. I've got to find this one turn. . . ."

They went through a half-dozen radical switchback turns— radical for their speed, anyway, and a truck that was modestly piglike in its handling—and then into a more densely populated, well-watered neighborhood, and Twist muttered, "It's right here . . . somewhere. Where is it?"

Down in the footwell, X rumbled.

"What are we looking for?" Shay asked. The BMW was still right behind them.

"This one road . . ."

"The guy's on the telephone again," Shay said.

"Hope he's not talking to a helicopter."

Another mile, then even more, and then Twist said, "There it is. That's it. The blue house. I'm pretty sure. . . ."

They took a left onto a narrow street, and then through a subdivision; a man was out on his lawn talking to a guy in a red shirt, and they both turned to watch as the two cars rocketed by.

"Watch for kids, watch for kids, watch for kids. . . ."

More turns, and then Twist said, "We're good, we're good, there's that old farm kinda place. . . ."

They went past the old farm kinda place, and more houses . . . and then the houses ended. So did the blacktop, and they launched onto a trail of mixed gravel and dirt, throwing up a dust cloud behind them.

"Still coming," Shay said.

"Gotta keep them coming fast . . . there's this arroyo up ahead . . . dry, lots of round rocks."

"They can't handle rocks? They're doing good so far."

"It's not the rocks they can't handle, it's the road. . . . Not if you don't know it." Twist took a couple more turns and said, "Get a grip on the dog, this is gonna be rough."

Shay got hold of X's collar and pushed her nose next to his and said, "It's gonna be okay, boy, maybe, if Twist's boy hormones don't wreck us. You can bite him if we get away."

The dog gave her a quick lick and then another throat rumble; he was with her, but he wasn't exactly sure that they were doing the right thing.

Twist said, "Here it is, and here we go."

The trail ran next to the arroyo, where earlier four-wheelers and other thrill-seeking drivers had beaten out a path through the rocks.

Twist shifted left onto the rocks, and the Range Rover began bounding like a three-ton rabbit but managed to stay upright. The truck was throwing up less dust as it pounded across the bare rocks, and the BMW began moving up as the driver's visibility improved. Twist's speed had dropped from forty or fifty miles an hour to the thirties, and then the twenties, and the BMW was almost on top of them, and Shay said, "They're coming! What're we doing? What are we doing?"

"We're about to go around a wicked curve," Twist said. "Here it is."

They went right. Behind them, the BMW found itself on an outside-banking curve that wanted to throw the vehicle off the road to the left, into the arroyo. The arroyo had dropped three feet below the level of the road, so if they went off, they'd take a terrific drop.

"If they stay on the road . . . ," Twist said. The BMW driver tried to do that, but the road grew increasingly banked, and the wrong way. "He's either got to take the jump, which will wreck him, or stay with the road, which will roll him . . . or stop. He should stop. Give it up, guy, give it up. . . ."

The BMW didn't give it up, and then, suddenly, it rolled, tumbling like a boulder into the arroyo, stopping with its wheels straight up in the air. Twist kept going for two hundred yards, then slowed. "Are they getting out?"

"Don't see anything," Shay said. They sat for a moment, then Shay saw movement at the back of the BMW. "Somebody's getting out. Somebody's— Twist, he's got a gun."

Twist hit the gas, and the Range Rover rumbled up the rocks. "He's going to shoot us."

But he didn't. They were on the tooth-rattling rocks for another quarter mile, then turned back onto the dirt road.

"Now. Let's see if they've got somebody out in front of us," Twist said. "They shouldn't, because they don't know the mean back-streets of Malibu."

They rumbled along the dirt road for a few more minutes, then onto a much better road, though still dirt; twenty minutes after that, they poked the nose of the Range Rover out onto a paved road.

"Not out of the woods yet," Twist said. A battered Xterra went by, carrying two blond guys with four surfboards on the roof.

"I have no idea where we're at."

Twist smiled at her. "We're about ten miles, give or take a land-slide or two, from the real California."

Shay: "The real one? I thought I was in the real one. What's the real one?"

"It's called the Valley. You can put the dog in the back."

After another long, rambling drive along Kanan Dume Road and then Mulholland Highway, they rolled up a ramp onto the 101 Freeway.

"This car is way too expensive to ditch," Twist said. "We've got to hide it, and there's no better place to hide it than a busy parking lot. I don't want to get towed, either. We need a place where it can sit for a while."

"How about an airport?" Shay suggested. "Long-term parking?"

Twist looked at her and said, "You really do have a criminal mind. That's perfect. I know just the one. We dump it at Bob Hope in Burbank, and Lou can pick it up in a week or so, when things quiet down. Get on the phone, call Cade and Cruz. We'll meet them there in an hour."

"And then . . ."

"Sacramento."

They left the truck in an economy lot off Winona Avenue and took a shuttle to the airport; the shuttle driver was not excited about X, but Twist said, "We'll *really* appreciate it if you just let us ride." He poked a ten-dollar bill at the driver, and it instantly disappeared.

Cruz and Cade were waiting when Twist towed Sean's giant suitcase through the main entrance. "We're in short-term parking," Cruz said. "You have any problems?"

"Pretty routine," Twist said.

"Nice scenery between Malibu and the 101," Shay added.

"We were freaked," Cade said. "We thought you guys were in trouble."

"Hey, she was with me," Twist said.

33

They headed north in a two-car convoy. Neither Cruz's used truck nor the Camry they'd bought from Cruz's connection could be counted on to be completely reliable, and if one of them broke down, the other would be there to help. Cade would drive the Camry, with Twist trying to get some sleep in the back.

Shay would go with Cruz, because X fit best on the narrow back-seat of the truck.

"Before we leave town, we should check GandyDancer and tell West we're okay," Shay said.

"And tell him that we're headed to Sacramento, but not exactly where—we want to make sure it's not a trap, so we'll want to look around when we get there," Twist said. "If we meet, it's on our ground, not his."

"If we're that worried, we should pull the battery on Shay's phone," Cade said. "If he's lying to us, they could track it when he calls."

"It's supposed to be for emergency contacts," Shay said. "It already saved us once."

Cruz: "If we're on the road, there's nothing we could do about an emergency, even if he called."

They all looked at Shay, who nodded, dug the phone out of her bag, and pulled the battery.

They made a stop at a Burbank Starbucks, sent the message, and then headed north. X sat up on the backseat, peering past Cruz and Shay through the windshield, watching L.A. thin out and then disappear like fairy dust as they passed Castaic and got into the Grapevine, and then down into the San Joaquin Valley and the endless farmlands. With the highway stretching ahead as straight as a ruler, X lay down and went to sleep.

Five and a half hours, up the Central Valley, the small towns, and a couple of big ones in the distance, flicking away in the growing darkness. They made one stop, for gas and coffee and the bathrooms. Twist walked around the parking lot, stretching his bad leg, and then they were rolling again.

During the first hour, there was some conversation between Shay and Cruz about what really happened during the car chase out of Malibu, and they listened to a Los Angeles AM station for news about a chase—there wasn't any—until they lost the radio signal. After that, they went quiet for a couple of hours, just the drone of wheels on pavement, neither of them uncomfortable in the silence between them.

• • •

"You sleepy?" Shay asked. "I can drive if you want to close your eyes for a while."

"Nah, I'm good."

"Cruz . . . can I ask you something?"

"*Sí.*"

"That tattoo by your neck, the one your mother didn't like—"

"That's not the one she didn't like," he said.

"Oh. So you've got two?"

"Two, twelve, seventeen—who's counting?"

"Seventeen?"

He chuckled. "You asking what's so badass about my tat?"

"Uh-huh."

He flipped on the interior lamp and raised up his T-shirt. She could see a five-inch-long cross and blue script on the right side of his rib cage.

"I can't make out the words."

"It says RIP GABRIEL."

"That's not so bad."

"It also says SANGRE POR SANGRE. 'Blood for blood.' "

"Oh."

After a while: "Did you?"

"No. Thought a lot about it . . . but no."

They went on into the night.

At eleven o'clock, West's phone buzzed. He looked at the screen, recognized the number. He clicked it on and said, "Yes." He listened, then said, "I'll be there."

At twelve-thirty, he pulled into the designated Walmart. Though it was late, there were dozens of cars scattered around the lot. As he'd been told to, he parked his black Jeep Rubicon halfway back in the lot, centered on the building, and got out of the truck. He waited a minute, then two, and then his phone rang and a man asked, "Where are you?"

"Right where Shay said."

"Guy's going to come get you in a minute. He's driving a white Toyota pickup. He'll get out. He'll park so you're between the pickup and your car."

"Don't run me over."

"One minute."

A minute later, a white pickup pulled into the parking lot, angled across the blacktop, and swung up next to West. The driver left the engine running, got out, and walked around the truck. A tough-looking Latino kid, who nodded at West and said, "I'm going to pat you down."

"What are you looking for?"

"Phones and weapons."

"I've got a pistol on my right hip, and two phones in my jacket pocket," West said.

"Put them in your Jeep and lock the door."

West did as Cruz told him, and then Cruz patted him down. West said, "You know, if I was bugged, the bug would be about the size of a fingernail."

Cruz said, "Doin' the best we can."

"Maybe I can give you lessons when this is over," West said.

"I'd take them," Cruz said. "Get in the truck."

They left the Walmart parking lot, took a left on Reed Avenue, crossed I-80, took another left on Stillwater Road, and then took a circuitous route through a series of empty parking lots, stopping under trees a few times, then returned to Stillwater Road, out to Reed, crossed the interstate again, and back to the Walmart parking lot.

"Let's walk," Cruz said.

"Didn't see anybody?"

"Doin' the best we can," Cruz said again.

Inside the store, Cruz got a shopping cart and told West to get one, and they pushed their carts into the grocery section, where they found a short man in a bowler hat, with a cane, looking at fruit juices. West said, "Mr. Twist. Pleased to meet you."

"Just Twist," Twist said. He tipped his head at Cruz, who pushed his cart around a corner and disappeared.

"I looked you up," West said. "You're fairly famous. Is Shay around? Or is this just the first stop?"

Twist took him in, then nodded, and Shay, from behind West, said, "Hey."

West turned, smiled, and said, "There you are. Didn't trust me, did you?"

"Still not saying I do."

"I can appreciate that," West said. "I *am* trustworthy, but it doesn't make sense to trust me."

"Where's Odin?"

"There's a whole story about that—I think I know, but I'm not absolutely sure."

"Let's move over to the produce department," Twist said.

"The Latino guy is checking for operators?"

"Not just the Latino guy," Twist said. "There are more of us than that. If Singular is here and they take us on, I can promise you national coverage, 'cause this Walmart's going up in smoke."

"Nobody here but us mice," West said, and they rolled his cart to produce. A tall, long-haired kid pushed a cart past them and said to Twist, "Nobody came in," and then kept going.

West looked after him, less amused, and said, "You weren't bluffing. There are more of you."

"There are," Twist said. "Tell us the Odin story."

West told about breaking into the logistics office and copying the hard drive, then analyzing the information on it and pinpointing what he thought might be a secret lab, and probably a prison. "It's across the river, in Sacramento. Not more than five or six miles from here. It's isolated, off to the side in a warehouse district. I saw them take a female in—too far away to tell her age—but they had her wearing leg chains."

"You don't know that Odin's there, though," Shay said.

"No, but it makes sense, if they have that kind of . . . facility. Also, the people who run the place are exactly the kind of people who would have grabbed Odin and held him. It's a group run by a guy named Thorne, who's ex-military, maybe ex-CIA."

"The idea of going in after Odin . . . is that just a fantasy?" Twist asked.

West shook his head. "No. I have an idea of how it might be done. But I'll tell you, it might involve a gun or two."

"We don't want to kill anybody," Twist said.

"Too late, cracker: people *are* being killed," West said. "If they've been trying to squeeze Odin about these thumb drives—"

Twist blinked. "Cracker?"

"I don't want to hear that Odin's been hurt," Shay said.

"I'm sorry, Shay, but the way people are acting . . . I think he's in real danger."

"We need to go somewhere to talk. Somewhere better than this," Twist said. "Someplace with Wi-Fi."

"Pick a motel," West said.

Twist stared at him again, then said to Shay, "Your call."

Shay said to West, "Promise me that this isn't a trap."

West looked into her eyes, put his hand on his heart. "I swear."

Shay said to Twist, "Whatever's closest."

They found a place called the Dunrovin, a mom-and-pop motel off the freeway. They got a room with a surprisingly fast Wi-Fi system, and closed the drapes.

West brought up Google Earth on Cade's laptop and spotted what he called the prison. "From above, it's not clear, but this is a ramp," he said, tapping the screen. "It comes off the parking lot and drops down below ground level. When trucks come and go, nobody on the outside can see what's being delivered, or taken out, or even that there's a truck in there. I was there in the middle of the night, and I saw three trucks come and go. Only one of them delivered a prisoner, but all of them opened that door. . . ."

"It looks to me like getting in there is impossible," Shay said. "Down in that hole?"

"It's not quite," West said. "But it'd be risky. If you come at the building from this angle"—he pointed at the far corner of the building, directly opposite the ramp—"you could crawl up this drainage ditch, right to the corner. Even if they have cameras, I doubt they'd see you. Then you crawl down the length of the building, right next to the foundation, and around the corner to the ramp. The trucks I saw pulled down into the ramp, then reversed and backed up to the door. The driver got out and identified himself at the door, then they opened the door and unloaded from the back of the truck using a dolly. If we wait until the door is open and the driver has pushed a load inside, and we drop over the wall—"

"Ah, I can only think of about a thousand problems with that," Twist said. "They *do* see us with cameras. They've got motion alarms. The trucks don't come. We go crashing in and find ourselves inside a secure room, like the entry rooms in real prisons."

West said, "I know. Judging from the security at Singular headquarters, I *think* we'd be all right. That's a pretty ragged area out there—all kinds of coyotes and street dogs, lots of stuff to set off alarms, so probably minimal motion stuff. I see cameras at the corners, but they're looking out, they wouldn't see us. The trucks . . . I think deliveries must be frequent. But I'm not sure on any of it."

"We have no idea of how many guards there might be," Cade said.

"I do know that. Thorne probably runs fifteen or twenty people. Not all of them are at this facility—they do other things, like try to raid Hollywood hotels. I think he probably has no more than ten or twelve to guard this place, and he has to cover three shifts, seven days a week. I'd expect to run into no more than two or three guys. Of course, with this kind of deal, it's possible that some guys bunk out here. We should be gone before they can get their acts together."

"Will they have guns?" Cruz asked.

"Yes," West said.

"You got any other ideas?" Twist asked.

"Only one that might work, but I'm not sure you'd want to hear about it," West said. "On the other hand, with your action history, maybe you would."

"What is it?"

"Here, back off the Google picture a bit, move it over this way."

Cade did that, and West tapped a point on the screen. "Bring it down to here."

Cade enlarged the scene, and Twist asked, "What is that?"

"It's a gasoline terminal, where tanker trucks fill up. They fill trucks all night, and they go out to the gas stations. So, they come out this gate"—he touched a gate showing near the gas terminal—"where we have this helpless but really good-looking young red-headed girl, limping, clothing torn, desperately flag down the truck. When it stops, I jump out, stick my gun up the guy's nose, and hijack the truck—and the guy, so he can't call anyone.

"We drive it to the Singular building, which is four miles away. We drive right up to the building, drop the filler hose, and start pumping out. These babies will hold ten thousand gallons of gas. We drive it around the building . . . touch off the gas . . . and call the cops and the fire department. When they arrive, we run through the rescue services screaming that there are people down in the basement. They knock down the doors, and there we are."

"My God, I *do* like you," Twist said.

"Since this ramp is belowground, what happens if the fire gets down there?" Shay asked. "Everybody gets roasted alive?"

"We'd have to be careful," West said.

Twist brushed back his hair with both hands and said, "The frying pan or the fire?"

"We gotta choose; we gotta move," West said. "I really don't think Odin or this woman I saw . . . I don't think they're in a good place."

Shay slipped out of the dry drainage ditch, gloves crusted with dirt, one knee bruised by an unseen rock, onto the lawn. She slid through the grass, with X at her shoulder on a short leash, and up to the building's foundation. West and Twist were already there, lying down, their backs against the wall. Ten seconds later, Cruz came in.

West had brought two pistols and, after some heated discussion, had given one of them to Cruz, who was familiar with the type. Cruz promised that he wouldn't use it unless it was a case of life or death.

"Won't even take it out of my pocket," he said. "Won't jack in a shell."

West also had a dozen keyed padlocks, some eight-foot lengths of chain, and several pairs of soft cotton gardening gloves, all of which he'd gotten at three separate Home Depots to avoid being the sort of customer clerks remember. He'd also stopped at a Target, where he bought nylon stockings to pull over their faces, like bank robbers did. Singular would know soon enough that Shay and Twist were part of the raid if they managed to free Odin, but they thought they might be able to hide out long enough to make further harassment unproductive.

West hoped to go back to Singular undetected. He'd find out more about the Singular operation from the inside than from the outside.

They'd decided that stealing a gas truck and kidnapping the driver and torching a building could lead to too many ramifications—like hurting innocent hostages, Odin included. West had suspected that would be the case, which was why he'd stopped at the Home Depots for the gloves, chains, and locks. Still, Twist had sort of liked the gasoline idea—more for the theatrical value than because he thought it might work.

"Can you see that? Hundred-foot flames, the fire department crashing into the prison section, the media coverage . . ."

Shay: "The people roasted to death, our trials . . ."

So it was option one: rushing the door at the end of the ramp, if it ever opened. They were moving in at two o'clock in the morning because that was when, according to West, human alertness was getting near its low ebb.

They would leave at five if no deliveries showed up.

Cade, much to his disgust, was sitting in the same burnt-out building where West had done surveillance on the Singular building. If the raid came off, he'd drive Cruz's pickup down to the building because they could get eight people—perhaps nine—and a dog into the pickup and its bed.

Cade had protested, and Twist had shut him up like this: West had to go, as the one who knew the most about this sort of action; Twist, because he was the boss and an ace in a fight; Cruz, because he knew how to use the gun if he had to; Shay, because she refused to stay behind, and besides, she could handle X, who'd proven to be valuable in a fast-moving fight.

"You're right," Cade had conceded. "I'm your driver."

Twist had extended a fist bump. "Damned *skilled* driver."

There were few lights around the building—barely enough to see each other at two feet—so they'd worked out some simple hand signals.

When Twist reached back and patted Shay on the head, she felt him move away, and she followed, crawling down the length of the building on her hands and knees. West had emphasized that they should move slowly, because quickness was more noticeable in the dark.

The building was two hundred feet long, but it took almost no time to crawl down its length. When they got to the end, West peeked around the corner of the building, moved back, and whispered, "Nothing."

They'd taken blankets from the mom-and-pop motel—Twist left a hundred-dollar bill on the bed—and tied them around their waists. Now they untied them and put them on the grass and sat on them; West knew from experience that they would get cold and stiff if they were sitting directly on the ground.

Shay and X settled on her blanket, and the men ahead of and behind her stirred around, getting settled.

They waited.

West had warned against talking—sounds carry at night—so they simply sat, staring at the lights of the city a few hundred yards away. The stars were brighter than in Los Angeles, but not much, and nothing like they were in the mountains of Oregon or Idaho. Once, Shay thought she saw movement in the empty field they were facing, but decided it had been a mirage. A pickup truck bounced around a building a quarter mile away, seemingly pointlessly, and disappeared the same way it had come.

They could hear trucks on freeways, and that was about it.

Shay got cold, as West had predicted, and snuggled up to X, who seemed to like it. She was scared, though she wouldn't have admitted it. She'd been scared the night she'd been cornered by the two thugs in the Hollywood alley, but only after the fact: when she'd been cornered, she hadn't had time to think about it, to be frightened.

Waiting here in the dark, she did have time to think. And brood. West thought Odin was inside—and he didn't seem optimistic about the prospect of finding him unharmed.

They'd been sitting for an hour and fifteen minutes when Twist's cell phone vibrated. He had the only phone among them—the rest had been left in the cars, so they couldn't accidentally go off at a bad time, or be dropped or lost or captured and used as evidence. Twist whispered, "Cade," then looked at the screen, which he held inside his blanket. "Truck coming."

"Stay with the plan," West whispered. He reached inside his jacket and produced a pistol.

"Coming in," Twist said as another message arrived. "Cade's going for the truck."

"Everybody cool," West whispered. "Let's get the nylons on."

Shay fumbled with the mask; up to this point, the raid hadn't seemed real. The mask came down over her eyes and chin, and she tucked in every strand of hair the way Odin had said she should. Her stomach clutched and she began to breathe hard. It was going to happen, and not some other time, but *now.* . . .

Then they heard it, a rumbling engine—a delivery truck. Lights flashed by the end of the building and then disappeared as the truck dropped down the ramp to the door. When the lights were gone, West said, "Move."

They left the blankets and crawled out after him, all but Shay, who stayed behind the corner of the building with the dog—X, with his gray coat, was too visible in the reflected light coming up from the ramp.

The three men crouched behind a low retaining wall above the ramp. Shay peered around the corner, keeping her head low to the ground, and saw West do a slow peek over the wall. He pulled back and they all listened, heard the delivery truck's door roll up, and then two men talking. West did another slow peek, then lowered his head and nodded at Cruz and Twist.

"When I say," he whispered.

He peeked again, and again, and then, "Ready . . . go."

The three of them crossed the wall and dropped the eight feet to the cement driveway. Twist's leg gave way and he went down on a knee, but West and Cruz kept going around the truck and Twist scrambled back to his feet with the use of his cane.

Cruz went around the front of the truck, West around the back, where they found two men in work clothes loading a dolly with cardboard boxes full of canned food.

West, intimidating in the mask and behind the muzzle of his gun, growled, "Hands over your heads and keep your mouths shut."

One of the men said as he raised his hands, "Man, we got nothing here but food. There's nothing to steal."

"Shut up," West said. He looked and sounded like a killer. He said to Cruz, "Chains."

Cruz stepped up behind the first man and said, "If you fight it, you get hurt. If you don't, you're okay." His accent had changed: gone cholo.

The trucker bought it: "Man, don't hurt me. . . ."

Cruz threw a loop of chain around his waist, locked it with a padlock, then threaded the other end through the truck's bumper and locked that, too. "Now you," he said to the second man.

While the men were attacking the truck, Shay and X had jogged around the ramp's barrier wall and down the driveway into the loading area. As they came down the ramp, Cruz finished locking the second man to the bumper. That done, Cruz patted both of the men down, found no weapons, but took two cell phones. "I'll put them by the door, where you can get them back," he said to the men; back to the L.A. accent. Attached to the short chains, the men wouldn't be able to get into the truck even if there was a weapon or a phone inside.

Twist was at the door and risked a peek. Inside was another room, with a steel door on the other side, but the door was ajar.

He said to West, "There's an interior steel door, but the door's open, if nobody pulls it shut."

"Then let's get inside before they close it," West said, and he led the way into the building; Twist was right behind him, then Shay and X, and then Cruz.

They were in a small room with concrete-block walls painted an

institutional yellow, smelling of disinfectant and something else—
something bad. A steel door led to two hallways, going away from
each other at right angles. West peeked, then pulled his head back.
"There's a room with a glass cage, twenty feet down the hall, and a
guy inside," he whispered.

Twist: "Hold the door. I'll be right back."

Twist went out to the truck and was back a minute later pushing
the dolly, on which he'd piled two extra boxes, so that they were
nearly head-high. "Good," West said. "I'll take it from here."

West put the gun in his jacket pocket and pushed the dolly
through the door and down the hall. At the lighted office, he
stopped, reached around, and tried the doorknob, which was unlocked. The man at the desk looked up when the door opened, and
West stepped out from behind the boxes and pointed his pistol at
the man's nose.

"Make any noise and I'll kill you," he said.

Cruz, Twist, Shay, and X hustled down the hall to the office, and
when the man saw them, he looked at the dog and then Shay and
said, "You're that chick with the dog." And to Twist, "You're some
kinda artist, you won't kill me."

He'd had his hands over his head but now he reached out to a red
switch and switch box on the far wall, and Twist snapped, "Don't
touch it," but when the man continued reaching toward the alarm
switch, Twist smashed him across the face with the cane. The man
went to the floor screaming, blood pouring from a broken nose.

The man tried to roll up, but X made a lunging move at him and
he fell back. Shay choked up on his chain. "Good boy," she said.

West stood over the dazed man, went through his pockets, and
finally pulled out an electronic key card. "Let's see what this does."

Cruz was chaining the man when Cade ran in through the door

and hissed, "Truck's ready." West said to Twist, "You and Cruz go that way, Shay and I'll go this way, yell if you find anything," and pointed down the intersecting halls. "Cade, start pulling files. Hard drives if you can get them. . . . Any records . . ."

They went running, Twist and Cruz one way, Shay and West the other. There were three steel doors on the inner walls of the hall that West and Shay took: one was a maintenance closet, one gave access to building power supply panels, and the third was locked.

"Try the card," Shay said. Just then, Twist reappeared at the end of the hall, followed by Cruz, and called, "It's a dead end down there—keyed door, no electronics."

Shay ran the card through the door lock and a green LED blinked at them, and West pulled the door open and stepped through. A woman was standing halfway down the hall with an odd-looking handgun and she aimed it at them and pulled the trigger and West said, "Taser!" and dropped and dragged Shay down and the Taser element bounced off the wall and Shay screamed, "Get her!" and X went down the hall like a leopard and jumped at the woman's face. The woman blocked him with her forearm, but the impact from the eighty-pound dog knocked her down, screaming, and the dog dragged at her arm and then Shay arrived and shouted, "No, no more!"

The dog wouldn't stop and Shay grabbed him by the collar and the woman half stood and struck at Shay, hitting her in the mouth, and Shay went down and the woman scratched at her eyes, but Shay rolled away and held on to the dog as West backhanded the woman, who fell flat on her back.

"Stay down!" West pointed his gun at the woman's face and asked, "Where's Odin Remby?"

The dog was still snarling at the woman as Shay scrambled back to her feet. The woman, frightened, stuttered, "Right here, right here . . . ," and waved her hand down the hall. "But there are no keys. The keys are upstairs. . . ."

"There are little windows," Shay said, and she ran to the first one and looked into a room that was empty except for a cot. She ran to the next, followed by Twist, and heard West say to Cruz, who'd caught up with them, "Pat her down and chain her to the door handle."

An Asian man was sitting on a cot in the second room, staring at the door. He seemed dazed, as though he'd just woken. As she looked through the window, Shay realized that it was silvered on her side, one-way glass, and the man couldn't see her. Just next to the window was a square metal flap. She moved it and found a speaking hole covered with mesh. She called, "Who are you?"

The man stood up and said something unintelligible: Korean? She didn't know.

"Not Odin, keep moving," Twist said. He was already running to the next window. Another Asian man, this one standing, his eyes wide with fear. They'd heard the screaming down the hall. . . . Would somebody else be coming?

The next room, and Shay was looking at Odin. He was lying flat on a cot but had lifted his head enough that he could look at the door. He was barefoot, dressed in what looked like yoga pants and a T-shirt.

She pushed the speaking flap. "Odin? Odin?"

Odin said, "Shay?! Oh my God, what are you doing?"

"We're getting you out."

"How?" He pushed himself up, but then fell back.

"He's hurt," Shay said to Twist.

West hurried up. "We've got to move, we've got to move—"

"Open this door," Shay said.

West ran the key in the lock, got a red light. Tried again, another red light. "Stand back."

He kicked the door, a karate-style straight-thrust kick, and the door rattled but held. "Again," he said with gritted teeth, and kicked it as hard as he could. The door held.

Shay said, "The dolly . . ."

She ran to the office, got the metal dolly, and pushed it back down the hall. West kicked the door again, and again it held.

"Battering ram," Shay said when she got there. "All of us."

West, Twist, Cruz, and Shay picked the heavy steel dolly off the floor and smashed it against the door. This time, the door bent and the glass window shattered. "Again," she screamed.

They hit it again and again and again, and with the last impact, the door blew open, the lock actually tearing out a piece of the doorjamb.

Instantly an alarm began screaming down the hallways.

"Ah, shit," Twist groaned. Shay pushed past him into the cell.

Odin was on the floor inside, trying to crawl to the door. His face was one large bruise. Shay knelt beside him. "How bad, how bad?" she cried.

"Pretty bad," Odin groaned. "Did this water thing to me. . . . Can't walk."

West said, "We'll carry him. Let's go. . . ."

Odin said, "No. No. There's a girl in the next room. Get her out, get her out—"

Shay said, "Odin, we don't have time—"

"Have to, have to, have to," Odin said. "They did something to her brain, they'll kill her, we've got to get her out."

"We'll look," West said. "Cruz, carry him out to the truck. Take it slow, be careful with him. Let's go look at this girl."

Shay said, "I'm going with Odin," and Odin said, "No, no, help them get her. . . ."

Cruz picked up Odin and hustled him out of the room and down the hall. Shay, X, Twist, and West went to the next cell, looked through the glass at a young Asian woman who was standing in front of the door, looking at them, though she couldn't see them. She was wearing a shapeless gray smock of thin cotton, and her head had been shaved. Her head seemed too large—swollen?—and was scored with dozens of lines from which thin wires emerged. The wires led to the back of her neck, where they were bundled almost like a pigtail and ended in a knot of connectors.

There was a chain around her waist, and her wrists were cuffed to the chain, and her feet were tethered together so she could only shuffle across the floor. She sensed they were there because she opened her mouth and screamed, "Help me!"

"What have they done to her?" Twist asked, aghast.

"Let's knock it down," West said.

Cade came running out of the office and down the hall. "Got a drive, but that's about it. We've been in six minutes. . . ."

"Knock it down," West said, and they began battering the cell door. They hit it eight times before it gave, and when it did, the young woman said in heavily accented English, "Take me or kill me, but don't leave me."

"We're taking you," Twist said.

West said, "You guys carry her—she can't run. I want to look at these other cells."

"I'll come with you," Shay said. "Twist and Cade can carry her."

Twist tucked his cane under an armpit and he and Cade linked hands and the young woman sat down in the cradle of their arms, and they scuttled, half sideways but quickly, down the hall toward the door.

The alarm was still screaming, but they hadn't seen any more Singular personnel. "We've got one minute," West shouted at Shay. "We gotta run."

They continued down the hall, looking through the windows. They found another Asian man, and an Asian woman.

"Why are they all Asian?" Shay asked, shouting above the alarm.

"I think they might be North Korean. . . . I think they might be lab animals."

The last room down was larger, and West looked inside, then caught Shay's arm and said, "Let's go, let's run."

"What's in there?" She pulled away and looked: benches and a tub and some hoses—no people.

West said, "Run, run, we've got no time. . . ."

West stepped into the intersection of the two halls and there was a sharp explosion and he went down, falling, and there were two more shots, and he pushed himself up and fired down the hall three times, and another shot came in, ricocheting off the wall above his head, and then he turned and looked up at Shay, who was still in the long hallway, and said, "Goddammit. Shay. Run."

"We've got to get you . . ." She realized he was lying in a puddle of blood.

"Leave me, or they'll get you. Call 911, get an ambulance down here."

She peeked around a corner, where the gunshots had come from, and saw a man lying on his back, and more blood on the floor.

West groaned and dug into his pockets, pulled out some keys.

"Take my Jeep—get it out of here. There's a hard drive and some files in the back, it's everything I took out of the headquarters. Ah, God, my legs are gone."

Shay crouched next to him. "Gotta get you to a hospital."

"You're wasting time," West said, and clutched her wrist. "I'm not gonna die, but I'm hurt, hit in the side, took out some ribs. The fastest way to get me to a hospital is . . . you gotta leave me."

A man shouted from the dead-end hallway. West: "They're coming—run. Call 911."

Cruz stepped into the hall with a gun in his hand. He took in West, and the man down the hall. *"Jesu Christo . . ."*

West said, "They're coming, combat guys with guns, get her out of here."

"No," Shay said, but West let go of her wrist and Cruz seized her arm, his grip like iron, and pulled.

West had been hit by three of the four shots, one in each leg, so that both were now useless, and one on the left side of his torso. He was on the floor, felt himself drifting into shock—he recognized it, it wasn't the first time—as a man stood over him and pulled the nylon mask off his face.

Thorne. Thorne was wearing pajamas. He said, "West. Heard you might be a problem."

"Need a couple aspirin, man," West said.

Thorne said to somebody he couldn't see, "Get him up to the lobby. Get Jackson up there too, but take it easy with him, he's bleeding bad. They'll be calling 911, we need to do this quick."

There was some talk that West couldn't make out, and then he felt himself being strapped to a dolly—he suspected it was the same one they'd used to knock down the doors. He was taken down the hallway, through a door, then up in an elevator. Couldn't feel much . . . starting to fade deeper into shock.

Then he was unstrapped and dumped on the floor.

Thorne said to somebody, "Gimme Jackson's piece."

West understood what was about to happen and fought back to consciousness. Thorne was standing over him with a gun in his hand. West said, "Man, don't do this."

"Lift him up by his neck. . . . Don't let your skin touch him, use your sleeves."

West struggled, but somebody unseen dropped a piece of cloth—a coat sleeve?—around his neck and lifted his head and chest off the floor.

"You dumb shit. What, you fall for that chick?" Thorne asked.

West said, "Don't . . . please, man . . . ," and tears leaked down his cheeks.

Thorne shot him in the heart.

Cruz threw Shay in the bed of the truck alongside the young Asian woman and Odin and Twist, helped X up and in, ran around to the passenger side, and jumped in, shouting, "Go, go, go!" Cade dropped the hammer and the truck bolted up the ramp toward the street.

Shay grabbed Twist by his shirt and screamed, "West is shot, West is shot bad, call 911, gotta call 911!"

Twist fumbled out his phone in the dark and punched in 911, and when the operator came on, he said, "There's been a shooting at the Singular building in the River Park Industrial Zone, the EDT Laboratory. Man's hurt bad, shot bad, we need police and an ambulance!"

The operator wanted more information but Twist shouted, "I can't talk, I can't talk, he's bleeding, hurry, EDT Lab, he's hurt bad!"

He hung up, pulled the phone apart, threw the battery over the side, then wiped the phone on his shirt and threw that too. "Nine-one-one tracks calls," he said to Shay. He was intent, but cool. "How bad is West?"

"He's bad, his legs are gone, he was shot in the side," Shay said. "There was all this blood. . . ."

She turned to Odin, who was lying next to the girl, their heads cushioned by Twist's scrunched-up blazer. Odin reached out and touched her arm. "I'm sorry I started all of this. I'm sorry."

The Asian girl was whispering several words like a mantra. X pushed his way between Shay and Odin, sniffed at Odin's knuckles, then licked his hand.

"Hey, bud, look at you, you're not wearing a muzzle. . . ."

"We've got to get somewhere safe," Shay said. She and Twist pushed themselves onto their knees, into the wind, and looked ahead.

"Parking lot coming up, we gotta be somewhat calm, but we gotta get under cover fast," Twist said. "Really fast. We'll move Odin into the back of the truck, on the bench seat. Cruz can drive it, and you and X ride along so you can talk to Odin. Cade and I'll take this lady"—he patted the arm of the Asian woman (*More a girl,* Shay thought)—"in the Camry."

Shay: "West gave me the keys to his Jeep. He said there're important files in it that he took out of Singular."

"Okay. You take the Jeep," Twist said. "We need to get away from here. Just get out"—the truck swerved into the factory parking lot where they'd left the other cars—"and we'll coordinate later. There'll be cops all over the place in two minutes."

The parking lot was poorly lit, which was why they'd chosen it. Cade braked to a ragged stop between the Jeep and Camry.

Cruz piled out of the cab and Twist told him, "Move Odin into the back, onto the bench."

Cruz dropped the tailgate and Twist and Shay helped move Odin into Cruz's arms and Cruz put him inside the truck. Shay ducked her head inside the door, gripped his hands, and said, "I'll see you again in a few minutes."

"Careful," Odin said. And: "I knew you'd come for me."

Shay squeezed his hands and said, "Stay strong." She backed away—and heard sirens. Not yet close, but not too far, either.

Twist gave Shay a hug and said, "I never understood how boring things were until I met you. Listen, do what you have to to get out of here. Go that way."

He pointed to the darker side of the industrial park. The sirens were coming from the other direction.

Shay and X climbed into West's Jeep. She jammed the key into the ignition and started it up, and then Cruz in the truck with Odin backed straight out and sped away. Cade and Twist were right behind in the Camry, and then Shay, rolling into the dark.

She was with them out of the industrial park, through two lucky green traffic signals. On the third signal, Cruz barely made the light and Cade followed him through, busting the red, and Shay was forced to stop by a line of passing cars.

The light seemed to last forever, the taillights of the other two vehicles dwindling in front of her. Then, a few hundred yards ahead, apparently realizing what had happened, they slowed, pulling right, waiting for her, and when the traffic light turned green again, she accelerated through it, but then a police car powered up behind her, its flashers and siren pushing her to the side of the road, and then a second one. Were they looking for the truck and the Camry? When she was rolling again, the taillights of the other two vehicles were gone.

Not a problem, she thought, reaching reflexively into the backseat for her backpack, with her phone and laptop . . . which was in Cruz's truck.

"Oh . . . no."

X looked at her, reacting to her tone, an obvious question in his eyes.

She'd lost Cruz and Odin, Cade and Twist and the shackled Asian woman. They probably all thought Shay had her laptop and phone, and so they weren't worried about becoming separated.

Two men had been shot, she thought. The Singular people would be talking to police, telling their side of the story, which meant the police might be looking for her.

She and X were on their own.

Sync and Harmon arrived from San Francisco by helicopter, called in by Thorne. The chopper put down in the Singular parking lot a half hour after dawn, and Thorne came walking across the lot, still limping a little from the hotel fight, holding a ball cap on his head against the prop wash.

Sync jumped down and said, "Tell me."

"Let's get away from the chopper," Thorne said.

They walked toward the building and stopped under a parking lot light. "The police are here, three detectives and a full crime scene crew. They'll want to speak with you."

"First: the female subject," Sync said.

"Don't know. She's gone. Her door was battered down, from the outside, so she has to be with them."

"And they got Remby too. . . ."

"Yes."

"My God, it's all coming apart," Sync said. "If they—" He seemed disoriented.

"We know that," Harmon snapped, bringing him back. "We've

got to get on them, right now, if we're going to recover. We've got a make and model on the pickup they used from a security video, but they'd covered the tags with mud—that was probably West's idea. Didn't see the artist's Range Rover, but they may have kept it off-site. Can't find West's Jeep, but we're looking for it. The problem is, there're about a million of them. . . ."

They were walking toward the building entrance, where a uniformed cop was standing, looking toward them.

"I gotta tell you what you'll see here," Thorne said, his voice low and urgent. "You know the basic sequence. My problem was that we had several of our experiments locked up, and we had that waterboarding setup in the back cell. If we let the police in there, we were toast. I had West and Jackson carried up to the lobby, where I shot him. He's dead. We shot up the lobby with their weapons, I made sure West went down with Jackson's, and I called 911. We found out later that somebody had already done that, but we managed to divert everything to the front entrance.

"When the ambulance got here, I insisted that West was still maybe alive, even though the medical techs said he was dead. I had him transported to the medical center with Jackson. That messed up the crime scene some more—we'd already tracked through it as much as we could, moving blood around. I briefed Jackson as well as I could before the paramedics got there, and he's on board. He'll say that West and his gang, wearing masks, tried to crash into the lab. We've already told them that we think it's this Twist and Shay Remby, who somehow subverted West—or vice versa, we don't know. Like I said, making it as confusing as we can."

"The police don't want to search the building?" Sync asked.

"Not at this point. We said they didn't get beyond the lobby—that West and Jackson shot each other and the others ran. I called our contact in Sacramento, the captain, and he came right over to vouch for us. So it's contained, but you might want to nail the guy down with a little more cash. I don't know what the crime scene people will find in the lobby that might make them suspicious. They will find blood spatters and lots of nine-millimeters. We made it as confusing as we could."

"If it just slows them down, we can clean out the cells, fill them with boxes of lab supplies or something," Sync said. "Get some wooden doors down there."

"I already checked on that," Thorne said. "The old wooden doors are still in the building, we can have them back in place in a couple of hours. I packed up the experimental subjects, loaded them into a van, and shipped them out. They're on their way to the port holding facility. We can't keep them there long, but they're out of the way for now."

Harmon asked, "If you hadn't shot West, think he would have made it?"

"No doubt," Thorne said. "He took one in the gut, but if they'd gotten him to the medical center . . . He was in shape."

Sync slapped Thorne on the arm and said, "Good man. I'll go talk to the police. You've got a heavy bonus coming your way. So does Jackson. I mean *heavy*."

"I appreciate it, but I tell you, we've got to walk careful. We gotta get the basement cleaned out. If Shay Remby produces her brother, or this subject that they took out . . . ," Thorne said. He was talking so fast he was spitting. "Or if they just call the cops in the next fifteen minutes and say, 'Look in the basement.' We're still out on the ledge."

"We've got the PR people already working on it," Sync said. "The goddamned Remby kids . . . Let's go. Let's go. Show me this cop I've got to talk to."

"Confusion," Thorne said. "Remember, everything is confused. We don't know what, or why, or what's going on. We want information from *them*. . . ."

Shay had no idea where the others were, but she remembered what Twist had said: *Get away from here.* She picked a freeway, the first one she came to, and turned onto it, hoping against hope that she'd spot the others.

She did not.

"We've got to find a place until we can get in touch," Shay said to the dog.

She didn't know how to work the Jeep's nav system, but she fiddled with it, and when it came up, she found that she was back on I-5 and traveling south, back the way they'd come about a million years earlier—or a few short hours in real time. Back toward L.A.

The gas tank was half full. She wouldn't make it to L.A.—she wouldn't even try. She needed to find a place in the area, needed a place to think.

She especially had to think about West. What would he do, and what would the Singular people do with him? Would they make a deal? Could West claim that he'd been kidnapped? That seemed unlikely—he'd shot one of Singular's guards.

If he was still conscious when the police got there, it was possible the authorities were already ransacking the lab, that it was all over, that Singular was going down.

In which case she should probably be calling the police, as should Odin, and the Asian woman with the wired-up brain . . .

She wouldn't make a move until they were all back together, until she better understood what Singular had done to her brother and the people in those cells. . . .

Forty minutes after leaving the industrial park, Shay pulled off the freeway and into a travel center north of Stockton.

She pushed her hair down the back of her shirt, cinched the hoodie tight around her face, went in and got a coffee and two cinnamon rolls, carried them back out to the truck, fed one roll to X, and did an inventory.

West had left a soft leather briefcase in the back, and when she opened it, she found his wallet with a thousand dollars in cash, a laptop, an iPad, and an accessory hard drive, along with a lot of personal gear—sunglasses, pens and pencils, two notepads and a legal pad, two small digital recorders.

She turned the computer on, and the first thing that came up was a password request. She turned it back off—West would undoubtedly have an unbreakable password. The iPad, however, was unprotected, probably because there was nothing on it, but it had an active Internet link. She thought for a moment, then went out to GandyDancer, found nothing, then out to her Facebook link with Odin. Again, nothing. She left a message for Odin:

Where are you?

She had no idea where the others were, except that they had fled Sacramento. She went to Google Maps to look at the Sacramento area.

Twist would make the call, but how would he be thinking? She peered at the map for a moment, confused by the possibilities, then closed her eyes, let it work through her mind . . . opened them again and looked at the map.

He'd stay on the interstate highways, she thought—only one set of cops, the highway patrol, and no reason for the highway patrol to be curious. If they got off the interstate, they'd have to worry about local police as well.

So they'd probably stay on the interstate—but which one?

Back to the map: They could have taken I-80 southwest to the San Francisco Bay Area, or northeast toward Lake Tahoe and Reno, Nevada. Or they could have taken I-5 north to . . . nothing big until they got all the way back to Eugene. No, Eugene was unlikely—it was too far away, and there'd be too many people who could spot either her or Odin. I-5 south was also unlikely: nowhere large to hide, until they were all the way back to L.A., where hundreds of people knew Twist.

She looked back at the line of I-80 connecting Reno, Sacramento, and San Francisco. Singular would have a lot of resources in the Bay Area. Maybe fewer in another state.

Reno? That seemed like the best bet, but who knew if Twist would use Shay's kind of logic? They could all wind up under a bridge in Yuba City.

On an impulse, she checked for TV news stations in Sacramento and found a sketchy report of a shooting at a building in the River Park Industrial Zone. No details were available, but two men had been taken to UC–Davis's trauma center.

Then her eyes snapped to her own name, drawn like a magnet: "Sacramento police are looking for two young so-called eco-terrorists, the brother-and-sister team Odin and Shay Remby, believed to be involved in a raid on a research lab in Eugene, Oregon, last month, in which a young woman was shot."

Shay clicked on the link to the story's continuation and found a photograph of herself taken by her last foster father, Clarence

Peters—her red hair hung around her shoulders like a wreath—and Odin's senior yearbook photo.

She felt as though a hand had wrapped itself around her heart and begun to squeeze. The police were looking for her and Odin? What had Singular told them? What about West—hadn't he told them what was happening in the basement laboratory? There was no hint of that in the TV report.

She fought down the panic. Now what? Nobody to talk to, no way to find out where the others had gone.

Hunted by the police . . .

She'd been with Twist when they'd located the no-questions-asked mom-and-pop motel the night before. She knew how to do that, how to look for a crummy motel. First she went back to the iPad, looked for a nearby chain drugstore. She found a Walgreens, drove there, and bought Clairol Nice 'n Easy hair color, a comb, and some shears.

A half hour later, she spotted the motel she wanted, a place where they wouldn't call the cops about anything unless they found a body under a bed. The motel was much crummier than the mom-and-pop of the night before, this one with a rawboned desk clerk who suggested that she might qualify for a free room.

When she walked out of the motel two hours later, taking a stained towel and a long rope of red hair with her, she was a different person, not anything like the red-haired, camera-friendly Shay Remby who'd wall-crawled the building on the 110 or lit a new sign over Hollywood.

She looked like a punk, pale skin and chopped black hair, like somebody who should have a Tiny Terror guitar amp stowed behind the rough-looking black-and-gray wolf that sat beside her.

She got back in the Jeep and found a Starbucks. She didn't go in; she could get the Wi-Fi from the parking lot.

This time, she scored.

On the GandyDancer site, an obscure statement:

The number on the curb plus 109.

Obscure to everyone but Shay and Odin. When they were young teenagers, they'd temporarily lived in a house with a 666 address, the number of the beast. Odin had been amused; Shay had been vaguely frightened by it. Now she added 666 and 109 in her head and came up with 775. She Googled it and, along with a variety of other things, learned that it was the area code for Reno.

The fear that had clutched her heart released just a bit. But where was the rest of the phone number?

She went to her Facebook link with Odin and found another Odin-only line.

Add El Primo Primo to the following number . . .

There followed a seven-digit number. And El Primo Primo was 3,631, a number that had frightened Odin, as 666 had frightened Shay. Thinking about prime numbers was one of Odin's pastimes, and 3,631 was a prime. It was also the ages of their mother and father when they'd died.

She added them, and now had a new seven-digit number to add to the area code she already had.

But no phone. The iPad had Internet access, but no voice capability.

Not a problem anymore, not in America, not if you have money in your pocket, and she had West's wallet.

If she could just get them all back together, they could work this out: Odin, Twist, West, Cade, and Cruz. If they could just get back to the Twist Hotel. . . .

She drove north until she spotted a Best Buy. With a new phone in her hand, she punched in the number. It rang once, and then somebody picked up. Said nothing.

After a few seconds, Shay said, "Hello?"

"You coming, or are you gonna stand out there like a lamppost?"

The fear let her go, and she sagged into the phone.

Twist.

"I'm coming," she said. "I'm coming."

Lights. Everywhere.

She couldn't believe it: they were staying at a shabby casino motel, under a two-story-tall pair of blinking red dice. GPS and a three-hour drive had gotten her to Reno, and now Twist, on the phone, guided her in. "We told them we had a handicapped woman and we needed to be on the first floor, somewhere quiet. We're on the back of the motel, room seventy—look for the truck."

The truck and Camry were parked side by side, and Shay fit into a slot next to them. She grabbed West's briefcase from behind her seat, then leaned over and smooched X on the nose. "We're back with the pack."

Twist was waiting at the door; he took her in, said, "Good God, you're so different. It's like seeing the night after knowing the day."

She wrapped her arms around him and gave him a hard squeeze, and she touched the faces of both Cruz and Cade as she went by, into the room, and knelt by the first of two twin beds, where Odin was sprawled on his back, his head up on two pillows. X came up and licked his hand. She asked, "How are you?"

"Better. Lots better," Odin said. His voice was stronger. "They were trying to wear me out. They just about had me. Sleep is bringing me back."

There was a high-pitched gasp, and Shay looked over at the other bed: the Asian girl was curled on her side, eyes closed, shaking uncontrollably.

To Odin: "What's happening? Do you know?"

"I don't know *why,* but I know it happens every few hours, then it just stops," he said. "She says it feels like bugs are crawling through her body."

"Bastards," Shay said.

"She's had it a lot worse than I have," Odin said. "We've been talking about what to do."

Shay stroked Odin's arm and continued staring at the girl, thin as a stick figure in the gray hospital smock, chains around her waist, wrists, and ankles, beads of sweat dripping from her forehead to her quivering lips. And her head . . . all the wires. They had to get her out of there—but rescuing her wasn't enough. Not nearly enough.

Twist was standing beside her now and Shay looked up at him and asked, "West—do we know how he's doing? I saw a report that said two men were taken to a hospital—"

Twist shook his head.

"We have to find out," she said. "He can testify against them, but—"

Twist placed a hand on her shoulder.

"He's gone, Shay."

For a moment, she didn't understand. Couldn't possibly fathom—he'd saved her brother's life. He'd saved her own.

Shay stood up and Twist said, "His father's done some interviews with reporters. Singular has put out a press release saying that they think he led some animal rights radicals in an attack on the lab. They said he may have helped organize the attack on the lab in Eugene too, that he may have been involved with them for a long time.

They're saying that the Remby activists might have been involved in the raid, but they're not sure of that. . . ."

Shay's face was like a stone. "He's dead. We know that for sure?"

"His father identified him. Said he didn't know how West could have gotten tied up with radicals. Said he was a hero in Afghanistan . . ."

"He was shot in the legs, which wouldn't kill him, and in the side—he believed he'd be okay if he got to the hospital," Shay said.

"That's not how it worked out," Cruz said quietly.

Shay took a step back from the three men and said, "No. He'd been wounded before. He knew what he was talking about. They murdered him."

"We can't know that—" Twist said.

"Believe me. They killed him," she said. "I owe them one dead man." She looked at her brother and the shaking, mutilated girl. "More than that. They've got more than that coming."

Twist: "Shay—"

She drew X to her side and said, "C'mon, boy, we're gonna take a walk."

As she stepped toward the door, Cade asked, "Where're you going?"

"Ten minutes to walk my dog, okay?" she snapped, without making eye contact.

She grabbed a key to the room and the door slammed behind her. The men just looked at each other.

"I should follow her," said Cade.

Odin pushed himself up and spoke: "No. My sister won't ever let anybody see her cry."

• • •

Sitting with X in West's Jeep, her face lit by the glow from West's iPad, Shay went out to GandyDancer and dropped a final message.

West, you were right: I am an exceptionally good liar. I made you think I didn't trust you. But I did, right from the start.

You are a war hero.

Shay

Then she cried.

Twist took a hundredth turn around the motel room, then snapped at Odin, "We've got to get the chains off this girl. I can't even stand looking at her anymore. Where in the hell is your sister?"

"She'll be back. . . ."

"She's been gone almost an hour. If she needed to cry, that's fine—but we've got things to do, and crying's a luxury right now," Twist said. "We don't know what Singular's doing, we don't have any communications, we—"

A key rattled in the lock and they all turned toward the door as Shay stepped inside. Her face was pink, but her eyes were dry.

She had a Home Depot bag and shook out a pair of bolt cutters.

"Let's cut her loose," she said, and unconsciously repeated what Twist had said: "We've got things to do."

"Like what?" Cade asked.

Shay snapped open the bolt cutters, like the jaws of a crocodile, and stepped toward the girl on the bed.

"Like revenge," she said.

DON'T MISS BOOK 2 OF
THE SINGULAR MENACE

OUTRAGE

COMING IN FALL 2015

The leader stepped closer. "We need to know three things *now*. How high in the government does all this go? CIA, military, politicians—where does it go? Who's paying Singular? We need the names, *now*. We need to know how many people are like our friend. How many human copies have you made?"

The woman in bed said, "I won't tell you a thing." She shouted, "Otto! Karl! *Herkommen!*"

The boy slammed the bedroom door, locking the dogs out.

The leader said, "We need—"

"Not a thing!" the woman shrieked. "Nothing! Never!"

The leader turned to the boy and said, "Give me the gun."

He slipped it out of his waistband and handed it to her. "What are you going to do?"

The sixteen-year-old girl thumbed the safety off with an audible metallic *click*.

"I'm gonna kill the bitch," she said. She raised the gun. "Say good-bye to Senator Dash."

Excerpt from *Outrage* copyright © 2014 by John Sandford and Michele Cook. Published in the United States by Alfred A. Knopf, an imprint of Random House Children's Books, a division of Random House LLC, a Penguin Random House Company, New York.